MARILYN'S RED
RED
Diary

MARILYN'S RED
Diary

E.Z. FRIEDEL

Sand Shack
PUBLISHING

New York | 2013

Doctor's Notes:

    A year ago today, at 3:40 a.m., I assisted Dr. Hy Engelberg in pronouncing Marilyn Monroe dead. By then, her personal files had been destroyed and her body was stiff and cold. Her phone records disappeared before sunrise. And twelve months later, after a massive cover up, this Red Diary is all that remains. How did her prized personal journal survive intact? Near the end, a terrified Marilyn begged me, as her psychiatrist, to protect her written words. I immediately locked this book in my safe at home. Still, Marilyn's insider knowledge of covert government activities was a continuing threat. Her death sentence was sealed and delivered to the Mafia. Her childish but powerful voice was stilled.

    Freud once described psychoanalysis as "an impossible profession." Treating Miss Monroe was twice that. Marilyn's life was so full of turmoil and crisis, I broke many rules just to keep her afloat. From the start, I urged my patient to keep a diary to help provide continuity in her therapy. Once she began writing, however, Marilyn would carry this book everywhere, detailing her roller coaster life.

    Surely I allowed Marilyn to cross barriers that could be considered highly unprofessional. But this patient needed help urgently; I quickly dropped my analyst reserve and became first a friend and then the concerned, supportive parent she had always sought. Unconventional? A definite leap but it seemed to work. I then looked to embrace Marilyn

into a close social unit. By absorbing her into my
own family, a healthy support system was provided.
My extensive treatment (up to four to five hours
every day) was aimed at negating her increasing
fears. But it took her death for me to realize how
much of her paranoia was justified.

Marilyn was blessed with a bright mind, a caring
soul, and great talents. A fierce drive and rare
beauty made her a world icon. It was this stature,
plus anger at her lovers' betrayals, that fueled the
security threat. I know she did not kill herself, but
the campaign to destroy her reputation persists. I
want to release this diary to negate the official
lies, yet I fear for my family's safety. All I can
do is make sure it goes public when it's safe. I've
added my notes at the end to help explain all I've
learned about her last hours. Marilyn deserves the
whole truth. Her life was a daily struggle, but she
was finding her path. Her Red Diary describes how
she handled her challenges, what she hoped for the
future, and why she was murdered.

Ralph Greenson, M.D.   Aug. 5, 1963

Marilyn's Journal of Her Final Two Years

Dear Diary,   *June 26, 1960*

New York, New York. Where do I begin this thing? More to
the point why am I having trouble putting down a few words. Is
it because its by me about me? For as long as I can remember I've
tried to hide my dirty mind. Now I'm being asked to dig up the
same painful memories I have tried my hardest to bury. Knowing
these feelings will then be poked and prodded only adds to my
doubt. Dr. Greenson is an expert free from emotion and much
smarter than me. He delights in playing twenty questions when
I have zero answers. The only thing I know for sure is having
this personal stuff get out would do terrible damage to my public
image. Destroying any trust I have in analysis to get me to feel
better about me. So its a big risk. Besides, right now I'm pretty
happy with my love life and surely my career. Another problem is
I'm afraid to begin kidding around because there is no one here
but me. Dr. Greenson does not like it when I try to use humor to
hide my pain. No crossing of emotion. He wants tears for pain,
laughter for happy, until he knows me better. And that's no joke.

It just stopped raining. Gentle, sweet rain. So rare in sunny
LA, so common on the East Coast. I love it, not when its coming
down but right now. The feeling of renewal as the rainwater shines
on the sidewalks and streets. Everything is washed clean, even my
regrets. So why do I sit here and ponder my screwed up thoughts
when I could simply go outside and enjoy this moment? Mainly
because I have promised my good Doctor I would try to do this
thing. Starting anything new is hard. But Dr. Greenson has been
urging me to keep a record from the very first day on his couch.
'Please, Marilyn. Get a notebook or even better a diary. Put down
some of your inner thoughts as they come up. Whatever pops into
your head, write it down. It will help me get to know you.'

I'm hoping it will help me get to know me. That would be a relief I can feel. Also I'm using notes to make my writing more orderly. Impulsive has never been my problem. Rambling is. Dr. Greenson has suggested I keep notes to help. Damn. I just realized I have another problem. Where am I going to hide you for safety, especially when I go from coast to coast or on a Hollywood lot? Here in NYC, I have a lock on my closet door. In LA, there's locks on both my bungalow doors. But there are so many guys from the various trade unions walking around the back lots, there's no real security. I'll have to ask Dr. Greenson what he thinks I should do.

Now that I've gotten this pre-production stuff out of the way, I feel the panic creeping in. Fear, my old buddy and worst enemy has returned in force. And its only page two. Ok, I'll do what I normally do when feeling this unsure. Lean forward, throw myself into the muck, and paddle my well padded ass off. My over admired ass, my under admired rest of me. Sure I'm afraid to write from my heart, to reveal my true self. My most embarrassing confession is I'm completely uneducated. Not stupid but working with lots less facts than most. I went to bad schools, had a lousy attitude and was absent more then I was there. And when I did attend and sat in those hard wooden chairs, I had trouble concentrating on anything but the boys. Then I quit to get married at 16. My foster family moving east gave me little choice. Still it was clearly not the easiest road for a teenager to travel. A foster home or a married bed.

Everyone thinks I'm a dimwit like in my films. Comedy farces are never very deep. And trying for humor I've been asked to act even dumber. Dumb blonde dumb. Lots of times I feel I'm about to go crazy, like my mother and her mother before her. Gladys and Della, the two certified loony birds have been locked up in nuthouses for years. Well, Della died there. Gladys, my mom, is trying her hardest to be just like granny. And even when I'm in control I feel completely misunderstood, defined by the roles I play rather than who I am. The woman who feels and thinks and struggles. I try to laugh at the weaknesses in myself. But its hard to look inward, and separate the good from the bad. Above all I want to feel fulfilled. Will it ever come?

Who knows the real me? I sure as hell don't. But the so called experts know far less. I've been called so many different things by the newspapers and fan magazines its become a bad joke. Do more readers want to learn I'm emotional or promotional? How about strong willed or weak and insecure? Its all a lot of baloney anyway. In some tabloids I'm a hopeless dreamer, in others a helpless drug addict. In the trades, I've been described as a major star that ran up the glass staircase on her own power (saved that one). Or a disaster waiting to happen who slipped on every step (burnt that one).

From the start I only wanted to get better and improve as an actress. Forget talent. I used hard work and an unbending belief in my abilities. It shocks me how or why I got this harebrained belief but I knew early on I was going to make it big. Not because I was more talented or prettier than the thousands of other Hollywood hopefuls. What separated me from the other girls was I wanted to be a movie star lots more than they did. And if I had to sleep with five producers to get one bit part, so be it. When people laughed at my bit parts, I got bigger ones. And I was down to two producers. Five films later, I had become an over-night comedy hit and a marquee name. So it all paid off. Well sort of. On the screen I'm fine. Inside my mind I'm not so sure. One of my worst nightmares is I've wandered into a zoo and I'm attacked by a pack of wolves. And I can't fight back because I don't want to hurt any living thing. I know I should at least try to kick them in the throat. Or gouge at their eyes or just go down fighting. Maybe some day I'll defend myself by lashing out but being successful is so much sweeter. At least with the wolves I'm used to.

In this business less apologies are better. A rumor can start from a tiny news item and almost overnight damage the way people view you. Fame. My past miscues have been blown up so much they've become a never ending storm. The media loves a circus making me the clown. The public would much rather laugh at me than with me. Still having my deepest secrets exposed would crush me. Any audience loves to see their heroes brought down but my dear fans are the most rabid of all. So fickle, they're capable of switching their support to the newest Girl Next Door before she's even moved in. A fully packaged phony bitch with bigger tits, fuller hips and rounder heels. Even my diehard faithful are way too eager to slice me wide open to view me fully naked. Once examined they can move on. Sorry, Marilyn, we've seen enough. New faces on fresher bodies are more appealing. This makes my blood boil. To leave me abandoned and alone, hanging by my toes to wither away. Then die, uncared for and unremembered. Still searching for the acceptance I have rarely felt. Except when the topic of sex comes up and that is not love or respect.

My worst fear as a child was to be buried without any marker at all. That's one scene I have managed to change. In my old age I can cling to some wonderful memories. Career triumphs, true friends and amazing lovers. I've screwed some of the best and in some of the best places. Even better, I'm hardly over. Clearly things have happened beyond my wildest dreams. Mistakes? Some I blame on two faced friends leading me down the wrong path. Well, their right path, my wrong one. Others I blame on me rushing into dumb decisions and taking too many chances. Makes me feel like I'm always living on the edge.

Still I will continue to reach for more. My Yankee Clipper says nobody counts your strikeouts. Its in the rules. Of course Joe, who is not terribly bright, believes baseball and life are one and the same. If you can call what I'm trying to achieve a game. Anyhow I will continue to swing away. When I fall it hurts but I pick myself up. Laughing away tears as I regain my clumsy feet. Dancing has never been my greatest strength. Surviving and attracting new men are my best skills.

Its night and I can't get to sleep. I've already taken two reds, maybe a couple more. Same stupid problem. Same constant terror. I just can't sleep. I often cry myself to sleep but within hours I'm tossing and turning like some troubled rag doll. Nightmares from my past rob me of any true rest. Present doubts add to the misery and make it hard to breathe.

This ongoing ordeal not only destroys my early morning beauty but leaves me exhausted all day. Adding years and making me look like dried up dog shit in my close ups. I try to give my best sultry smile and hold my eyelids half open and many admirers think I'm winking at them. Don't most people believe what they want to? I believe I'll get it together tomorrow. And Jack will marry me after he becomes President.

Dear Diary, *June 27, 1960*

I just woke up. Its 2:20 in the morning and its raining again. This time not so pleasant, harder with thunder and lightning. My foster mom called it cats and dogs so as a kid I kept looking out the front window, waiting and praying Tippy would return. My dear black and white puppy was found dead behind the side bushes. I always blamed my neighbor. Would Tip be sent down from heaven? Don't think so. Anyhow I'm reading what I wrote because sleep is no longer an option and the pills aren't helping. Many questions remain. The most obvious is why am I so alone when I'm the world's number one sex queen?

I'm aware I don't deserve the title but I am prepared to fake it. My sex persona was created fifteen years ago. Me and Nana fashioned the Marilyn character in the Karger kitchen when I lived there. I was madly in love with her son Fred, my music coach. Probably still am. Much of '48, I prayed he would marry me. But Freddie, with his magical hands and extra long, piano playing fingers played me badly. Sent me to heaven and later in the month drove me to the abortionist. Me and Nana were a girl secret team. She would talk me up, then disappear at certain times to allow nature and romance to build. But Fred refused to marry me because he thought I had a shady reputation and his kids would be tainted. I was heartbroken. So was Nana. But then came Jack to really light my fire and he was turned on by anything lusty including my past indiscretions. The more checkered the better. He just wanted to join in. So I quickly fell in love, again. Soon enough I felt linked to him like no other person before or since. He was even smarter than Fred and he wanted to help people and make the world better. Peace, equality and financial aide, with a big smile sprinkled on top. He was a congressman, soon to be senator from the East and I was about to become something more than a bit part actress from the West. Neither had the fame we now have, especially around sleepy California. I was in my twenties, and even though I had been married and done other things (not nice), I felt around him like I was a teenager. We used to get really drunk at one of the pier bars off the beach and stagger into a cheap motel, which only added to the excitement, the fear of getting caught. And because I loved this smart, beautiful man and because he said he loved me I did everything he asked. It wasn't that we did anything really way out, but the inner feeling of youth and energy, and promise was at a peak. He was definitely in command but I went willingly.

One of the best times, we wandered over to our favorite second rate Santa Monica motel just off the beach (known by all as the Porn Palace). But before Jack could go to the seedy office to pay and get our key, we sort of fell into a room with an open door that some maid had probably forgotten to lock. Once inside Jack kicked the door closed and we embraced, laughing the whole time. Thinking we were getting away with something so daring, raising the ante. We were necking, and petting standing up. Sort of swaying, dancing without any music. And of course fully clothed. Me afraid he'd notice I gained a few pounds as he brought me closer to caress my ass. Squeezing like he was weighing each cheek. Me trying to be perfect, trying to excite him with everything I had.

He walked over to the poorly lit far corner, bent over and began fiddling with something. I moved closer to see. There was a beat up 16mm projector perched on a small round table, one leg duct taped together. After he managed to turn the thing on, there was just a blinking light like from an early silent film. But without any film, just the blinking light in an empty projector. Then he gestured to the bed with an open palm. Jack had this slightly cocky smile that warned me something more was going on. He just seemed so pleased with himself. All of a sudden I got it. He had staged the whole thing. The open door and the projector and that he had come early and paid for the room. I went along with this pretend scene happily. After all, I am a dedicated actress.

In seconds I was naked, shorts and halter-top on the floor, me on my back, on that thin mattress with the stained single sheet. He moved over. We kissed slowly, hesitantly. Like we were testing the waters. The blinking light casting a carnival feeling to the whole experience.

Then he went to the top drawer of the nightstand. He pulled it open. I waited. He took out a thin pink ribbon and small rust colored feather and laid both on the tabletop. He slowly tied my wrists with the ribbon, palms together and lifted my hands above my head. He told me not to move. Standing over me, off came his shirt. Then he leaned over. Out came his tongue, lightly licking at my nipples, blowing on them until I could feel each harden. Until I shuddered.

Then he took the feather and began to tickle my mound in a wide circle, slowly edging inward. He continued this for a while, his strokes becoming stronger and more concentrated, enjoying my discomfort. Several times he almost accidentally let the tip of the feather slip, brushing the very tip of my sex, so gentle I couldn't be sure anything had happened. But when I looked down and saw his smile I knew.

And I knew even better when he moved his head down and lightly licked me, so fleeting, I wanted to grab his ears and drive his face all the way inside me. He shifted his tongue to my thighs. But always moving back to my center. I could feel my entire opening responding. And could even smell my arousal, of sex going out of control, definitely out of anything I could stop. He began licking at my love button, pulling it away from the rest of me. Sucking and twisting, making me feel raw and exposed.

Finally he slipped the feather inside. Moving in wide strokes up and forward, pressing harder against the inner wall of my pubic bone. He started squeezing and teasing my hot pussy. I was groaning and whimpering. Starting to feel these contractions all over my belly and breasts. I then felt the waves tighten, starting near the tip of my clitoris and fanning out. I was electric and poised to be set on fire. And I reached this massive climax. Like I was having a giant seizure, from my vagina straight up to my brain and every muscle in between. Last to contract were the toes, digging into my soles, scratching at the cheap sheet. And when he removed the feather, it was totally bent and matted and looked completely useless. I was a wreck, sweaty and thirsty and so terribly vulnerable.

He undressed, and came to me. Me going crazy. Crying out please. Please my love. He riding me slowly, partly in. Then quicker, deeper. He finally giving it up inside but again so deliberate. So fucking cocksure because he knew he had me, then and forever.

I came a couple of times, which I had never done before. I was so thrilled he had gone the extra mile to show me he loved me. And orgasms of any sort are extremely rare to me. So this was like magic, when we were entwined and after, when he washed me down with a wet towel, like I was a helpless baby. Perhaps washed me up is a better term. Massaging the back of my head and neck at the same time with his free hand. Telling me how much he enjoyed it and me. How I was the perfect woman to excite him. And how I made him feel he could do just about anything.

Thinking back, it wasn't what he did or how because I've been done in every which way. Sure, he was a lot of fun to be with because he showed imagination and warmth. And yes, he showed me I mattered. He took great care with my body, complimented my mind, but clearly best by far, he treated me as a kindred spirit. A partner in his social dreams for a better, kinder world. Where all people had equal rights and opportunities. Men and women, old, young, all colors. That's what won my heart, because there was a real chance we could work together and openly, making it our life's mission. Me and my commander. And I've clung to that belief, more than eight years and counting, hoping each second it will be now.

When I calmed down I asked about the props. The ribbon came from a gift box of chocolate fudge from some elderly widow in his dear state of Massachusetts. The feather came from the tail of a European thrush. This he had pulled from the hatband of an aide's fedora as he rushed out of his DC office to catch the plane to LA. And the vintage old projector came from, no surprise, The Porn Palace storeroom. So there was a worldly aura to Jack's stage props. Then my darling looked at the bent, matted feather and said, 'I'd better get him a new one.' And I said, 'While you're at it, could you get me a couple, also?' And we both laughed like school kids.

As to other memorable climaxes, several times just as we were about to vacate one of the rented or borrowed rooms wherever, back into the world, he hugged me at the door. By my love. He, much more important, always leaving first. That's when I was able to reach a mini orgasm, partially dressed, my palm pressed into my groin, because I knew it was over until the next time. Besides the sadness at separating, there was such an emotional relief because I had tried as hard as I could to please him. And hopefully did. But it was hardly like the time he cast the blinking light on the headboard to kindle my dreams and tell me how much he cared. Making me feel so lucky and needed.

We ended each date planning when we could see each other again, like all hope driven people in a love affair are bound to discuss. But this time he only said 'See you soon, darling.' Which was special in its simplicity. It made me feel he wanted us to stay together for the long haul, as lovers, perhaps more. Because I was already sure Jack would begin to take majestic flight. He was getting ready to conquer and lead the world. My red, red robin, his chest all puffed out, bobbing across the empty parking lot, ready to soar. Almost perfect, minus one small feather. And me.

If Jack ever saw this entry, he would be angry about what I revealed about the sex. So lurid, so revealing. Almost like I was trying to excite myself. Which I was. But Dr. Greenson has urged me to put down whatever comes into my head. After all, this diary is for me and him and my inner self. Maybe Dr. Greenson can find some trait in Jack that I can use to help me capture and keep him? The truth is I love my man in every way. Its Jack who loves to get laid more than anything. He's the one into anatomy. I'm into feelings.

I'm going to try to go back to sleep. Wish me luck because the storm outside continues to howl. Is it a terrible warning? Or just a normal act of Nature? Either way, I'm tucking my toes in so they're all the way under the blanket. And I'm pulling this 'blanky' up to my neck. Even if its hot as hell I'm going for safety over comfort. If Tippy comes back, he can find me under here.

Dear Diary, *Morning of June 28, 1960*

Alright, honey. Let's get you a better name. Its been driving me crazy. So what do I want to call you? Dear Diary sounds way too ordinary and corny.

You belong to one of Hollywood's biggest stars. You deserve something special. In the store I was immediately drawn to your red covers. After all a nude photo on a red velvet throw put my name on the marquee. Red is about love, passion and devilish pleasure. Its also a color which suggests some weighty (and I don't mean fat) person saying something of importance. Now I just have to write my thoughts down in you. Pray they make some sense so I can start climbing out of that rattrap of my mind. Getting smarter by choosing smarter. Doing fun things that make me feel good. And good things that make those less fortunate feel good too.

I can't get Jack's red feather out of my mind. Am I stuck in the past? Well I'm definitely stuck on him and those lovely afternoons. Perhaps I'll simply call you Red and leave it at that. Hold it, I really like that name. Red. Am I starting to think of you as a friend, not just a collection of mostly blank pages? A cool new pal to bounce my thoughts off. Please my lady, help me achieve my goals as a person, not just as an actress. I'd love my own family to love. Not just a studio one.

So tell me, Red. How do you think its going? Not so bad for a high school drop out, right? Well, I'm sure you'll be a lot less impressed once I let my hair down. And I show you my dirty underwear. That is when I put some on.

Dear Red,   *June 29, 1960*

Damn it. I can't believe I lost that bottle. I'm an idiot. Now I've got to get more sleeping pills from Doctor Kris and pronto. I have an appointment with my caring psychiatrist, tomorrow afternoon. No, way too long. I'll call and have her send the drugstore my script. Then I'll have a messenger service pick up my Seconals for me. Funny, Red, but I call them red's too. Not so funny that I have to go through all these hoops just to get some.

When will these devious drug companies invent some products that do what they are designed to do with no hateful side effects. So I can free my afternoon calendar of all my doctors. Each a different specialty. Each with few answers other than my other doctors don't know shit. And why should anyone so successful need anything to help her go to sleep? Do they think I count armored trucks passing into Fort Knox in place of sheep? Or film credits?

The only chance I have to be normal is to break away from all their double talk and triple billing. I want my life back to enjoy, not to suffer anew. I'll stay calm by drinking some champagne. Then I'll go for a long walk by the East River. Its warm and sunny. May as well enjoy it. I should have my new bottle of Seconals in a few hours. I'll feel better when they're in my pocket with a couple dissolving in my stomach. Pills in place of love. My other problem, where do I hide you, Red, to keep your pages safe from falling into harmful hands? A safe deposit box at a bank would be a continual pain in the ass to get at quickly. Greenson has a safe behind a painting in his library. Perhaps a small safe in my bungalow. More thought required. Maybe I could hide both Reds together.

Dear Red,   *July 1, 1960*

I must be honest as I write each line. I have to be truthful so
Dr. Greenson can help me. A great actress is always seeking the
truth. Acting is my destiny. Its what I want to do now and when
I'm seventy (my hair's almost white already). Good roles may be
difficult to find but I can produce good film projects long after my
charms have gone bye-bye. As for faded beauty, I'll shift to being a
character actress. I'll still be me. So I won't be a star. In most ways
I'll be happier. Is my worst fear to be uncovered as some deeply
flawed very ordinary human being? Too shallow to care about. Too
boring to pay to see. Fragile, needy, all those faults I continue to
find. Got to go, Red. Phone.

It was Arthur. He's on the farm in Connecticut finishing
up the script for The Misfits. Poor dear. He's been working too
hard. He rewrites for days on end. Well, I told him about us,
Red, and he seemed amused. Even encouraging. He thinks it
would be wonderful to have two great writers in the family, one
right handed and me a lefty, like matched bookends. Arthur's
still plenty annoyed about my LA trip next weekend. I know my
Poppy's concerned about Yves and me starting up again. Like
I could possibly still care for that old frog. He can't even speak
decent English, let alone be someone I could care about for very
long. This became quite clear after wrapping Let's Make Love.

There were so many problems. Going behind Simone's back
made me feel terrible. She's a true lady, smart and well read. In
complete control of not just her career but her entire being. This
supremely confident woman somehow understood I had to have
her husband in order to get him out of my system. Now I know its
over and we're all free to move on. I want to concentrate on serious
acting, not cheap berlesk. Besides Yves will never leave Simone
despite his promises. As I've come to grips with this final truth, I'm

hardly upset. Yves smokes too much and has bad teeth. He's too old and lumpy, with not near enough sense of humor. Why you can't even tell him a dirty joke he understands. And he's French. Its scary how quickly my leading men lose their glow once the spotlight is turned off. Every actress should be made aware of this if she wants to survive. Mr. Montand gave me the old song and dance and I swallowed hard. Well, he wasn't that hard. When will I learn? Marrying an actor would be like marrying myself. Boring and vain.

The only star I was romantically involved with and still continue to adore is Marlon Brando. And we just slept together. Never worked together, so there was no blurring of issues (as Dr. Kris would say). Unfortunately, my dear wild one is too often hiding out on some remote island, playing shipwrecked sailor with unclad native girls. Plus neither of our studios was all that pleased with our deepening friendship. Now that's a major understatement. Everyone seemed so frightened we would dirty each other's reputations. Like me or Marlon were ever that pure to begin with.

The studio execs try to tell us exactly how to live our lives. They only see us as money making puppets with a pulse. I'm sure I could understand and accept this a whole lot better if I was paid a regular weekly salary. Management should provide their feature players with month long programs for their down time. Divide the calendar into days for working, days for community projects and charity work, along with acting workshops. And family time if you're lucky enough to have one. Pay us like we're regular workers.

Which would take much of the ball and chain feeling out of a long-term contract. And help the public to appreciate the business so much more. The heads get paid weekly. Why not the tails? With all the reporters, critics and photographers at my heels, I'm working full time all the time. Yeah, Red, being famous isn't all its cracked up to be. But living unnoticed was far worse. Now I have a tub in my bathroom and a few decent pairs of shoes in my closet. Plus somewhere to go in the morning.

And my handprints in a Hollywood sidewalk. I share that billing with my good friend Jane Russell. Beautiful girl but such a goody two shoes, she's out of this world. She helped get me involved in all these children's charities which have become such a big part of my life, the best part. I like to kid her that she's like the Good Book with a very flashy cover. Just before immersing in concrete, when we were getting ready to kneel down, I suggested she add her breasts and I do my bottom, so we'd be T and A together, forever. After laughing it up we bargained with the publicity man in charge, doing our high heels instead. Hands and feets and forget our seats.

Regarding dirty jokes, I've developed quite a collection through the years. Starting with Groucho and Milton Berle, two of my earliest admirers. Great entertainers and the dirtiest old men to ever pinch a girl. These wacky stage clowns understood plenty. Groucho taught me how to walk like a woman and Milton taught me what to do when I stopped. Johnny Hyde, my agent and lover taught me everything else, including how to cry when he died.

Dear Red,   *July 2, 1960*

One thing's always on my mind, I want to marry Jack Kennedy but I don't know what will get him to want the same thing. Its clear we belong together. Jack's so handsome and smart and sexy. He deeply cares about the common man, not just his rich friends and old schoolmates. From the time he was a kid congressman from Massachusetts he could really light my fire. He's such a great kisser. And since I've started to see him again over the last few months, at Peter's beach house and around LA, its been wonderful. He's so well read and keenly aware of everything, so alive and exciting. Jack's the complete man in every way, even with his bad back. He still kisses me with fiery lips.

I pray he's growing as crazy about me as I feel about him. When we're together we laugh and have fun. And not just in bed. He listens to what I say and thinks I'm smart. Well, at least not dumb so I'm halfway there. And definitely not boring and highbrow, like the privileged deb who always seems so utterly perfect. A woman I could never be, let alone be friends with. If she would ever consider letting me near her dream world. Her beautiful daughter Caroline, the apple of Jack's eyes. Fat chance I belong anywhere close to them. I'm sure my man's fair lady would never be my fair friend. She'd choose to see me as a giant threat, not a welcome ally. In the past, great kings often had harems and all the girls learned to get along. I wonder if a woman ever had a harem. I'd really like that.

Back to Jackie. Lucky stiff can't be afraid of being wrong because even her mistakes are drop dead wonderful. So how can you call them errors at all? Well I'd take Jack off her hands in half a heartbeat. Even with his wandering eyes. Soulful eyes full of passion and mischief. And that haunting laugh that leaves me utterly limp. He has the most beautiful hands. Fingers like the great Rodin, lovingly molding my body into the finest marble piece of ass ever viewed. Leaving me glowing with joy long after he's come. I want to be the First Lady, Jack Kennedy's wife. Screw Yves, who's a second rate Maurice Chevalier at best.

I wonder if Arthur knew what I was thinking right now, would he be hurt and angry or feel far more threatened? Probably all three. Would serve him right for constantly dwelling on my temporary lapses. My husband delights in making me feel bad when I'm trying to feel good. Only time he shows any real emotion is when he thinks he's caught me cheating. I sometimes pretend, like when we make love to get his goat up. He's a writer so he's thrilled to see me as completely selfish. A distrustful tortured tramp, screwing everyone including myself. When at the deepest level, I'm just giving pleasure to some other needy soul. I can't be closed up and frozen like some rock fossil. I need to explore my world and my self. So sometimes its with another person. How else do you stay current? I've confessed to sleeping with lots of men before Arthur. Along with a few women. From this varied group I've gained both enjoyment and knowledge. Why stop trying to improve myself now? What can any of us catch that penicillin won't cure?

Dear Red,   *July 3, 1960*

I admit to being a lousy wife. But there's not a woman
alive who can be faithful all the time. Especially not in her
private thoughts where she's often considering another lover. Of
course there's a good chance he may be attached. In my limited
experience (ha), most of the good ones are. Shameful? Well, more
like unfortunate. The flirting game is just a temporary daydream
to wile away some time. You'll see, Red, only a few progress to an
actual audition. Or a call back if they show promise. I say if my
brilliant playwright needed someone constantly panting in his
corner he should have married Lassie. Arthur is the one who says I
live just for the moment every moment. So why try to be true blue
faithful and then weigh myself down with pointless guilt when I
stray? We should never fake what is clearly impossible as it will
come out even more false. Guilt is not just harmful to the spirit. It
can go straight down your spine, numbing everything in its path.
Large amounts of gas can collect inside your colon and around
your ovaries. Terrible cramps can press on your lungs and kill. My
dear absent mother, who was a Christian Scientist, taught me these
things before she moved to the 'mental hospital'. Well, perhaps
escorted would be a better term. As regards the gas, I've learned
to use salt-water enemas (high) and vinegar douches (low) to fight
off the bloats. So sometimes I feel like a seafood salad. At least I'm
clean and regular. And not so loud.

Dear Red,   *July 3, 1960 (evening)*

I just got finished pushing Paula off the phone. Paula Strasberg is my part time Jewish mother, personal acting coach and constant nudnik. (Hebrew for pain in the ass). She wanted to know if I had written anything yet. We bought you together when we were out shopping at Saks's which remains my favorite New York store. She thought I should choose one in ostrich leather but I thought your red cloth covers perfect. Like me, ordinary stock but daringly beautiful. She's shocked at my progress. Perhaps I'm discovering a whole new talent. One thing's for sure. I'll never let her look at your contents. I consider this secret stuff I've been writing down. Especially about Jack and even her husband Lee. Paula's too damn nosy to be trusted. In fact she's one of the biggest gossips in the history of the business. And the business has had a long line of gossip stand outs. Sometimes I wish she'd just go away and never come back. And I always wish I had the nerve to stand up to her. She's such a terrible know it all and not just about acting. Paula thinks she has all the dirt about everybody and everything. What an attitude. She's such a self-centered bitch! Some observers might even surmise she thinks she's Marilyn Monroe. At least I'm not a know it all. In truth I'm more of a know very little. And I try not to talk behind people's backs. Not like that cheap no talent lunatic bitch witch in black robes. There, I just did it myself. Well, Lee did dump her on me. Which means he couldn't take her either. One good thing, she will not desert me. Of course if I had my own kids, they would not desert me either. Because I would go wherever they went to try to get away from me.

Dear Red,   *July 4, 1960*

I read over some of my stuff. Not bad, pretty good in parts. Ok, Papa Hemingway, better move over for Mama Monroe. You've got some female competition. And not just as an author but as a keen observer of the human condition. Besides, I can sing and dance. Along with sucking cock with true relish when I'm in the mood.

Especially like now when its late at night and I'm thinking about Lee Strasberg, another fan of the human condition. (Is this a negative reaction to Paula??) I just got a great thought. Wouldn't a threesome of Lee Strasberg, me and Albert Einstein be thrilling? I, of course, would be in the middle, center stage. Lee could teach me all his subtle acting moves from behind and Mr. Science could work my head from the front. Getting my brain purring so I'd be smart enough to grasp all of Lee's acting pearls, along with The Wizard's energy and time stuff. All in one magical night. So by morning I'd wind up with an armful of Nobel's and a neck full of hickies. I just have to trust my two geniuses will be able to balance their thrusts, thereby reducing any chances of my back going out. Still being able to incorporate their lessons into my performance, becoming the character I'm playing has to come from inside me. There's no shortcut to good acting, even in daydreams. The main thing I work on is observing others, trying to capture their smallest gestures. I've also learned to try to fall in love with my character, even if she's not so good or normal. I hope these efforts will add up to trusting myself and going for more. Never been fully satisfied with my work. Never been satisfied at all with my life.

Back to the 'mouth to meat' or oral department. When I was first trying to get into the business I'd straight out swallow for any role. Lap it off the linolium floor if it was a speaking part. Later I'd do it with a certain few men for the right role. And now I'll just do it with the right man to win his heart. So I'm definitely moving up, or down may be closer to it. But its definitely higher on the respect ladder. As my first female therapist, Dr. Hohenberg taught me, as long as I continue to strive, I'm at least alive. By the end of my time working with her I had stopped doing things in bed for bargaining chips. Respect comes in simple steps. My Freudian whiz took me to the point where I had become a star. Definition: I no longer had to bend over or blow just to get into the show.

The good psychiatrist came with me to England but when we returned I had to drop her. The problem was she was also treating Milton Greene. Fox very much needed me back in their house. And they were willing to give me the world, at least in acting terms, to get me. Total project and director approval. Milton, my co producer, was the one who got me these unheard of clauses. The terrible part was in order for me to have and enjoy them, Milton had to be fired. And he was one of the true loves of my life. A few weeks later the studio bigwigs demanded I resign from my own company. Me fired too. Marilyn Monroe Productions was formally closed and any threat to their way of doing things was forever removed. Its a rough tough business. And success doesn't make it any easier. But I did learn how to produce films. Easily as well as those young executives.

Back to blowjobs. No guy ever got seriously ill let alone perished from being on the receiving end of a good half and half. But especially when its me, the Grand Dame performing this sexual division. One of my real specialties if I do say so myself. A performing art finely tuned at the Hollywood School for Call Girls and Want-to-be Mistresses that I was forced to attend for nearly half a year. After that son of a bitch Zanuck fired me for dating Tommy Zahn, my too cute friend from acting class.

Unfortunately for my career, Zanuck's wife of thirty years had earmarked Tommy for their daughter. After we were discovered making out in the small lunch room, I got fired from the studio almost before I could push my knees together. So I lost my twice a month paycheck and my free singing and acting lessons and my pride. Tommy wound up in Hawaii working days as a lifeguard. I wound up in a small modeling agency off Santa Monica Blvd., working nights as a convention pro. Me and the other 'entertainers' exchanged favors with Kansas pig ranchers with funny straw hats and big horns. And oriental salesmen with big tippees and little dickees. Well, I did have to eat, but it was a terrible job.

I just got a call from Arthur. He can be so sweet, then suddenly turn into a mad man from a horror film. Especially if he's pressed with a writing deadline like right now. The Misfits screenplay is due to be finished two weeks from this Monday. After that we're no longer in pre-production. The clock is ticking.

One can rewrite original plays for years trying to get things perfect. My Poppy's learning in film the screenwriter is almost a side attraction. Like ketchup. Its the actors and actresses who have to get it perfect. I'm sorry. On The Misfits its THE ACTRESS (along with the rest of the cast). Joke, Red. Even I'm not that conceited. Well, I am but would never admit it. And I'm not narcissistic either. Mainly cause I want to do it with others, not just myself. And I want my movie to be the best ever. And I want to help kids and women, especially the uneducated hungry ones.

July 6, 1960

Hi, Red. I'm on the Connecticut farm in the large, sunny kitchen with my coffee. House and Gardens lovely with the beautiful garden right outside the screen door. My garden planted with my hands, all in bright colors. Anyhow, the mail just arrived and I'm looking at pictures from my luncheon date with Mr. Khrushchev and some of the film community on the Fox studio lot. The Red Head's or Head Red's luncheon was over half a year ago but the photos somehow got lost.

Paula again. Madam Buttinsky and Miss Supreme Know It All. She must call twenty times a day. And the plumber, who has to hook up the sink in the barn. I'm converting a portion of it into a baby nursery just in case. Please God, give me a child. I called several architects, asking for an estimate. Each of them said knock it down, the wood was too old. But I have stubbornly resisted touching the frame because the beams are truly beautiful. Why does everything have to look brand new? This has nothing to do with me being scared over losing my looks. The public has to stop thinking of actresses as frozen statues. There is not a single living thing that does not age. I'm just trying to age well. So should each of them and stop saying I won't be able to. Watch me sing and dance in the old age home, you nonbelievers. Grind your false teeth while I celebrate my hip grinds. I'm sure I can seduce an aide.

Back to my Russian admirer, Mr. K. Usually, I like older men. Less in a rush and kinder. But he really frightened me, even though he kept looking down at my breasts and letting me know he was attracted. Still, after seeing his wife Nina, I can easily understand. I wouldn't be surprised if he forced her to carry a potato sack around. Well, at least ordered that she have it nearby as required intimate apparel when he got hot to trot. She's that dumpy and unaware of her appearance.

I, on the other hand, require over three hours just to make up my face. And I always use five different shades of red lipstick because my lips are actually quite thin, especially my upper one. Nina comes in wearing what looks like plain Vaseline on her lips, part of which is smeared on her cheeks and teeth. And her hair is in a thick bun like a coil of worn rope. Poor dear. Now there's a lady who would definitely benefit from an expert make over with real American professionals. We might win the cold war with eyeliner, mascara, blush, and a good bra. Lot better than bullets and bombs and breasts to your knees.

Still, her husband scared the pants off me. As if I haven't been scared my whole life anyway. Sometimes even simple things like going out shopping or making a call from a different phone, let alone being with an ugly BEAR who kills people. Stalin, his boss, made Hitler look like a choirboy in the murder department. And now, Russia's become a country where basic rights do not exist. Least of all the right to keep breathing if you piss off some big shot party member. Tell the truth and risk viewing the firing end of a rifle squad. The direct opposite of the good old US of A where you can criticize almost anyone. Just as long as its partly true. Thank God for our constitution. Along with the press, hungry for a scoop. Shame because socialism seems more in sync with the masses. Equal food for all. Clear case of right idea, wrong outcome. Least when it comes out as Communism. A steel curtain with mind control has to be a horrible place to live. Still, I begged the Bear to work harder for world peace. Why, one atom bomb could wipe us all out. The ultimate enemy seemed far more intent on trying to rub his sweaty body against me. Like I could possibly be turned on to such a mean spirited dictator with 20 years of bloodletting and mass executions on his hands. Don't want those stained fingers coming near me.

I'm quite proud Arthur wasn't asked to attend this luncheon because the studio felt his politics infuriate so many. Hooray for him. I've always felt one of Arthur's best qualities was his concern for the under-privileged. Me? I firmly believe in equal rights for women (we should get paid the same as men and have the same number of bathroom stalls), children (who should be loved, protected and cared for always), and animals (ditto, with an exercise pen). We need good schools and hospitals for everyone who lives here. Or comes for a visit. Make our citizens healthier and wiser and they'll also be happier and do better work. See I too am a devout liberal and constant bleeding heart. Of course in order to be generous, you need some money in the bank. So I also have a career to think about. And I'm a much better businessman than my husband. Sorry, Red, businesswoman. Anyhow, its important to be seen out. Especially in the entertainment business where short term memory is the gold standard for getting roles. So I keep making appearances and blowing kisses. Hey, at least I'm doing it on my feet. I've got to do a few chores. We will resume later, new friend. I have to take care of my blessed hound dog who is howling for some exercise and to get his big belly rubbed.

(After walking Hugo with the lovely ears)

While walking in the woods, I was thinking about the end of the Khrushchev party and the sour after taste that remains. It started while I was waiting for the elevator, trying to get downstairs where the limos were being loaded. The door opens, out pops Frank Sinatra. The little wise ass had wrangled his way into hosting the whole shindig, like some UN peace maker from 'Joisey'. Smut dealer is more like it. Frankie Boy was even cockier than usual. Talking about how he had wanted to invite my husband to his party but 'the Pentagon pricks nixed his coming.' I informed Frank that Arthur had character and wouldn't come if the invite had come directly from President Eisenhower. Talk about Mr. Obnoxious. He's like a kid brother you love one minute and want to strangle the next.

There's still an awful lot of bad feelings between the two of us from the 'wrong door' raid, when he broke down the door of that nice old lady. And I was in a different apartment, upstairs and one down. Frank said he was just helping me and Joe get back together. How? By trying to catch me screwing someone else, when we were legally separated no less. What an idiot. Only good thing about that mess was it just about killed things between my former husband and Frank and they were best buddies. Giuseppe never forgave him, which is hardly a surprise. Anyone who knows Joe knows he has the memory of an elephant about upsetting incidents that leave him feeling slighted. Or treated with DISRESPECT. A word I heard from my he-man so often he was like an Italian tenor leading a Greek chorus.

And even though I forgave Joe rather quickly, I realized we could never get back together. I would always be his friend. I might sometimes be his lover. By the way, he does excel in that area, with power and stamina. Plus rather impressive equipment at the bat rack. Shows that sex isn't all that important, even for a sex queen. The present day Eros, Symbol of Love, needs tenderness, understanding and appreciation. Both mental and physical for this lady. True romantics and I am one, seek the emotional part of coupling. Dr. Greenson taught me true sexual arousal (the act which ends in climax) arises from the mind, not the genitalia. Kindness and consideration mean a lot more than a forceful pounding of my insides. I'm no cement mixer.

Ok. The real reason I could no longer spend married time with Joe is he beat the crap out of me several times. My baseball star turned out to be a rather lousy sport in the game of love. Lot better hitter than fielder. If a man hurts you physically and emotionally, I don't think things can ever be the same. When the Yankee slugger felt the slightest bit hurt, he lashed out. This behavior was simply unacceptable. Bruises can not just be covered up with carefully applied make up. The ones done to the heart remain forever. And violence or the threat of violence really scares me. No one deserves fists as punishment even if caught cheating, which I never was.

The issue guaranteed to bring on one of our terrible arguments was my work. Giuseppe hated my film career and demanded I retire from acting. Too painful and not acceptable. When I realized his attitude wasn't going to improve, I pulled the plug.

Mi amore only wanted me waiting in the kitchen, wearing frilly lingerie, greeting him, swaying to Steam Heat. Some life. Lounging in the 'on deck circle' until he finally drifted home from some country club bar, wearing sweaty golf clothes and that stupid glove. Like I've come all this way just to boil spaghetti, darn socks, and be available so he can get his rocks off. I need to spread out my mind, not just my thighs.

Besides, Arthur was at that moment getting a divorce from his first wife. And he was so much more appealing. A real intellect who was respected for his social beliefs, honored as a writer, and much more sensitive to my needs. So we got married. I prayed he'd be the answer to all of my prayers. My 'beshert' or chosen one. Well that was a long time ago. Now all my hopes seem to be going up in smoke. And I feel at a real loss. Perhaps I'll turn inward. Say the hell with love and give my soul and vagina a rest period. Get involved in more charities for kids. Or Ban the Bomb protests for the world.

Dear Red, *July 8, 1960*

Arthur seems more accepting of my California trip. Resigned may be a better word. Looking back, I'm sorry I ever started with Yves. Why do I always seem to make things more difficult for myself? Now I'm sure Poppy doesn't trust me like he used to. Which means it will be a lot harder to screw around behind his back. Still, where there's a will, there's a way. And I've got to do what I think best, especially when I'm back in action searching for my soul mate. Eyes open, tits and ass jiggling enough to catch my prey's attention. Panties in the bottom drawer or casually draped at my ankles. A real class act from top to bottom.

My sometimes socially conscious husband has it coming. He never should have broken the Writer's strike by doing the Let's Make Love rewrites. Overnight, my great liberal hero had become a scab, peddling his wares to who ever. Course he said he did it only for me. But I know better. Since then, I've been unable to view him with the rose-colored glasses necessary to make him my modern Abraham Lincoln. My true hero had become no longer true or a hero. When we got married, I believed he would free me up from all my insecurities. And rescue me when I fell to demons, real or imagined. Now I find out he has trampled on some of my dearest values. So he's not all that trust worthy himself. Some payday, climbing over the backs of the writers he stands with. Those struggling hacks, who either through lack of ability or just dumb luck find themselves less in demand then he is. That's not to suggest he's not a great writer. Just two faced and frantic.

All the miscarriages sure didn't help our marriage. That's a major understatement. Lord, I want a family so much, I would give absolutely anything to be blessed with that one forever gift. Not to point fingers but I'm pretty sure our failure is pretty much all Arthur's fault. My doctor, who is a lady herself and a very good doctor, has suggested he might have weak, inactive sperm. Something about the little guys decreased movements past a certain age. No tail action which I have retained to the max. I've also noticed his come seems a good deal more watery than most and I do know seamen texture and consistency. My doctor's not sure that's all that important. I tend to think more and thicker has to be better. I do know we've failed repeatedly.

Then to add to our troubles in bed, after getting the commitment from John Huston to direct The Misfits, Arthur's become frigid. Frozen into the script rather than trying to make our marriage the center of our life together. He seems to need an artistic success far more than he needs me. But wouldn't it be wonderful? I mean if the film won the Pulitzer like Salesman and I won the Oscar, like I should have for Bus Stop.

After all, he is writing it just for me. Sometimes he'll come into the bedroom and ask me to say a line. Then we'll go back and forth and finally I'll just blurt it out the way it feels easiest to my tongue. And we both start to laugh because its clearly better. The beauty of my character, Roslyn, is she's so much like me I can be more of an expert than even the author. Above any film I've done, this is going to be an A project. The Misfits, the number one dramatic project of the decade, perhaps even the century. An all star motion picture with me as the No. 1 performer and major star. Clark Gable, the handsome King, as my co-star. A wonderful supporting cast of little stars. Great director. Terrific director of photography. High powered producers. Experienced production crew. I have to admit its very exciting to be looking out, not in.

I hope its not too hot in the desert. My hair is bad enough, breaking off in the back, and brittle everywhere. George will have a fit. Well, its his job to make me look beautiful, no matter what. And in the role of Roslyn, my character can look a bit weathered. It should only make my performance more believable. This one's about deep down go for the core feelings. Not posing or going for cheap laughs. Phone. Got to go, Red.

I'm back. Paula again. With nothing. Hope I don't call too much. I know I spend lots of time using the damn phone. But its my way of connecting with lots of people in lots of places for business and pleasure. And doing it fast. Red, you're my real friend. I don't ever lie to you. You and my good Dr. Greenson. Actually I don't ever try to lie to the world either. Might lay it on and twist the truth to make me look better. But so do lots of public people. As Joe E. Brown said at the end of 'Some Like It Hot' (after finding out Jack Lemmon, his love, was a guy), 'Nobody's Perfect.' OK, so sometimes I just make stuff up. If its good stuff no one cares and if its bad stuff they like it even better. If you don't believe me look at the tabloids. I never came close to screwing a mariachi band. Or the entire USC football team, like others are rumored. I hate football. The players are way too brawny, with their jocks of steel. Besides I'm much more discreet than screwing in an open field. You can get burrs or bites. Major confession, over the years my sex drive has to a large deal diminished. So now I only sleep with men I love.

MIDNIGHT

I JUST GOT THE VERY BEST NEWS! ITS TOO WONDERFUL.

Peter Lawford called from LA minutes ago. He just reserved a suite for me at the Hilton. If JACK wins the nomination next week, and who can stop him now, I'll share in his triumph. And his bed!! Everyone says I have a great ass but the Senator's is like two ripe melons. How come men don't spread? It isn't fair. To marry him would be a dream come true. In my heart the Senator is the all time perfect mix of Joe and Arthur. Jack Kennedy's my true Prince Valiant, who will make all my lonely days and nights worthwhile.

I want be the First Lady. And one of the great actresses of all time. Then I won't be asked to play whores or mindless sex objects in vulgar comedies. Only major dramatic roles worthy of a gifted artist and CHARISMATIC female lead. (I stole that term from an article I read about Jack that came out in one of the magazines).

When I used to see him, we could walk the beaches and nobody seemed to notice or care. I don't think we'll be taking that stroll anymore. Definitely not in broad daylight. He's very virile but not a hugger like Arthur or some of my other boyfriends. I mean sometimes he won't even wait till my pants are off. Bang. He's inside. One thing's for sure. Jack enjoys sex any time, any position, any combo. I refuse on more than us two. Too confusing. Plus I've never been known as a great sharer. Of course that's one of the few times I've set any limits with my man.

Bottom line we're pretty much the perfect couple. In all the important things we think and act like we arrived here from the same womb. (He of course much earlier.) We're both shameless manipulators with huge career drives. Never even close to feeling satisfied with what he or she has already achieved. Looking forward, we share enormous visions for our future selves. To the point of being quite annoying to those who can't see as far. I want to star in and produce important films and eventually try directing. Something light, maybe a comedy. He right now (well, in six months) wants to direct the entire world. But both of us are always striving, always grabbing, always moving forward.

Maybe it was better that I never had a baby with Arthur. The press could accuse the Senator of being a home wrecker. As if any individual could be responsible for breaking up a solid marriage. The problem is Jack and I are far too much in the public eye to risk being exposed. The Senator would wind up getting terrible press that would totally kill his election chances. I could never allow myself to injure my man's image like that. That's why I have to play the loyal soldier, to protect my lover and commander. Step back from my dreams and ours to assure his.

But it would be marvelous to be a mother. Forget who the father is. So my kids would have to go it with only one name. He or She (fill in the proper name), child of Miss Monroe (family name). See, Red, I keep thinking I'm running out of time with my tortured ovaries and tubes. Along with the tortured memories from that pregnancy roller coaster. Arthur being so caring and kind and eventually disappointed. Then I'd get frightened I would never be able to get pregnant. And I'd stay drunk from the time of my damn period for almost a solid two weeks. Then, we'd try again, during my fertile period. No alcohol, no pills, no lubricants. Just Sinatra and hard core humping, with me on my back, cheering Poppy on. And after, afraid to move for the next half hour. My feet up, wiggling my toes, counting the seconds off, hoping, praying. Little joy. No success.

Our worst fate, to be a barren couple. No one who knows us doubts that our child would be bright and socially kind. Arthur's one of the world's great geniuses. And he always says I'm as street smart as anyone he's met. Its obvious at times I still love the guy. So where did we screw up? Its complicated but according to my world respected L.A. shrink, Arthur made the ultimate mistake. He began caring for me too much, until he lost his own identity in the process. Dr. Greenson says I have a tendency to bring this on, having noticed the same thing happening during his treatment of me. To add to our problems, Arthur can be terribly moody and withdrawn, especially when under pressure.

Also my husband made me stop being friends with Milton Greene who I deeply trusted. Not only was Milton my partner in the production company but I loved him as a human being. He was always encouraging, upbeat, with such a great eye. And marvelous sense of humor. Along with some of my lesser friends who happen to use drugs and alcohol, but are also fun to be with. Many, surprise, surprise, happen to be very successful in the film business. Pretty soon I had no one to laugh with anymore. Arthur managed to get rid of lots of wacky people, but destroyed a big part of me in the process. Losing comrades hurts, even if most of them were two sided, undependable louses to begin with.

Which brings me back to the baby issue. We were not able to make a baby together which is the one thing I want more than anything. Still as my good Doctor constantly reminds me, I must take my cards as they're dealt. I have to start learning to roll with the punches. I can still champion children's rights because all the world's children are important. Besides I could easily adopt. Any agency would be more then thrilled to have me as a client. Think of the publicity, especially since I've chosen to breast-feed.

But one from my own body would be such a special gift. Please, God. I'd be forever grateful. Am I being punished for all those abortions when I was just a dumb kid? Or when I, … well, maybe I'll let you in on one of my most closely guarded secrets when I know you just a bit better. Let's say I'm terribly sorry for all my misdeeds and miscarriages and leave it at that.

I'm going to try to get some sleep. I got these new pills from one of my other doctors to take. I only hope they work better than the damn reds. I'll try to write more tomorrow. I'm getting nervous already. But Red, its such a good feeling. After all, the next President of this wonderful country has asked me to come and be by his side to celebrate his nomination. Talk about history. The youngest candidate to ever run for the office of President has called out to me. This leader is clearly one of the smartest most handsome men to ever grace the halls of Washington. So I've got the most dreamed about man in the history of our great nation. How many girls can say they're going to meet up with their handsome prince right after he is chosen King? I'll be with my hero, casting all my hopes up to heaven. Lord, please help me bewitch him.

Sunday, the 12'th, I think

Damn, I'm so woozy I almost started at the bottom of the page. The pills didn't work, only made me more confused and a little less anxious. So now I'm fighting exhaustion too. Well, at least when I'm back in LA I can see Dr. Greenson. If he knew how many different doctors I see, he'd flip. Sometimes less is more. Sometimes not. Especially when certain MD's, like my dear Professor of the Mind, don't like to medicate. Working through analysis, freeing up my demons, rather than masking them through sedatives and sleeping pills. So painful most times I could scream. If this would do any good in terms of him changing his approach to my treatment. And I've been doing drugs like reds (aka dolls) as long as I can remember. Shit, everyone in filmland is on them. How can they be harmful when you never hear any bad stuff happening to any of us? The other abusers can't all be dead. I see them everywhere.

July 12, 1960 (evening-this time I'm sure)

Red, you're becoming a routine but I do like the feeling when I sit down and read the stuff I've already written. And then compose my present thoughts to make new entries. So I can see right in front of me I'm capable of developing good habits, just like I got my old bad ones. Arthur tried to sneak a peek at your first pages but I made him promise to never try that again and he put his hand on our bible and swore.

Can you imagine him reading about Jack? That would be simply terrible. My saving grace is he'll protect and preserve anything that might help me put down on paper what I'm trying to capture. He respects the great problems in writing anything. Most especially something as personal as a diary. He says creation is G-d's greatest gift. That's why he insists that a writer's privacy can never be trampled on. Especially after I found his wrinkled, angry note where he compared me to his first wife. Someone I know he hates, which caused such a ruckus in our first year of marriage. Hinting I was a floozy slut when I was just doing what the Studio calls immersing in your character. Analysis and breathing exercises for the ACTOR and immersing for the CHARACTER. How could Arthur be so ignorant of his friend Lee's major teachings?

He also seems to forget I was the only one who stood up for him against those crazies from the government, especially that horrible Joe McCarthy. He and his insane crusaders, especially J. Edgar Hoover, tried to put Arthur in jail. As a Communist, citing him for contempt. I urged Arthur to refuse to testify in any form. Say nothing, give up nobody. You'll be seen as Gandhi, Nathan Hale, and Jimmy Stewart all rolled into one national treasure. Arthur finally stood up and said 'I've done nothing wrong. I will not cooperate or name names because there are none.' Front page headlines galore!

We wound up with wonderful publicity and the Un-American's were called bullies by the news. Soon the charges were dropped. After I paid his lawyers, that whole bi-coastal bi-sexual firm of leeches, we were free. After close to three years. Speaking of red, for a while that was the most hateful of words especially around here and the N.Y. apartment. Some of his dearest friends, like Eli Kazan, turned on him in fear. I do hope that had nothing to do with the fact I had slept with Eli previously. Some men can be so strange with issues like that. Bottom line Arthur is a very loyal citizen. I mean he thinks America has faults. Especially in terms of care for our poor and less fortunate. Still its a hell of a lot better than any other country. Anyhow it was ridiculous because Arthur is in many ways the most moral man I've ever met. Square, stuffy, a little superior (especially brain wise) but always decent.

Besides, his father is very religious, a Jewish Rabbi. In my experience people of the Jewish faith seem to be a bit more moral anyway. At least the ones who have managed to keep their fat asses out of show business. That's why when it came to our wedding ceremony, I chose to do it in Arthur's faith. Not to please his parents, although I'd do just about anything to please 'Izzy'. No, this was for me and my inner self. I wanted to learn how to worship in the same manner as Arthur did because I thought it would help to cement our family together. So I did a rather intense 'mini conversion' for two weeks, in order that I understand the Hebrew words when I said them. And in Hebrew and English I promised to raise any children from our union in the Jewish tradition. Next in tribal importance is the caterer so I chose me and made sure not to serve ham or lobster to our guests. See, Red, I gave up being a 'shiksa' for my 'dahling mensh'. But in the end it didn't really matter. Turns out Arthur was far less religious than me.

One funny note about diet laws. I'm at my second Seder (Passover) ever at my future in laws house. And I foolishly ask if there was some other part of the matzo we could eat in the soup, not just the balls? Big laugh from everyone. But I honestly thought the balls were like scrotal sacks, you know, that hold the nuts, or testicles of the matzo. Which I had been told by Izzy's cousin was a wild animal that looked like a small desert zebra which through the centuries had been tamed by the nomads. And these matza (pleural) were now kept in herds.

I can be a real dunce and people like to kid around and use my gullible nature. And I fall into their trap cause I'm too trusting. With this lack of caution I often wind up looking like a total jerk. Which I've worked into my humor, playing the over the top dumb blonde who doesn't have a clue how stupid she really is. But in real life it can be a most dangerous weakness. Because some people try to take unfair advantage especially because I'm a celebrity.

Like with you, Red, my book of personal secrets and fears. I suddenly realize I have to be extra careful in protecting you. In fact I think I'll start carrying you around in my bag. First off, I can write down any insight (spur-of-the-moment) that comes flashing into my brain, which might become important later on. Once I've had the chance to look at it in black and white and think about its meaning. But more important, I sure don't want to take the chance of losing you now that I've begun to bare my soul. Why if you got into the wrong hands, I could be blackmailed big time. Or given up to the newspapers.

I used to have a diary years ago that was green leather. And it had a small lock. It was a present from Amy Greene, who always has such perfect taste. But I've already written more in you in weeks than I did in years with it. Johnny Hyde, my wonderful agent and lover, used to say, 'Kid, everything's timing'.

So, I can't trade you in now. We already share one of the most important bonds there is. Trust. And what protection is a flimsy lock? I'll start carrying you around in a small leather case. Of course if you, my dear 'Red' ever turned up somewhere too embarrassing? Well, I'd simply call a press conference and state you're an out and out forgery. Act angry and hurt and insist I've never set eyes on you. Lie my ass off. The nerve to suggest you were my personal diary. People are always doing that with some supposed article of mine. Clothing, luggage, a used Kotex. Damn hustlers, always trying to make a buck. And you'd understand why I said what I did. To protect both of us.

I just spoke to JACK!! MY ALL TIME HERO…

It was just for a moment, but it was so exciting!

First, I'm going to open a bottle of bubbly to celebrate.

We're going to be together Thursday, when he locks up the vote (mind you there no longer seems to be any doubt). Right after his formal acceptance speech, his ass, and penis, will be mine. After all, my Jack wants to spend his biggest night ever celebrating with me in his bed.

And then he told me he loves me. Isn't that wonderful? Not that I'm really counting (hah, I'm such a liar) but he's only said that two times before. And one of those I can't count completely because he was drunk and I refused to give him his precious BJ unless he stated it with meaning. So did he like my little thank you that followed this forced declaration? Obviously yes, because he's not only continued to hang around, he just told me he loves me. Which makes three of those magic moments, and three, as any gambler knows, is a very lucky number.

Now I wouldn't be spreading this around, but I've been thinking Congress should appoint a sex expert (me) to testify during the coming presidential race. After conducting a thorough survey, I would declare on prime time television which candidate had the biggest balls. Because that's one of the most admirable things people look for in a leader. Surely not traits of honesty or consideration for others.

Its really not fair. A woman has to be beautiful all over, inside and out. And a guy just has to have 'cajones'. Big brass balls to fire the fiercest emotions, ranging from simple threats to murderous rage. I personally feel male hormones are grossly overrated. Our leaders should be patient and slow to anger and try to compromise with people from other nations.

Haven't there been too many Hitler's and Moossolini's already? We should give the mothers a chance to run things. I'm including myself in this group because number one, I feel I will be a mother in the near future and it is important to think positive. And number two, I care about all the people on this planet, especially the little ones, so I am a mother to the world's people already. And a little girl to the men. Wonder why I'm confused?

My unschooled view of history. The Roman Wars only stopped when the mothers refused to allow the brutal behavior to continue any longer. Tired of seeing their sons being destroyed in terrible conflicts, they finally said no. No to the military who were using their kids as human targets, no to the leaders who used the soldiers for their own false glory and most important directly no to you, my dear child. You are not going. I won't allow it. I'll give up my own life before allowing you to risk yours. And then there was peace for many years.

Still until that blessed day comes, I do want my dear Jack to win. He is the total opposite of both Lyndon Johnson and Richard Nixon, two faced horrors who I'm sure would delight in leading us into a big war. Just keep making it bigger and bloodier. Shift the attention to some makeshift enemy as cowards and crooks need to do. Sell themselves as protectors of our freedoms. Wave the American flag, salute crisply at our country's graveyards and steal the taxpayers blind. It sure won't be their kids carrying the rifles. Or winding up permanently crippled.

My hair in back is in horrid shape, despite the protein and beer rinses. Maybe I'll let it grow out completely so I look more proper and subdued like a First Lady should. Oh my word! What will I wear? Perhaps the little black Chanel sheath. I can't wait. More later. I have to make plans. This is my most important date ever.

Dear Red,   *July 13, 1961*

I'm back in New York City, getting ready to fly to LA. Its all too wonderful! George and me fly out tomorrow morning. He'll start working on my hair while we're airborne so I have a head start. (No pun intended)

I'll need the works, times two. I'm really worried I won't look my best. I mean when the soon to be President of our wonderful nation calls me the most beautiful woman in the world, meaning not just his world but everyone's, I have an obligation to look the part. Its my patriotic duty. And while I'm there, I'll be able to see my brilliant Doctor Greenson with you under my arm. Hey, I just realized you're a virgin, Red. A true innocent. That is you've never undergone analysis with me on the couch. I'm sure he's going to enjoy going over some of our entries. Then my handsome Romeo (true given name, Romeo Sammy Greenschpoon, can you die? That's why he got a stage name) will try to render some profound insight into my crazed thoughts. Maybe he can even help me plan strategy. Although, what does any man know about love? They can be so naive.

Unfortunately, my sweet, caring doctor has learned considerably more about achieving emotional goals than marital ones. Even if he did train at the school of the great Freud. Besides, he's been married for ages. Its interesting but he's one of the few men I'm attracted to but have never wanted to sleep with. Well, maybe fool around a little. But that's a normal part of the shrink process. Its called transference. And especially since I've never had a father around to care or to teach me right from wrong, Dr. Greenson's been there for me. But, also like a good Daddy, he constantly maintains his own rigid rules of social behavior. Fortunately for both of us. Drives me a little crazy, because these boundaries as he calls them make him even more enticing.

Sometimes by the end of a session I want to just reach over and give him the biggest sloppiest kiss possible. If for no other reason than to make him realize I'm a woman. Similarly I jumped into the lap of the skilled Life photographer, Al Eisenstadt, just after finishing Gentlemen Prefer Blondes. One wiggle and 'Eisy's' face stayed red for hours. And he messed up the f stop for color. But we got some truly great pictures together, on that simple patio in natural light with no backdrop. Me in a plain black sweater sitting on an old chaise lounge in high spirits over my ability to arouse people of all ages. Sexcess.

Anyhow from his side of the desk, my world respected doctor remains far more concerned with tapering my medicines which he thinks are still way too much. I've actually changed plenty under his care mainly because he has no idea how out of control I was before. If he knew how often those quacks on the set would inject me with heavy doses of barbituates to keep me working like some robot, he'd have their medical licenses taken away. They made me feel like an out and out junkie. Although the shots did help for a while. But the rebound was vile, leaving me a tearful unsure wreck. Especially by the end of filming, after we wrapped whatever movie I was doing at the time, the next two weeks were pure hell.

Jack is my absolute dream man, along with being the most important leader of modern times. Well he will be in a very short while. Then we can see each other whenever we want. He'll have his shiny new airplane to fly him into my highly toned, slightly used vagina. So after awhile he'll want to be married to me instead of little Miss Perfect. The present Mrs. Kennedy, a true blue ice statue and poised debutante, who has never had to struggle one damn day in her entire blessed life. I'm sure she doesn't have to worry about split ends. Let alone severe menstrual cramps which seem to be getting worse each month. Damn endometriosis. Often so bad even the Demerol shots don't start to take the pain away.

Being a woman is hard enough without being all alone in this insane business, facing an army of pencil pushing pricks. A male assault using their cherished erections as weapons. The studio chiefs want you to do whatever they say and do it at the exact moment they say. And if you don't, they run to the press calling you angry and withdrawn and extremely difficult to work with. As they whisper to themselves that you're an over indulged spoiled BITCH, constantly on the rag, who only delights in fucking up the works. Actors may be second rate citizens but women are worse than dirt. Making actresses the lowest of the low, to be used, abused, then discarded long before they hit forty. Dumping us into the gutter like other street vermin, once our boner appeal starts to fade. And we become human.

That's the reason I broke ranks and started my own production company. Not because I was seeking to be a trail blazer for the film community let alone the entire business world. I'm hardly that noble or brave. And it wasn't the money. I simply had to get away from the studio because they never listened to what I wanted to do as a performer. Wouldn't even let me try to be a real actress. Great, they gave me a little bigger dressing room on Gentlemen. But then when I saw what they gave Jane, I was furious. Besides I was the blonde in the title and had equal billing. So I said something. They refused to listen.

I continued to fight for over a month for the 200 more square feet. By then the movie was a third in the can. Jane fought by my side cause she thought it was extremely unfair, also. The studio boys finally gave in but was it worth the battle? Why couldn't they just offer it up without making it so damn difficult?

After being pushed to the edge time after time, I finally said 'Screw it' and began to fight back. I took a stand to keep my remaining sanity because I had no other choice. I had to get all the studio dickheads off my back once and for all. I had no doubt I didn't need them to keep working. But I had to demonstrate it to them. Which I did rather easily almost the day I left. Major projects started falling into my lap without any help from any of them. So now I have project approval along with director approval plus I make ten percent of all the profits that the film makes. And no one gets that except Marlon. So I wound up getting a fair share of the profits as an added bonus. Well now that I have the revenue, everyone seems to respect me a whole lot more. Especially the other actors and the crew and their families. Look, I'm happy I could break new ground. Use my clout to help others get to a better position while financially bettering me. But it always came down to simply having a say in what I did. I needed to at least feel I could try different things. I know people like me in comedies and they buy the tickets but it isn't only about receipts. Its also about increasing my range and helping me to be proud of my work. So now all the studio executives hate my guts and say very mean things. But I've had it with all their bullshit. Many of these bastards consider it their duty to keep all their women employees on their knees, helpless and gagging. Now I've licked their puny peckers for the last damn time. No more humiliations.

Thank you Milton and Amy Greene, who helped me break the status quo. They gave me the courage and the know how to make a film. And I did a good job on The Prince and The Showgirl. Its a real film with Sir Lawrence Olivier as co-star. What a stuffy asshole he turned out to be. Besides being just about the worst director I've ever worked with. No fun, no spontaneity. He yelled at me continuously which just got me more and more nervous. To do great comedy you have to be loose as a goose with buckets of imagination. Not some castrated constipated Macbeth. Anyhow the film did well at the box office and was ours from the beginning and I get receipts each month to prove it. Because best of all, I own it. Super tight ass knight of the square table worked for me but I wasn't going to tell him that. Just went about my own strictly unprofessional business making fans of the Brits by making them laugh, along with curtsying to the Queen.

So there, screw you Larry and all those Fox execs. Now I can say what I think is best for my career. And who I want to work with and what films I want to do. So much fairer in every way. My triumphs, my failures, but most important, my decisions.

Jack just WON THE DEMOCRATIC NOMINATION!

On the very first ballot. Wyoming, the last state, put him over the top. His brother Teddy pledged the final votes. Praise the delegates and pass the bubbly! My honey's going to be our next President. Holy shit. I can't believe this great thing is really going to happen.

My love just called me, ten minutes ago and less than one hour from THE MOMENT. Jack, my true angel. He said he can't wait to see me. I told him how thrilled I was and how I love him with all my heart. He thinks he has to choose Johnson for his running mate. Blackmail of the worst kind and kind has nothing to do with it.

Something about the Texan's threat to release some of Hoover's FBI files to the media. (LBJ and Hoover, Washington's two merchants of evil, linked at the hip and mind.) Revealing Jack's dad Joe's illegal activities, of all things. Who cares if he was a bootlegger? Also something from Jack's youth about an affair with a married woman. I'll find out more tomorrow. I just can't wait to be in the same city as my darling. This will make all my years of emptiness and over striving worth something more than just becoming a star. I've worked awfully hard to get to this place. And now I'm finally going to have the man of my dreams to share it with. I'm getting hot just thinking about him. More later.

I've got to go pack. I've narrowed my wardrobe down to a simple black Chanel evening dress and my most comfortable pump heels. Simple pearl necklace. For my cosmetic case, travel size jars of noxzema and vaseline, night shades, and of course my trusty vibrating massager. For pelvic stimulation and relaxation. One thing's for sure. On this trip I don't think I'll be needing a nightie.

July 14, 1960

Red, I'm in downtown LA outside the Convention Center and its a madhouse. I'm waiting in the back of the limo for Jack to finish his acceptance speech. It took Whitey and his wife over five hours to do my make up. But it was worth it. I look beautiful.

Peter keeps coming out to check on me. And sneak quick drinks from his flask which he stores in the bottom pouch of the rear door. He's in such bad shape its a joke. But he plays the go between role perfectly. I've known him since my starlet days when we were both at William Morris. For a while he even tried to date me. Fat chance. He's a shallow groping moron, with no character or talent besides speaking old English, staying tan and smiling like a mindless dummy. But we're going to use his house for the evening so I have to be nice. Five minutes in his presence, I'm sick to my stomach. I can't believe Pat Kennedy married him. What in the world was she thinking? He takes so many pills, he could open his own private drug store. What he spills would cover his lights and rent. The only two people in the entire universe Peter's loyal to are Jack and Frank (the Rat) Sinatra, so at least he chose one good one there.

Together Jack and I will change the world. And you, Red, will hold the down and dirty history of this wonderful trip right here between your covers. My knees are shaking. I hope I make him happier than he's ever been with any woman. So he won't be able to live without me for one moment more. Got to go. Our President is coming out.

July 15, 1960

Oh, Red, it was one of the most wonderful nights (and mornings) of my life. So where do I begin? In the limo before my man came out, I kept trying to hear his speech on the radio. Very difficult over all the standing ovations and roars from the adoring crowd who just love him. And why not? He's such a powerful speaker and Ted Sorenson writes almost as well as Arthur. Well different but definitely powerful. Very stirring slogans. Especially when Jack delivers them, with his crisp Boston accent and index finger pointing. So believable and honest and unforgettable when you hear him in real life. The President to be, (Jack informed me that Elect is only after he's won the vote so I've already started calling him 'to be'.) Anyhow Jack came out with confetti all through his hair and looked so royal and handsome. Like he had just descended from the ceiling as a Greek god might in one of those early plays. I almost jumped on him right there. And he was so happy to see me. On the ride he kept kissing my ears, which he knows drives me crazy, and grabbing everywhere. I was hot and heavy, wet and ready by the time the limo hit the beach. And I did everything I could to make his next several hours as enjoyable and memorable as possible.

He's so commanding. A lot of times I don't like feeling vulnerable (that's a word I got from my good doctor) or even brainless. Cause he's so smart on so many topics. Sometimes he's cute and funny like a little boy. But he's always a mature man who knows how to pleasure a woman. Really enjoy her in every way. He said he ranks it up there with fine Cuban cigars. One of which he smoked in the limo while getting me sick to my stomach.

So after we drifted into the bedroom, I pointed out the error of his recent campaign speeches. About Castro and how bad things were in Cuba and how the Eisenhower-Nixon team had totally missed the boat. Putting all of us citizens in grave danger. And now the President to be was secretly supporting the enemy and their socialist economy. He only laughed and pushed me onto the bed, lifting my hem to my waist. And he kissed me down there. Then we made love. He even held me afterward until he fell asleep. Poor Jack. He was so exhausted and we didn't get to speak about his commitment to making us a married couple. But we plan to see each other very soon.

OK, Red, the painful truth is I don't know if Jack will ever be able to get divorced, at least not for the next eight years. Right now it sure wouldn't be possible. No man appreciates being pushed into a corner with no way out. But especially with Jackie pregnant and my darling just beginning his campaign. I sure don't want the Pope coming out in support of Nixon. Wait. How could I forget Tricky Dickie's a Quaker? Along with being a very big faker. I'm giddy and silly but it feels great! Jack truly cares about me and that's all that matters. The energy between us was the greatest.

Oh, and I told him that joke about Speedy Gonzales who was so quick to jump into sex with anyone, anywhere. And he laughed and said he had heard that was J. Edgar Hoover's (who he HATES) nickname, or his gay lover, Toll House (he's the cookie with the tight ass, we think, and Hoover's the one with the nuts). Well, one or both of those weirdos can manage to come in less then thirty seconds of sloppy head from the other. Hence comes the nickname 'Speedy'. Wish I had been that lucky with some of my early casting directors. Anyhow, the very first resignation he's going to demand after he takes office will be from Hoover. Then the FBI can finally start serving the public interests and not that blackmailing bulldog despot. Jack told me a story about this woman Helga, who he loved when he was just a kid, a teenager really, and how FBI agents did all these foul things. The President to be calls Hoover a senile closet queen, grossly over suspicious, mentally unbalanced and extremely dangerous. Only concerned with his power. Along with being so totally corrupt its horrible.

Oh, and we did it again in the morning. It was even better because we were well rested.

Jack's really into his Dad. Not like Arthur who treats his father dreadfully. Instead, with absolute awe. The soon to be President gets Variety and the Wall Street Journal (just like Papa Joe) wherever he goes. The papers are saying he's starting eight points behind but Jack should get a lot more respect once the campaign gets rolling. Nixon is such a soul less ghoul and everyone has to see the difference, especially when the two are face to face. As I well know, a lot of anything is in the look. And Jack's so young and handsome and dynamic. And supremely confident. I'm sure all the women will just go crazy for him. Too bad he can't show his bare backside which I consider one of rare beauty. And believe me, Red, I've seen a good number in my day.

But I lie to him and tell him only about a few encounters because it amuses him. I sure don't want him to know all the risqué things I did while starting out. We're not even talking naughty here. Straight out slutty and whorey, especially to get my career going morey. That's something he might not understand, being born into such wealth and privilege. Besides, if you peel back the layers, Jack's just a guy and the double standard persists.

Anyhow, I told him if we were married we'd have both beds covered. I'd get the men's vote and he'd get the women's. He smiled and said he was far more concerned with getting Texas, which was shaping up as the major swing state in the south. Johnson is corrupt but could be extremely helpful to the ticket. Texas is where he controls the ballot boxes. Jack HATES Johnson but his brother Bobby HATES him worse. But because their Dad, Joe, felt it would balance the north/south divide, and block any chance of being blackmailed once they got in, they offered Johnson the V.P. spot. It was a token gesture, a formality to get the Texan firmly on their side and not use the dirt he had obtained. And then, out of the blue, Lyndon Johnson accepted. 'Just a heart beat from the President', he told the reporters, flashing a big smile. This was a disaster for the brothers' plan to go through a whole list of 'big wigs'. Thereby gathering more support from more key players. Slang for rich contribution.

Obviously, politics is pretty tricky business. Especially when you find yourself dealing with some of the biggest tricksters ever. Anyhow, Jack's going to order Johnson to stay below the Mason-Dixon line until the votes are cast. But I told Jack to be extra safe he should try to keep his running mate solely in Texas. Cause he still has an early lead in Florida and Maryland, two states with a good number of black and Jewish voters, who might not cotton to the tall Texan's shenanigans and hatreds.

Mr. Johnson could prove to be a very big weight round Jack's neck if word gets out about his boys, Bobby Baker and Billy Sol Estes. You can't even get an outhouse built in the state of Texas without going through one of their outstretched palms. Bobby, Billy Sol, or Lying Lyndon: The three musketeers of sleaze and full out corruption can and will deliver. Anything, anybody can be bought including souls. And easily as important, VOTES.

Still, the biggest problem is winning the state of Illinois which the MAFIA pretty much controls by way of the voting booths in Chicago. Now I'm hardly an expert on crime but Chicago was the mob's first home base in America. This is going back over a hundred years. In the twenties, Al Capone created a major crime ring using his gang of thugs. Loyal to a man and if not, face the wall and quickly say your prayers. With prohibition they tripled in size. Paying off officials and running off or shooting rivals was their favored way to do business and they did a good deal of business. Now, Capone's old driver, Sam 'Mooney' Giancana has become boss of bosses, stretching this criminal cartel around the world. My dear admirer and benefactor Joe Schenck, already terribly ill when I first met him, spent time in jail rather than squeal on his syndicate friends. Loyalty mixed with fear.

Joe was the one who introduced me to Mr. Giancana nearly fifteen years ago. So I've known Sam (the gang guys call him Mooney) awhile. He was a big help at the start of my career. After getting Howard Hughes interested, Sam and Joe combined to get Fox to sign me up. Sam then arranged some of my earliest roles in musical comedy. And he's kept an eye out for me ever since. One time there was a pushy fan and another time there was this horrid reporter who was writing all this vile untrue stuff. Sam's boys apparently had a talk with him because he never bothered me again. Sam is crude as shit, dapper and no nonsense. Ladies man and gunman, powerbroker and body breaker. Quite a mix.

I just ran into his right hand man, Johnny Roselli, was it yesterday? Day and a half. Right after I checked in at the L.A. Hilton, he called me, pretty much out of nowhere. In five minutes Johnny's up in my suite, asking if he can get me anything--you know, drugs or booze or tickets. Most important, he wanted to make sure everyone was treating me nice since (he begins to whisper) they own a part of this place. And Johnny and Sam wanted to make sure everyone's going out of their way to make sure I'm happy.

Like they don't own a part of every place in the entire universe. He was very curious about what was going on with Jack and that 'pipsqueak Bobby', and that 'fag piece of shit' J. Edgar Hoover. Bobby has just been taken off the Senate Crime Committee (which Johnny said was running nails up their ass) to run Jack's campaign. Apparently that's the deal, that Jack will control both Hoover and Bobby and stop any investigations into the mob's operations. And in return he'll have the Mob's help getting him elected.

The Mafia controls the vote count in certain key downtown precincts of Chicago so they can guarantee that Jack will wind up taking the whole state. They'll work backwards with the count after they know how much they need. With that Jack should win the national election and become President. The political analysts are saying Illinois is the key. Well, this is the key deal. And the Mob already refused Nixon's request and he worked with them plenty as VP. They like Jack for the job cause he's a stand up guy. And they're patriots. Along with being Catholics. And, above everything else, just damn good businessmen and proud Americans.

Johnny said Mooney had it all set up. Something about old business and Joe, the dad, was almost rubbed out, as Johnny calls it. Mr. Giancana stepped in and had the contract Costello had on Joe Kennedy canceled. Saved his life with a simple phone call. Mooney's everywhere and has been for years. He's a real gangster, the biggest. But he's no all-out monster. Mooney's word is considered as good as gold so he's got to have a certain amount of character. Johnny left with a quick kiss and a wad of hundreds thrust in my palm. These are not the guys you want to say no to.

I had suggested to Jack that he might use the Giancana thugs for certain national security problems because they're the real pro's. Managing to get the dirty jobs done clean as a whistle without any messy witnesses. Jack smiled and said he was thinking about doing that very thing. Something about Castro and creating a private police force with the mob as soldiers.

I told him I was quite surprised he would work with men of such questionable character. These guys are flat out dangerous. Cold-blooded killers who'll gun you down just as soon as shake your hand. Especially if they think you're screwing them over.

Jack laughed and said he wasn't worried in the slightest. 'A President holds all the cards, including four aces. The Army, Navy, Marines and if all else fails, the Air Force. Bombs away.' His first act as President will be to make his brother Bobby the Attorney General, number one lawman. That way the family (that is the Kennedy clan) will make sure of keeping Mr. Giancana and his cronies (the bad family) in line. And he wasn't forgetting his own tainted running mate, the future Vice President Johnson.

How could you? Shortly after the inauguration, (Lord, that word just gives me goose bumps), brother Bobby will start a discrete, under the radar Justice Department investigation into Bobby Baker's activities. Then spring it on Lyndon once his agents have the goods. So Jack will wind up having all those creeps by a tight collar. He'll be everybody's boss. Shame you can't win an election this important honestly, but Jack's dad, Joe, says that's the way its always been. A real down and dirty, no holds barred catfight. Using anything you can find, obtained by any means, to gain the slightest edge.

Jack also talked about a few other things before leaving this morning. While sipping coffee, he asked what I thought about Frank Sinatra. Frank had helped the campaign plenty in the primaries, especially in rural Pennsylvania and West Virginia. Worked his ass off. Did I think Frank Sinatra would make a good ambassador to, let's say Italy, if and when that decision had to be made? I almost choked on my spoon. Then I told my Jack about the episode with Frank when I was breaking up with my husband Joe, and they tried to catch me cheating on him. How Joe and Frank and those Mooney goons went to the wrong apartment in my building and broke down the old lady's door below me. And then Frank arguing with Joe on the lawn while getting drunker and drunker and more and more uncontrollable. Egging Joe on by insulting his manhood. And then kicking the private detective they hired to follow me across the lawn, using his pointed alligator shoes. And once the police arrived, him shouting, 'Hey, paisan. Keep me and Mooney's name the hell out of this, you know what's good for you', as he ran away. And everyone in the whole neighborhood could hear. Jack just shook his head, grimacing. So I don't think Frank will be appointed a diplomat in the near future.

Sam probably ordered Frank to do everything he can to help get Jack elected. Because deep down I know Frank is a staunch Conservative. Ugh. I used to think that everyone in the Republican party was just so selfish. Now I realize everyone's pretty much the same. The Democrats being just as bad, just a little less obvious. And its a criticism game they both play to make sure we don't notice that they're all in cahoots together. I suggested Jack should go after all those bigshot crooks heading major corporations. And he replied not a bad idea but only after he had received a huge campaign contribution from each and every bigshot. Then he laughed before kissing me goodbye and leaving in his limo.

Well, I'll write more later. But it was wonderful, the entire beautiful night and morning. I couldn't sleep much but does it matter? I just held Jack to my chest and gave thanks. My man chose me to begin his quest to lead the free world and heaven knows this world needs his leadership. I take this as a true sign that God wants us (Jack and me) together. So I can be of help in this historic mission. Something this important has to have deeper meaning.

I didn't get to see my good Doctor as I hoped, but I did manage to speak to him on the phone. Actually several times. He sounded encouraging, a little, and concerned, a lot, mostly about my relationship with the candidate. He's afraid I'll get hurt in the end but what the hell. Its hard to reach for the stars when your feet are firmly planted in the ground. To the point they're completely buried over. Well, that's what I told Dr. Greenson. He told me to be absolutely sure I was doing this because it was something I wanted to do. Not something I felt I had to do, like following the lines in some script. But Yves has his wife and Arthur has his writing, and I have no one. And here Jack wants me and I want him far more. So, Red, what could be simpler? I mean I haven't done all that badly up to now. I have to believe in my instincts about us, together, as a couple. And hope my Jack does also. So if he asks for me, wherever and whenever, I'm going to be at his side just as quick as I can for as long as he needs me.

July 18, 1960

Hi, Red, I'm back in New York. Home sweet home. My maid, Aunt Lena is so kind and helpful. And she makes great meals, like her vegetable lasagna which I'm nibbling on. I'm her little bambino and she's my sweet loving Italian momma. She loves to hug me and I love it when she does. She talks to me long into the night and we laugh. I can tell her anything without being embarrassed or feeling guilty. We read some parts of you, various pages. And I can tell Lena really likes you, Red. She thinks you're helping me come out of my shell. Getting me to take down the defensive wall and all the dead wood and bad baggage, as Dr. Greenson calls it. She's also one of the very few who knows all my secrets but I'll leave it at that.

Speaking of Italian, Joe just called. He wants to take me to dinner and I told him I'd love to see him. So I have to start to get ready for my Yankee slugger, with his big bat, and famous staying power. I mean aside from my one marvelous night and morning with Jack, I've been celibate for over five weeks. Which is an unhealthy condition, one sure to bring on frayed nerves and pimples by the pound.

After all, as the world's reining sex queen, I do have an obligation to keep myself in training. That is keeping my birth cavity firmly toned, along with having gas in the tank and the motor purring. Ready for action. Or reaction if he's still in the mood, like my Irish Prince was two nights ago. Shit! I haven't dated you in days. Its Sunday, the 19th, I think. Bye, Red. I'm just glad you don't care about stuff like the days of the week. Or even the months. Well, I do know 1960's the year and it seems to be getting better by the minute. Nice thoughts to wake up to.

Dinner with Joe started off surprisingly nice. He can be a dear when he cares to listen rather than control. And for a while, he was acting both supportive and almost tender. No, even if he was like this always, I'm not going back. Along with the hitting, he's still too limited in his interests. What's even dumber than a dumb blonde who can wiggle her ass and make people laugh? A dumb jock who refuses to read anything but the sports pages. Whose buddies are men with loud ties and even louder belches, who ogle me like I'm raw meat. Sure I'm a cock teaser but I like to choose the cock I want to tease.

Sometimes you have to laugh because Joe can only talk in sports phrases, no matter the topic. Like Henry the Eighth threw a 'no header or Lee got beaned by Grant. Well, this time he starts at dessert, 'Your boy Kennedy is being thrown a screwball or a wicked change up. And he's going to have it break against his head. I just don't get why anyone wants to be skipper of this crazy country, even a phony like him'. Things quickly came unglued when Joe added, 'too many headaches from the uppity spades and reds and pinkos, trying to turn everything around'. I asked him if he was referring to Good and Plenty's. Joe says 'no, the damn Negroes and Commies and pushy broads, trying to grow dicks'. I told him I refused to listen to ugly demeaning terms, especially not in public. Now I know Joe can sound like a hate monger without even meaning it. I also know I cannot change his lack of a developed brain or inject kindness. But prejudice like he shows is offensive and hurtful to everyone. And I said so rather emphatically. Then I left him in the restaurant. He said I was acting like a dumb ass. Well, I may not be the most educated person alive but I know not to hate certain groups of people just because they're different. Actually I try not to hate anyone. I hope to continually expand my mind and don't want to bean anyone. I want to help make a difference. Joe can just remember some old ball games and how many curved balls or second bases he hit in each.

I'm really happy I'm home. My phone has been going crazy but I must admit I love hearing the rings. Suddenly everyone seems to want me. The Misfits is finally just about ready to go into production. So a lot of the calls are from Poppy, that's Arthur when he's acting nice. He's up in Connecticut, excited about the script and especially the ending. Other calls are from John Huston, from England, no less, and CLARK GABLE, from LaLa Land. That's Hollywood, honey. I almost fainted when he called. He was so nice. And he's very excited to work with me and he knows its going to be a great experience and a great film. He can't wait to have a couple of drinks and just sit down alone with me. So we can work on our ideas about our two characters, Roslyn, my character and Gay, his character.

He wants us to play a bit with the dialogue so it sounds more natural. And also some of our physical interactions need to be worked out, so we should start thinking about the key ones. Maybe we can get together even before we fly out? And I totally agreed. Especially cause I'm really playing me this time. And it would be great fun to play anything with Clark. He's a perfect Adonis. Past handsome. As for the physical moves, come on, Red. I've been told so many times I think with my ass. Now's my chance to study for finals.

So later, after I relayed this harmless conversation to Arthur, he became somewhat annoyed to outright hostile. Bad Poppy screaming accusations. How I was always changing everything around because I could never be satisfied. But especially with anything he did for me. How dare I question his Valentine gift, his very best writing. He thought the script was quite tight and definitely ready to go into the next phase. After all, he (Arthur) knew a good deal more about crafting a powerful drama than me or some other dumb actors or even the Strasberg's, for that matter.

And I don't have to tell you, Red, with his critical acclaim and records for theater attendance and, of course the major drama awards being brought up about every other minute. So I finally had to remind him that regarding his career, all of the legs had been pretty much set in bronze early on in his twenties. This must have struck home because he started insulting me, calling me dumb Dora, who uses her hippy body to get any work she could.

After over an hour of hassling, I had to give him the bitter cold truth. That he hadn't done shit in close to ten years and Clark and I were the ones reviving his career. And if he didn't allow us the freedom to explore, well, it would be an extremely uncomfortable set. I, for one, would feel completely handcuffed. The true beauty of Roslyn is she's a free spirit. Arthur simply does not realize how much that conflict will show up in the film, feelings of restraint and constraint. All shackling down my inner core, especially when the finished film is projected onto a huge screen. I mean that camera sometimes is so close, I feel its been shoved deep inside me like some giant organ. And how can I act my part and maintain my own inner being when my husband is harassing me with nervous fidgets because he's insecure? Uncertainty always upsets me greatly. Yelling at me even worse. Besides, he was going to upset the entire cast, not just the headliners. Then we got into a real shouting match, a free for all.

Of course, the biggest problem is not the film directly. We haven't made love or even held each other in well over a month. Mostly because we haven't been together for more than a few hours, let alone a few nights, during the entire pre-production period. Like soldiers getting ready for a battle, staying apart in case events go badly later on. Depressing if you want to be reassured and cared for a little. And we know how the rest of my sex life has been going. So unless I start doing underground films or start latching on to Jack or Clark, I'm (un)screwed.

But as long as Arthur was intent on pushing me aside for his art, I needed to start working on preparation for my artistic performance also. After all, I had my own demanding role. He could continue working like a maniac on this stupid script, probably making it worse. Fact is he had done all he could. And he had to stop this compulsive rewriting over a few words or phrases, changing them ad nausea. But I think I called it 'jerking off' 'cause that's what it is. Dry humping an ultra dry, harsh script.

Clearly, it is the director's turf as to close ups and background and tempo and feel. Pace, emphasis. But even he, the boss on the set, would normally be eager to listen to others involved in the project. Especially suggestions from the actors and actresses, whose mission it was to convey his message, and who had also been living with the characters for a while. I've got to go eat. Arthur's coming down for the weekend. We're going to make up. Ugh. The sacrifices we make for our careers. But it sure is better than fighting, where no one wins even if you're right. I wish I had never fallen' in love with him in the first place. Now I just feel this incredible anger for letting us both down.

The only man I ever truly loved besides Arthur, for a while, and Jack forever was Freddie Karger, my first singing coach. But he kissed me off before we ever really got started. Blaming my past when I was a call girl after Zanuck axed me. Hell, I had to have money to live on. Fred never gave me a chance, even though Nana (his mom) loved me to death and still does. And his sweet kids adored me, and I adore them. It still hurts, especially when I see pics of him with Jane Wyman. Arthur, on the other hand, cared about me so much he forgave me for all my bad decisions. Ever.

So now Poppy has to pay up on my anger meter, for him, me, and everyone else. Because by forgiving me, he's set himself up as someone quite superior. Now, as we've slowly become aware, he's just as needy and even weaker for seeking my approval. The bottom line is Arthur's not much more together so he shouldn't have tricked me into believing he was. I need the extremely rare man who's both smart and inwardly strong. So he knows how to keep both of us afloat when the sea gets choppy. Especially after he gets me pregnant and we begin our family. Then, when our babies start to cry, he can rock them back to sleep. Holding all of us in his arms, protecting and shielding us from the devil's fiery breath. And making each of us feel safe and secure and loved. Amen.

I'm just lucky Jack's so bright and virile and dynamic. Its clear he doesn't have sluggish sperm. And he's fiercely independent. Too much so. Surely I don't like my men clingy. But Jack only calls a couple of times a week. I worry he's losing interest and falling out of love.

Carl Sandberg just called to wish me luck. He's such a brilliant man. Poet, writer, expert on American heroes like our 16th President. But he's also sweet as sugar. We spent a weekend together last year. No sex, he says he's too old. Mostly we talked about Lincoln. Abe I'd marry in a second.

Dear Red,

Something very interesting occurred Saturday morning just after Joe left. Yeah, after our big fight in the restaurant Friday night, I came home, alone. I come in and plop on the sofa. I spend over an hour and a half writing in you. I had just laid down to go to sleep. It was about one in the morning and there was a knock on the door. It was Giuseppe telling me how sorry he was and promising to watch what he said and I was right. And could I please forgive him? So I dragged him into my lair and let him attack me. Actually then and in the morning, which is often my best time. Then we had coffee and he smoked three cigarettes and he was out the door. And I felt terrific.

Two hours later, the bellman calls to let me know Mr. Sinatra was downstairs in the lobby. Almost like we had a lunch date planned which we didn't. Then Frankie gets on the house phone and says he was in the neighborhood and would like to come up for a minute. Seems he had been thinking about me a lot lately and wanted to give me a little present. Some choice emerald earrings that he bought because he thought they matched the color of my eyes, which in fact are hazel, not green. But I didn't correct him on that small point. I'm not that stupid.

So when he came up to give them to me, he noticed a pair of male sunglasses on the coffee table. He almost flipped when I told him whose they were. Cause there was the chance Joe could just float back up to retrieve them. They might have to start calling Frankie Ole Black n' Blue Eyes if Joe ever got his mitts on him. Especially if he found Frank alone with me. Well, anyhow, it was good to see the Chairman sweat a bit. Plus he invited me and the whole cast up to his show at Cal-Neva when we're shooting.

And he didn't even get frisky or annoying. And I got these beautiful earrings for nothing because he was out of my apartment in less than fifteen minutes. Frank is also not a bad lover but I still only dream of Jack because he has the mind and soul to match.

Frank is hell-bent on becoming someone important. I asked him if he'd accept the job as Chief Pimp. Said we're both grabbing for the same brass ring and to lay off. So I had to remind him I was going for a simple gold one based on love. He said Mooney thought the Kennedy's were dirty dealing liars and not to trust any of them. I shouldn't expect too much because my boyfriend was in it for himself. Couldn't change even if he wanted to cause his father would never let him. I told him I already had a shrink for advice. Actually, two or three. Now who am I going to believe? My almost perfect Senator, who is getting ready to lead the entire free world or the King of Sleaze, who has a nice voice and no heart or morals? Who quotes Mooney like he was some great prophet. A lot closer to the devil. Poppy, my dear beautiful man, arrived around 1 o'clock from Connecticut. He's made some really important changes in the script. And the story is much, much stronger. Arthur can be such a sensitive and powerful force with words. And the fact he really listened to me is great. The N.Y. Times is coming out for Nixon, only a matter of time. I wonder how Mr. Lincoln would feel if he had an army of old trolls from the biggest conservative newspapers to contend with. Its hard enough being honest. But my darling Senator said it takes time to change things. He jokingly called me 'a fiery crusader rabbit'. But even Arthur's going to vote for him and he rarely votes because he thinks everything's fixed. Nighty-night, Red.

Dear Red,   *July 21, 1961*

Early Sunday, we were lying around in bed drinking coffee. Feeling more lovey then we had in months, almost like the old days. It was so nice and easy and cozy. A beautiful sunny summer day with big lazy clouds floating across the bedroom window. Half the city must have taken off for the beach or the mountains because the streets were empty. And so quiet.

Then Arthur gets this call from the coast requesting a quote about an article in a Hollywood gossip column. And our lovely weekend instantly dissolved into total crap. That complete shit! I can't believe Yves could deceive me so badly. It wasn't that he screwed me but a hundred times worse how he talked about me after. To Hedda Hopper, of all the bitchy, deceitful, spreaders of negative news and slime. I just despise her pen point lies, cruelty and bad taste. That phony wrote three columns, increasingly distasteful but this last one is absolutely revolting, truly vile. Arthur became furious. I mean can you blame him? He comes out looking like a total fool. And I look like a home wrecker with a goosed up, out of control pussy.

Before I met Yves he was a run of the mill song and dance guy, a mid-level actor and nightclub entertainer who could not utter one complete sentence in English. Now, all of a sudden, when his career starts to gain a little attention, especially in the States, he's spouting speeches like he's standing on top of some mountain. Calling me a child, and saying he could not risk saying good-bye because I was too much in love with him. How nothing could ever break up his beautiful marriage, which has given him so many wonderful years. Never, ever trust a Frenchman, especially a spurned, desperate one. I thought only low class hustlers stooped to play phony 'kiss and tell'. Not MEN OF CHARACTER.

But Hedda got together with Yves for tea, and they hatched a plan to serve me up instead of those flaky empty pastries that fall apart in your lap. Lousy bastards. I'll never forgive either one for their betrayal. But it definitely got to Arthur like a fierce kick in the balls. He threw the script on the floor and started screaming. I tried to defend myself, explaining it was just a brief flirtation that was long over. He reminded me of the time he caught us kissing in our bungalow at the Beverly Hills Hotel when he came back to get his stupid pipe. And he was fuming. I mean right then and with the very same pipe which he then threw down on the just cleaned rug near my naked feet. And several embers caught fire, while leaving a trail of charcoal. Ruining our rug and our weekend. Me feeling so disloyal and selfish and trampy.

I truly care about Simone, but now I'm afraid I can never be friends with her either. Definitely not like we used to be. How come a woman always blames the other woman rather than their own man? Both Yves and Milton Greene came on to me a lot more than I did to them. Yet I lost Amy when she found out and a little later when I bought Milton's shares of the company back from him (for a dollar), I lost him also. Even though he was always completely fair and took nothing from me. Now Simone is lost. And she was one of my most favorite people ever. Someone I deeply respected. She had just borrowed my pearl scarf, one of my favorite accessories. I wore it often and it was very lucky for me. But the hell with it. I mean the karma's pretty much destroyed. And I don't dare ask her for it back. Serves me right for caring about some stupid possession when I really care about losing her.

So Arthur went storming out to catch his plane to Nevada. Guess I'll meet up with him in a few days. But this is not the greatest start to our film project together.

Well, at least it was a good thing that Arthur left when he did. Definitely decent timing. Because the phone rang and it was

Kenny O'Donnell from the president's office. Twice in the last two weeks he's sent messages of caring through his aide.

I don't want canned declarations and excuses from his aide. I want the President to be locked between my sweaty limbs, whimpering like a love starved pup. While pledging vows of complete fidelity, one on one. Well, one on two. His wife I can accept. At least for now. I'm a realist. But by this time in our relationship I want to know I am his only girlfriend, not one of a troupe.

Well, I'm off to the desert to make this difficult film in this suffocating summer heat. Depressing all around. Wish me luck, Red. The person I'm most excited about working with is Clark Gable. He's been my idol since I was a kid and I carried his picture everywhere. He had become my substitute dad. Mainly cause my dad looked like Clark if I am to trust my crazy mother's word. My real dad, who I never saw, split right after I was conceived. Had a nine month getaway period.

Clark has been more than kind the few times we've gotten together. We started being friends at the wrap party at Romanoff's to celebrate the Seven Year Itch. When was it, four years ago? I couldn't believe all those stars, Bogie and Bacall, Claudette Colbert, William Holden, and Gary Cooper. Even Zanuck and Meyer. All the Hollywood royalty. They all came to salute ME. And they signed this big cardboard cut out, the one of me teetering on the subway grate in high heels, with my skirt blowing up to my ears. Like a jackass I left it somewhere in the studio, and it quickly disappeared. Lord, I wish I'd kept it for when I'm old and nobody gives a damn about me or my films. It was signed by forty of the biggest stars in the business.

The King of Film said he'd love to work with me and be my co-star. I almost wet my pants. I informed him that I was planning to leave Hollywood, go East and start my own production company with Milton Greene. Thereby freeing myself completely from the Studio monopoly. I would become two people, a serious hard working actress and also the newly elected PRESIDENT of an independent film production corporation. So someday he might wind up working with me for me. An incorporated me with a reserved parking space.

He laughed and nodded approval and called me 'Boss Lady'. He said we had an awful lot in common including big ears. And we both laughed. He also said I had Carole Lombard's sparkle and brilliance. Well, I just started thanking him because Carole was the girl of his dreams and a tremendous actress. Doing comic and dramatic parts equally well. A feat I'm trying to accomplish with The Misfits.

The other good thing is he drinks as much as me. Of course, no one drinks as much as Monty. Actually the only one who doesn't drink is Arthur. And he's the one who should because he needs relaxing the most. He's so rigid and withdrawn, especially since the pressure of this film has set in. Monte and I have been friends since our N.Y. Studio days, so Paula has someone else to bore with the history of drama, B.S. and A.S., that is before and after Stanislavski. Hopefully, Eli will be able to shut her up because he's known her for decades and by now is totally unimpressed with the Method school. He considers the whole thing a total crock. So anyhow, that's why when we were considering various veteran actors with major credentials to play Gay, I said it simply had to be Clark. Arthur quickly agreed. And then, there's John Huston, who believed in me from the start. He was the obvious choice for director. After all, 'Asphalt Jungle' was my break through role. Though at the time I was petrified of all of them. He's an absolutely marvelous artist and everyone respects and fears him. Though he's always been understanding and kind to me. Now he doesn't mind downing a shot or two himself, before lunch. So I'm starting to get excited. A serious, meaningful role to show the world I can really act. And leave those dumb blonde characters in a bottom drawer of immature, early stuff.

Front and center with my soul and acting prowess. So any viewer who watches and dares to laugh out loud...Well, they'll be asked politely to leave. Still giggling? Fine. Then I'll kick in your Adam's apple and severely damage your voice box. Am I class or what? Only crying is allowed while viewing my new drama. And staring at the star. See, I still have my lovely breasts and buttocks which don't sag at all. True wonders of nature, defying gravity. So T and A is still OK, just being packaged different. Well, its good to think I still have some trace of humor, cause we're going to be needing something to break up the tension. It should be hot as hell in the desert. And there's a lot of screwy people involved in this film.

My maid Lena is such a good cook. She made her very best, the vegetable lasagna and chicken cacciatore. But this time for my farewell meal. Paula's flying with me so she can protect me from the other travelers (she's that obnoxious). And myself. I always get nervous when I start a new project. But nothing like now. Clearly, this is the On the Waterfront of the decade. A big time serious production that will be remembered, studied and dissected. And hopefully honored. Can't forget those little naked statues, can we? Thank you, Academy. Mostly because I've been completely ignored up to now. The critics call my films 'pedestrian and predictable.' I call the critics 'fuckheads filled with venomous shit' and my films 'comic masterpieces' with a human, loving edge. I hope Jack calls. I'm always thinking about him.

Dear Red,   *July 23, 1960*

Well, we've arrived in the desert. And its as barren and God forsaken as I feared. Maybe worse. Just above 102 degrees in the downtown Reno shade at ten o'clock in the morning. We're going to be driving some thirty miles into the country, up to some dried up basin in the foothills where it will probably hit 115. John has to decide whether its the right site to shoot the finale, the mustang roping. Personally I don't give a damn where the hell we shoot it. Its just background for the main characters. Everyone gets so caught up in the little stuff, they often forget the real stuff, like the dialogue, the characters and most of all the story. If I have to wait for one more perfect sunset I'm going to throw up. Which is something I've been doing rather constantly for the last ten years anyway. This morning, after I unpacked and said hello to Poppy, I rested. Then I saw this quiz in a women's magazine and it was about bad eating habits and digestive problems, I think they called it. I rated over 100, see your doctor immediately! So I called Dr. Greenson and he told me to forget any article like that because it wasn't directed towards specific medical problems. And I should be less sensitive to tricky articles and tricky people, and just go with how I felt in my gut, which after his reassurance continues to work well.

Foremost, I'm getting more and more concerned with my character. I can't seem to get into her or find many parts of her personality I can identify with. Roslyn seems far too, well, emotional and sappy. I fear Arthur may be too close and he's made the character so complex. She may appear just dreary. Is this his ultimate revenge? Did he subconsciously make Roz out to be a severely damaged waif. A woman completely out of touch with anyone she seems to care about. Unable to give anything but sex in place of love. Only caring about animals, not people.

When you add all the elements up, the story sure doesn't show a very positive side to the heroine. Like kindness, sense of humor, and strong spirit. Having a love for all living creatures, and being forgiving of their faults. Solid attributes I cling to and hope I can show and make the viewers feel.

But above anything else, the major problem regards Gay's (Clarke's) job or vocation. The rounding up and killing of the wild horses to make dogmeat is vile. The theme is so terribly depressing it seeps into everything. The hunt leading to their slaughter, using an airplane to flush them from the canyon is out and out cruelty. And for what end, dog food? Don't they have grains? Or ground bones from cattle and chickens? Dogs like marrow. Even when a few horses are saved, its sheer torture. I fear Arthur wants something ultra dramatic and killing horses is symbolic of the death of the West or of the country. Or his innocence. Who knows? But many in the audience will be horrified. Justifiably so. Is this his hidden motive, to turn everyone against the film and me, well the four of us, me and the guys?

More later. I have to go learn my lines, which keeps getting more difficult because Arthur keeps changing them. For the last two nights, he has not gone to bed at all. Just sat at his desk, typing like a madman. Then this morning he refused to show me the changes. Instead he ran over to John Huston who was eating breakfast alone, and went over the new lines with him. So there they were, both laughing and patting each other on the shoulders and nodding. And I felt like a total outsider. Then he came back to our table, sat and began calmly eating his breakfast. Finally I asked, 'So, Arthur, are there going to be any more changes in the script?' He shrugged, and said, 'Why no. Not that I know of,' and turned back to his eggs. Weird? We have been rehearsing for over ten days and there have been maybe fifteen changes he's made and unmade and now after this whole two day buildup there's none. Talk about bizarre behavior. Maybe that's his real plan, to completely upset me. I'm sure he's secretly hoping to turn everyone in the production against me and over to his side. Well at least I have Paula to stand up for me. Of course, with her there is one extra problem she brings to the table. Everyone hates her. Including at times, me.

I don't understand what's happening. Arthur originally wrote this script for me and me alone. My Valentine gift as he constantly calls it. So maybe its just his own personal insecurity. But at this moment, I need him as rock hard and supportive as he can possibly be. And definitely not this nervous Nelly who seems intent on abandoning me in pursuit of saving his own personal artistic career. Most men are head cases. Most writers are out of their minds. But put any writer deep into the movie making circus, and they become certifiable lunatics. Arthur appears to be a candidate for a mental ward as he twitches and turns. Believe me, these qualities I'm able to recognize as easily as the veins on the back of my hand. See, I got the right bloodlines. And experience gained through visiting Grandma and of course Momma. Talk about crazy, one night a bad policeman climbed in the window of my apartment when I was just an inexperienced model. He was just about to attack me when I screamed and he ran out. I went to the phone. Soon a police car with two cops in it arrived. One of the two was him, the would be rapist, acting all official and in uniform, not jeans. And the sergeant thought I was making the whole thing up and wouldn't make out a report. Two days later I moved out of that dreadful neighborhood into Joe Schenck's mansion in Beverly Hills. No sex, he couldn't really get it up or keep it up long enough to do anything. But he was so kind and didn't care if I saw Bob Slatzer or others and he helped my career a great deal. And he cared about me and loved me and wanted to marry me. He said I'd get millions but I never cared about money. What a kind sweet man.

My Dear Red,   *July 26, 1960*

Filming so far has gone all right. Not terrible but not perfect, either. We're about to start our fourth day, actually only a half day behind schedule. Which really isn't all that bad in a big production. Still, on the second day I encountered a huge obstacle. From the very first read I felt there was a problem regarding this one scene. Any script snafu translates into a serious acting problem for me. Before I can show the right emotion I have to understand the situation and feel it makes sense.

Now I very much like the fact that we're trying to shoot this film in sequential order. Usually its all so hodge podge and its only after they edit that you even have the slightest hint as to whether its good or bad. Of course, The Misfits, a serious drama, could be an instant failure. There's a much tighter circle we're aiming at than in a light comedy. All our two years of hard work could be for nothing.

We're about to film my first big scene where I'm walking up the courthouse steps to get my final divorce papers. I'm with my friend, Isabel, (Thelma Ritter) who owns the boarding house where I've been staying. I meet my husband, Raymond, who has just flown in.

He is upset and hoping to stop me from going ahead with our divorce. And I just blow him off, telling him, 'he never noticed me, and I was no longer going to feel sorry because I had to think about myself'. Like a total uncaring bitch, I just toss him aside. Even though he really cares for me and still loves me. A real hard worker, he has made a huge success of his life. So generous, he gave me a new Cadillac convertible as a going-away gift. Had it delivered to Reno, where I'm waiting to establish residence to get my divorce. And he is very very sad about our state of disunion.

Heartbroken. Well, anyway, this was the scene I had trouble with from the first time I read the screenplay. And Arthur and I have argued about this ever since. Because I just know I would never do something that callous. I could never be that mean to anyone, even if I hardly knew the person. And I just say 'you weren't there for me. And if I'm going to be alone, I want to be truly alone. Just me.' Arthur insisted on this because he felt it explained my later actions. And I may have said this once to him in real life. Anyhow I think it makes Roslyn look like a heartless, angry self centered bitch. Especially when she ends the scene and dismisses him with, 'Go home, Raymond. You can't make me feel sorry for you anymore'. And then I wheel around, turning my back on good 'ole' Ray, and run up the courthouse steps. Real cold like I'm the vicious wacko from hell. Rather than the poor, misunderstood heroine I'm trying to be.

So its time to shoot the scene and I'm walking up the steps, and ROADBLOCK. I just couldn't say the lines out loud. So instead I sort of whispered them. And John got really upset, especially after about fifteen takes, and pulls me aside. 'OK, kid, what gives?'

So I explained how by talking in a very low voice, I could show I was totally torn and tortured about saying these mean things. And we could easily do voice overs to get the dialog, but my inner psyche would not allow me to do it any other way. Mr. Huston smiled and said,' fine'. And ordered the sound crew to run a mike up Kevin McCarthy's (the actor playing my husband) trousers, continuing up to the lapel of his suit. So this time when John said 'action' and we went through the scene, the sound people were satisfied they had gotten everything.

And the next morning, John came by, smiling like he came from Wonderland and he said he was really happy with the dailies. And I definitely looked like I was in knots over casting Ray aside, very sympathetic and not mean or angry. And I did it just right. It was a terrific opening, and a beautiful job of acting.

So great to hear this from a cinema genius. I love film when it comes together even when its a painful struggle to get there. Especially when someone with real experience recognizes my work, and it is work.

Today we did the short scene on the bridge where a dejected Roslyn (me) throws her wedding ring into the river. This is on Isabel's coaxing, after the divorce proceedings. No problem. I can throw old relationships away easy. Next we went to the scene in the bar where I meet Gay (Clark) and his dog, which is over four pages of script, meaning about four and a half minutes of the film. So its a pretty big chunk. Eli has been very supportive and respectful of my feelings. After all, he knows how difficult it can be to get into character, especially in this mad house. We studied together in New York and we've learned a lot from each other and Lee. What the Studio accomplished was to take all the skills learned in doing plays through the centuries, sift out the key ingredients, and condense them to work for movies. Well, Stanislavski and Chekhov and a couple of others got it started. But the Strasberg's have taken it to the next level. I think every serious actor or actress should be forced to study with them for at least a year. It takes the cast a little more time in preparation but its well worth it in the end. I can tell Clark thinks its all a crock of shit but he's so kind, he humors me. And us.

Eli's confided he thinks its mostly a lot of hot air but he goes along with the program to get roles. Speaking of the Studio, Marlon Brando is simply the kindest, most considerate man ever. He sent me this huge flowering plant just because he said he was thinking about me. Its funny. Everyone thinks he's a rude pig. But to me he has always been the perfect gentleman. Down right sweet and very considerate. With a beautiful body when he's nude. Great chest and tush. I think I'm much more of a butt gal than a dick chick because that's the first place my eyes go when I'm studying a man. That and his inner spark. Traits which in Marlon's case enable him to be a marvelous actor.

I think one of my proudest moments ever was when Lee started telling interviewers that Marlon and I were the best actors that he had ever seen or worked with. So what if I've never been nominated for an Oscar? I did win several Golden Globe's, including one for best over all performer and that's the big one. Now, I'm sure my critics will quickly add as a comedian. And they're right. Still, I know they're going to have to start respecting me some day. I hope this film is that beginning.

Since the film seems to be destroying my marriage, I'm hoping its a hit. Arthur desperately needs to achieve a major success. I want him to succeed for his sake. Even though I'm starting to hate him for my sake. He's so different than a few years ago when he was carefree and fun to be with and interesting. During my career, I've managed to work with some extremely fanatic people, like my first acting coach, Natasha. Arthur's becoming even worse. Thinking of me more than the project in the beginning, and then the project far more than me now. Maybe I have to stop sleeping with people I work with. At least the fanatic ones.

I'm sure Arthur's buttering John Huston up so they can tag team me, ganging up emotionally from morning to night. Trying to make me think like they do. But I still have real doubts about the theme lines of The Misfits. And I refuse to go down easy. My continuing problem with Roslyn is she's so cheap, its disturbing. I mean right after her divorce she gets involved with these misfit drifters, and you get the feeling she could wind up sleeping with all THREE of them. Possibly all together and not give it a second thought. I personally don't find her very courageous or admirable. And she sure doesn't convey much caring, which is the one absolute thing I'm trying to achieve in any of my roles. So I don't see how this is all going to work out.

Its still pretty eerie to be saying lines I know I've said in real life. At different times and for different occasions but my very own words. Strange but it doesn't mean as much as I thought it would. I rehearse all my lines to all my films so often and so many different ways that after awhile they feel like my own words anyway. Unfortunately at that point, when I'm finally ready to deliver them, I sometimes forget them completely. Like I've overworked them past exhaustion. I need some brain tricks to stop repeating that nervous behavior. Maybe hypnosis. But the main reason I've gotten to the level I have is because I work damn hard to keep improving. So I'll continue preparing for my hopeful triumph, with this piece or the next. Now its true you can find a great lead role in something less than a tremendous film. Three Faces of Eve was like that for Joanne Woodward. Which could easily be the case here. Its the actress's ability to show her different emotions that's the key. So maybe the critics will like it or at least like me. Clark thinks its one of the best screenplays he's ever read. And he's still the King of Movies. So who knows? I'll just keep my fingers crossed and pray my judgment is soured by my marital problems and the fact I miss my Jack so much.

Well I'm going to turn in now because tomorrow is a busy day. I do hope I can get some sleep. I seem to be using more reds each day. Each night is actually more like it. I hate the doctors who started me on this crap. And I'm starting to hate Arthur who has lost his focus along with the thrust of our story. I can't believe at this late date he has begun reconsidering what the ending should be. Thinking maybe I should NOT wind up with Gay after all since he's so much older. I keep saying Clarke is the co-star and that's the way its always been. Star and co-star. Man and woman. Perhaps that's the author (Arthur) voicing his personal self-doubts? We've discussed this issue ad nausea. Especially when he's tried to blame me for the baby or lack therein. I have not raised the other possibility because I'm way too kind.

Back to the ending. Arthur says I can't wind up with Perce, cause he's too young, and already completely broken up inside. Not Guido either, cause he's too numb from the war and the death of his wife. I personally think everyone should split up at the end and go his or her own tortured way. Like the few wild horses who are freed.

But this is a movie and the public likes a happy ending, probably because they're so darn rare in real life. Most important they do vote with their ticket purchases. So Arthur will have to do the tried and true if he wants our film to have any chance of success. Me and Clark will ride off into the sunset, with the wild stallion following faithfully behind. And one of the mares and her foal running to catch up.

Whoever said comedy is much harder to do than drama should come to the desert. And deal with my estranged husband for me. Once we wrap, he's ancient history. Let's see Arthur write about that. My luck, he'll probably get the whole horrid thing down in one perfect weekend draft. Make me look like an absolute monster, foaming at the mouth, and chewing at his nuts like they were apple seeds. Well, out here in the desert its probably cactus seeds.

Very bad morning, Red, *August 5, 1960*

Speaking about my monster side and how I can suddenly get so frustrated I burst into pieces. Well I went totally crazy on the set. Didn't burst, too mild. I flat out exploded. The sad part is it was over nothing at all. Still I just couldn't stop myself from screaming at Arthur and crying and continuing to whip myself into an absolute fury. Uncontrollable. Wailing like a baby without a mother. Which of course I was for a long time. So now I'm the opposite, a mother without a baby which is equally bad. Actually worse because your early years are limited. I've got decades to be childless.

It was so hot in the bar we only shot half the scene. By the second hour everyone wilted. Even the dog was panting loudly. John Huston is furious at Paula because she yelled 'cut' out of nowhere, and that rightfully is the director's domain. She thought I had a momentary twitch which of course you can edit out. He hates her anyway and was just waiting for the right moment. Seems she called him right after he agreed to be director to welcome him into the family. Wanted to talk about how Lee might want to visit the shoot once we began shooting. To see how I and the rest of the crew were handling everything. He hung up on her cursing like a sailor. Months later it still remains a thorn because he throws it up all the time. So when Paula screamed out for no reason, John totally lost it. He cursed her in several different ways, her phony techniques, her overinflated ego, her philandering husband, which I don't believe, and demanded she get on the next plane out of town (and this isn't even a town). So I asked him nicely to please take a deep breath and be kind. It was just a stupid mistake on Paula's part. He glared, then turned on me and my arrival time the last two mornings. Truth is I did come rather late to the shoot but they just couldn't get my hair right. I knew this would happen with the sun and the wind and sand everywhere. Bad climate for an over bleached peroxide queen like myself.

While this was happening Arthur was pacing in front of the entire cast and production crew. Then he looked over at me with the most disapproving glare like I told you so. I looked at my feet, scratching at the sand. Embarrassed, pressured because he also hates Paula. And I was pissed at her myself.

Fifteen minutes later, after allowing this to fester deep inside, I was beside myself. Arthur was still flaunting that annoyed superior look. Like he's Mr. Creative Genius and I'm a worthless, neurotic mess who needs a jackass like Paula as a constant crutch. And since I'm so needy of support and reassurance, I'm no longer worthy of his love. Damaged goods need too much time and effort to keep from falling apart.

Actually I've seen these signs of acting superior with other guys who I later found out were screwing around behind my back. Shit, was that it? Why, the sneaky swine. He's having an affair with someone. I'M ALMOST SURE OF IT. So I leapt on him in a full frontal attack trying to flush him out. Accusing him of doing it with that cheap script assistant. I think her name is Angie, who works for John Huston. A real moron. Was he screwing her bouncy body behind my back? I stared into the tramp's eyes. She twisted her head with its little brain towards Vegas as she looked away in guilt. May they both burn in hell.

So how does dear Arthur react to my fears? Instead of trying to reassure me he becomes even angrier. Starts yelling curses directly in my face, spitting madly. And then he uses his upper body (he's a lot taller than me) to try to push me over. Obviously I was pressing on a very sensitive nerve. Then my demented husband steps back and tries to shift the blame completely back around. Saying I was the one who had dashed off to LA to see Yves last weekend and who was the unfaithful one around here and everywhere else? When in fact, I needed desperately to see my good Doctor Greenson to make some sense out of everything.

Later that evening when I called my good Doctor, he said there was a lack of communication between Arthur and me. I was angry with Arthur for neglecting me emotionally. And the fact he needed to work on the script didn't make it any better. Still this was hardly an uncommon problem, but especially when making films, where there's such pressure on both of us because of time and production costs. Even in normal environments many couples find they can not work together. It was hardly a sin to admit this and make plans accordingly in the future. We could just go on sharing beds but not careers. I said that was a nice thought but total rot at the present time. After all, we had a movie to make.

So he said, 'Well, Marilyn, taking three 'reds' a day was grossly excessive and had to be a major negative force on my psyche.' I tried to explain that's exactly how many Paula has doled out on major shoots for years. And she knew my performance level better than anyone. He replied that working as an actress is not nearly as important as living comfortably with myself. I had to learn to love myself, and protect my health. Surely more than any career or love interest. Even a husband. And so it wasn't such a great session. Besides I had lied about the number of Seconals which during this crisis has gone up to four. Three to three and a half to sleep and one or two around noon. I'm swilling them down with champagne, and I'm in a stupor over Arthur's betrayal. Pure hell. Lets say for the last three days. Besides Yves refused to see me Saturday night even though he was in town. Refused to even take my calls. Which was another HUGE REJECTION festering just under my skin like a giant splinter. Lousy bastard.

Then the next morning outside the saloon, before we start shooting, there was Arthur's angry face right in front of me. He was purposely and rudely shaking sweat in my direction. And there was me, totally frustrated and helpless. So I started screaming back curses and telling him to get his clothes the hell out of our room. And his stupid pens and that dumb ass leather blotter, with all the match burns from his dumb ass pipe. And from now on, to consider our marriage over. Fini. End of story, master story teller. You've killed the dream and the hope that was us.

So he offers this blatant lie, 'that he still loves me, even now.' Complete crock of shit. I was livid. 'This was hardly love. You deceived me badly. And I've had it, finally.'

He counters by saying, 'You need major psychiatric help.' I replied, 'Utterly ridiculous. That's the one thing I happen to have in abundance.'

During this exchange we have been circling each other, staring eyeball to eyeball. All at once he leaned in a bit and then I did the same and we started to physically go at each other, screaming and kicking until we were pulled apart. And I know I would have won cause I know how to fight dirty, with my knees or foot in his groin and my thumb raking his eyeballs. Pulling his thinning hair out from the back of his scalp, making him pay for my frustration.

But afterwards I felt even worse and I was completely ashamed of my terrible behavior. The rage passed and I was totally lost and confused. I found myself walking around the set in a spent daze. Not able to remember much of anything but so emotionally exhausted, like a rung out dishrag. By then I was feeling very badly about my behavior and quite guilty. Much too embarrassed to just hang around. The trees began to swirl faster and faster. Then I fainted. And after they revived me with ice water on my brow and cold tissues on my forehead and a lemon to suck, I felt a little better. Finally I could stand, shaky but able. I pushed the crew away and started out moving away from this disturbing scene where I had lost my grip and embarrassed myself. And then for a moment lost my mind, embarrassing myself even worse.

I went back to the Mapes Hotel to find my husband to tell him I was truly sorry. But when Arthur saw me in the hallway, he backed up toward his writing room. Backpedaling and slipping on the wooden floor, grabbing the knob to steady himself. Looking terribly upset and afraid, almost without any color in his face. He turned away to open the door, then spun into the small office area. He slammed the door shut and locked it. And he never did learn I was simply coming back to apologize for being so out of control.

Dear Red,   *August 16, 1960*

I'm unable to get out of this funk. Often I can find a light, happy spot in some part of my mind. Enjoy a few laughs with the crew, especially my personal staff. These are the people I love and who love me. My true family, my healthy support, people who care and I care about them. Real people who weren't trying to get something from me. But yesterday, we totally shut down shooting so we weren't together to work or hang around and joke. And it became a long confusing day, or daze cause it wasn't like a day, closer to a haze.

It started when a huge desert brush fire produced a cloud of smoke completely covering Reno. So thick and harsh, it was hard to breathe let alone move. Then as the sun came up to high-noon (cowboy talk) the massive heat caused the electric power to go down by frying the lines. Which further overloaded the whole system, burning out more stuff. I mean everywhere there was quiet.

So by nighttime no repairs have been made and it was dark and spooky, with a burned rubber smell like a haunted town in Hell, Nevada. I can understand there are very few stand-by generators in this wasteland, like who would anticipate a movie shoot coming to town? But because of the shortfall, the only lights are at the hospital and, of course, the blessed casino. Couldn't possibly risk losing any business over there, now could we?

It was late, almost midnight and eerie and I had been walking aimlessly around the town for hours. I ended up standing on the bridge over the Truckee River at the site where the divorcees throw their wedding rings.

I was standing next to Rupert, my loyal press agent, who's been my friend for a very long time. We were just talking but I kept sneaking looks over at Arthur's window. Everything else was dark, but Arthur had borrowed the production generator so he could have light to continue his endless revisions. My totally fixated son of a bitch husband has to keep churning out more confusion. More inconsistency. Can't take a rest or quit. Can't put it or himself to bed.

I couldn't see him but I knew he was there because I could see his shadow through the curtains. He looked so old, dark and bent over, faintly moving. And I realized it was over, and said that to Rupert. He replied, looking down at the river, 'well, there's always another fish.'

Also, my sad conclusion is Arthur does in fact have a girlfriend. Just don't have the proof to nail him. Not yet. I was wrong about one thing. Its not that script assistant. But someone a lot worse. A class act, tall, thin, pretty. A well known photographer from Magnum who is doing the stills. A true blue (eyed) Germanic slut. Even younger than the other one. Damn her. And a lot smarter than me, damn him. I hope Arthur's penis falls off and his mind turns to jello. If it hasn't already. And he misses me terribly.

I was afraid he'd betray me the first chance he got. And now he's done that very thing. I feel completely humiliated. And stupid because I did contribute a bit by throwing him out. Now that I don't have him anymore, I miss him dearly. Yeah, bad night's a coming. I can feel it right down to my bones. I'm pretty sure I won't be able to sleep at all.

Dear Red,   *August something*

Its been more than a week since my huge fight with Arthur, and one day after the brush fire and I'm in the Reno Hospital hiding out. I'm hooked up to an IV so writing is difficult. John Huston suggested I admit myself to get some rest along with letting the doctors check me over because I looked a tad run down. This place is a real dump and there's not one single private room in the whole damn building. The Head Administrator cooperated by taking one of the beds out of a double so at least I'm alone. But my good Doctor Greenson has gone on vacation to Europe (another abandonment) and there is not one trained mental doctor on the entire staff. Just a young GP who has done a thorough physical and a bucket of blood tests that reveal nothing except my blood count is slightly low. This could not in itself explain my fainting spell. So I've been started on iron and B12 but I still feel horrible. Dead tired, both body and soul.

My only happy moment came when Peter Lawford called to let me know the President to be was very concerned about my health and how was I doing? Jack hoped to see me next weekend at either Frank's Palm Springs getaway, or more likely at the Cal-Neva Lodge where Frank was singing. If of course I was up to it. Jack is getting ready to kick his campaign into high gear starting officially on Labor Day, which I think is September 5. And I explained I wasn't really sick, just upset because my marriage had ended and this shoot was a toughie with many technical difficulties.

John Huston had suggested we shut down for a few days on the premise of making sure I was OK. But the real reason was he was gambling like a madman night and day, day and night and losing huge amounts at the Reno Casino.

Presently my skilled director is in debt to the house up to his eyeballs. And he had to get out of town to get the cash to wipe his markers and make good with the mob boys. John was the one with the problem. Cards and dice turned on him. But I was fine, both in my body and head. Mr. Huston was the one trying to keep his thumbs.

Then I told Peter to call me the moment he knew which site was better, but I would go anywhere to see my darling. I miss Jack so much. And him and Pat, too. (Two monster lies. Actually three cause I detest Peter most of anyone presently alive. So the lie about him counts double.)

Now as regards my fainting problem, Arthur has already talked with the Doctor who admitted me. I'm sure he's told him a pack of lies, hiding his guilt about being unfaithful. And acting all loving and supportive like the hippocrit he is. Besides grossly exaggerating my pill and alcohol intake. So far this doctor has only talked to me about my medical state and just a little about my current medications. We don't exactly agree on maintaining my present level of Seconals which he thinks are way too much. So I had Paula speak to him and try to explain how long I have been using this rather large amount. And that's why they no longer worked. And the Doctor agreed, and called it 'ackomodation', which was a very common side effect with addicting medicines. But he wasn't going to order any more because he didn't want to be responsible for killing me or letting me kill myself. Another coward in a white coat.

Most important, he cleared me for duty. He thought I could start working again just as soon as I thought I was ready. He had seen some of the filming near the bridge and could understand some of the huge pressures being placed on me. With over a hundred people milling about and horses in the pens and the food caterers and don't ask.

So he ordered an enema, times two, and one chloral hydrate, half a gram, times none to help me sleep. The stingy shit. Well, fortunately, I still have near a hundred of Paula's reds stashed away in her 'Bubby bag'. Straight up honest, I'd never go on a shoot without them. That's why I can never fire my dear acting coach and pal. Paula sometimes suggests good things to try as an actress. But I all the time want to guarantee my fairly unlimited supply of reds, just in case. They work better than anything to let me rest. So I'll sleep through Sunday and be ready to get back to the grind once the workweek begins.

A little while after he left, I heard some nurses talking in the hall and I clearly heard the phrase 'crazy as a bedbug' which I found rather disturbing. Could they be talking about me? I pray they don't think I'm insane. But, of course, what else could they be thinking with my family background and all?

Dear Red,   *August 26, 1960*

We've been working for close to two weeks straight trying to catch up on the shooting schedule. And we're finally just about there. Everyone's in a groove and working their butts off. Seasoned pros doing their best, grinding it out.

We just did this great scene with Clark when he talks about dying. His lines are 'if a man's afraid to die, he's clearly going to be afraid to live.' Arthur sort of stole it from William Shakespeare in Julius Caesar. But its still really powerful the way Clark says it. So after he finished, we just sat in this extremely hot station wagon for a moment, waiting for John to yell 'cut.' But he didn't so we waited. And I could see a small tear form in Clark's right eye and I moved closer and we just hugged each other. It felt so good and only then did John call 'cut' to end that part of the scene. So we got out of the front seat of the station wagon. I just knew the tear was real. And this small sign of weakness meant so much to me that I ran around the front of the old Chevy and I kissed Clark square on the lips. Sometimes really fine acting can be so great and it does something funny to my insides. And he gave a quick laugh like he was a bit embarrassed but also like he was getting turned on at the same time. Well he sure didn't push me away like he could have. I mean his wife, Kay, is ready to give birth, for gosh sake. It was one of our first scenes when our characters are getting to know each other. So sometimes life does imitate art, just like visa versa. Then we were back in the car for the rest of the scene. Monty and Eli came up to my car window to ask us to come to the bar. But they started hooting and shouting and saying it was their turn. Jokers.

Then we all laughed, and I got out and kissed Monty and he turned scarlet red. But Eli took it like a trooper because he loves women. Then he grabbed my ass so I did the same thing to him. Equal rights, womens rights.

Arthur and I have partially reconciled after Jack shot me down, flying down to Florida instead of coming to see me in Nevada. Externally, I didn't even flinch. I'm taking all the disappointments I have ever suffered and funneling each and every one of them back into my acting. Paula thinks I'm doing some of my best work ever. At times I even think I'm as good as Clark. As she reminds me, I even held my own with Lawrence Olivier and he was knighted for his dramatic performances. So I'm proud of my progress, especially after all this huge hard work for so many years. And torment. I can honestly say I've become an ACTRESS and in the right pieces with characters I can believe in, a good one.

Montgomery Clift is a marvelous actor. On Monty's first scene, in this old phone booth talking to his mom, he just belts it out. And its a one take, and that's over a page and a half. Unbelievable. I, on the other hand, for one scene in Some Like It Hot demanded 36 takes, even though Billy Wilder said it was great after two. But that was also to piss off Tony Curtis because he was acting pouty and annoyed, like he needed a good spanking. I wanted to let Curly Cutey Pie (who loves himself past Bogart) experience just a little of what it was like for all us real girls, decked out in fancy make-up, high heels, and compressing under garments.

I hope the critics like my performance this time as much as they liked that farce. Arthur says its a sad western but he only writes sad things anyway. That's cause he thinks sad even when he's amused. Which is very, very sad. I'm not looking forward to the mustang scenes. I do hope none of the animals are hurt especially the wild ones who are extremely unruly. Beautiful but also uncontrollable, much like Jack. Of course he has legit reasons to be flighty, like winning the national election and leading our country and world forward.

After wrapping for the day, I went over to the corral with cubes of sugar and two apples. But no horse from the herd would come close enough to let me feed him. I tried throwing the biggest, the stallion, a few sugar cubes. But Jack (my name for Mr. Unruly)) just trampled them with his hoofs as he charged around the corral, looking even more agitated.

Then, like a dunce, I tried to slip between the rungs. I was hoping to go over and comfort him. Give the big guy a little hug. I hadn't got one foot inside before the Security Policeman starts to frantically blow his whistle and wave his hand. Which only managed to spook the horses far worse. So I just left them all in the corral and went back to my trailer. Like in many other circumstances, my presence seemed to only make matters worse. Its so hard being a lightning rod.

Half an hour later, I was sitting around in my trailer going over lines with Paula. When HE called, from Texas of all places, the President to be. First he used Kenny O'Donnell to make the call, on the pretense of thanking me for my twenty-five thousand dollar donation to the campaign. Arthur was so pissed about that. Not because it was for Jack but because it was for so much. We're not rolling in chips right now. Also considering Arthur and I split a total of five hundred thousand for this entire picture. While Clark pockets seven hundred fifty for just acting. Easy cash for him. Which is another reason I'm annoyed at Arthur, because he is a very poor businessman. I am the leading star, darn it. And he is the top writer, if he'd just write Fade Out. We wasted two years in pre production, and now we're bogged down in shooting. Get to the climax, my ex honey. Let's move on. With the film and our lives.

Suddenly my DEAR JACK was on the phone, asking me if it was all right to speak. And I said it was fine and how thrilled I was to hear his voice. How I missed him terribly. And he told me he loved me and missed me very much. (That's four!) And I totally melted, and said I felt even more the same. I asked him how the campaign was going, and he replied OK. But he was real nervous about the first debate which has been scheduled for the last week in September in Chicago and did I have any helpful hints.

So I told him to speak slowly and firmly, opening his mouth to shape the words (ala Natasha). And to stand up straight and look right next to the camera, about one and a half feet off center. And not to be afraid to smile.

He laughed and told me he'd take my suggestions to heart. He said he loved to speak to me, but even more to be near me so I could direct him in a dress or perhaps even better an undress rehearsal. But his hands were tied and he had never worked harder for anything in his entire life. Of course I told him I understood.

Then he said, oh, by the way, he was going to be in California on a whistle stop train tour on September 8th and 9th ending in LA. And he knew I was busy filming but was there any chance I could arrange to be there so we could get together? And I told him if there is any way at all, I'd be there. If I have to pedal through the desert, I'm on my Schwinn with giant tread tires. Training begins tomorrow. He laughed. I'm suddenly excited and thrilled and oh so happy. I have somewhere to be with the man I love.

The second we phone kiss and hang up, I'm on a instant mission to get the hell out of this blasted desert just as soon as I can. So I can rest up before being with my true love. Then I can comfort him, rubbing his tired body with my hands and toes. And hopefully warming his soul with my love.

I look up at Paula, pleading with my eyes. She really knows me so she gets right to it. 'OK, Marilyn, how can I help get you to Loverboy?' So we start to work on various ruses. Finally going with the tried and true, we decide on a moderate overdose of sleepers. And after a fair amount of haggling, we then agree on three additional Seconals, which in a normal person could perhaps be dangerous. But to this girl, its pretty much my normal allotment. Because I'm down to two to four a night, once again.

By next morning, two hours before noon, it was already over 105 and I was wrapped in a wet sheet being carried by stretcher to a two engine airplane waiting to whisk me off. Next stop, Westside Hospital in dear old LA. Paula reminded me to shiver. She figured that would be a convincing touch. But I already knew that part, cold.

Dear Red,   *September 6, 1960*

My hospital stay was a bore, but I was finally able to talk
Dr. Greenson into discharging me just in time to meet Jack.
The Kennedy Campaign will pass through central and southern
California. And the Whistle Stop Train Ride will end right here
with an election speech in some North Hollywood shopping mall.

Maybe I'll jump on a train to Merced or Fresno or one of
those other small farming towns and just hang around the station
like a farm girl. As I think about it some more, though, its better to
have him on the hungry side. I'll wait until he arrives in L.A.

Dear Red,   *September 10, 1960*

The last two days and EVEN BETTER nights have been great. Whew. Just wonderful for my spirits and libido. My Jack seems so energized by the campaign he's simply bubbling over. Total enthusiasm for what he's doing. And big love for me. We stayed at Peter's house below Malibu and the weather was close to perfect. Warm and breezy. We walked the beach at night like the old days and he kept his arm around me and I felt so adored. And appreciated as a complete woman. His woman. We talked about so much. The country: regarding everything from the present election (we're going to win because Nixon is a fraud) to the three greatest presidents in the history of our nation. (Past presidents, obviously.) Jack picked four Democrats and Jefferson but then I talked him down because of Sally Hemmings, his slave mistress. He agreed Jefferson was a big hippocrit on that important issue and no one should ever be a slave. We both agreed on number one being Abraham Lincoln, no dispute there. I had seen a picture in the newspaper from Spokane Washington. Jack addressing the people in the main square next to a statue of our 16th president, his high hat in his hand, his long coat with tails so dignified. I told Jack how for the longest time I had thought of dear Mr. Lincoln as my number one father figure because he was so smart and kind, and treated everyone fairly. I had even won first prize for the best essay on 'your true hero' in Erickson Junior High when I was in the seventh grade. And the Senator from Illinois was my choice. Decades later, I still believe Honest Abe was our history's most memorable leader.

In the same way, I believe Jack is the one to lead us in modern times. I think his appeal to the poor and downtrodden is the key to his future greatness. Along with his ability to inspire our youth.

I suggested when he took the presidential oath, maybe he could also wear tails and a top hat just like you know who. JACK laughed and said he would as long as I didn't ask him to grow a beard. He asked if I could come and keep him company that night. I told him I had to respectfully refuse because I would be using that opportunity to get my divorce from Arthur. I sure didn't want to in any way INTRUDE on his wonderful triumph. It was his show. And he would be busy enough. Besides I was difficult to hide away.

Near the end of our wonderful weekend, we made plans to see each other in New York, probably in about three weeks when he barnstorms through. But there were factors to keep in mind. After all I was still shooting a film, and the producers wanted to strangle me. And I wanted to get it wrapped too. He had heard I was having difficulties on the set. I replied Arthur had become a huge problem, knowing nothing what so ever about movies.

Jack just nodded and said Arthur was lucky to have me. I answered he doesn't have me any more and I explained our sleeping arrangements. He quickly corrected himself, saying he meant for the film. But that was the same way with him and Jackie, when they were together cause she was already as big as a house. I replied she was still the blessed one to be carrying his child inside her. He shrugged and said 'Sorry its not you, pumpkin,' which is his loving nickname for me.

He countered that making love was a big part of his expressing care and affection for someone he cares about. But since I was such a steamy sexpot, it kept his hormones flowing. And most times he felt like a teenager around me because I was such a unique combination of… let's see if I can remember this, Red. OK, beauty, wit and sparkling personality. Wait, this part I memorized in my mind, front wards, backwards, and sidewards. Dah dahm, 'And I would make a great First Lady'.

Jack always knows the perfect thing to say to allay my fears. I rolled onto my back like a seal in heat.

I cried for almost two hours after we parted but I would never let him see any of my dramatics. Never, ever let him see how he gets to me so much. Because romantically he's very much like me in one crazy way. Once he recognizes that someone has fallen completely, head over heels in love with him, he'll lose interest fast. Guaranteed. No more game. No more thrill. No more love of my life. Once he knows I care so much it hurts all the time, he'll never look back.

Dear Red,   *Sept.15, 1960*

Well, I've returned. Back in Reno, the divorce capital of
the nation, finishing up The Misfits. I've stopped fighting with
Arthur. We both agreed to leave the script in whatever state it was
presently in and shoot it just as quick as we can. So we can just get
something in the can and get the hell out of here and go on with
our lives.

I've also stopped coming late to the set. This change occurred
after my good doctor suggested I was perhaps doing my tardy
routine just to punish Clark, who was my substitute father figure.
Mainly because I had been waiting all these years for my true dad
to show up. I realized Clark hardly deserved that kind of treatment
because he's a real gentleman and a great actor. So things are going
a whole lot smoother. Plus John Huston is having more luck at the
tables so he's a good deal happier. And we're just moving through
the script as per the schedule. Very professional and seasoned. One
scene after another.

I've completely given up on Yves. Jack is the only one I think
about and almost all the time. I've only spoken to him once over
the weekend because he's been practicing his short replies to each
of the major debate topics to be addressed. He is intent on making
the first debate a showcase for his knowledge of world issues. Plus
he's getting prepared to go on the attack about failed policies and
promises from the Republicans. Mano a mano, as he says. And the
first to flinch is the loser. Jack was made for television because he's
so handsome and elegant. Besides being a great speaker, direct and
to the point. Straight forward but with an impish sense of humor,
which he uses to completely disarm an attacker.

Like right before the first roll call at the Democratic
Nominating Convention, he appeared at the Texas caucus for the

Kennedy-Johnson debate downtown. And Lying Lyndon starts right up stating one of the two candidates present had a horrible attendance record in the Senate. Then Jack got up and said, 'well, it was true but the delegates shouldn't take it out on Senator Johnson because he was busy doing deals elsewhere.' And even Johnson laughed. By the way, Johnson, as ordered, has stayed completely in the South to campaign, referring often to his pappy's Confederate roots. Ugh. I'm surprised he hasn't made speeches in his white robe and hood.

Dear Red,   *September 26, 1960*

I started in the middle but what the hell. We just watched the first Presidential debate in a small unadorned room off the overly elaborate casino on three small TV's. JACK WON, hands down, on each and every one of them. Plain and simple, he was so much more appealing.

First off, Nixon looked absolutely horrible. He looked completely unsure of himself like he needed a massive tranquilizer, sweaty and ready to pass out, with this pasty skin and shifty rat's eyes. Jack had heard Ike had tried to persuade Tricky Dick not to debate him at all. Good suggestion but Dicky is an ass for never listening.

Cuba was one of the issues where Jack definitely had the upper hand. Citing Castro's increasing friendship with Russia. But of course Jack didn't mention the MAFIA or the United States gun running. He just boldly stated we must do something to stop Castro's aggression and suggested a naval boycott.

At that point, Nixon really started to fumble about. And my Jack looked like a true white knight, riding in to rescue our nation's interests, which of course I always feel he is doing anyway.

And twenty minutes after it was over, my Jack had Kenny O'Donnell call my room to tell me that the soon to be President of the US would call me tomorrow morning. Meanwhile, Kenny was kind enough to give me some background gossip. In other words, the dirt, which I always eat up.

Nixon had refused to use any makeup, none at all. So they tipped the custodian who raised the heat in the room to the max to make Dicky sticky and he began sweating buckets. Jack was wearing short sleeves (he usually wears long ones with French cuffs) and was deliberately tan, aided by a pancake base. I stated I thought the Candidate appeared extremely rested and confident. He said his whole staff thought Jack had won handily and Henry Cabot Lodge, who was in the audience, was overheard cursing Nixon and saying that 'the know it all son of a bitch had just lost their team the election.' More later, Red. I have to go to sleep now. THIS WAS A GREAT NIGHT if you care about our country, and the entire world. Also the future of politics is clear. It will be framed in rabbit ears, and will unfold in black and white with a few cigarette commercials before and after.

Dear Red,   *October 11, 1960*

We just finished a series of scenes leading to when we return from the rodeo, the men drunk as skunks, me just a little. All of the cowboys are in their own private grief stricken world and Roslyn tries to comfort each in turn with very little success. Perce is mourning the death of his father, who was killed in a hunting accident. Three months later his mom takes up with a con man who marries her to get the farm, which has been promised to him since his birth. Completely lost he starts wandering about the West. Finally, unable to hold a job, he becomes an alcoholic rodeo performer. So drunk he doesn't feel fear. But also so drunk he often gets hurt. Gay has met his two kids just before, at the corral. But they leave him before he can introduce them to Roslyn. He realizes he has been a lousy husband and worse father and wonders if he has the strength and desire to try it again. Now that he is weathered and tired and Roslyn's a lot younger. And Eli, with his war wounds and love losses, using his airplane as a merchant of death for all the brave wild horses.

Drunk, they all fall asleep and I walk out to the car to shut off the lights. Then I look up to the sky, and cry 'Help' 'cause I'm still desperately lonely. This part of me Arthur has caught just perfectly. Concerned about all those around me but myself totally lost.

Jack has managed to call a few times since the debate. I can hear his confidence growing by leaps and bounds. He said perhaps we could rendezvous at the Carlyle, our old trysting place, on Oct. 19 after his ticker tape parade. I replied, I will try my hardest. Nixon has continued to drop in the polls and Eisenhower's bad heart has stopped him from running to Dicky's rescue. The race is now neck and neck. Jack has one more debate scheduled for October 21 in Manhattan. His staff thinks he's gotten about as much mileage from the TV debates as he's going to get. I don't.

In my line there's no such thing as over done publicity. My nude calendar photo continues to show I'm a shameless show off and I love every well lit inch of it. Elizabeth Taylor, who is supposedly my biggest competition, thinks I'm one of the few women who looks better without any clothes on. And she should know. We became loving friends in Vegas a few years ago. Nice tits and she definitely enjoyed our night together. Got to run, Red. They need me on the lot.

Dear Red,   *October 19, 1960*

We've just finished shooting! I'm so relieved I can actually feel this tremendous boulder lifting off my chest. But nothing ends well. At least on this project. We had a major crisis near the climax that is continuing to haunt all of us. A terrible twist that won't go away and just seems to get worse.

In one of the last scenes, Gay fights the wild stallion. The horse drags him across the plains before the cowboy is finally able to take control. Only then does he decide to set the horse free. Well, Clark, like a stubborn mule, (and probably adopting the character of Gay) decides to do his own stunt work. A very unwise decision, even though we all pleaded with him to give it to one of the much younger professional stunt men, who train for things like this. And are much more supple and athletic.

Clark winds up getting dragged maybe a hundred yards on this desert surface, which is like hard irregular sand paper. And there's no give what so ever. Its like diamond bedrock. By the time the handlers were finally able to take control of the over excited horse, add on another fifty yards of being dragged and jerked about by the whole group, frantic animal and crew. Swirling, breaking, screaming, sliding, and praying. A terrible mess.

So Clark's just lying there in a heap and I hear this low moaning as we all come running up. Seeing how pale he is, I begin to cry in fear. Then we help lift him up, and nothing appears broken. I mean in terms of major bones, but something was different about him. Clark suddenly looked so old and tired and, yes, thoroughly frightened.

He kept saying he was fine but I could clearly see he was not. Clark continued to clench his chest and remained ashen for almost half an hour after the trauma.

I kept checking on him, and made him lie down on this cot in the shade. Then I pulled John Huston aside and made him promise to film the close ups scheduled for the next day using a dummy horse with Clark. And he said he would have readily done the earlier scene with a stand in but Clark had insisted. Above any and all of his protests, this time he had to absolutely insist because he was the director and had the final word. Clark was no longer the spring chicken he wanted all of us to think he was. And we had to look out for him and protect him. John promised he would.

But I am still thrown out of whack because I sense the real damage has already been done. And I feel responsible and terribly guilty. Bottom line, this was our story (me and Arthur) and our movie. And I was pretty sure we had done something extremely harmful to a wonderful man and a great actor who took it farther than he should have. But that is his nature. We were the guilty ones because we knew Mr. Gable and still let it happen.

So last night, it was Arthur's 45th birthday party which I thought was truly ironic. Like he's not old at all even though I keep thinking he is. And since we were through with all the major filming, it was a wild party from the very beginning, fueled by a lot of drinking. I had switched to straight bourbon cause we were in the West and what the hell. Real cowboys drink real liquor. I'm not sure about cowgirls.

One of the film jesters is this cameraman named Russ. He's been on like five of my films and he's usually truly sweet. So he stands up in front of everyone and asks me to please wish Arthur a Happy Birthday, by singing the birthday song. 'Just start and we'll all join in,' which I just can't do. No words. No sounds. Nothing.

I was so tied up with all my emotions about Arthur, I couldn't breath. Disappointed with him and this film which I always felt was our own special project. So important, it held us together. Almost all the other films I've been on, I felt it was a major collaboration of many different people. A big group to share the blame.

But this one was Arthur's and mine alone. A dreary morbid Western from a dreary morbid Easterner. And, of course, mine because I needed to do a serious major drama. Had to prove I could cut it. Prove I could make audiences cry. But hardly one about killing wild, beautiful horses. It was too wretched a theme. A little like the Holocaust. Or Korean War.

I just sat there at the birthday table and like a total idiot shook my head several times. Well, finally Russ gave up and started to sing Happy Birthday by himself and everyone joined in and even I sang the last line. Still, I was unable to do anything after but hang my head. I felt my face turn bright red. I couldn't look into Arthur's eyes because I was so embarrassed by my behavior. Not just then but through the whole shoot. And to get to this ending, with simply great acting by the entire cast and yet each member finding his own very worst disappointment, it was so sad. Also it was clear to me we could never stay together for even a moment more. It was over, fini, time to pack up and move on. Time to start looking again.

Then I told Paula to get us two tickets the hell out of there just as soon as possible. Because we were going back alone. And Paula, whose marriage to Lee seems to have dried up ten years ago understood completely.

As for my present performance I can just hope I'll be better from here on out. Learn better how to pick them, especially the right scripts. And be patient if they don't come quickly. Hell, all I've got left is my career.

My need to find my true voice as a dedicated actress remains strong. Its a journey, not a single test, as Dr. Kris always reminds me.

So I'll continue down the path, searching for the right projects to define my movie career. And the right leading man for my life. Amen.

This is crazy bad but I just flew back to New York to be told on landing that Clark Gable has been admitted to a hospital in LA with a heart attack. And he was in ICU in critical condition. Oh, God, this is terrible. I already tried to call his wife Kay but there was no answer at their home. Damn. I knew this film had bad karma but I hardly expected something like this. I suddenly feel so totally beat up. I pray I wasn't in any real sense responsible for what happened. Far more, I pray he'll just be OK.

My dearest friend Red,   *October 26, 1960*

I'm in New York City with my Jack, the President of the U.S. to be who almost is, in our elaborate penthouse love nest. We are appropriately enough, in the newly renamed Presidential Suite at the Carlyle. Very chic! This has been the most incredible two days. I heard Clark is getting better. And soon after, I became one hundred per cent positive, for the first time that JACK WILL WIN. All doubt in my mind has completely vanished. And my Jack knows it even more so. Amazing good luck at exactly the right time and I was there as it happened.

It all started yesterday after we got news that Dr. Martin Luther King, Jr. had been sentenced to four months in jail. His crime, failing to stop the car he was driving completely at a stop sign. Jack immediately called the Reverend's wife, Coretta, to promise his support. At the same time, his younger brother Bobby was calling the judge who had ruled on the case. He passionately persuaded him to free Dr. King, setting a minimal bail. (In exchange for future considerations including a Federal appointment which, of course comes with a life time pay check and lifetime benefits). Well, Dr.King was out in less then an hour. The morning papers went crazy.

But word got out way faster than that. Boy, oh boy, did it ever. Especially in the black community. Reverend King's father called Jack in the late afternoon and promised him a suitcase full of votes. He would deliver them by way of the black church goer's. Their ministers would implore them to get out of their homes and churches and playgrounds and where ever they gather including bars, and numbers parlors, and houses of ill repute. Everyone must go vote for JFK for President because Nixon was a closet racist.

This is really funny. When Jack relayed the message, I got so excited I ran over and jumped in his lap, in my birthday suit. And he playfully tried to push me off, saying there wouldn't be enough room down there real soon. His reason: the good Reverend had just promised to dump all of the Negro votes from clear across the country into his lap. Especially from the Bible carrying church goers. And he didn't know if the choir ladies would approve of my outfit, let alone move over.

But for right now he liked fully naked. And he hugged me, but his fingers were already wandering down to my crotch. So WE CELEBRATED. But this time it was for real because of this important new support. Along with the fact there was going to be a huge ticker tape parade through the garment center scheduled for tomorrow. So we started to really feel it at almost the same moment. We very near had the victory and could see the light at the end of the tunnel. President of the United States of America. Top Dog. And me as his Vice Mistress. Second Bitch.

Then later that evening, we dined downstairs with Jack's father, Joe, and he was as excited as the two of us. Still he repeated at least three times, the only thing left was to take Illinois and his son would be President. Most powerful man on the earth. But the way he said it was a little scary, like it would really be him, Papa Joe. The power behind the throne. Him and only him.

Well, Jack won the first debate in Chicago, which began his triumphant march so this was a good omen. But it was an even better thing that he, Joe, was such a close personal friend with Mayor Daily. Along with some other powerful people who could really get the vote out up there. Neither father nor son ever mentioned their names and I didn't ask. Mainly cause I already knew. He was talking about Sam Giancana and his gang of mobsters. Old Blue Eyes, Frankie boy, keeps me pretty well informed from the Mob side, bless the Little Rat Packer. Appropriately named, don't you think, Red?

Next day, watching Jack's big parade through the garment center on the rather large TV in the living room of my 57th street apartment. Me, in my bathrobe and curlers, a thick mud pack caked on my face, getting ready for our evening together. Jack, sitting on top of the backseat of the open convertible, reaching out to the horde of excited admirers. With his charismatic smile radiating up to the tops of the highest buildings and clear across the mid-west plains. So exciting knowing everyone wants him but he'll soon be back in my arms. George Masters flew back just to do my hair, and it turned out beautiful. I looked like Wow. Time to practice your penis up salute, my Commander.

I was elated when I walked back through the underground corridors under the mid town New York City streets to be with my guy. Happy as hell, edgy with excitement, and ready to suck my lover's brains right out of his skull or his graceful neck and ears. Or somewhere a bit lower, like just above his balls. Jack was like a young stallion taking me several times during the night. Interrupted by a fair amount of champagne sipping and caviar snacking. And just plain laughing. Truth is, he probably stopped off at Dr. Jacobson's 'Feelgood' office for an 'energy shot' just before returning to his suite. But Jack denied it. So I didn't want to press the issue. I'm not his mother.

And as you know rather well, Red, I'm hardly the one to cast stones on the use of intoxicants. Besides even if it was partially drug induced, it was with me and it was glorious. But now I'm getting competition from the whole nation. And pretty soon, the whole world will come 'A' flocking. Will I be screwed in the end, left as a memory, like Dr. Greenson warns? Refuse to think about it. Because if it happens, its still a great, great memory. These two days were simply wonderful and I'll remember them always. Arthur says I live just for the moment so I'm going to enjoy my time in heavenly bliss. I'm really worn out from all the sex. Actually, my entire bottom feels like its on fire. Could my perfect prince have given me the clap? Damn, another doctor visit.

Anyhow, I can't open my mouth wide enough to eat an apple cause the back part of my jaw is sore as hell. Besides, the muscles in my groin feel like contracting steel bands. Especially when I walk or is it hobble. But I feel totally alive. This guy, when his time comes, should be stuffed from top to bottom, then lovingly bronzed. With an extra layer of bronze on his erection. Like those Revolutionary park statues, our leaders swords drawn.

Its two days after we parted, and I'm still thoroughly satiated. Not bad for a lonely foster kid who dropped out of junior high. Even if I just remain Jack's mistress forever, I'll be satisfied. I'll make myself be satisfied, just to remain a part of his world. See, shrinks don't know everything. I really got it for my man, even when he hurts me so by leaving me to go to his family or work. Great love sometimes means greater sacrifice.

Dear Red,   *Nov. 8, 1960*

Its election night. So far it seems to be a dead even tie. Shit. I'm sitting on my sofa, with Paula, on absolute pins and needles. I mean I'm sure there'll be a winner, but when? Every time Jack manages to take a little lead, some Republican stronghold comes through with big numbers for Tricky. Then we're back to 'Even Steven', neck to neck. As Jack prophesized, Illinois is going back and forth like a fierce ping pong game. Jack is hunkered down at the family enclave at Hyannis Port, with his mom and dad and all his brothers and sisters and in-laws, including little Miss Perfect. Ready for the photo-op. Even brought the home dogs in from Virginia. Peter's called me several times to relay messages from Jack and to keep me informed. Also pretty clear from his changing tone, to take a couple of quick swigs.

They have this new thing called an exit poll where they ask some of the voters, after they voted, who they voted for and why. Not very scientific 'cause they seemed to have sampled a lot of farm boys from Bum Fuck, Montana and very few from the main cities. But under this straw vote, Nixon has a comfortable margin. Boo, Tricky. I'm sure there's a lot of irregularities in that tally.

Well, the vote in the key state of Illinois is shaping up as a contest between the rural south, for Tricky. And urban Chicago, for Jack. Now, normally a lot more people vote from the sticks. Don't ask me why, but this time everything seems to point to a record turnout in the Chicago precincts as well which is very encouraging. New York has gone solidly for Jack, with or without Carmen DeSapio's help. It was mostly without. The New England women's vote seems to strongly favor Jack, and not just in the urban areas. Across the states, which shows all women, wherever they live ain't stupid. I mean who in their right mind would want to get into bed with Dicky for four years?

I just got a phone call from Frank Sinatra. He was so excited! Says the vote in Chicago is going to come in overwhelming for Jack. Over 80%, but they're going to hold off the final count. At least until they can see how much they're going to be needing, 'yuh know', to seal things up. Still, I can rest assured, right now, Jack's going to win it all. Seems they got a huge turnout from the Teamster's, and, big surprise, all the 'shines' in the ghetto. That's Frank talking about the black citizens of our democratic nation. And the minute he said that, I could visualize some of the toughest Teamster's using baseball bats and herding some of the Blacks to the poles. Disgusting. Maybe some day we'll have a Negro President. And a lot of that hatred will finally stop. Please.

They also had four buses of convicts on a day pass being bussed from precinct to precinct. Casting multiple votes and having a few drinks along the way. Plus harassing and threatening some of the straight up normal Republican voters. Quite an effort. Frankie says its still going to take ten or twelve more hours to get the official tally. So he thinks I should take some 'reds' and get some shut eye. But they did it, stole the election for Jack and it was money in the bank. Funny but he pronounced money like Mooney which I guess was a little slip.

So I thanked him for calling. But I wanted, needed to hear it from my darling, from his own lips. Being the other woman sure isn't all that great during a time like this. But Frank finished by saying, 'looks like your lover boy is in. So this is going to be good for all of us, huh kid?' But when I hung up the phone I wasn't really all that sure anymore.

My dear friend Red,   *Nov. 11, 1960*

I'm nervous as hell. Today's the day! I spoke to Earl Wilson several days ago and this is the morning his column comes out in print. He's going to announce that my marriage to Arthur is kaput, over, finis. And I know there's going to be a feeding frenzy of reporters after that tidbit gets out. I could have sworn there were already some reporters waiting outside my apartment last night. All night and I live on the 13th floor. Who's superstitious? Besides how did they know already? I think I'll take a look out the living room window. Be back in a second. Now, Red, don't start writing anything without me. Ha. When I get nervous and scared sometimes I get stupid.

OK, I'm back. Guess what! Not ten, or twenty. There's got to be over a hundred over eager cockroaches out there on the street, milling. And I do mean the street. The entire block has been cordoned off. Shit! Some of them have bullhorns. There's a lot of noises. Well, seems they definitely want to talk to me. So I'd better get dressed and go down to my public. But first off, I'll call Paula. For this little press conference, I'm going to be needing some support in my corner.

Got to go, Red. Somehow I'm afraid it will be a Roman circus, me being fed to the raging lions. Most reporters are so uncaring and they have absolutely no boundaries. None at all. Then there's the ones from the foreign press. They have boundaries but not emotionally. Absolute animals in heat. But they always give me the greatest reviews imaginable, so I'll be nice and give them what they want in return. A few tears plus some T and A for the cameras. A big smile and a little wiggle, aimed at getting their readers all steamed up. I'm going to base our breaking up on artistic differences, plus incompatibility. The usual crap celebrities use instead of saying we were both simply fucking around.

Dear Red, *the 16th*

I've just been awakened by John Huston's call. Terrible, terrible news. Clark Gable died in his sleep. What is it, after three o'clock? So its past midnight on the coast. At least that part's correct. He dies in Hollywood where he ruled. I'm sitting here, totally numb mainly because I really loved him and I don't want to believe this happened. For my entire youth, as I lugged his picture from one temporary home to the next, I kept thinking this guy Gable was some sort of hero, a real saint. But when I started working with him, I got to know him as a person. So patient and concerned. So incredibly kind and gentle with me. Like a real father.

I'll try to call Kay, but I probably won't get through. John said it was a madhouse there, with Kay getting ready to give birth so soon. And he, they, had so many friends and admirers. Shit, this is a real tragedy. Rhett Butler is dead. No one can take his place. A one of a kind movie star and leading man has left the stage. I feel so damn guilty.

I'm going to call Dr. Kris and get in to see her tomorrow. In truth, I definitely feel like I'm partly responsible. Even though I became far less tardy near the end of shooting, I still never apologized face to face. I know he wasn't mad at me when we wrapped. He called later to tell me we had done a great job. Still, it would have taken away some of the awful guilt of this present moment if I had been more professional from the start.

No, it was the stallion scene that caused the heart attacks. We were all crazy to allow him to go through with it, rather than a professional stuntman. Spend so much time and money and caring and then, you think stupidly or not at all. Thirty seconds, a minute. Bullshit creativity trumps common sense. In the name of art, we think like idiots. Not trying to be safe but trying for the most creative, the purest way.

And Clark's mortally wounded. Not killed but just a matter of time till he goes down, succumbs, like the bull in the ring. Like all of us, wounded and wandering around, carrying the arrows and picador lance tips and banderillas of other fights and hurts. Why is life such a damn struggle??

Dear Red,   *November 23,1960*

I still feel beyond awful. What a terrible loss for not only me
but the entire film industry. So many seasoned pros are totally
stunned by this void. Along with millions of fans throughout the
world. My God, he was the King. Everyone knew to call him that.
John tells me they're just about finished with the film edit, and
our modern western drama looks good. Real good. Great acting
performances from CLARK, possibly his finest, and me, too. It
resounds with depth and power. The director sounds like this
tragedy has hit him even worse than me, if that's possible. Clark
used to watch John gamble and whore around and stay up all night
and said he'd kill himself in a few years. Told him right to his face.
I was there and heard him.

And a few weeks later its Clark, who always went to bed at
nine or ten, dying from his second heart attack in just a few weeks.
I've also heard Arthur is seeing that cheap Magnum photographer,
now openly. That Aryan dirty blonde mass murderer, Inga. Some
Jew Poppy turned out to be. I'm sure Izzy's just overjoyed about his
boy's choice, a blue eyed Doberman Nazi Storm Trooper. Probably
one of her most appealing virtues, in Arthur's mind, to give his
aged father a stroke. So I was right all along about those two
devious shits. Even worse, they had to take my dog.

Hugo, my beloved Basset hound, who I truly miss. Much
more than Arthur. That dog had the softest ears.

Dear Red,   *Dec. 5, 1960*

I can't believe I haven't written in almost a month. So clearly
its catch up time. I'm so lonely. Jack's only called me twice and
each conversation was extremely brief. Terribly disappointing,
almost better if he didn't try keeping it going since its been so half-
assed. On the other hand, I need to be more understanding. He's
very busy picking his cabinet and other key members of his team
so he can hit the ground running.

But its really almost unbelievable, after all the checks and
back-checks and studies and heated discussions, the first two men
he winds up naming, not to fill a vacant position but to continue
in their present posts are J. Edgar Hoover and Allan Dulles, from
the FBI and CIA. Ugh. The two men I know he hates the most
of anyone in public service. And thinks the least of in terms of
good character. So now he's got a Vice President he hates, and
the Chiefs of the two major spy organizations, who he also hates.
So I asked my President right on the phone (which, who knows,
could have been tapped by either one of them), 'Jack, why those
two, you know, Hoover and Dulles?' Jack replies, 'my dad'. Great,
so the only person from the family and team of advisors who feels
totally different than the President is Papa Joe, who has done many
questionable things himself, and rules with an iron will. Why the
hell is it his business? No one voted for him. I just don't know why
Jack couldn't surround himself with people he truly wants and
trusts. I mean what would happen if all these ambitious pieces of
shit band together? In Rome's golden times, Julius Caesar made
that mistake and it cost him his life. Et tu, Brute? God, I hope not.

Jack has become the most powerful man on earth and that's
both good and bad. Good for him and clearly the nation but
obviously not that good for us, as a couple or just as friends. Or
me, as his lover.

Yves has called several times and just before Thanksgiving, we did manage to be together for a weekend. It actually was glorious, until the very end, of course. He starts packing, I get up and leave. He's flying back to Paris and Simone, and where the hell am I? Again on the outside, looking in.

Christmas is in the air and I have no one to share it with. Shit, its like I've come full circle back to my foster child beginnings. Its very nice, I can buy just about anything I desire. Everyone knows me. What I really want is to be the center of a loving family. Now what's the price of that? Nothing and absolutely everything. The whole nine yards if you don't have one. I mean you've got to be lucky.

I'm keenly aware that there's a great many people capable of achieving this state over time. But I've never, ever been close. Of course, I'll still keep trying. And hoping my particular loved one, the man necessary to turn things around, is just around the corner.

Maybe this entire quest is screwed up because anyone who wants me, and a baby, is just saying it to use me. Stop. Thank you, Norma girl, paranoid child of Gladys. I probably should just adopt. Forget men, forget me, go straight to someone else's innocent abandoned infant, who needs someone, to love and protect. Just like I was decades ago. And I won't screw up my body or my head or my heart anymore.

Dear Red,   *December 18, 1960*

I just had the most distressing call from Simone Signoret begging me not to see Yves again. Ever. First of all, the call came totally out of the blue. I hadn't spoken to her in nearly half a year, my dear old former best friend, who I used to speak to maybe four times a day. Yves had been calling me numerous times over the last three weeks, pledging his love and saying he had moved out of their Paris apartment. And the French papers and tabloids were all screaming about their eminent divorce. My God, he was supposed to fly into Idelwild Airport in just three days. So we could be together for the holidays. I was really looking forward to it, extra hard, and that's a huge understatement. I mean every thing else has gone so badly for me and here was Yves, who I had already written off as a totally lost cause. And suddenly he had come back to me, saying how I was the love of his life. And always had been.

I really started to feel excited that someone wanted me, for a change, over someone else. Which in Yves' case was something spectacular, because in truth, Simone's a dream woman. She is a very classy, smart, wonderfully talented lady. One of my most favorite ever.

Dr. Kris has suggested I might care more for her than for him. And I might be displacing my attraction towards Simone by going after Yves. I rejected the suggestion, saying it was Yves coming after me. But she insisted it was a distinct possibility and I should at least consider it. There is definite admiration but still, I don't want to go down on her. Or match souls.

And now I have that same Simone on the phone, completely breaking down, pleading with me not to lead him on anymore. And I'm trying to say, well, I think I really love him. She's whimpering, in total agony.

Saying if I ever meant anything to her, please don't do this. Don't break up her family which would just destroy her whole life and she'd never be the same.

And I try to explain I really had very little to do with his decisions. But she replied that she knew I had tremendous impact on everything he decided because he was hopelessly in love with me. Like every other man who's ever come close to me. And if she ever mattered to me, could I, would I leave him alone? After all, I could have any man in the entire world, whoever, whenever. Many, many way better than Yves. Younger, more dynamic, more fun to be with. Who smoked less. And didn't always stare at the prettiest girls in the room. Pretending he was brushing a wisp of his hair.

So this went on for close to an hour, and I felt utterly horrible. But then, when Simone finally hung up I FELT FAR WORSE. I mean what about me? And was Yves now coming or not coming? Was he listening in to our conversation, and, if so, how would that effect his decision, if at all. I didn't know anything anymore, and uncertainty is the cruelest feeling of all. But I NEVER WANTED TO HURT ANYONE, just grab some happiness for myself. Still, somehow in this exchange I think I've lost everything, once again.

Dear Red,   *December 22, 1960*

I just know he isn't coming. Not a chance. Yves is supposed
to arrive in New York a little before noon. Its early morning, little
before nine. Lena, my maid and cook and dear friend says I can't
be sure until that time comes and goes. But I know that he would
have called if he was still coming, at least once before to check that
we were still on, especially after that painful call from his wife. So I
feel utterly devastated. I really couldn't sleep all of last night, taking
pills and drinking. Trying to call a few friends but no success.
Waiting. Hoping beyond hope. I'm all alone, as always, and no one
wants me. I want to die. I deserve to die. I've screwed up my life
so badly. I feel completely devastated. I want to have a family of
my own. Like Jackie, like Simone, like Jane Wyman, who married
Freddie Karger, like just about every other woman in the entire
world. Why do all the basic joys like having loving parents, both
a mother and father, and a caring husband with loving beautiful
children seem to completely allude my grasp?? Each failure to
surround myself with loved ones only plunges me ever deeper into
myself. But not just me. Into the worst part of me, housing the
most severe loneliness and despair. Christmas is almost here and
I HAVE NO ONE to share it with. Fucking Frenchman fried me
good.

Dear Red,   *December 26, 1962*

A miracle. Joe came back to save me, as he has so many times before. Bless him so. He may drift away for awhile, but he never goes that far. Around Christmas the bond between us is particularly strong. He's knows its my most important holiday and has been since I was in those horrid foster homes. Its the same with him. Once the family I was with, they had four kids of their own, gave me absolutely nothing. So one of the kids gave me an orange 'cause he felt bad for me. And another family, they were so cheap, she, the foster mom, gave me a couple of wooden cuticle sticks, can you imagine? So all their kids and cousins and friends of theirs are sitting in the middle of the floor next to the tree, showing off all their expensive loot, and then inviting the others to play with it and them. And I'm sitting off by the side, watching them out of the corner of my eye, while pushing my cuticles back, not even allowed to have nail polish.

Well, Joe, my handsome lover, my ex-ex, showed up at my door on Christmas morning, without any warning, with this absolutely massive poinsetta plant that we had trouble dragging through the front door. I was crying and laughing at the same time. And then he gave me a gorgeous white leather photo album, with enlarged pictures of me with his whole family, his handsome son Joe Junior, his sister Marie and several cousins, taken around the Christmas holidays past. He also brought in a desktop size ornamental tree and two bottles of eggnog which he had been hiding in the hall.

I was just hugging him, tears coming down my cheeks and he had the slight uneven smile I love so much, when he's real pleased. Then I dragged him in.

I sat him down on the sofa and kissed him, again and again. We started to reminisce about our first Christmas together. I think it was 1952 and I had attended a studio party at Fox. I came back to my one bedroom hotel suite, all alone and feeling miserable, same as now. And I walked in and flicked on the lights. There it was, with this large, glittering star on top. A fully decorated tree in the corner of the room. So I'm thinking how did this get here? Well, I go to the closet to hang my coat and open the door. There's Joe, crunched up to fit, holding a beautiful mink coat. And he says 'Merry Christmas, darling.' I'm utterly shocked because I was sure he was in San Francisco, celebrating with his massive family of fishermen and all their children, I call them the minnows. Since then, I've always told everyone it was the nicest thing anyone has ever done for me.

So we kissed some more. Then I went in to get him a cup of coffee and two of those Christmas star sugar cookies that I know he likes. And from the sofa he starts asking me if I've seen Frank Sinatra lately, except Giuseppe calls him the Rat. And I said no. And he said good 'cause he's complete garbage. Then he asks about Montand and I told him the whole story, at least the basics, truthfully as I could without hurting Joe's feelings. And he stalks into the kitchen as I was just pouring his cup. His face is all red and he sweeps the cup filled with the piping hot coffee onto the floor of the kitchen.

Then I started to cry again, but this time I asked him, don't you think I feel horrible enough without you getting furious with me for being so stupid also? Cause I feel that way, already. Just so horribly dumb and so used, by both of them, including Simone. Sandwiched into some desperate family drama and then I became the common enemy. So I wound up strengthening their relationship by falling on, well not my sword but definitely my ass. How absolutely dreary and morbid.

Joe says he's sorry, and hugs me. Goes back, turns on the phonograph, listens to parts of a Peggy Lee record, skipping, picks one of the middle songs in the album. We dance, hug at the end, go back and sit on opposite ends the sofa.

He looks down at his shoes, then asks, 'So how's your bigshot boyfriend, the politician from D.C., you seen much of him?' I say 'no I haven't and he was plenty busy getting ready to run the country.' Then he said, 'Good, 'cause he's as big a piece of shit as any of the rest. Bigger. Just a playboy, using everyone he can. Women, girls, pro's. If she was willing, he had the time to squeeze her in.' Then he looks up to check my reaction. And I nod, head down. 'You're absolutely right, Joe.' And I said it to myself maybe five more times in a row, hoping I'd learn something from this present humiliation. Another emotional roller coaster ride with me crashing at the end.

So we made a fire and called Joe Jr. to wish him a Merry Christmas. And then we made love, which I didn't much enjoy, just something to do as a thank you 'cause he expected it. And I didn't want him to abandon me also. I knew my mind could not take another crippling blow, definitely not in the foreseeable future.

We took a short, maybe one hour nap together. And when we woke I gave him his present, which was a silver bracelet. Antique and quite handsome.

I had it engraved, 'true love is visible not to the eyes but to the heart, for eyes may be deceived', love Marilyn.

Joe read it twice, then looked up at me, with his eyebrows all scrunched and asks, 'Its nice but what the hell's it mean?' I said it was the theme of my most favorite book ever called The Little Prince about a lovable space traveler which was done in French verse.

And what it meant was we would be together for many more Christmas's because we truly loved each other, heart to heart. Not based on how we looked or how some of the things we do appear stupid to the other person but how we cared for each other. Deep down in our core.

He shrugged, then asked if we could keep seeing each other, at least until I got back on my feet. And I said by all means. He was the true man for all time, my knight in shining armor. The love of my life.

And in truth he is. Well, him and Bob Slatzer, friends who accept and love me unconditionally. That's probably why, years ago, they got into a big fight over me.

In the late forties, Bob and I pooled our meager funds and bought presents for the kids from my former orphanage. And the thrill and gratitude those little ones showed when we gave them out remains with me to this day. And in the fifty's, I did the same with Joe, who made an extra big hit with the kids, who seemed to adore him even more than me. So as you can see, Red, Christmas is a very big deal to me.

Dear Red, *January 20, 1961*

Well, here I am. Beginning the last leg of my trip to Hell. I'm in the waiting area of Love Airport in Dallas, Texas. And I'm waiting for my Air Mexico connection to fly me and Pat Newcomb, my some time too close friend and press aide to Juarez, Mexico. There I will obtain my divorce from Arthur and become a free woman. Again.

We are watching history on the TV. Jack has just taken his oath of office in snowy, ice cold Washington, D.C. He looks so incredibly handsome, so dashing in his tux and tails and his silk high top hat on the chair. He kept his promise and I love him for that. And I'm listening to my Jack make this beautiful speech, 'ask not what your country can do for you', and the camera is scanning the list of hot shots and there is former President Eisenhower and Supreme Court Judge Earl Warren who is getting ready to give the oath and the new Vice President Lyndon Johnson. Johnson, who is tall with shifty eyes, looks so uncomfortable in his tux, sitting on this small chair.

I realize here I am in the heart of Texas and there are murals of gushing oil wells and cattle ranches on the walls and Mexican food on the menus in the cafeteria. And this is the state Lyndon Johnson has totally controlled for over fifteen years. This is his support base. No wonder, 'cause its hardly a sophisticated spot, compared to New York or LA or Washington. The airport is really quite small and lacking a decent restaurant or rest room or bookstore (don't ask) and the newspapers are a few pages and very centered on Texas goings on and even the gossip is boring. One even talked about Johnson taking office today. As if he were the President.

Sorry, Red. Have to go catch a plane and make it official that I'm alone once more. Out with the old and nothing to take its place. For now.

Dear Best Friend,   *January 31, 1961*

I'm getting dressed to go to the premier of the Misfits, and
I feel like crap. I'm going in all black, black bra and panties,
black gown, shoes, black fox wrap-all to match my black, black
mood. Let me tell you, Red, I'm only doing this for Clark's
memory. Forget all the dreams. Its at the Capital Theater on
51st and Broadway so its at least close. I'm attending with one of
my best friends, and one of my most preferred escorts anytime.
Montgomery Clift is the most handsome, polite, and sensitive
man I've ever known. He's thrilled he's accompanying me. So am
I, visa versa. No sex, obviously, which takes the edge off. I mean
the pressure to do it. Its been a little over a week since my divorce
from Arthur and I've been assured my ex won't attend. If he
brought her, the Inga bitch, I'd kill them both in the lobby. Make
the carpet a little redder. Bury the hatchet in their hearts. My
real fear, I'm petrified the film and my performance will not be
appreciated, nor understood. Or even liked. I surely don't look or
act like the old Marilyn they know and love. Will they understand
its me, as a more sensitive, vulnerable woman? Besides, all the
historyonics about the making of this film has got to dim some
of the luster. Then the post production staff screwed things up
royally by not getting the sound and editing finished in time to
qualify for this year's Oscars (deadline two weeks ago). Instead,
we're bringing it out so early, tonight, that its dooming us to sure
failure in next year's race. The studio heads, such a sensitive lot,
say they NEED TO CASH IN on the public interest created by
the untimely demise. RIGHT NOW, not a second to spare. Down
goes Clark, up goes attendance. So, Red, what the hell. It was a
failure from the start. Hopefully Clark, at least, will be awarded a
posthumous Oscar.

Well, Red, its morning and the reviews have come out. Extremely favorable up to truly excellent. Basic feeling is very good film, great performances. The Daily News says both me and Clark have never done anything better, and the screen vibrates with our male/female duel. And the New York Herald Tribune says its a great American film and we're all at our very best. My performance was MAGIC. And the Times says 'could become an American classic.'

Variety and the Hollywood Reporter gave a very commendable acting, outstanding production, definitely worth seeing pair of reviews. And Clark and I were powerful. One bad one. Some NY columnist from the Mirror said it was memorable in parts, but succeeded in expressing my neurotic individuality. Where in the hell do these clowns dig up this garbage? Like they're medical experts rather than two bit hack writers with fat asses and doughy brains from sitting in theater seats way too long. They don't even pay for a ticket or refreshments. They surely don't agonize for months over getting something good on film, let alone perfect. Truth is not one of them can write or act or sing or dance for shit. Well, whatever, its over. With the film, with me and Arthur, with Clark, with Yves, even with me and Jack, who has managed to call only a few times since taking office. So busy running the country there seems to be very little time for us. So, my hopes have been dashed to smithereens.

I have to see Dr. Kris more often. No, Red, not just for the pills. For real help so I can stop acting in this truly destructive manner.

Dear Red,   *Feb. 3, 1960*

I just got through a terribly upsetting visit from Frank
Sinatra. Slimy son of a bitch. I feel numb all over. He came to
show me candid photos of Jack from the various inaugural balls
and others. Thought I'd enjoy seeing them. Get to take a peek at
my guy enjoying himself. I opened a new bottle of champagne
and we started drinking. Mainly so I could brace for this visual
smorgasbord. 'You know Jack's been pretty busy. Here's some of the
after party.'

Pictures of Jack, in tuxedo, and a few beauties, including
several pro's, in a lot less. Kissing and hugging. I wait as he gets
more pictures ready. Then, 'I hate to be the one to break the news,
girl friend, but your boy Jack has been busy shacking up with
Judith Campbell.' Then he shows me four photos, one where she's
in the back seat of a towncar being driven off an estate grounds,
one with her entering the lobby of the Carlyle (worse than the
estate one 'cause this is our special place, me and Jack.) Two with
her and Kenny O'Donnell, on different occasions because they're
both dressed differently but no specific background, and I'm
getting sicker by the second.

He gives it a little time to settle in. 'Yeah, he's got her carrying
FBI reports to Mooney. Suitcases full a dough back n' forth. Hell,
she's his private party mule. And he's screwing her every chance he
gets.' At that I gasp. Jack had me carrying close to half a million in
hundreds in a satchel on a east to west coast flight only a month
ago. He said I'm never searched by Customs. Guess neither was
she. Anyhow, when I arrived in LA, I handed the bag to Johnny
Roselli, who was waiting as I entered the airport. And this in turn
was to be given to Mr. Giancana.

So I'm quite aware this is not only possible but one of my Jack's favorite ways to transport 'important papers'. I'm stunned, completely nauseous. I knock over the bottle and the contents are all dripping on the pictures. 'That's horrible, how could he do that to me?' I can hardly speak. And he replies, 'Hey, kid. Its not like he's Snow White or her Prince. Dumb to trust him in the first place.' And then he gets up and goes to the door. He turns back to me and says, 'Sorry, but you know how much I care for my best girl. Don't want some clown makin a fool outta you.' He reaches in his coat pocket and throws me a bottle of reds. Numb, my arms hang down by my side as the capsules are strewn on the wet floor. Then he leaves as I sit there, rocking and crying and wishing I was dead. But I'm not giving up without telling that louse exactly how deceived I feel. Cheating pig, slimy former boyfriend!

So about an hour later, I get up the nerve and call my smooth talking Democrat at the White House. I'm told The President will call me back just as soon as he can. So about fifteen minutes later Jack calls. Concerned. He of course denies everything. Says we have to get together and he misses me very much. And when he hangs up he says 'I still love you, pumpkin.'

Like he still loves me even though I had the nerve to question those disgusting pictures. I call Johnny Roselli. 'You saw the prints? Hell, honey, she's in and out of the White House more than Jackie. Cause that's what she is. A hoorish JACKIE. A broad who can't say no to nothin.'

I knew it was the ugly truth. She looked like Jackie, she sounded like Jackie, and just like the pure perfect one, she was taking my Jack away.

Dear Friend Red,   *Feb. 6, 1961*

I just left Dr. Kris's office for probably the 50th time in the last two months. Now I'm in the lobby waiting for a private hospital towncar to take me to my apartment. I'll be damned. Without the slightest warning, I'm now on a time deadline to get to the hospital. My long time doctor has just cut me off from all further medications. Says its because I've increased my intake since I returned from Nevada. I'm now at dangerous levels. She's afraid she's lost control of me. I'm feeling about the same about her.

This is very same Marianne Kris who has been ordering these very same drugs for months. Not really questioning me at all about the prescriptions I asked for. Without warning, she has suddenly changed everything. She's become convinced I need to go under the immediate care of these two, not only highly respected, but brilliant psychiatrists who only practice at the famous Payne Whitney Clinic. No time to think. Because I'm suddenly an emergency case. Get me to an ambulance!

They will presently take me back to my apartment to pack up a small valise and report to the admissions Office by 2 o'clock. Here its already twenty minutes past noon. Hurry, driver. Get me to the Asylum in time.

But I'm sure my Granny's smiling in heaven. Her little Norma Jean has finally made the grade. She's being admitted to the nut house, just one with a fancier address.

Dear Red,   *Feb. 13, 1961*

It was absolutely the most horrid experience of my life.
Criminal. The facility was not a hospital in any sense, just a vile
psycho ward where the nurses were sadistic jailors. They shoved
me into a cell and treated me like I was an uncontrollable animal.
And I never did get to meet or even speak on the phone to either
of my two genius Doctor's for my entire stay. What was it? Three
and a half days of humiliation and torture. I never felt more out
of control. That's cause they had me tied down and drugged out
almost the whole time. I'm reporting all of them, the bastards for
medical and psychiatric malpractice. Along with gross stupidity
because they inexcusably let me live to talk about their crimes.

OK, Red, let's start with the admission. I enter the lobby, walk
over to the admissions desk. There is a plain looking middle aged
frizzy haired lady, who is sitting in a cloud of smoke, (no cigarette,
no ashtray, no eyebrows) reading a magazine. I state 'My name is
Faye Miller'. This is a prearranged pseudonym, given me by Dr.
Kris. Admitting lady glances up, tilts her head to the side, like she's
asking why I'm there. 'I've come here to stop taking drugs'. She
gives me an uneven smile, revealing very bad teeth and matching
breath. In a gravelly voice, says 'Why, yes, Miss Monroe, we've
been waiting for you. (Emphasis on you.) Allow me to call an aide
who will escort you to your room. Excuse me, your junior suite.'

She lifts the phone and dials a number. Tells whoever is on the
other end 'Yeah, she's finally here, in a mink, no less.' Hangs up the
phone, and puts both her hands flat on the desk. 'I just saw your
movie, The Muskrats.' Big sigh. Exaggerated shake of her head, like
she had a tick in her scalp.

'Total waste of my time. Plus my two bucks. Don't you folks
read the script before you sign on to do something? You ask me,

there wasn't one good laugh.' I don't want to reply I hadn't asked. 'Step back,' she orders. I do, while scanning this slick pamphlet she's just thrown me about the hospital. Like its a spa. I read for a couple of minutes.

Suddenly, this massive She man gorilla, has to be tipping the scales over 250 pounds, comes up behind me. No warning. Just lifts me by the waist, twisting my other wrist behind my back. Like I just shot the Pope.

Next she works my fur coat off and drops it on the linolium. This is in the main lobby, mind you. There are people seated on a sofa in the corner. They look at each other, not knowing what to do. The guard half drags, half carries me to a padded elevator which has been waiting with the doors open. Throws me in. Turns key, doors close. Up we go to the fifth floor, housing the MODERATELY DISTURBED PATIENTS. (Big sign with a few nail scratches on the disturbed part.)

Our well designed treatment area is a Mecca of personal and individualized treatment modalities, which are offered on a case by case basis. (I'm reading from their bullshit pamphlet they hand you when you first sign in.)

Godzilla then pulls me down a corridor, lined with numerous heavy steel doors and small windows. Behind a few of these I hear some of the most God Awful SCREAMS, women in total torment. From a few not even words, just guttural sounds. And my stomach is in total spasm. Zilla pushes open a door near the end of the corridor with her foot and says, 'This ones for you, sweetie.'

I peer in and its like a small closet with a cot bed and small chair, an overhead fluorescent light, barred window at the end. No coat rack or hangers for my clothes. No telephone. No door to the tiny bathroom immediately off to the right with just a simple sink, no mirror, small john. So I ask where's the bathroom door and she replies, 'Get used to it. We have to be able to view you at all times'. Then Godzilla orders me to take off my clothes.

Throws down a simple gown which I'm supposed to tie in the back. When I step out of my things, miss ugly monster grabs my slacks and sweater, and my panties, and storms out, not waiting for my bra.

The door is slammed shut, then locked from the outside. I push against it, at the same time trying to turn the knob. Doesn't move an inch. INSTANT PANIC. I'm locked in this cell, wearing just a bra, my soiled tampon string hanging down. And I cry out, 'Wait, please. This is some horrible mistake. You must speak to Doctor Kris. I'm not crazy.'

And the monster growls, 'Wrong, sweetie. You're under the care of Drs. Goldstone and Finch, and we treat strung out junkies all the time. You're nothing special in here.' And then she laughs this really sadistic laugh and I'm ready to wet my pants, except I don't have any on. And I ask, 'Where's my phone?' and she looks at me through the bars like I'm from Mars and replies, 'Phone calls are restricted, miss glamour girl.' Turns, comes back. 'Break the rules, YOU WON'T LIKE WHAT HAPPENS NEXT.' And then this she-ape lumbers down the corridor, probably to go comfort some one else.

I'm totally alone. I hear the shrill cries of the anguished human discards caroling down the hall. This is over my pounding heart. And I'm more frightened than I can ever remember. I hurl myself against the door, using my shoulder. Again and again, screaming for someone to open the damn door, promising I wouldn't make any trouble. Banging and kicking, crying for help, sliding downward.

So after fifteen minutes I'm completely exhausted and sweaty, and I'm laying on the freezing floor. Sobbing. And I realize no one is coming.

So I stand up and the feisty fighter, the movie star diva takes over. 'OK, the lousy bastards want to treat me like I'm crazy. Well, that's a role I know by heart.' So I pull off my simple gown with my teeth while ripping at the knot. Then I throw that ridiculous rag down on the bare cement floor. Sobbing, I run to the outside window and stretch my arms up so my boobs and pelvis are pressing flush against the glass. And I start screaming, again and again, five floors down on the sidewalk, 'Please someone help me. I'm Marilyn Monroe and they're keeping me against my will. Call the police. I'm a captive.'

Then, realizing no one can hear me through the window, I run to the bed and grab the chair. I run back, and proceed to throw the chair through the window. The damn leg gets all tangled in the outside screen, and I try to pull it free. That's when I feel a huge hand clamp over my mouth and I can't breathe. Godzilla is choking me. 'I warned you, you crazy cunt!' Then I feel this sharp stick in my buttock and I remember falling downwards towards the floor and then I remember nothing.

I awake in a daze. I'm in a drugged state like nothing I have ever experienced. I slowly look down at myself. I'M IN TOTAL RESTAINTS, just lying there, my arms pulled across my body and attached to the frame. My gown riding up, useless. I am unable to move. I can kick with my legs. Slide down a little. But where the hell was I going?

Over the next three days there is a procession of hospital personnel. Aides, nurses, doctors, even house keeping, all coming by to gawk at me through the small window. All devoid of any human concern. Talking among themselves. Looking with pity.

A few even laughed, such a mocking, degrading response. These are health workers who have sworn to come to the aide of people behaving in this cruel manner. And I remember hearing that same laugh coming from my mom, old crazy Gladys, when I was a toddler. And her friend Grace, from next door, wound up taking care of me. But this time a different woman each shift comes and give me an injection of tranquilizers rather than a bottle of warm formula.

In that bizarre hospital, lying on that horrid army cot, I totally stopped being a human being. I was just a curiosity piece for a staff of mean spirited monsters to toy with. And I remained a helpless prisoner until the third morning when they finally allowed me one phone call.

And that was only 'cause I kept demanding the right, the privilege, explaining even an ax murderer gets one phone call. And threatening to sue. After about an hour I finally reached Joe who was in Miami. He jumped on the next plane and came to the hospital and signed me out of that hellish place. My hero then got me transferred to Columbia Presbyterian, where I've been for two days now, in this sunny private room, with two phones and a large TV and a private bathroom with an extra large tub so I can, at least, feel human again.

Now as one of my exercises to free my head of the demons caused by that nightmare, its been suggested by the Chief Resident, who is quite caring, to use my diary to document what happened. He suggested that I put down on paper some of my experiences in dear old Payne Whitney. Well, now at least I know where they got the Pain part. I don't think I'll be sending a contribution to their research wing.

Dear Red,   *March 4, 1961*

I'm meeting Jack tomorrow at the Carlyle. I was discharged
from Presbyterian Hospital at noon and I have a day and a half to
get ready for my big date. Dress, accessories never matter much to
my guy. I just have to worry about my hair and make up and get
out the vinegar.

Because any time I'm with Jack, all of our activities pretty
much center around the act of intercourse. His choice, hardly
mine. Like we'll have dinner brought up from room service, a
good French champagne, caviar, we may even have one dance with
Dean Martin or Frank providing the ballad. But, sure as the sun
will rise, so will my Jack. And we are going to be in or around a
bed, me fully naked within half an hour. Getting ready to begin
sex, or getting his penis ready or actually in the act of, or just
finishing. And I'll be wiping down, or up as the case may be.

I don't want to think about it because its sad, even a little
humiliating. But this is one man who is pretty much ready to go at
it any time there's an open, unoccupied vagina in the near vicinity.
Still, you've got to do a lot more of the work with Jack, mainly due
to his back. Definitely more than some of my other boyfriends.
Take Giuseppe, who just about does it all for you, willing or not.
With him you'd better just lay back and enjoy the ride. Pray you
don't lose a tooth.

Anyhow, in order to get discharged, I had to promise to see
her at least twice each week, that is Dr. Kris. I think she finally
realizes how harmful the last experience was to my psyche. I told
her I definitely feel it was her responsibility to know what those
two idiots were doing to me and she should have interceded. And
if she recommends another patient to those absentee Nazi's, she's
the crazy one. They're out of control quacks.

I also let her know I'm still considering making a complaint to both the Chairman of Payne Whitney and the doctor licensing board of America. I think she feels sufficiently guilty 'cause she's already given me my normal amount of pills, same as before. I'll try to raise the count in a few weeks just to see if she'll go along. But I'm not depending on only her ever again. I'm not that stupid. Besides I'm sure within hours after I've been with Jack, either Frankie boy or Johnny Roselli will pop up and want to chat. And in return they'll be more then happy to deliver me some Seconals, so I don't get caught short again. Or I'll go to one of my internists, if necessary. Even a General Practitioner. More than one way to skin a cat. See, Red, everyone's a form of barter in Hollywood.

My Dear, Best Friend Red, *March 5, 1960*

It was magic just like it always is. Dammit. And damn him. My Jack, the new President, is so smooth he could charm the pants off any girl. Charming, attentive, with good manners and oh so intelligent. Funny about everything and everyone including himself and all done with this incredible inner confidence. Makes everyone else average.

My love has deep blue bloodlines (almost purple), was schooled in only the finest prep schools, then onto Harvard, Harvard Law. All his different recreations, skiing, sail boat races, golf, where he's playing with all the other set up for lifers. So privileged, so easy. See, Red, they to a man (and maybe to one or two women thrown in by accident of birth) enjoy one basic freedom that the rest of us can only dream about. They don't have to work. Ever. Nor do their kids. Or probably their kids kids. Unless they drink or gamble or marry and divorce too much. Which they all do.

And then, add in all the famous people he's been meeting since taking office. Sprinkle his mischievous joy in giving choice tidbits of gossip about each one on top of this. And you have a fascinating and most entertaining evening. That is once he fully apologized, almost breaking down, stammering in probably our most emotional moment ever. How truly sorry he was. Especially about Judith, who he only used because he didn't want me to get 'dirty with this Giancana stuff.' Couldn't bear me risking a lot of bad publicity if I ever got caught, making me out to be some sort of mob floozy, which Miss Campbell clearly was. And he was only protecting me because he truly loves me.

So I forgave him. I mean by this time we've both had drunk two, well two and a three quarter glasses of this really fine French

Chardonnay. And we're both half undressed (he has his shirt on and I have my pearl necklace) and he looks so appealing and he knows it. I mean this is the only man who can easily have over ninety-nine per cent of the population of women on this planet of consent age on their back in less than ten seconds. I gave him a little going away present I know he'll remember. So at the worst, we're fuck buddies and great friends. At least we talk, at times like this quite a lot and enjoy each other's company immensely. And have a long history and memories. And he listens to my viewpoint and at least respects my thoughts.

So what the hell, this is one dream I cannot just give up, especially when all of a sudden Jack is really asking, no, imploring me to be with him. A man who is clearly the perfect over nighter. Ever.

So before and after sex, naked on the bed we talked about his work so far. Jack has doubled the allowances for underprivileged children, including providing balanced school lunches. And its high time. I mean this is the richest nation in the world and some of our poor colored (that is really an obnoxious word) children get only one skimpy meal a day. And no clothing, just throw away rags.

Mr. President has given free rein to his brother, Bobby, the dashing Attorney General, to dog Hoffa and the whole Mafia Empire, who profit from robbing from the weak and poor. A campaign which is long overdue. My Jack says he's sending secret FBI reports to Chicago to keep Sam from suspecting what the other hand is doing. I told him to still please be careful cause Mooney and his Black Hand soldiers have ears everywhere. And trigger fingers.

Dealing with national threats, Jack has taken away the huge central office for emergencies created by Ike. He prefers to deal directly with any crisis. As he says, 'Cuba is here, Vietnam is coming, and Khrushchev is lurking.'

Mostly he has Castro and his revolutionary Red army on his mind and, as he later let slip, in his sights. They, the CIA, have been training a force made up of former Cubans who want their homeland back and may invade (and conquer) sometime soon. And Castro might be put against the wall, like he did to so many innocent families. Castro might even, and I quote, 'be neutralized by other means.' That's when we had our most heated disagreement. Let's say in a very long time, actually ever. 'Cause I was so taken aback by that term.

I asked him directly, 'Jack, you don't mean kill him, do you?' and he gave this half assed shrug. 'Not me but why not? We can't allow that crazy dictator to just go on. Why if he's allowed to build a huge arsenal almost next door. With Russian weapons that could wipe out our entire nation. It would be almost suicide. How could he as President allow that to happen?'

I said I felt horrible because I know he has the highest values and principles of anyone. But it was morally wrong to murder anyone, even some crazed tyrant. And there had to be some other way to solve the problem. And he said, 'fine, pumpkin' like in forget it, let's get down to the screwing action. But I wouldn't let him come close to me until he swore he would not have anyone killed unless he had exhausted every other avenue. Then he put his finger to his lips and confided 'he was speaking to Khrushchev on the sly. And the two of them were working to keep things quiet and safe. Away from the generals.'

So then we made love, riled up, passionate love, like the old days. But he knew I wasn't kidding. Men can be such bullies if you let them.

Anyhow, during all this, I've been thinking of moving back to California. First of all, the weather in New York is still wet and chillingly cold. More important, I've had a lot of bad experiences here over the last several months. No longer fun. Hollywood is still my home and LA my birth place. I'd like to do a new comedy, something light, to get me out of this funk. Also I can see my good Doctor Romeo, whose basic common sense advice I miss desperately.

Dear Red,   *March 8, 1961*

Is this intuition, or sixth sense or what? I move back to the coast because I have a contract at Fox to fulfill. They have a picture ready. (They always have a picture ready.) And the first person to knock on my door (I'm still living out of boxes) in the Old Deheny Complex (but now I'm in a new two bedroom corner cause I got the bucks) is FRANK SINATRA. Double surprise! He is holding the most beautiful white toy puppy (mix of maltese and poodle), a little girl, and I'm thrilled. Actually I'm in love with her already. Such a little itsy bitsy thing and the second I take her up in my arms, she begins to kiss me all over my face. And Frank is giving me this gift cause he feels bad about upsetting me the last time we were together. Even though he was only thinking about my well being, giving me the word about that Campbell broad who was nothing compared to me, anyhow. But if it was anything like the punch to the balls and turmoil he felt for months after he heard Ava was making it with that young Spanish bullfighter, he was real sorry.

He understands Jack is madly in love with me, again. (An embarrassed laugh.) And he was happy for that and he, The Prez, now knows he (the Rat) will stick up for his friends. Me, especially, and not let anyone screw around and crap on me or even try to take advantage. And the Pres was now only using Judith to deliver shit to Mooney. Money and reports but no sex, from what he knows. So I kiss him and say all is forgiven. And he flips me a big bottle of reds. I mean BIG. He says there's over two hundred fifty, but I'm not going to be rude and start counting.

Instead I take the plastic container into my bathroom and put it on the counter. I take three pills out and bring them back to the kitchen. There Frank and poopy (she's already christened the floor) are waiting.

I take this pin from the counter drawer and start pricking the bottom of the capsules ('cause reds kick in so much faster when dissolved). Then I dump them into this glass of water, swirl and gesture to Frank. He shakes his head and I swallow the whole thing down. What a chef.

We sit down on my new white sofa, puppy between us, in the living room. First I name my new baby Maf 'cause Frank and the Mafia are one and the same. He snarls and warns me to watch my kidding around about the Mob. And I remind him Mooney has helped my career as much as he's helped Frankie's. By now, I'm feeling little pain. So I start playing with her little paws, staying distracted. Frank begins by asking, 'Did I hear Jack and Bobby put out a contract on Castro and gave it solely (horrible choice of words) to Mooney to fill. 'Cause these CIA clowns are such total screw ups. Wasn't no different than Ike and Nixon trying the same thing. Hell, what was the biggest thing the Outfit did to put my boyfriend in power? Forget fixing the vote. It was holding off on iceing Castro before election day.' Big laugh. No response from me or Maf.

Mooney stalled and told the CIA jokers they had to refine the poison pills before they could slip them into Castro's food. They, the spooks, have some Midwest chemist who makes all this fancy shit. Deadly potions and exploding cigars. Mooney saying they needed to be able to dissolve them in both hot and cold fluids. Then with no taste, finally no after taste. So the kid genius is finally almost finished making the perfect take out dish but its too late. I tell Frankie he needs to hire a good comedy writer to help with his off the cuff remarks because most are DOA. Now the Agency clowns are looking to get some island queen to drop it into the Beard's afternoon beverage. After she screws him senseless so he isn't thinking about the danger. I continue to get more and more upset. So he says, 'Don't worry. Castro's always got some lackey political prisoner tasting his food first. Like the loser canary in a mine. So it probably wouldn't work anyway.'

He asked if I wanted to use his house (mansion) up in the hills until I unpacked. I said no. Then he invited me back to Cal-Neva which he now owns with Mooney. (Don't think they have any worker's benefits or waste collection problems.) This time Jack is going to be up, probably with brother Bobby. And maybe even the dad, Joe, making it a family affair. I said maybe, but don't think so and thanks for Maf. I look at my watch. 'Sorry, friend, but I have to go for fittings for my new film.'

Frank says, 'Great, what are you doing?' and I said I don't even know but its with Dean (Martin). I also don't mention I feel horrible that Jack has continued using Judith Campbell, who makes me look like a PHD, as his trusted courier. So let her be part of a planned murder. I know I would not be able to live with the guilt. Oh, excuse me, Red, I meant to say neutralization.

Dear Red,   *April 14, 1961*

Since moving back to the coast, I'm back in therapy with my
wonderful Dr. GREENSON. He's made me feel the healthiest that
I've felt in years, well, ever. We now call it Constant Treatment
which means I've become a full fledged member of his beautiful
family while, at the same time, undergoing at least seven to ten
hours of therapy a week. That's a minimum. Lots of counseling,
lots of crying and Kleenex, lots of bills.

Started out simple enough. A few times I went to his home
to have dinner, and it was wonderful to just be included, help
do the dishes (only one broken glass, Mazel Tov), give a little
helpful advice to the two kids. Joan is a teenager (I taught her the
Mashed Potatoes) and Danny has just entered full manhood (24).
He is already as smart as his Dad but prides himself on being
a social radical. Even thinks Che is 'cool'. (They're both in med
school.) Me and his dad think the rebel is a lot closer to a mass
murderer.

As to my therapy, each day, usually at the end of the Doctor's
regular hours of practice, we both drive over to his home and start
where we left off. He'll give me one or two hours, on his leather
tufted couch in his private library. So after a while, its evolved
into a more extended form. I'll remain to eat and talk with all
of them, watch TV, exchange clothes with Joan. Just be involved
in their lives and they in mine, except I would never discuss sex
or anything private. With these simple restrictions, my brilliant
innovator has agreed to take me on fulltime.

So I'm seeing him so much, he knows me as well as I know
Paula. Actually better, because he doesn't borrow my clothes or
jewelry. He cares about the inner me. Well, all my inner self's, the
three very different me's.

I'll list them. First and worst is the self centered, narcessistic ugly monster. Me with clenched fists, like at the end with Arthur, fighting for my life. Desperate, inflexible, and possessed with only one single purpose. That is to stay alive. Next there's the film actress, Marilyn, the dumb, lovable but always calculating sexpot. The cartoon character me and Nana Karger invented in her kitchen ten years ago. Naïve, much too concrete, and oh so predictable because we know her oh too well, Marilyn, with a wiggle here and a wiggle there and not a single thing between her ears. And third, the real Marilyn, who is so insecure, so lonely for real relationships, I've readily adopted not only his entire family, but Dr. Greenson, as both the physician in charge and the Dad. And my heart belongs to Daddy.

My Doctor thinks I'm looking for my future husband in all the wrong places, like around Pennsylvania Avenue, Washington, DC. He fears my thing with Jack is just to punish myself and take away any chance for a lasting relationship. In the end I have to know it can't happen the way I want. That's become just another reason I'm drawn to the Commander (our new code word). To side track, as a byproduct of my recent time in Payne Whitney, I'm also angry at the limits of his profession. That plus anger at myself for winding up there, in large part due to the many drugs taken and all my other destructive behaviors, like drinking, promiscutey, and wasting my abilities. So I'm punishing myself ever more, dating you know who, not giving anyone else a chance.

The one thing my good Doctor can not understand. Jack is someone I need to continue to see because I love him. He's obviously never loved anyone to the point of nothing else mattering. But then he's a man. Men love with their cock and testicles. Nothing above the waist. No heart. No soul. Little truth. They're often taught to lie to get some. Women love with their heart and soul and they don't tire. Rarely lie, not about love. So deep down I know Jack won't be able to leave his wife or his life as a world leader. I got it long ago. I can be happy with crumbs.

That is if they're his crumbs. I just need to know he really likes me. That he cares. So I'm pathetic for accepting so little. Meanwhile, I'm going to keep looking for the right husband. Two is better than one, especially a fraction of one.

So we're sitting around watching the evening news, me and the Greenson's, and you, Red. Is this crazy or what? We've gone ahead and invaded Cuba. Well that's one way to neutralize Castro. But I thought we wanted to appear a bit less obvious. This is playing out like a poorly planned movie shoot and poor Jack is taking all the blame. 'Cause even at this time, its apparent this is a total embarrassing failure.

I remember watching the President's second press conference where he was talking about supporting General Fumy (I don't think I spelled it right) from Layos and we would start sending troops to fight the communists there. Jack, pointing on this huge wall map, surrounded by big Generals with bigger bellies, nodding mechanically. So there he is again, My Jack, with his long pointer, and the maps. Just a different region. True its closer to us, but still, are either a real threat.

Its now hours later, and the terribly sad newsreels of ex-Cubans killed, bodies floating in the water is playing out on all the news stations. The bodies and the captives, now prisoners of war, hands behind their heads. The Cubans laughing, in relief and disbelief, pointing with their guns, leading them away.

Its morning and the Cuban invasion is completely squashed. All the invaders have been arrested. Castro's men, laughing, poking rifles in the rebels backs, tripping them. And the newspaper editorials have been simply brutal. I'm really pissed at Jack for lying. Of course he's lied to me about other things, like making me his constant companion. So maybe my good Doctor and even Frank the Rat are right. Still, I feel really bad for the President 'cause I still love him with all my heart. Besides, I want him to do well for our country. And the world. Am I a dunce or a nutcase or just a hopelessly lost romantic? Well, maybe all those foolish things. I can be a freaky mess, because I think so often with my heart.

A very important relationship has blossomed in my new surroundings. I have a girlfriend, a real one! Now, don't despair or start to feel threatened, Red. 'Cause its a true live person and a wonderful one at that. Her name is Jeanne Carmen. I knew Jeanne from studying at the Studio in New York years ago. Now she lives four units down from me in the Doheny Apartments. And we've become great buddies, staying up to drink and do a few red's which she loves as much as me. She's slightly younger (seven years, bless her) and does these golf tricks for TV and live shows, like in Vegas. Does real well with it. The only thing I can swing are my hips.

One time Maf stayed with her when I went out of town to see Frank at Cal-Neva. Jack and his brother and Dad were no shows. Frankie has become much more of a friend recently. I know he's bad for me, but I even slept with him, once, about three weeks ago. In his suite up there in the mountains. One side in Nevada, the other in dear old California. And it wasn't bad, not bad at all. Plus his singing to me at his nightclub show was very flattering. Then he gave me these diamond hoop earrings, very simple and lovely. So I put both of my heels in different states and dug my ass into the Great Divide and let him come in. So we could go riding together.

And he was nice both before and even nicer after. So that says something positive about him. Plus he is more than eager to fill me in on all the Mafia social dope and mob going's on. Who they killed, who they robbed, who they fucked over. And who they're lookin to do more to.

Like a month or so before, the Outfit 'TOOK OUT some rabble rouser in the Congo.' Which Frank swears to me was ordered by the present administration (that is Jack ordered the murder). But I don't believe him. Even if he showed me hard core evidence, in pictures, I'd believe it was simply forged. Which it very well might be. I've watched film editors enough.

On another unpleasant note, Frank's still a disgusting klu kluxer, even though many of his friends are Negroes. The little hippocrit's also been playing the liberal card like a total wild man just to gain Jack's favor. If he winds up as the Italian ambassador, I'm giving up pasta. Which I probably should do anyway, since I'm like 8 pounds over movie weight. Not that I have a project ready to go but its better to think I do.

Dear Red,   *April 15, 1961*

Regarding work, the movie Fox originally wanted me to do, the one I came back to LA to prepare for has now been put on the back shelf, probably to gather dust forever. It was Freud, written by Jean-Paul Sartre. Naturally I leaped at the project when it was offered. Freud was one of my huge heroes. Sartre, of course, ranks up there as one of the great writers of this century or any century. So two of my BIGGEST heroes on the same project, got to do it. Studio says not the right time. If you knew how often I've heard that ridiculous line.

I read Sartre's script and was thrilled for weeks. I would play Cecily, one of Freud's earliest and most psychotic patients. Lots of moods and parts of characters, all mixed into one small person. I'm absolutely perfect for this role. Besides, Sartre recently said that I was one of the greatest actresses alive. So I figure he wants me to do it, too.

Problem is Dr. Greenson is strongly opposed because he is a dear friend of Anna Freud, Sigmund's youngest daughter. She has followed in her father's profession, working so diligently with children, doing her own brilliant studies and attempting new treatments. And Anna hates the script on a personal level. She feels its very unfair to several of the real patients, who are still alive. She isn't all that pleased with Sartre, either, because he insulted her. Once at some left bank party in Paris, he was rowdy and spilled wine on her blouse and did not apologize. Shows even together people are quite insecure.

Anna feels the story should be done in ten years. Also my doctor thinks playing an uncontrolled psycho might be dangerous for me, personally. Especially because of my total immersion approach to acting. I take on the character being played and try to stay in her for the entire shoot. That is as long and as strong as I can. So I told the studio I pass, but it was a terrific role.

Turning to other work offered, there are a few possible projects. CBS has been urging me to play Sadie Thompson in the Somerset Maugham's short story, Rain. They want to do an original film, themselves. I mean first they wanted to do it as a live performance, but then they said, NO. Way too difficult, especially with you. You have to hit it on the nose, first time out. I said, 'Why would I accept such restrictions? Go away.'

Then a month later, they're back. 'We want you to do it on film and we'll air it at a special time, OK?' They have this specific week each half year where all the stations are judged against each other and this is a big deal with sponsors. I said fine. Month after they said they somehow couldn't get the script right. What the hell could be so difficult? I mean they already have the whole story. BUT they're petrified of the censors, 'cause Sadie is shady and its television. So Rain has been put on hold for the foreseeable future, even though I signed a letter of intent a while ago. Looks like I'm still in the same place, playing whores, just better written ones.

This delay is probably a blessing. My internal health is crying out for medical help. I just saw my GYN, Dr. Krohn. He feels my tubes may be blocked due to scar formation, which might be preventing me from conceiving like I want to. And he feels he should go in (operate) and free them up. So now I have an operation facing me in the next two weeks, dammit.

But if it would enable me to have children, please Lord, it would be a miracle.

Didn't God let Sarah conceive with Abraham when they were like a hundred? Now, of course, a hundred then is probably like being forty years old now, because of all the pollutants. And bad foods, and street drugs and even prescription medicines but still I have a date at Cedars of Lebanon, in LA, for the first week in April.

And Jeanne, my best friend, has been very encouraging as she knows the whole story. About all the abortions when I was a kid, with Freddie Karger. Even the part about me having to give up my only baby when I was barely a teenager.

How that horrible episode has tormented me all these years. Yikes, I don't think I've ever told Dr. Greenson. Holy smokes, I don't think I ever told you, either, Red. Sorry but I know Dr. Greenson's going to jump on this one. Well, I guess I wasn't able to come to grips with this distressing issue until now. So I'll bring it up with him this afternoon. I just hope he believes me.

Dear Red,   *April 18, 1961*

Well, I've been seeing my good Doctor almost continually since I brought up the topic of my baby, the one I gave up when I was a teenager. Not surprising, its been a big roadblock in my emotional development. Therefore the only thing is to work through it, so I can get on with my life without the guilt.

My grandmother gave up on my mother, and then my mother gave up on me. And I gave up on my little baby son. Doctor Greenson has pointed out that in the first two cases, granny and mom gave up on their baby, little Norma Jeanne, because of reasons of health. Their mental health. I gave mine up for legal adoption because of financial concerns, my age and my lack of a male to help me. Simply I could never offer the support and help that a full-fledged family could, especially not at the age of fourteen. So my reasons were very different. But it did prove I can conceive so there is real hope for my pending operation.

My good Doctor asked if I ever tried to get to see or even trace the where-about's of my baby. I said no because all the records were sealed. At least, they told me so at the regional Catholic church where they did the adoption. I had to swear that I would never bother the family, or check on my son, even when he was older. And Doc replied, 'Well that's too bad but its probably for the best, anyway.' And I had to agree, sort of. Because I would still love to see him at least one more time, and hold him in my arms and explain to him the reasons why I had to give him up.

I could see what he had grown into, and tell him I was there to help if he ever needed me. And that I was sorry, really very sorry. But the nuns wouldn't hear of anything other than give him up to a nice observant church family. I fought the bitches. Honest I did. They had my baby in his new parent's arms twenty minutes after my child was born and cleaned up. And, of course, the contribution check had been signed by your new poppy. It was a big business back then. Probably still is.

Dr. Greenson says that sometimes discussing a long buried trauma can free up something deep in your subconscious, enough to quiet the demons. And I must say, I do feel better. Let's hope this feeling remains. So its off to surgery I go and may my tubes open like my big mouth.

Dear Red, *May 4, 1961*

I'm one-day post-op and despite some pain in my incision, I'm feeling marvelous. That is after I got the news. My surgeon came in to check me over and tell me what he found, etc., etc.

There was a lot of scarring around my tubes and he removed all of that stuff that didn't belong there and cleared my tubes. Most important the spermies should be able to sail up my vagina, passing through my now unclogged tunnels to my beautiful unfertilized egg where it will worm its way inside.

And this precious fertilized egg will then set up residence in my uterus wall, where nine months later, my beautiful baby will come off the assembly line. Singing and screaming and laughing and making me the happiest woman in the whole world.

God is the great creator. I mean the more we learn, the more we realize we know very little. And sometimes I've doubted my Maker, like recently in response to the question, 'what religion are you?' I answered, 'I'm an atheist Jew,' which I'm truly sorry I said, cause now its not true. I honestly have hope. When you don't have it, and suddenly it reappears, that is truly wonderful. And spring is my most favorite season, and I'm right near the beach. So I'm going to enjoy it and get my body in shape. And as always, hope to find Mr. Right. So I can put a name to the spermies and even a face. A real sweet and good face. And a kind heart.

My Dear Red,   *June 7, 1961*

I'm back in New York, because I missed the Studio, and Lee and Paula. Also because I have a Children's Charity dinner to attend this weekend. But to be honest, and when have I not been with you, my Dear Red, its a good deal easier to get to see Jack if I'm on this coast. With all my hospitalizations, I've only spoken to him a few times. I miss him, but he's been rather busy, going against Khrushchev and all the Republicans.

Still, we could write letters, which I once suggested, mentioning I thought they were very romantic. He said bad idea, pumpkin 'cause if the wrong people ever got hold of one of them, it could become a very embarrassing situation. I also got the idea he deep down didn't think I could write anything worth reading. Mainly because his book won the Pulitzer (although Jack told me Teddy Sorenson helped considerably, which I understood to mean his assistant wrote pretty much all of it). And I would never want him to know how hooked I am on him. Therefore I would never allow him to see what I've written about him. Better. You're for me, alone.

Anyhow, here I am, planning several Madison Avenue and Rockefeller Center shopping days with Paula, and several visits to Dr. Kris and there's a Rodin exhibit I desperately want to take in. (He's my new artistic heart throb.)

And last evening I ate at my favorite Italian restaurant down in the West Village with the Rostens, Norman and Hedda, who first took me there years ago. I had the baked clams as an appetizer because the waiter recommended them. They were spicy, maybe a little too much so, as if the chef was trying to disguise something. There was also a long aftertaste, a very unfamiliar one.

Now, I'm mentioning all this because I think they may have been tainted and I may be having early signs of food poisoning. When I woke up all my sheets were literally soaked with perspiration, and I felt chilled which is extremely unlike me. And I felt this burning irritation, not in the area of my bladder, which was sore for about two weeks after my GYN surgery, but higher. And when I put my bra on and I twisted to do the snap, I felt this sharp pain in the lower back part of my rib cage. And it was piercing like a knife wound and for a second, I couldn't seem to catch my breath.

So I walked out to the kitchen and made a cup of coffee. And I waited around for about an hour and tried to call the restaurant but there was no answer. Then I realized they probably don't come in until noon. So finally I called Norman 'cause he had eaten one of my clams when I couldn't finish and I was wondering if he or his lovely wife or even Pat, their daughter, had been having any symptoms and they both said no. And Pat was sleeping at a friend's. And Norman said there was a virus going around because one of his writer friends (no, not Arthur) had had a wretched time last week. I hung up and decided to go back to sleep but by now the coffee was kicking in. So I decided to take you out and write.

Now I've decided to take an early walk along the East River. I've put on some slacks and a simple sweatshirt and sneakers. And I'm going down to the first floor as I'm feeling a little better. Thinking maybe I just need a good high colonic enema to rid my body of all the toxins. Anyhow, I'll write more later.

HEY, Red. You won't believe this but right now I'm in the emergency room of Polyclinic Hospital waiting to meet my General Surgeon, who will explain his plans to cut me from stem to stern. That I am about to undergo what they call an abdominal exploring, or exploration, something like that, which could wind up being a big deal operation. How did I get here? Well, I started to walk down the little jogging path from about 50th to 65th street and damn, there it was again, that stabbing pain but now it was in my front. When I pressed on my belly where I thought the pain was coming from, I fell to my knees because my entire stomach area was like fire. Apparently one of the policemen who was patrolling the area saw me go down and came running over and called an ambulance. And they took me here, where a host of interns and residents have poked and prodded and my temperature is 102 and my white count is around twenty-one thou where normal is less than eight. And they think I have a nice figure but a surgical abdomen, meaning it needs surgery to get better!

So I called the Rosten's and my maid Lena, who brought you to me, Red, so I can keep you instantly informed. But the entire staff is sure its not from my recent reproductive system clean out and every thing feels non tender down there, thank God. So now I just have to worry about saving my life. Joke. I'm still plenty nervous 'cause so far I haven't had all that much luck in Manhattan hospitals. Well, I'll write more later when I know what the hell is happening.

Dear Red,   *June 13, 1961*

It was a badly infected gallbladder. If I had waited a few
more hours I might have died of shock cause the tip could have
ruptured. So its a very good thing that policeman found me.
The doctor's had me up in ICU for near three days, with several
intravenous lines. My surgeon is Dr. Cottrell. For a little joke I call
him Dr. Cut. Well when I first met him in the ER I also made an X
on my right side with his pen, to make sure he cut on the correct
side and asked him to sew a zipper in, to make it easier in the
future. Anyhow, we're now good friends.

He said it was necessary to drain the liver bed because if
we didn't have a pathway out for all those bad bacteria and dead
tissue, he might have to open me back up in several days to drain
a huge pocket of pus. You only have a couple of chances before
all your systems start shutting down. This is true even if I was the
healthiest specimen in the world. So I quickly told my surgeon,
believe me, I'm not. And we both laughed. Damn, I'm not having a
very good summer. Not at all. But Joe has visited me every day and
I'm fortunate to have some good friends come weekends.

Still, once I'm out of this hospital I'm going straight back
to the West Coast to rest and recuperate. Not only get to change
my luck but I can speak person to person with my good Doctor
Greenson. Frank's also been calling to encourage me a lot. And he
can be fun during the times when I feel lonely, like almost always
recently. Old Blue Eyes can party with the best of them. Besides, he
gives me really nice jewelry, which doesn't mean that much to me.
But it does show he cares and he's been taking care of Maf for me,
and that says even more.

I miss my baby, with her cold nose and little tongue. You
thought I meant Frankie boy? His crooner's tongue is much longer,

and its not his nose that's cold. Ever hear of a man who has ice in his heart? Well, I'll let you in on a little secret, Red. My sometime friend, Frankie, has it in what passes for his soul. No wonder he's Mooney's Godson.

Dear Red,   *November 10, 1961*

Well, I haven't picked you up in months, which has to say it all about my present dating my old beau. Along with my present state of mind. Afraid neither is all that much to write Red about. I've been seeing a good deal more of Frank over the last weeks, months, and I guess you could call us an item. But I think of our relationship as too much alcohol (him), too much pill taking (me), and too much jetting to Cal-Neva (both). Where we often meet up with the very same Mooney Giancana, who is Frank's silent partner in this enterprise. Its a breathtakingly beautiful place outside the casino and theater areas. The mountain trails are majestic for walking and just thinking. Especially the California side, which has lots of small waterfalls.

I'm not overly happy with Frank because he continues to openly screw several other girls, while he's supposed to be my steady guy. This pisses me off along with knowing the guy is programmed to obey Mooney's slightest whim. The way he fawns and grovels makes me want to puke. And he's so erratic. Especially when he decides to suddenly go somewhere, like on his huge cruise boat which he keeps docked on the Hudson River in New York Harbor. Now the skyline views are nice but he expects me to drop everything and jump on his private jet. Then we have to land at Laguardia, when I hate that airport as compared to Idelwild. There's always a long line to land, and you just sit there, strapped in, and circle in the sky and wait. And Frank smokes like a chimney, strong things like Lucky Strike, so its not the most enjoyable experience, even though the plane is quite comfortable. And the pilot is sort of cute, and single like me and very competent handling the flying and seeing through the smoky cabin.

I still don't have a great script, or even a good one to get ready for my next film. There's this bland thing called Somethings Got to Give going around and I've accepted. Not because its original or funny, but because they think Nunnally Johnson can fix it up, which is never a great sign. I'm the wife who returns after being shipwrecked for years. And my hubby has a new lady of the house. Dean Martin is the hubby, actually former hubby and he is the sweetest guy to work with. A real dream. George Cukor has agreed to direct and he's near the top of my list for comedies. But he yells and can wind up concentrating on the clock rather than what's going into the camera. Still we've done good work together in the past.

In truth, a lot of director's get pissed off at my delays. He's hardly alone regarding that problem. Before I'm ready to go on the set and perform, I can take considerably more time than many others. But that time is necessary to get me ready to portray the feelings of my character. Many in the business think you don't have to prepare at all for comedy, especially dumb blonde roles. I totally disagree. Comedy is way harder than regular dramatic acting and if you over act, you're dead. George and even Billy Wilder don't get it, and they're supposed to be great comedy directors. I know when a scene works for me. They also have to understand, EVEN COMEDY IS DRAMA.

I must knit together both internal and external stresses (some not even dealing with the character but with me as a person), and make them all mix properly. There's no getting away from the simple fact that being a good performer in any piece takes a lot of emotion. Constant work for occasional joy. Pain and attention to details. Like even singing a cheery love song, my specialty in the musicals.

Perhaps this is because love is a big problem in my real life, outside the business, worse than anyone suspects.

Jack is flying to the west coast so in three days I'll see him. I miss my baby, even though I hear disturbing things from several spies. Frankie and Johnny. Hardly the lovers in the song. Frank

Sinatra and Johnny Roselli both swear my Jack is still seeing Judith Campbell, often. The big boss, Mooney Giancana, is also screwing Miss Campbell, who has never met a prick she didn't like. From the rat's mouth, Ol' Blue Eyes knew she was a special lay from their first go round. That is among the shiploads he continues to sample. Then, the instant he saw how much Jack was attracted to her, she was it, Miss Criminal Chest for the 60's. Because that's what the mob boys were looking for. Someone to give them inside juice around The White House.

What am I doing with Frank?? I love Jack and will do anything to keep seeing him. Fine. Frank is a horse of a whole different color. Doesn't figure, Red, does it?

I mean here I am, a Best in Show many times over and I'm giving Frankie boy some of my good stuff and he's still chasing back alley strays. Jerk. Frank the Rat returns to his former and true self so now I'm trying to unload him. He's hardly a dependable companion, and I'm being overly generous with that rating. Well, I knew that going in.

So Jack will soon be in my bed and I'll give him all my best stuff, and more. I know I'm a sad example for womanhood but I so love the guy. Maybe he's my just reward for all my bad behavior against some of the other men in my life. I'm in love with a fickle Casanova, who takes my breath away. But what the hell, this is something I'm supposed to be, the reining SEX QUEEN. And I require a KING.

Now remember, for this President, there's always an army of female competition. And all the entries are drop dead gorgeous. I know I photograph far better than I look. But still, I'm 15 years older than many of these good time girls. Some are just babies. And its getting more difficult to stay up with them all the time. I can act more beautiful and think more beautiful but there is just so much any one can do. In the long run, you still have to go face to face, tit to tit and gravity is never flattering.

Besides, I want a loving, settled husband, not a party boy. I don't want to feel there's tough competition all the time, or even anytime and I'm always being graded. Who needs bullshit like that, to have to look your most beautiful every minute? I do know my good Doctor Greenson is right and I should drop both Frank and Jack. Well, I'm one for two on the plans to cut off relations. And 500 is a pretty good batting average, even in the BIGS. Hey, Red, in my ten months married to Joe, that's one of the few things I learned from him. That and how to tape my thumb like a trainer after he twisted it during one of our fights. How typical.

I've also started to call in to one of the local radio stations and I've made friends with this very nice DJ, Tom Clay. Relax, Red. I know its healthy cause we're just friends. No pillow talk, just everyday chatter.

I like to hear all about his home life and his young baby he's nicknamed 'Rebel' because the young man definitely does not behave so well. And his loving wife, Lily. And all the things a healthy loving couple needs to do for each other, to create a solid enduring relationship. Which I've never had so I want to listen and learn how to do it.

Damn, so far this has been a rather bleak year. But I'm scheduled to see Jack and meet Bobby at his home in Virginia for a family pre Christmas Party.

Its sad but typical that the last time I saw Jack, at Peter's and the day before, at the Beverley Hilton, it ended badly. After screwing me silly for two days, he waits 'till the end, then tells me, 'Oh, by the way, pumpkin. Have to give you a little bad news. We can't be together for awhile. Because the FBI continues to press their investigations into mob activity. And J. Edgar Hoover has highlighted my relationship with Frank Sinatra, who, of course, has major ties with Mr. Giancana.' In response I said 'Now, wait just one damn minute. Your family's the one working with that other family, not me.'

So he shakes his head and sighs, 'But Hoover is all over me. Apparently they taped us once when I was at the other Hilton, in downtown LA.' I remember, Jack had come up for a quickie. That meant fifteen minutes, from the first zipper to the last button. 'And Love, SEE YOU SOON, BYE.' A Jack refrain I know by heart.

Anyhow, his brother Bobby 'was simply dying to meet' me. Jack even said it was a real crush, and he never gets those 'cause he's stubbornly faithful to Ethel.

I have to admit, I was a bit excited. You know, Red, he, our boy Bobby, looks very cute.

So hopefully I'll have some fun and meet someone interesting. Then I can dream of this new dreamboat to get me out of my doldrums. Unfortunately Jack will never be that man, Amen. For many reasons but first, because he is the President of the U.S. and he could never leave Jackie with those two young, adorable children. The public would never accept that of THEIR LEADER and rightfully so.

Also 'cause Jack's already quite impeachable, morally, with pictures of him with at least several different girlfriends he's seeing presently. Probably even with me. And Hoover has shit on him with many others, starting a very long time ago. Once again, probably with me and definitely many others. Bobby's fresh meat.

Seems he is the only man who isn't terribly afraid of that Sick to the Bone, Closet Queen Dirt Monger Hoover. So Bobby's got one very good point going in. No dirt to be used against him. Two if you count his cuteness. Well, that's what's on my calendar for the near future. But Jack will have to be left back there in DC to run the country.

To be honest, I'm having a good deal of trouble accepting his approach to Mr. Castro's leadership. Especially if what I hear from Frankie Boy, and Johnny Roselli is even partially true. Jack's trying everything possible to kill the Cuban leader. Mainly because he got shown up at the Bay of Pigs.

Now, I personally feel our government (starting with Ike and Nixon) should have given Castro more time to see if he could make Cuba better for his people. Surely before deciding he was just some Khrushchev puppet and putting the poison to his ear, or the serum to his cigar. Whatever the method of entry may be for that specific murderous attempt. That's just me. I'm sure I was a social worker in some previous life. Or a nun. Haha. Well, I'm catching up if that was the case.

Castro is a real disappointment. And it's obviously not an ideal world for anyone. Our great country does not behave in all matters according to the Nuremberg code. Take the Mafia-CIA secret missions. Also take a few of our commando military units, which are allowed to act under the very dangerous blanket of complete secrecy. While the administration denies all knowledge. The U2 spy planes are also wrong. I know I'm talking out of my ass, but this issue is very disturbing.

I truly thought Jack's term would be different, because I had idealized him to the point of pure perfection. Dr. Greenson says this is a major part of my personality disturbance, being able to see only good and bad, when most people and things, including countries, are varying shades of grey and darker grey.

Now, as regards the ill-fated history of my personal relationship with Jack, he led me on. No doubt about that. Primarily by telling me he wanted to leave his wife. He loved me deeply and we were birds of the same feather, and had so much more in common. He loved the way we made love and he loved my quirky sense of humor.

At the same time he always said 'Sorry, pumpkin, but we'll have to wait a while to get together.' With slightly different twists.

This time it was, 'I'm the President. I have a reelection to win and Hoover's tailing me.' Or in the past, other contests that must be won. I would never damage his legacy but I was always so let down. Because I believed the love part.

So I said to Jack, 'Hell, you only have one election left and you could win that one like the last. With a little help from Mooney and company.' In anger, he turned quickly away, and in doing this, his shoulder struck me on my chin. There was the loud sound of my teeth jarring together. And he quickly realized what he had done and said he was sorry. But I couldn't stop crying, not because the blow hurt so much. But emotionally, after what he had said about taking a break, it killed my insides and my hope. My biggest hero had huge cracks through his spine, and even worse deficiencies in his character. Shit. So, it was a total, sudden destruction of all my dreams.

Once I regained control, Jack tried to console me by foolishly bragging that his Dad had paid Jackie over a million dollars just to stay with him. Cause he's behaved badly for years. And she's an emotional wreck.

So I'm thinking if he and his family are willing to pay his own wife millions just to stay with him, Jack does have a real problem with commitment. And that will never change. He is also addicted to SEX, and, like the ketchup, which is one of his love's, all 57 varieties. There are many pictures out there documenting these activities. Mooney has shown me pictures of girls from over five different countries in a hot tub with him. This President can scan the UN secretary pool and get hard.

At the same time, and as difficult as this is to believe, he also needs to keep his reputation perfectly spotless. So he and his family will do absolutely anything and everything to insure it stays clean as newly fallen snow.

One slip and then the flood. Now that's the true reality of my long history with this dynamic person.

His career always comes first, last, and always will. I am, at best, only ONE of a very big fan club of friends. Almost all of the girl friends are willing and eager to put out for him, whenever he whips it out. And if he doesn't they can find it. The general terrain is pretty well marked out by now.

Jack, and his large family, during the few times I have been around them, all seem to have an extremely loose and distorted definition of marriage. Especially regarding the state of commitment to the female partner. Including Pat Lawford, who is obviously a bright, decent girl, and who apparently helped cover up for her father's (Joe) cheating and even helped him get new girls (and I do mean girls). Well, I don't want that now or ever. I could never live under such a cheap charade. I won't.

My good Dr. Greenson thinks I've made a major breakthrough from my days of being utterly powerless to Jack's allure. Now I know I have been led (or laid) astray but I also went willingly. And willingly I will come back down to earth, and start to look elsewhere. Perhaps in Virginia. Perhaps abroad. Until then I can see Giuseppe if I need male companionship and sexual stimulation. Although them there nights seem to be getting fewer by the hour.

I'm afraid my last true, body shaking orgasm was over a year ago and that was with myself. In the bath, with my natural sponge. And my not so gentle fingers pointing the way.

Dear Red,   *December 6, 1961*

I met him in his own living room. He's wonderful, Bobby! I
called him His Excellency, Mr. Attorney General, and he laughed
and said he was probably half that title. Jack introduced us, then
left almost immediately.

Didn't take that long to realize Bobby was extremely
intelligent and intense and funny. He quickly reminded me we had
met in the summer of '54. It was on the set of Bus Stop. Milton had
just done these marvelous photos of me, and I was poring over
them. He (Bobby) came up with Josh Logan, the director, and they
knocked on my trailer door and I told them to come in, please.
And he reminded me the first thing he said to me was 'You're even
more beautiful in real life.'

And he thought I looked even better today, and of course I
thanked him and told him I was floored over his memory. And
he said, 'Wait. I remember a good deal more.' So he told me he
recalled looking over my shoulder at all the Green photos, and
saying he liked the dancer group best. And then he had glanced at
a framed photo of me and Joe taken at Niagara Falls that sat on my
little trailer desk. He remembered remarking how we both didn't
look very comfortable together. And I said, 'I'll say. He wanted me
to quit acting. Then and now.'

Bobby shook his head sadly, before gazing at me with a
radiant smile. 'Miss Monroe, its a good thing for all of us you
didn't listen.' He didn't pause for an instant. Rapid fire, like a
machine gun, and all good to hear. He simply loved my work and
thought I was wonderful in my last few films. Maturing and able to
take on much more difficult roles.

Had I written any of The Misfits because some of my speeches
seemed so natural? I told him there were many parts Arthur and I

had worked out together. And many were pure me, for I had said them often enough. Just not in the context of the film. Which is the bitter truth.

So then Bobby got me another glass of champagne and we started a tour of the house. Pretty soon we were in the kitchen. He grabbed an almost full bottle of Dom Perignon and led me out the garage and down the driveway. We were laughing and drinking and bumping into each other the whole way. And Bobby was telling me about some of his run-ins with Director Hoover, who he truly despises.

The time he kept playing darts while Hoover addressed him about Martin Luther King's infidelities. Hoover wanted permission for the FBI to bug Dr. King's phones. And how the General refused, saying not on your life. And he was appalled at how Hoover had his field agents trailing the Reverend wherever he went. Hoover hates all Negroes and would do most anything to embarrass Dr. King. The FBI was also trying to photograph the Reverend with a white hooker, who they hired to pose as an ardent supporter for Negro causes. She would seduce Dr. King and they would get it on film. And use the pictures to pressure him or his would be followers.

Well, Bobby had to establish right off who was boss. So the General ordered a red phone and had it placed on Hoover's desk and explained it was a direct line to the head of the Department of Justice which, of course, is Bobby. And when he called to speak to the FBI Chief, the present Director damn well better answer, in three rings or less. Or his days at that desk may be ended.

Bobby seems so intense and honest. And when he believes in something, he really believes. Then he has the courage to follow through. My likely new boyfriend (wait, I'll get there) exhibits the moral strength necessary to stand up to bullies in general. Even government sanctioned ones, who could be the most dangerous enemies of all. Like Director Hoover, the arch villain of freedom and truth and protecting everyone's rights. You know, I think its called a democracy.

He's quite a guy, my spunky General, my new man. On the outside a fearless bulldog. But on the inside, tender and caring enough to not only want to watch over me, but seeming to enjoy doing it. Putting his arm around me when I shuddered from a sudden chill.

So we slipped into the backseat of one of the sedans parked in the driveway, and started to neck like we were school kids. Keeping with the innocent mood of the moment, I gave Bobby one of my super intense handjobs, where I started by lightly brushing his shaft. Going on to use my nails to pinch the skin area directly below his tip and he came in less than a minute. Then I bent over and licked him clean. He was still obviously quite sensitive 'cause his little tush was jumping around on the plush leather of the back seat.

Then we just held each other until he had calmed down. Well, enough to zip up, stand up and return to his guests. He said he had never met a woman like me and I really had him coming (obviously) and going. We laughed. And I told him likewise, and next time I'd take him even further, like possibly around the world.

Then, when the party was coming to an end, before we parted, he slipped me a small note saying, 'I think I already love you,' and he signed it the General.

Which I kept rereading on my flight back to the coast. Because it seemed so bold and straight to the point and so romantic. As compared to his brother Jack who carefully measures each 'love you' like it was a unit of his own blood. Probably because he was cooing and screwing half the world's female population at the same time.

Of course, since it all happened so fast, I do have questions. By using the word 'already' in Bobby's note, did he mean he had planned to fall in love with me? Or that it was love at first kiss or that he so rarely did this, fall in love? And it was love on that first true meeting and conversation with me. He is so damn cute, 'cause he's a good deal shorter than Jack. Also he has this huge tassel of hair in front, which is so unruly, he always has to brush it aside, like a little boy. (I called him mopsy in the car as I played with it.) And he has that cocky manner kids in a playground might show, like a cigarless Edward G. Robinson taking over the swings. Yet, he was already willing to risk his reputation just to tell me that he cared, putting it down in black and white, on paper. Making a record that others might view and question.

And with Yves, and Arthur, and Frankie boy, and even the big boss, meaning our President, I have had a lot of romantic disappointments recently. And the General seems so utterly different; straight forward and honest. So flying back to LA, my spirits are soaring. I can't wait to discuss this with my good Doctor Greenson, so he can see that I'm on to bigger and better things.

Dear Red,   *Dec. 12, 1961*

Doctor Greenson is not happy over the news of my new love interest. In fact, he seems quite concerned I may be making a serious mistake. First off, he thinks I'm probably doing this just to get back at Jack for treating me so cruelly. Which I concede, is definitely part of it.

But we've already had three long phone conversations and Bobby just wrote me another love letter. And he has managed to call me every day, even if its just a quick 'thinking of you, love you, have to run'. Of course I realize part of throwing myself so enthusiastically into this romance is the fact I presently lack a leading man.

Then, my Doctor asked me if I wasn't worried it might turn out to be more of the same underhanded treatment that I received from Jack. After all, Bobby was another highly respected official in our country, and had much to lose. Also his father, Joe Kennedy, was infamous for chasing and bedding movie stars and dumping them when he got what he wanted. As the father goes, so goes the sons? Alright, maybe I am being a little quick to decide he's a totally different Kennedy concerning his approach and attitude towards women. Truly caring about proper behavior. But I keep thinking about what Jack said, actually several times through the years to me. 'Bobby's different, he doesn't screw around. Its not in his nature. He's been faithful to Ethel since they got engaged.' Stuff like that.

So deep down I say to myself, you can just go to hell, my stick in the mud shrink. Because this brilliant, intense, honorable public servant will be my next, and last, husband. And the LOVE OF MY LIFE. So I just nodded but at the same time, I was also checking my watch.

Bobby usually calls at 4 in the evening, which is 7 Eastern time so he's just getting off work. Ridiculous because he works around the clock, which is definitely not like Jack. By then, he's usually ready to leave his office. So I wanted to get home because I didn't want to miss his call.

Turns out he's planning to return to California between Christmas and New Year's just so we can be together. He has a beautiful present for me and he misses me terribly. As a matter of fact, he told me he never felt this way about any woman ever, in his entire life. Now he may be laying it on a bit. But because of all these wonderful things he's said to me, I do believe I'm in real love with someone who feels exactly the same as me. And, thank you, LORD GOD, its a simply wonderful feeling. I can't say I fully understand it, myself, because I've never even slept with him. But this has to be a good deal more than mutual infatuation. This one seems destined, to borrow a term from those over the top producers I loathe, to have real legs. Wait till Bobby sees mine.

None of the great thinkers understand the love experience. That's why people say its magical. Powerful and mysterious. Its surely what brings the movie goer's in. Books, paintings. Love is big business everywhere. Because its the best damn feeling in the whole wide world.

Dear Red, *December 25, 1961*

Its Christmas day, tra-lah, and Joe and I are going over to the Greenson home to celebrate with their family. Bobby already called early in the morning, so it had to be really early back in Virginia, to wish me a very happy holiday and he hoped I was not feeling too sad, or lonely. Because we would be together very soon. And he's never felt this way about anyone and there he was, yesterday, sitting in on some boring meeting with all these boring investigators and even more boring officials and all he could think about was me. And his penis has been aching for over a week from our first encounter and he could only wonder how incredible it would feel after a whole day of being in bed with me. And I said, 'Hold on, I've got to come up for air, too. I'm not just a sex machine. I require nutrition and intellectual stimulation. And some humor.' The General laughed and promised me that and the moon. And I said not so fast, because the Russians may beat us there. With a monkey. So he promised me his heart and I said I'll take that in a heartbeat. Wasn't that just the sweetest thing?

Anyhow, I'm looking forward to this afternoon because Joan has a new boyfriend and they've just started petting, like to second base. And I can definitely identify with her because I'm sort of at the same stage with mine. So we can share experiences but I'd never let on to her who my boyfriend is. That information is strictly for her father. Because I cling to the very real safeguard of doctor patient rules regarding anything I choose to discuss about the General. Just as important, some things are meant to be private. For Joan, also. They have to be, otherwise they wouldn't be brought out, ever. I'm sure you can understand that, Red.

Dear Red,   *December 27, 1961*

    Wow. It was simply the highest energy and most exciting
evening I have ever spent. We met at Peter's house. I arrived first
so I just lulled around for an hour, getting comfortable, drinking
some bubbly and waiting for my man.

    Then he arrived, (driving an open convertible) and at
the entrance doorway,(open shirt, hard nipples) he gave me
this bundle of letters, wrapped with a beautiful blue ribbon.
There were seven days of I love you's and a few notes about the
weather and one brief note saying he was beginning to hate all
lawyers. I really laughed at that one. Then he gave me a simple
scalloped gold heart on a chain, engraved Love, Gen. It was a
lovely necklace, and I let him put it on me. Then I gave him
his present, which was a beautiful stuffed tiger, which I told
him would protect him from all the evil people in this world,
including Khrushchev and Castro and Sam Giancana and Jimmy
Hoffa. And he loved it, because the tiger had a beautiful red satin
collar saying 'MY HONEY', and he promised he would take it
everywhere. So I knew every time he looked at it, he would be
reminded how lucky he was to have found such a loving and
beautiful woman who was thinking only of him. Oh, I forgot to
tell you, I was naked, in high heels, when I greeted him at the
door. So I took Tiger and began to rub his head and back lightly
between my legs as I danced around the sofa and pretty soon, like
a minute, the soft fur working between my vaginal lips got me
real hot. I even had a mini climax, which has become so foreign
to me over the last few years, I thought I had lost that feeling for
good. But it gave me a true shudder, and my legs got weak. And
I groaned a real groan. So I took the tiger for a steamy little spin
around my love nest. Using his ears as a rudder.

After awhile, I held the tiger up and said 'now that I've christened him, he'll always hold my juices. My scent of arousal for my dream man. You'.

I took Bobby's hand with my free one and led him and the tiger to the bedroom. There my guy did a little strip tease which I thought was just adorable. And I showed my appreciation by kneeling in front of his already firming penis. Then I went down on him, alternating between those tiny thumbnail pinches directed below his head (I mean of his dick), along with tickling around his ass and serious deep pumping with my whole mouth, and cheeks, taking him all the way in. Not surprising, after a few minutes he was rock hard.

So I went over to that stuffed tiger where I had thrown it on the bed and unclipped his collar. Then I pushed Bobby down on the bed, on his back, erection up and bobbing slightly to the right. I wrapped his whole package real tight with the ribbon which magically I was just able to clasp and catch under his balls. Then I continued to work him with my mouth and tongue and cheeks and palate and fingers and palms and nipples and breasts and even the crack in my ass for 20 minutes and I know, 'cause I glanced at the clock on Pat's nightstand before I began. Then, he took me there on his back, doggie style, on my back, on his side, on my other side, partially standing, sitting, every which way and I really enjoyed myself 'cause he's quite fit and athletic. And not in a cave man way, like Giuseppe. Tender and gentle. We easily screwed for close to an hour before he finally came. And it was real good, especially 'cause I've been missing a real fuck fest for too darn long. (I used to have trouble using that term but my good doctor has cured me of that particular neurosis. Fest is not a bad word.)

And when we were finished, he just kept saying how beautiful and sexy I was as he held me firmly to his chest. And did I have fun and he was sure he loved me because I was all he could think about for the last month. He didn't know if that was good or bad.

Especially because now that we had at long last had sex it was far better than he had ever imagined, so what sort of condition would he find himself in now?

And then he asked me how he compared to his brother, which I knew he would do sooner or later. But not so immediately after shooting his first wad deep inside me. Excuse me, Red, second shooting. First direct hit. And while his stuff is dripping out of me, onto the 300 thread Egyptian cotton sheet, I tell him 'he was better than his brother 'cause he was younger more athletic and able to move about and balance, and more caring', and then I smiled and waited. He just stared so I went on, 'coupled with your greater stamina, giving me all the time I needed to warmup.' I stopped, he stopped. This was getting to be more difficult. I began again. Less smiling, more grasping for the right words. 'At the same time, you're exciting because you're kind and concerned with my pleasure. Which makes you the most appealing man I've ever been with.' Now he ate it all up. Big smile and kiss. How come every guy, however minimally smart or talented or successful, thinks his penis is made of pure 24 carat gold and his in and out moves are totally different from anyone else's?? Even with my vast experience, if I did a double blind test right now, I'd have a problem comparing the Attorney General to the two blind guys.

He waits again, like he is looking for the right words. Smiles a silly boyish smile. 'So you still madly in love with that dirty dog?' For a split second I was unsure what dog he was talking about. 'My brother, Jack?'

I shook my head and replied that the President was like a schoolgirl crush you have for the King of the Prom. And I idolized him but Bobby was the man I knew I could love for my entire lifetime. And my new lover agreed. He said he could love me for a lifetime, too. And he had to admit he had often felt jealous of me and Jack. And it didn't seem fair, 'cause Jack had a flock of girls, coming and going, and he only wanted me.

It was the same in everything they did for as long as he could remember, even growing up with their Nanny. He ran interference, Jack scored. Bobby was the hard worker, the dependable one. He made sure everything got done while Jack took all the bows. During the election, he brokered all the backstage deals with the difficult locals and the reporters and the wealthy contributors while his brother was making the pretty speeches up front and screwing the college coed volunteers. And after the Bay of Pigs disaster, he started running the entire Cuban campaign, 'because the CIA was such a bunch of incompetents jerks, top to bottom. Including Bobby's own secret plans to screw up the socialist economy, by messing with their wheat and milk and blaming it on Castro's stupidity.' I winced, my mind saying be careful, Marilyn. Don't criticize. He's as insecure as you are. He nodded, sensing my uneasiness. 'Well, its only one crop.' I half smiled, silent. 'Look, nobody's going to starve. The Navy, along with the CIA, have been slipping small exile groups back into their island to rile up the peasants. He and Jack hope they can remove Castro from power. One way or another'.

I replied 'Please, I'm not that anxious to hear the specifics, especially if 'other' means what I think it means.'

And he said, 'better for all concerned.' And I replied 'you're right' and blew him a kiss. He smiled and moved close and hugged me.

So by the next morning we're back at it, on the bedroom floor, and Bobby is revved to the nines and a good time was had by all. Aside from the fact I got some pretty bad rug burns on my knees and coccyx and elbows.

It was, all in all, a pretty spectacular experience. And it wasn't just that he thought I was a lot smarter than he imagined. But for the entire eighteen and one quarter hour time period while we were together, I was also a lot smarter than I imagined. Well informed and interested in his difficult tasks and, in many ways, his equal.

I also made sure to not challenge Bobby about any of the activities that he talked about. Its too early in our relationship and I think he wants me dumb. Also, I have this feeling Jack is a lot easier to confront about negative issues that the administration supports. If the President is uncomfortable, he'll explain why or laugh it off. Bobby might just as easily (and quickly) get angry and take it as a personal confrontation. And since I'm running for wife and not Senator, I want to hold the tension to a minimum.Before we met, as I studied Bobby's statements and interviews in the magazines and papers, it got more and more exciting. We think pretty much the same on everything. And we're interested in the same things, like equal rights for Negroes and women, hell, for all people.

And taking care of our poor children, providing decent doctors and medicines and food. And HOPING TO OBTAIN WORLD PEACE. So what if on a few things we differ. I don't know everything about Russia and Cuba. Maybe they are that dangerous and are planning our destruction. If so, we should try to catch and stop them. I have difficulty with some of the ways we may be pursuing it. But what do I know? I'm a junior high school drop out.

All in all the weekend was GREAT! So I'm thrilled and can't wait to speak to Dr. Greenson and tell him how incredibly wrong he was.

My Dear Friend,   *Jan. 3, 1962*

Its a brand New Year and I'm starting to get excited. After all, its got to be loads better than the last one. I don't think I could take another year of disappointing failures and not fall to pieces. Wind up in some loony bin, helping to complete the family wing.

I spent the Eve with Joe, roasting chestnuts, watching the party in Times Square on my TV, acting very much like any old married couple and it felt great. Around midnight, Joan came by with her boyfriend, Keith, and we all drank champagne.

They looked so grown up that I was going to offer them my bedroom to use for a little while, as a special treat. But Joan's still a minor and Dr. Greenson's daughter and youngest child. Even though I knew they were dying to make out (they're still just rounding second base) but had nowhere to go, except the back seat of a car. But there was this little voice in the back of my head saying, don't do it, Marilyn. Right now you think you're offering a refuge just to be kind. But you're also promoting and giving your permission for some form of sexual activity. And no matter how innocent it turns out, you'll be sorry. A lot of times I act out just cause I get so frustrated with all the phony morals of today. But that's about me, not another person, who is not only young and immature, but who also happens to be my doctor's flesh and blood. Someone he has consented for me to be close friends with and encouraged our talks about everything and confiding in each other.

So we watched television for awhile more and then we all hugged and wished each other a Happy New Year for the umpteenth time and then the kids went home. And Joe and I went to bed.

But it was a nice night and I felt content cause I knew I was going to be seeing the General in a couple of weeks and thoughts of him make me absolutely giddy.

I was happy for Joan because I had acted like a parent to her, showing I cared. She seems to really enjoy my company and advice, more all the time. It is a wonderful feeling to be concerned about someone other than the usual, myself and my big causes. Just someone normal and nice. With this big sister development I've come to realize Joan's a terrific girl. I wish I had had an older, wiser friend like me who was concerned with my welfare to grow up with. Probably would have helped a lot, developing a constant sense of self worth. It would definitely have helped me feel easier around older people. With a solid base, I might have challenged myself more later on. Harvard College here I come? And, perhaps most important, I might have learned to rely on fewer drugs. My first psychiatrist, Dr. Hohenberg, constantly harped on this. Her message boils down to greater fulfillment for me based on the confidence to be me. Hey, looks like I'm not really sick after all.

Well, I'll find out tomorrow because Dr. Greenson comes back from vacation. He needs to pay for his trip. And I need confirmation of my dreams.

Dear Red,   *January 7, 1962*

My last several sessions with Dr. Greenson have been very upsetting. He's not at all convinced Bobby is a good match for me. At this point, I don't know if anything I say will change his mind. The biggest problem is he hasn't had the opportunity to get close to Bobby to converse with him and get to know him better. Which my good Doctor has reminded me would be a violation of medical ethics. But if he did, he would soon appreciate the General's incredible mind plus his great sense of humor. Along with his growing commitment to me and us as a couple.

The Doctor keeps saying 'life's not some script or book that has to be followed to the letter. And just because this extremely attractive man wants to have an affair with you, does not make it equally good for you to go along.' Sure, he can understand how the General fills my over all needs for intelligence, with strong social goals. And his convictions would give me inner strength. At the very least, determination. And it was nice that Bobby was exciting and socially relevant in many of the same areas as I was. The doctor could understand that attracted me. Still, despite all his attributes, he was a very public figure with a very large family (father of the year two times). And this family was in a highly prestigious larger family that guarded its image fiercely. Making it even more difficult was what I had discussed with him before. The entire group was ruled by a single man, a most unusual one in Joe Kennedy, who had the mind and morals of a sleazy Roman emperor during the excess years. On this point I was able to counter with, 'not anymore because Joe's mellowed in his old age. Besides he seems to have suffered a stroke. Actually, a rather severe one. This complication that occurred last month is being kept secret by the family. That's because their considerable news control team has largely been successful in keeping it out of the papers. But at present, he can't walk or talk.'

Doctor Greenson shook his head, like he wasn't buying into this at all. 'He may die but his influence won't.' I shrugged, then said, 'You know I want to quit Hollywood and settle down with a man I can look up to. And I'm absolutely sure the General's the one.' At that point, Dr. Greenson reminded me I had been fooled before. But in this case, 'there was such added potential to be used. And no real up side.'

I tried to describe how we've been speaking on the phone for hours. And already, he is talking about our future. How he'll divorce Ethel and we'll marry and I'll have his children. (Lord knows he can produce on that end). And my Doctor looked down several times before suggesting Bobby might be trying to do his brother one better. In fact, he was quite possibly even more dangerous, since he seemed to be trying to get me to fall in love with him. He was painting a beautiful but false picture, giving me all I ever wanted. Promising me a permanent, legally sanctioned relationship, while at the same time fulfilling my most basic needs as a woman.

And this has been my quest for a very long time with several previous, painful disappointments. He was afraid caution may be giving way to desperation. I countered by saying, 'I'm sure he's going to be the next President, after his brother, and he doesn't lie.' So then my good doctor started beseeching me to 'go slow, because it may not happen the way I want it to.' Fine, I'm duly warned. But I'm still going to see Bobby again in ten days and we'll see who's correct.

My Doctor does not know everything, most of all, who and what is best for my future. He's an analyst, not a fortune teller.

I just heard Arthur is marrying that bimbo Nazi, Inge Morath. Even worse, she's pregnant, which is a huge dagger to my heart.

This clearly shouts I'm the flawed one regarding Arthur and our infertility problems. Its me. Do I carry this curse with whomever I'm with? The possibility is something I find extremely difficult to consider. I continually blamed Poppy for all our difficulties. To now find out its all my fault is the worst possible news. What I deep down always feared. I may never be able to get pregnant and carry a baby to delivery, ever.

This assault comes along with the news Frank, 'The Rat', has just announced his engagement to that cheap chorus girl, Juliet Prowse. But this is far less of a loss. Her heartache. Bet it won't last three months, tops.

Whew. Well, onto more concrete and less heated topics. My good doctor thinks I should buy my own house. He feels this would be good for me in several ways, providing security and comfort. And as I furnish it with my own stuff, it would become a source of great personal pride. (I've never owned something like this before.) Well, I've agreed, so I've started looking, and he suggested Malibu because I've always loved the beach. But I got really nervous because I'd be pretty far away from where Dr. Greenson and his family lived. I want my new house to be close to his. At a minimum a few miles. Especially with traffic in and around LA continuing to be a problem.

Well, I didn't challenge him on this but just started thinking, 'Was my Doctor, deep down, planning to get rid of me, using this house thing as an excuse?' So it took three tearful sessions for me to come to the conclusion he wasn't in any way trying to end my therapy.

Red, between the conversations about the General and the purchase of my new home and the feeling I was no good in terms of bearing children, I had become afraid that Dr. Greenson was getting increasingly annoyed with me. To the point he was trying to sever our relationship altogether. Simply put, I was getting to be too damn much trouble. This now seems to be more a problem in my warped thinking.

Mostly due to my inability to accept even the slightest hurtful behavior or questioning in any of my key staff or friends, who I depend on for support. Support? Hell, Red, I require unconditional, 100 % pure love. I may be screwed up but at least I'm unwavering in my all encompassing needs. And total loyalty is paramount. People have a habit of turning on me somewhere down the line and it gets too painful. So I've decided on taking this approach to protect myself. Dr. Greenson thinks I'm nuts, but let him try walking in my shoes. Still I agreed to work on this.

Dear Red,   *Jan. 24, 1962*

   Well, I've been house-hunting for several weeks now with the help of my new assistant, Mrs. Eunice Murray. I mean my new full time assistant. I elevated her from part time because with the house and Bobby and everything, we feel it would be better. She's allright and she does seem to want to help but she's very frozen and old fashioned. Hardly someone I'd choose for myself but my good Doctor had suggested I hire her as a constant companion. She has extensive experience with emotional patients or people under emotional stress. Whatever the hell that means. We are attempting to find my dream place and it hasn't been as easy as I thought or hoped it would be. A lot of stress.

   Some people don't react well to me even though I've never done anything to them, personally. Never even met them. So many seem to have major difficulty separating me, the quiet, stay to herself, insecure person from the head lining actress. Some of the film roles I've played where I've acted outrageous or extremely seductive or just plain crazy seem to frighten them. A couple of the people refused to show me their houses altogether. One lady screamed at me from the front porch to 'get off her property this instant.' We had responded to an open house notice stapled to her front tree. Sale by owner. Should have added NO FILM PEOPLE.

   But I finally found one in Brentwood, a charming rambler done in a Mexican motif with a tiled roof and ceramic tiled floors, and a small pool in the back. Its quite manageable and homey, with a large living area with impressive wood beams and two small bedrooms in the back. I loved it the second I walked in. And its eight minutes from Dr. Greenson's house and maybe ten the other way to Peter's on the beach.

Its quite private, in a quiet residential area at the end of a small cul-de-sac. So last week, I put down a deposit and I signed an offer sheet.

Well, I've just been informed the owner has accepted. You can congratulate me, because I'm a homeowner to be. Tears are flowing down my cheeks because I would have liked to be buying this with a husband, or some meaningful companion. C'est la vie. At least I can afford the place. I'm almost thirty six so I can't keep acting like a child or waiting for my dream man. If he comes along we'll buy a bigger place and I'll sell this one or rent it out. And if he doesn't I don't have to keep looking. I'll have a solid, secure base I call home. My home. And I can have my friends visit me here, in my neighborhood.

By the way, the General and his wife are coming to California this weekend to kick off a ten day world tour. They're staying a few days at Peter's home before they take off. And I've been invited over for dinner, along with Gloria Romanoff, who has always been a dear friend and Kim Novak, who has often been compared to me but still has a long ways to go as an actress. So I want to make a good impression on the Attorney General and the other guests. See, I haven't written Bobby off because he keeps calling and writing me these cute love letters, on Department of Justice stationery, no less. I wonder if the taxpayers would be annoyed if they got wind of the misuse of government paper? Anyhow, my good Doctor has finally accepted the premise of me and the General as a couple, and has even become somewhat supportive. That is he's helping me with my 'key questions to ask my man during the dinner meal.' Like I was the youngest child at the Seder.

Dear Red,   *Jan. 26, 1962*

The dinner was terrific. I mean for me. I had several intelligent questions listed on a small index card in my purse and I was placed right next to Bobby, on my left. Which is my best side because of my tiny birthmark, which I help accentuate with my black eyebrow pencil. Along with the fact I part my hair on that side. I am a lefty and always felt it was easiest to do it that way. Interesting, I also like to start making love with me on that same side, but we sure weren't doing any of that at this high class function. Especially with Ethel seated on the opposite side of the table, two people down from directly facing me, casting occasional glares and constant frozen scowls of absolute hatred. Brrrr.

Its tough to be the other woman, but its even tougher to be the wife. Or former wife as in my three (actually four) cases. Anyhow, everything was catered with two to three help per each diner, and there were twelve of us, including our hosts, so the dining area was packed. Dinner, needless to say was excellent. I had the fish.

And Kim Novak, the transparent little slut, was boring everyone about her beautiful new house on her beautiful new cliff located a hundred yards above the ocean. And by evening, the beautiful sunsets, which were only enhanced by her extensive new landscaping, designed by some famous old Japanese gardener.

I said very little, content to nod and smile at the General, who was trying to act very cocky and above it all. Until I dropped my silver napkin holder and he almost dove down to get it, fondling my inner thigh in the process. No alcohol, though I cradled a glass of white wine, more as a prop. And he was even acting somewhat immature when he had a phone brought to the table where he called his father.

Then he greeted him, sounding real excited. 'Dad, guess who is sitting right next to me? Marilyn Monroe, the movie star. Want to speak to her?' And then he thrust the phone into my hand. Now in truth I've already met him a few times when I was with Jack, including one at their beautiful Hyannis seaside estate. I had the feeling Bobby was doing this little show for the benefit of his wife, Ethel but it was still flattering. Especially because Miss Kim stared buckets of envy at me. So I just said, 'Hello, Ambassador. Happy recent birthday. I hope you're feeling better,' and I think he said 'Tank yoh' and 'Like taste in boise' but he was slurring real bad. I was happy when Bobby pulled the phone from me, 'cause I really didn't know what else to say. Seems Ol' Joe has taken a bad hit and I don't think he's getting up so quick. Well, he did his share of plundering and grabbing ass where and whenever. I heard that from Frankie boy and my longtime friend, Robert Slatzer. While working as a magazine reporter, he learned several damning tales of Joe's maltreatment of different girlfriends.

He attacked Gloria Swanson in the hall of her hotel floor after their first dinner date. And he pulled the same 'rape and ravage' routine with Marion Davies, William Randolph Hurst's former, when he first met her. I've never told any of this to my Good Doctor. Out of fear he'd just use it as ammunition against my argument to stay with my man from Justice, even when he was treating me like shit. Using his saying about the apple or in my screwed up case, apples, not falling far from the tree.

Finally, when the staff started to clear the table before dessert and coffee, I turned to the General and asked my first and biggest question, which I had prepared mainly with the help of Danny Greenson. Danny is starting Med School and is a real genius. 'Mr. Attorney General, could we talk a little about Vietnam?' Bobby nodded and my voice rose loud enough for everyone to hear above the clatter of the staff and the dishes being piled and taken away. 'Many of the South Vietnamese soldiers and Buddhist monks are claiming Diem and his brother are uncompromising rulers and there's no real freedom in their country. So aren't you concerned that the Diem regime might turn out to be far more of a dictatorship than a true, freely elected government? And, in light of possible unfair treatment of the masses, do you still plan to continue sending military aide, if they are found to be using it badly?'

Bobby slowly turned his entire body towards me, while his eyes opened in total amazement. 'Well, Miss Monroe, is that a question in two or three parts?' I held up two fingers while giving him my freshman (should be freshwoman) earnest look. He seemed like he was getting slightly uncomfortable, but at the same time even a bit aroused over the unexpected intellectual challenge. 'Miss Monroe, I'll have you know Diem has been a friend of the Kennedy family for the last twenty five years, mostly spent in forced exile from his homeland. He is a devout Catholic, a fearless anti-communist and staunch defender of his people. His brother Nhu was just ordained as a bishop. They are considered, by Ho Chi Min, as the number one and two most wanted war criminals still alive.'

I looked at him calmly. 'Then, I guess you plan to continue sending 'military advisors' to help him maintain his control?' Bobby gave a little shrug and said 'if necessary.' So I responded with an innocent shrug and said 'Well, hopefully there won't be any further need.' Now Danny had told me there were reports of little brother's (Nhu's) secret campaign of physical abuse and jailing of Buddhist monks and other religious leaders. But I didn't want to embarrass Bobby, just show him I was smart.

Then we both nodded and he put his hand over mine. And he led me out to the pool area because the three-piece band had started playing. He held me tightly, and part of his support team including Peter and Pat (always loyal to the Kennedy man in any relationship, no matter how long or brief) shielded Ethel away, and we were pretty much alone out there. Then he asks me, snippy and clearly annoyed, 'OK, Marilyn. We both know you're a real ditz.

So where did you get that crap from?' And I told him 'I had read it somewhere a few days before. But I would go carefully in 'Nam' cause the area was real screwed up and Diem's brother Nhu was one of the worst screwers. And choosing sides based on anything Ho Chi Min hated might turn out to be foolish.'

And he nuzzled my ear, and suggested we go there together, to enjoy the screwing. And I said I was serious, and I was learning you always had to watch the younger brother.

But later, when we went back to the table, he reached down and grabbed the index card from my bag and pulled it out. He started reading to himself while laughing in relief. Then he pulled me back out for another dance. As he held me, he said in a mocking tone I did not really appreciate, 'no wonder you talked like some genius reporter rather than the dunderhead I crave. You had me thinking I was on the hot seat.' He smiles. 'So when I get you alone, you're going to pay.'

And I smiled back and replied 'you call me a dunderhead again, you'll be the one to pay. A parting kiss and return my campaign donation, please.'

So, that's how we left it. He's off to the Orient with his long time angry wife and I'm off to Mexico with my press agent, Pat Newcomb, and Eunice Murray, to buy some furniture for my beautiful new home. And we (Bobby and me) should get reacquainted in about eleven days. Hopefully, he'll start to have more respect for me, both my brains and my substance.

Buenos Dias, Roja,   *Feb. 14, 1962*

I'm in Mexico and I'm having a very nice time. Just lovely.
A respite before I begin filming Something's Got To Give, which
Fox is demanding I do 'cause they're losing millions on Cleopatra.
They want me to uphold my old contract. I come cheap, only one
hundred thou up front. Nothing like Elizabeth Taylor and Richard
Burton, who claim a million and a half between them. (And now it
looks like they'll be sharing that.) Well, anyway, Nunnally Johnson
finally got the script to a B level. He did a beautiful job on Three
Faces of Eve. He also did Marry a Millionaire and that's been one
of my most popular roles, ever. So if George Cukor approves the
script, we're green lighted for the middle of April. We're waiting on
Dean Martin to get free from his present shoot so I'm hopeful we
can get rolling.

Anyhow, at the Mexico City Hilton, I met this wonderful
Connecticut couple, the Fred Field's. Their help has been
invaluable, especially in locating skilled local artisans to make
some of my dining room and kitchen pieces. Which of necessity
have to be smaller than usual because my house isn't all that big.
More than that, I seem to have found a kindred spirit. Fred, born
into the Vanderbilt wealth, has become a man for the common
people. His wife is an Mexican intellect friendly with Frieda Kahlo
and Diego Rivera and their very talented and very, very bright
friends. This entire socialist group thinks with their heart and not
their pocketbook. Well, the Fields are just charming. And I told
them of my disappointments with Arthur and Giuseppe. Plus
the loss of my babies through miscarriages and the fact I'm tired
of Hollywood and the rat race. Probably even sicker of all the
scurrying rats.

Then some spice came into my life. Through the Fields, with a
little help from Pat Newcomb, I met the extremely romantic writer,

Jose Bolanos, who is quite the rising Mexican talent. An author and playwrite and director and bon vivant cutey with a great chest (hairy but muscular). And real character.

Pat was seduced by the beautiful yellow roses he sent on a silver plate, which turns out to be a family heirloom. As she passed them on to me, she kept repeating 'this guy's gorgeous. Tall, dark, handsome.' (There she goes again.) I'll add sensitive. He has subsequently followed me all through the country side, hiring bands to serenade me with Spanish songs and reciting beautiful poems (in both Spanish and English) to warm my insides. And delivering more yellow roses at each stop.

So I've become intimate with him and he is a charming companion and thrilling lover. I'll say, he's almost eleven years younger than me. Yet he's already accomplished so much, including an award winning script done by the legendary director Luis Bunuel. I think it was called La Cucaracha. Anyhow, I can be myself with him and don't have to feel this overpowering need to please him in bed. So I can concentrate on my own pleasure and he goes down on me for hours. Now he's got a nice mind and hands, too, but his tongue is delicious. And with his full lips cradling my most sensitive clit, besides shaping a most beautiful smile. I'm starting to feel like a woman again, and not just some sex symbol. Not bad for an older gal.

On his prompting and before I left, I visited the Institute for Orphans, and got so carried away I made a donation of ten thousand dollars. Actually I would have adopted one of those beautiful children right there on the spot. If Pat, (the bitch from the East) hadn't stepped in to throw ice water over my dreams.

Saying I had to think very carefully about this adoption and I absolutely must first talk it over with Dr. Greenson. And I couldn't even take care of Maf. So how could I ever???

Then I said Adios to my new friends and started drinking that last evening, mainly brought on by my desire for motherhood.

Maybe I should treat this state of bareness like I did my need for a home. Take a deep breath and just adopt a baby for myself. And love it to pieces. And screw everybody who doesn't like the idea.

Anyhow, I threw up on the choppy flight home, and I just hope that's not a harbinger of stormy weather ahead. 'Cause I was pretty bombed and suddenly quite miserable. I kept thinking I should have listened to my heart and not stupid Pat, who hasn't a motherly bone in her body. Some expert. How could anyone say I'd be a lousy mother when I've never had the chance?

Well, I've now been home two days and the vision of those children remain, haunting in their innocence and need to be loved. I spoke to Jose on the phone just before. Jose loves all children and comes from a big family. He said he would be thrilled to help me bring any of them up. And would also help in the adoption. This hombre is so sweet. Excuse me, Roja. Muy dulce.

Dear Red,   *Feb. 28, 1962*

I'm in Peter's bed at his Santa Monica beach house with the General and you, my trusty diary. He has just dozed off after a fairly long discussion. About politics, what else. Our scholarly session was capped off with a lovely romantic interlude, which started when he said he was cold. I went to the bedroom closet and there was an old mink hanging in the corner. SO I MADE HIM WEAR PAT'S MINK COAT AND HE WAS NAKED. (It almost fit him.) After a few minutes of stroking him with the free sleeve, he came up ready for action. Up, up and horny. He almost came in the fur and then the silk lining, but I made him save his stuff for me. I put the coat flat on the bed, fur side up and then put him down on it, butt side down, and I rode him like a bucking bronco.

He is now wearing his boxer shorts and I have just put my bra back on. So I am bare butt and he is bare chested and we lie, satiated with each other. My head rests on his thighs, using him like a pillow, my feet dangling over the side. You, Red, are wearing your usual red covers, front and back. Now that I've used over half your pages to write in, you fall open easily in my lap. I know, honey, so do I.

But I just can't sleep when I'm near my Captain Dynamo. He gets upset when I write in you while we are discussing some little thing that I find interesting. But I don't want to forget. I'm now of the feeling its best to transcribe it immediately, while everything is still fresh. Much better than trying to remember some little detail tomorrow or even later. He finds my behavior more then just annoying. 'Rude and distracting.' Yet, in truth, he brought these actions completely on himself and, as he can see right here, I'm much more accurate this way.

At the very beginning of our affair, Bobby chided me about remembering some stupid little detail about Lyndon Johnson and Bobby Baker getting paid off by some major Texas oil company, (drilling to refinery to you, the consumer) who wanted to get a big Army contract.

Bobby was secretly investigating this criminal act and others, including the murder of an investigating official in his home county. The goal is to get enough shit on Lyndon to force him off the ticket in '64.

Anyhow, Bobby assaulted me about being dumb 'cause I couldn't remember which company when he mentioned it a month later. Like they're all not the same. Buncha of thieves. And saying just maybe I should start taking notes when he spoke to me, so I'd remember something, anything. I said never you mind because my good Dr. Greenson, who is far smarter than him, had awhile ago recommended my keeping a diary for my therapy, which I had faithfully done. So from now on, you, Red, would become a part of us, especially when we were involved in discussing some particularly involved and complex matters. Such as Bobby's behind the scene daring do's, with the CIA and the Mafia. Also there's this young chemist from the Agency, who makes all these concoctions, and then the daring do agents try to give them to some unfortunate party with the first name of Fidel. Or Lumbago. Or Trujillo. Or who knows who else we decide is not worthy of continuing in office. Another task force continues to be fixated on catching LBJ with his hand in the government till or cookie jar. Or oil field.

Must also remember, he and his family had chosen Johnson as their running mate in the first place, and at the very last moment. So who was the dumb one, I ask you, Red? I will not ask Bobby that same question.

Anyway, for the last month or so, you've been by my side. Haven't written much but you've been around, nevertheless. Well, now Bobby's getting annoyed at that.

So, to compromise with my honey, I'm going to start taking some notes on a pad and then I'll fold them in you, Red, so it won't upset him. Because he already hates you as you must remember from the time he threw you across the floor, cursing. Temper, temper. And I'll write them in you later.

Dear Red,   *March 12, 1962*

I am presently trying to transcribe some scribbled notes from
the last three weekends when we got together. Either Saturday or
Sunday, usually both. Bobby has managed to get away from his
home in Virginia so often on the premise of working on his script.
Hey, we're in Hollywood and everyone and his brother has a script.
His is based on The Enemy Within, Bobby's book dealing with
Jimmy Hoffa's control of the Teamster's, which was a best seller.

Actually it just might be done by Twentieth Century Fox. At
least, they had a meeting over it, somewhat on my suggestion. But
there's no love story at all. And little action. No character changes
or arcs. Not even a cat and mouse suspense. So its not exactly up
anyone's alley as a film. In fact, this project more closely resembles
a phony make up to be used as an excuse with Ethel so he can
come out here on weekends.

For Bobby and me, its been a delightful bender of sex and
talk, at Peter's whore home on the beach. I'm presently attempting
to transcribe onto your sterling white pages much of what I've
managed to gather over the last three weeks, on notes totally
illegible. I have promised to burn you before allowing any of these
conversations to ever hurt him or the family, but I did have my
fingers crossed.

So he, Bobby, has gradually gotten used to my constant
attachment to note taking, with you in the far background. And
has given me the OK to write as we talk on these small note
papers. Just as long as it does not interfere with our lovemaking
or his discussions. He seems to have accepted you as a girlish fad.
Actually, in some strange way, I think Bobby may even be flattered.

I greet each revelation with awe, his thoughts and deeds. (I'm
such a little actress.)

He often says his brother gets the glory but he's the one getting things done. Especially through his harassment of the criminals using big investigations. Pressuring Hoover to keep his agents tailing the Chicago mob boys. For example (as the General puts it) when Mooney goes to the can. And anyone dealing with Johnson in Texas. Also all the mob boys in the south.

Just to be extra annoying, Bobby had Carlos Marcello thrown out of the country, in an immediate capture and flight to the forests of Guatemala. (Totally illegal but who cares.) There he was released deep in the jungle, in just his pajamas. We both had quite a laugh 'cause Marcello is a no holds barred gorilla who controls all of New Orleans and in Texas, the brothels, docks, and unions. (LBJ has the bars, and restaurants and anything else you need a license for.) Its amusing to consider how ridiculous Mr. Marcello must have looked, running through the woods, with his shriveled penis bouncing around beneath his huge jelly-belly rolls beneath his torn jammies. And the fact he couldn't call any of his expensive mouthpieces made it even better. He should be out of the country for awhile.

Which leads me to a very special showdown I was witness to, here in Peter and Pat's family room last weekend. Sunday to be exact. The main opponents were my summer wind romance of last year in the person of Mr. Frank Sinatra, and Bobby, my true romance of this year, squaring off.

Bobby told Frank he could no longer be seen in public with the President because the Department of Justice, under Bobby's direction, was conducting major investigations into Mooney and the Mafia. Plus the mob's connection into the Teamster's, led by Jimmy Hoffa. And since Frankie Boy worked with Giancana and even owed a major casino with him, Frank was squarely in their sights. This could prove highly embarrassing once charges were handed down. Especially if the newspapers got wind of all the secret connections. This might quickly come back to the President's front door, embarrassing him severely and destroying their cases.

Part of this dilemma, always present, but unspoken is older brother Jack's continuing hot and heavy romance to that absolute whore, the mindless Judith Campbell. Whose greatest charm is she's mobile and likes to stay busy. Judy was causing huge problems 'cause she was also fucking Mooney, and his godson, Frankie boy and his right hand man, Johnny Roselli. Quite a lot of action for this sweet young girl who appears to have only missed the College of Cardinals and the LA Rams. This tramp should lie on a lazy Susan mattress, naked and legs apart. So the various interested men can just spin her into position. But not in the White House. President Lincoln would die all over.

Bottom line, this was between Mooney and Jack but Jack is the President of the United States and the most influential leader in the entire world. So Bobby had to insist they cut off all contact between his family, including Jack, with Mr. Sinatra, the middle guy. 'Cause it would look like everyone was in bed together.

So Frankie asked, and not without some truth. 'Well, weren't they?' Bobby said 'of course they are. Actually so much so, they can't all appear to be in the slightest. And this was just a bad time to have our President sleeping in the same bed, at Frank's Palm Spring's Estate, when only a few weeks ago this was where Giancana had slept'. And Peter, who was there only because it was his house, added 'it was important for the President to appear impartial.'

Frank became real snippy, saying 'this was a hell of a time to pull this bullshit turn around. Why the hell was he investigating Mooney in the first place? Didn't Jack promise to lay off before the election? Yuh know, when he needed their help? He and his big brother were just a lousy bunch of dirty double-crosser's.'

'Nobody's going to jail.' Bobby explained. 'It was just important that Jack appear to be doing an honest job.'

Frank yelled, 'the Fed's aren't just looking around. They're hounding Mooney and had been ever since the first week you micks took up the reins.'

Bobby remained firm, not giving an inch, and Frank's cock-sure edge seemed to drain right out of him. He became visibly frightened, saying 'this might wind up being his own death notice. 'Cause Mooney did not like to be screwed over. Especially if it made him look bad. And his goombas could take it out on Frank, personally.' Bobby said, 'hey, that's your problem. But he'd (Bobby) would resign from Justice if there was any continued friendship. Even though the entire family understood Frank had done a lot to get Jack elected, and appreciated it. But the President would be staying at Bing Crosby's from now on.'

Frank screamed, 'You'll all be damn sorry for this. And he couldn't wait to see the day they got theirs, in spades.'

And Bobby said 'don't even think of threatening the Kennedy's because we're the legitimate ones. And your boy Mooney and his pack of goomba's were the crooks.' So Frank went storming out.

And I applauded and hugged my honey and the General was so pumped. Well, we almost threw Peter out the front door of his own home. And at two in the afternoon we started screwing on the living room rug, in front of the artificial fireplace, like twenty year old's. And the next morning, my hero was out of there.

But I finally came. I mean not a full climax, but something fairly close, this morning when Bobby said goodbye. He hugged me as he was ready to leave and I just went off. Just like I did so many times with Jack. But this bit of news I did not share.

So now I have to go rest. And wait for my First Commander's arrival tomorrow evening. At Frank's, of course. He's only sleeping at Mr. Crosby's. Jack's screwing me at Frank's. And to be quite candid, I don't know if my female muscles can hold out past this weekend. If I was a mercenary soldier I think I'd be asking for special duty pay around now.

Dear Red,   *March 13, 1962*

Switching to a more frightening topic, I think the phones in my home are being bugged. Seriously, I've heard this metallic sound like a click more than once and then there's total silence, which lasts several seconds. Then, there's the person on the other end finally talking. This is quite obvious, especially on my bedroom lines, both of them. And its very unsettling. I tried to warn Jack, but he could not care in the slightest. He called me paranoid.

As for Bobby, who knows? He might be the one who's been bugging me. Actually I was warned about this a few months ago by a friend and business associate of mine. He told me to be extra careful. That someone was listening in on me in my bedroom or trying to get some bugs into my home so they could listen in. And now, with Frank's threat, I'm starting to get real nervous. So I'll mention it again to both my dream men. I hope they take me seriously. And have a way of checking to make sure my lines are private.

Bobby is my best hope for phone safety and kids. But meanwhile, he just left and his brother Jack is pulling into LAX in less than two hours on Air Force One.

So I've got to go get ready. I'm seeing him tonight, in less than seven hours. Gee, I wonder what he'll want to do this evening? You know, Red, for entertainment? Hah.

Great weekend. And Bobby, my true love, my husband to be, called less than an hour after Jack left. He's put in a private line (100% bug proof) in his private office. (My boy works fast.) News flash. Johnson is almost gone. New evidence to send Bobby Baker and that Sol Estes character up the river has been found. Hopefully they'll sing like canaries and bring down the vulture. At least get Johnson to resign.

The General is also handing down a thirty-page indictment on Jimmy Hoffa, which will be filed in Federal Court this Tuesday. Hoffa is history with what they've managed to dig up, especially about using the Teamster's pension plan as his own private piggybank.

Oh, and he loves me so much he can't wait to be with me again. He knows there will come a time when we'll never part. And we'll be the best team ever. How come Bobby becomes the most romantic when Jack is around?

Dear Red,   *March 16, 1962*

Last night I attended the Golden Globe Awards. I was both a presenter and recipient, World Film Favorite, my second of those, which is the Grand Prize. Nice when some of the trades have been hinting I'm all washed up. I went with Jose Bolanos and it was a wonderful evening. I met many old friends and people I've worked with. Its nice and I love to be honored as an actress. Hell, I just love to be honored, washed or unwashed. And Jose made sure I was sopping wet afterwards, from inside out. Its great how the entire entertainment business loves to honor themselves so much. I'm not complaining in the slightest. I mean I still have lots of room on my mantle. And in my closet. No, there I have my shoes. Just kidding, Academy. I'll make room. Or build another room now that I'm a home owner.

Oh, Joan Crawford, who I once had a little romance with a long time ago, met me in the ladies room, when I was touching up at the mirror. She came up behind me and playfully caressed my breasts (creepy) and said, 'Hi, lover.' I replied. 'Hi, Joan.' She winked, 'Your new guy looks cute. But he's just a boy. Is he old enough to drive?' I shrug. 'Where did you find him?' I squeezed her hand. 'Can you keep a secret?' I asked, blushing. 'No one ever asked you about us, right?' she replied. So as I turned to leave, I blew her a kiss and said, 'OK, I met him by the bike rack.'

Dear Friend Red,   *March 17, 1962*

This could turn out to be a momentous day for me! I think, no I just about positive. I'm PREGNANT with Bobby's baby! Its all too thrilling. Well anyhow, I'm almost a week late and this morning I woke up and I was terribly nauseous, and I really hadn't eaten. (Or drank, Tah Dah.) And so it just has to be. And I made an appointment with my Ob/Gyn doctor to get my tests, but I've been pregnant before, about six times with the miscarriages, and more with my childhood pregnancy and other short term ones during my early modeling days.

So I'm thrilled and can't wait to speak to Dr. Greenson and of course, THE FATHER ROBERT. Can you believe, that cocky son of a bitch pulled it off? He's so virile he was even able to get me knocked up and hey, that's A OK. Chances like this don't come around all that much at my age. Just about never. So hail to the potent little father of the year. Bless his little bouncing balls, which behave lots bigger than they look. So all of a sudden I have a morning of exciting things to do. And at the same time I have fittings for all the dresses for Something's Got To Give and color tests and don't ask. But that's all so insignificant compared with my feeling of jubilation at having helped create a new human being. The knowledge I'm carrying this rapidly maturing person right at this moment is overwhelming. See you soon, Red. I'll keep you posted.

Dear Red,   *March 18, Night, 1962*

Bobby was horrible. Totally frozen in overcontrol and negativity. Refused to talk about it until we knew for sure from the tests. Couple of days. Still it was disturbing news. He's coming out this weekend. 'It was something we, together, will just have to deal with. Of course he still loved me. Not a question of that. Only timing. Controlling when things like this happened. Not letting them control him and us.'

Maybe I'll write tomorrow but I'm terribly depressed. Little prick has cut me the deepest. Still despite his rejection, I'm absolutely thrilled I'm pregnant. Screw him. I'll have the baby on my own. He or she'll be a beautiful love child who is mine, all mine! I will carry this child with even more joy and care. If for no other reason then to spite the gutless son of a bitch. Let each inch I grow be a dagger in his heart. Fetus grow on. And later, if it becomes too big a deal, I'll marry Jose and have him claim the fatherhood. Spanish men are so much kinder about family, loving kids without reservation. Adds so much to their manliness, to love a woman even when she's breathing for two.

Dear Red, *March 19, 1962*

Well, I'm pregnant! The first tests reveal my urine shows evidence of the pregnancy hormone, trace but definitely present. So now we just have to inject a rabbit to make sure, and I'll make the announcement in the gossip columns. Just kidding. But I am thrilled. Which is a good thing because Bobby wasn't exactly swept off his feet with joy. Still, he was much better than a few days ago when I gave him the news. More loving and even positive, saying, 'he was thrilled for me and happy for us. But we'd just have to discuss what to do next.' He even apologized for his curt, unemotional response when I first gave him the news, blaming it on the fact he had been working too hard. 'And my maternal status seemed to come out of left field. So sudden, in the beginning, it felt like a kick in the stomach. But now that he has had the chance to mull it over in his mind, it was grand news.' And I told him I was elated and he still wasn't acting like I hoped. So he said 'he would be there with me Friday evening (tomorrow) and we'd discuss the matter fully and make a mutual decision on where to go from here. But he had to run right now and finish up all the work he was planning to do over the weekend before this came up. Above all, he wanted me to understand he loved me and always had my best interests as his first priority.'

After I hung up, I called Dr. Greenson. And he said 'we have to wait and see, of course, but not to be too surprised if Mr. Kennedy wants you to have an abortion.' And I said 'I'd rather take an arrow to my heart.' I have already stopped all prescription drugs because I know they could damage the fetus and even alcohol. So I will do all that is necessary to assure a healthy, happy baby. And I really don't think a razor sharp curette is all that good for his development.

Dear Red,   *March 20, 1962*

Friday evening Bobby came storming in from the airport. We sat in Peter's family room, and our discussion went from bad to worse in a matter of minutes.

He could never divorce Ethel right now. It was a bad time, one of the worst. I reminded him we had talked about this blessed event so often. He had always seemed as positive as me. And I simply didn't understand what could have changed so much now that we were faced with the reality of it all.

He tried to turn it on me, saying I had a movie to do. I quickly dismissed that idea, replying there always was another movie, and besides, I wouldn't show for several months, and they could always shoot around my condition when it did. Besides I could always wear a girdle. And at the worst, they could delay the stupid movie for awhile. It wasn't Gone With The Wind.

Then Bobby switched back to his own personal reasons for wanting to, as he put it, 'delay our child for the foreseeable future. It was a difficult time politically and there was bound to be adverse publicity. And all their enemies would jump all over this, rather than the real issues, civil rights and his crusade against organized crime. And it would be political suicide and make him and his entire family look ridiculous.'

So I said, 'We were just talking about two people who are in love, doing exactly what God intended them to. Which was bringing children into this world to love and give guidance to. Giving them a proper home.' Then Bobby got really upset, like I've never seen him before. And he started screaming, which got me even more upset. Saying 'I wasn't listening, and that he couldn't divorce Ethel now. And divorce was a very sensitive subject, especially to Catholics.'

So I dried my eyes and got off the couch to face him and said, 'Fine, then I'll have the baby myself and it will be my love child. He or she will face the world with only one name. But with one hell of a loving, generous mother. Ingrid Bergman did it and it didn't kill her. I was coming to an age when I wanted a baby desperately. This little being growing inside me was the answer to all my prayers and I so wanted to just be a parent.'

So Bobby gets up and starts shaking me by the shoulders, hard, saying 'I was crazy. And that I was going to have an abortion, 'cause there was no other way. And it was his kid, too. And he had the right to decide what was best for everyone.' Then I broke away, pushing against his scrawny chest, and stared him right in the eye, and yelled, 'Did the Catholic church approve of abortion? Is that a sensitive subject, too? And he wasn't going to kill this child, just so he could weasel out of his responsibilities. And I was fully able to raise a child without him. So he could just fuck off.'

Then Bobby grabbed both my wrists and started to twist them and said 'he was going to protect the two of us, even if I was too stoned out of my mind to comprehend the danger.' And I said 'he was totally full of shit, and I understood completely, that he was rejecting us, me and him. But even crueler me and my newly conceived child.' Then he released me and took a few steps back.

He took a deep breath, 'Look, you've got to take it easy. And listen carefully.' He would take care of everything and get a specialist from LA to fly down to Mexico, and 'the surgeon could do the little procedure there. And that I was going to be in the best of hands.

He would never forsake me. We'd just be delaying our family for awhile.'And I replied, 'killing my baby was not some little procedure. It was cold blooded murder.'

So then I went over to Peter's liquor cabinet and started to slug down a couple of reds with some vodka from the bottle. Bobby came running over and asked, 'What the hell are you doing

214 | E.Z. Friedel

now?' then screaming, 'Be careful, dammit.' And I replied, 'I have insomnia and with this horrid news, I'll never fall asleep.' Then he said in this cold, cruel voice I can't get out of my head, 'I'm warning you, don't overdose again.'

So I took the bottle and threw it at his head (missing) and ran into the bedroom screaming, 'Just leave me alone. And didn't he realize he was really hurting me, and he was a bastard and a lousy liar.' And he countered with, 'You'll get over it. After-all its hardly your first time. And to just trust me on this.' And I cried out 'I've learned long ago to never trust any man who says trust me. And it was my first time I got pregnant in over fifteen years. And things are way different now. Now I want a family, and I can't get pregnant when I want to.'

He walked over and said 'I'll make it up to you. We'll have lots of babies together. Promise, Marilyn, this is just a temporary delay.' So I just shrugged. I mean he had already knocked all the fight out of me. And the rest of the weekend was a bloody nightmare, but I wouldn't let him come near me.

Especially after he started to call these doctors and get, as he snipped, everything rolling. Like it was some Democratic croquet party on the beach he was organizing.

And Peter and his wife Pat came back to the house to help him, and even that bitch, Pat Newcomb, who works for me, helped book the hotel rooms outside Juarez. While constantly repeating, 'Honey, its the best thing for now. And later you'll thank us.'

I drank and took pills the whole time because it sure didn't matter to my baby's health. Not anymore. Hell, in a few days Marilyn Monroe and Robert Kennedy's child would be torn apart and flushed down some Mexican sewer. As would all my hopes and dreams. The only dream I ever really wanted to live out. I just spoke to my Doctor Greenson for a few minutes. He urged me 'to show sufficient caution', whatever that means. 'And how important it was for me to feel I was part of any decision we came to. After we explored all the possibilities.'

He seemed far removed and had no idea of the pressure being put on me. And either I wasn't conveying the urgency or he simply wasn't getting it, so I hung up. Then, when Bobby flew out Saturday night, by way of a helicopter landing on the beach, I felt I wanted to knife him in the back or even better the belly, just like he was doing to me. His only passing grace was he didn't try to palm the responsibility for this child onto his brother. But the more I thought about that, I realized they both were acting as one, all the time anyway. And what difference did it make now?

Dear Red,   *April 4, 1962*

Well, I'm back from Mexico, with my womb scraped bare and my soul cut in half. I can always look at the bright side and say I'm four pounds lighter, down to 116. But I can't even try to joke because my spirit seems almost completely crushed. So much so that I tried calling The Orphan Institute right before I left. My luck, the Director doesn't work on Sundays. So my dreams of adoption have been returned to the bottom drawer. Yes, I'll put them back in action once the film is either shot or scrapped. I promise.

I'm right now in Hollywood, getting ready to make a movie. This is what I always do, so I will continue. Although this time any excitement seems to have been replaced by cold, clammy fear. I remember that John Huston often said, 'Honey, if you're not nervous you might as well give up.' So I must really be ready to fight my heart out 'cause at this stage I'm getting real scared.

All the magazines seem to be featuring Elizabeth Taylor on the cover, especially since they finally wrapped Cleopatra. I can't knock her. I mean I think she's a fine actress and a decent person. And I know how the press loves scandal (her dumping Eddie for Burton). Even more, any studio fiasco where huge budgets are blown in a matter of a few bad months. But I feel over the last year or so I've been moved somewhat out of the center of the storm, the mass market frenzy. Hard to believe, but I miss it. So I do hope this film puts me back on top. Then I can act like it doesn't matter at all and start to complain about all the attention again. And how pushy those damn reporters are.

Dear Red,   *April 15, 1962*

I must be suffering from some sort of deep-seated virus, with my front sinuses feeling like they're ready to explode any time now. I really haven't been the same since my forced trip to Mexico. On and off fevers, shaking chills, nightmare headaches-to the point I feel like a train wreck.

Beneath the surface, the reminders of what I've done with my pregnancy haunt me far more. My devil lover, Bobby, continues to call and check on how I'm feeling. We are scheduled to meet this coming weekend, so we'll just have to see how that goes. At least he continues to talk about his feeling guilty, so that's something.

In the mean time, I'm scheduled for a script conference with George Cukor, the director of my new project, and Walter Bernstein, who has been brought in to help salvage the script (the seventh or eighth screenwriter, I've lost count) which has been set for tomorrow morning. I personally liked Nunally Johnson's version a great deal and don't understand why they keep tinkering. It was quite even and favored my character, Ellen, as a caring mother and faithful wife. We're supposed to start filming on April 23, but this would indeed be a minor miracle. See, I have just spoken to Dean Martin and he assures me he's not going to be free for at least ten more days. (They're still shooting in Mexico, ugh.) Hopefully, they can hammer out the script by then but I'm not reading it through again. Not just yet. About a month ago, Dr. Greenson got Mr. Levathes, Fox VP, to hire his friend, Henry Weinstein as the producer, replacing David Brown.

Weinstein is kinder and more of an artist. He produced Tender is the Night. He also walked me around my living room one long afternoon after I took a couple too many reds and a fair amount of alcohol, combined. When I was trying to scare Arthur into being nice. Actually I did that with Poppy a few times, not 'cause I meant it, but because he was treating me like a precious porcelain vase.

This was nothing like the couple of rather major attempts to dose myself into a stupor, when I was younger and Joe Schenck had died. And I felt so guilty for treating him like shit. Those came a good deal closer to what I would call a suicide attempt, but they were still far more dramatic than true. Natasha was always around to save me. Sure I had temporarily given up much hope and thought I might welcome death, if it came. But I also knew you have to go way down past the last level of despair to truly consider ending things. I was never near that point. At my core, I've always wanted to keep living. And to be honest, I loved myself way too much. Death sure wasn't going to get me anywhere and I had things I wanted to do. Sure didn't do anything for my foster mom, Grace. Grace and my mom Gladys, drinking buddies crippled by the liquor they had to have. Buzzed all the time, screwing whoever wanted them for the night. Grace taking a bottle of sedatives and leaving a simple note. Sorry, people.

The sickness affecting me is more internal and eternal. My spirit has such severe ebbs and flows, and has done this for my entire adult life. One constant: I will pick myself up from the floor no matter how hard I get knocked to my knees. After all, its not like this is a rare point of view for me to view life from. Nor an unfamiliar body position either. Head up, knees down. Mouth open. The human receptacle, not on wheels, but in heels.

I've been seeing my good Doctor often, sometimes our sessions go on for two or three (or three or four) hours at a time. A lot of shrink bills. And a lot of tears.

He thinks I should unload Bobby right now. Give him his walking papers like he did to my baby. Start to take back control of my situation. But he (the General) has been so damn remorseful, I almost feel sorry for him, not me. Shows what a nutcase I really am.

So on with my movie and my life. If I didn't feel this great need to be the most desired woman in the world (long live Liz Taylor), I'd quit this nasty show biz life altogether. Go live in some dark, quiet cave. Find some friendly Poppa Bear to crawl up next to. And hibernate for six months. Well, maybe I'd start to get a little hungry after about a month or two. But to sleep, uninterrupted, would be glorious.

Dear Red,   *April 18, 1962*

My weekend with Bobby was stormy, but, by the end, these little boy eyes that just well up when he's sad won out. He's much more touching when he's kind and even a little insecure. These are the times I find him almost irresistible. Especially when he started to plead his case. Saying I was blaming him for a lot of things that he had nothing to do with. I told him 'you were responsible for saying you didn't want our child. That cowardly act continues to tear at my insides. To the point I can't sleep anymore.'

Then I swallowed a couple of reds, right in front of him to show my defiance. He tried to pull the bottle away, saying, 'you're taking too many of those damn things.' So I threw the bottle at him and spit the pills out on his shoes, and cried that they didn't work anymore, anyway, thanks to him. And I even tried LSD and that didn't do anything, either.

The anger in Bobby left in a flash, and he became both curious and concerned. Asking where and when. So I related my experience with Timothy Leary, the professor from Harvard. Rah, rah. For a drug guru, he sure didn't seem to know beans about pills in general, let alone upper's and downer's. And how I gave him a few Randy Mandy's, well actually we traded. I got a small dose of LSD which I swallowed immediately.

Disappointing, 'cause I really didn't get much out of it. Dr. Leary said it was a small dose but I think it was mainly due to the fact I just couldn't relax. I explained how I was having a lot of troubles on the lot and I sure didn't need a drug charge in the papers to top it off. Bobby seemed quite concerned and said it sounded like I was trying to hurt myself. And I agreed, saying most likely that was my great fascination with him.

At this he seemed genuinely upset, saying how sorry he was. That he loved me more than ever. And how he never wanted to hurt me. But I still kept turning away from him until he promised me, on his knees, he would get a divorce from Ethel, right after Jack's reelection. He begged my forgiveness and called me wife to be. And kept explaining all his problems, foremost being his Dad's stroke. He was sure Winchell's column had contributed a great deal to his condition. Writing about possible mob money from the big crime families going to Jack's campaign. Too bad Walter didn't mention a word about Judith Campbell as the go-between, the willing messenger. The snatch with the dirty cash. Anyhow, J. Edgar Hoover and Winchell have been working together forever. Well, as long as the rabble rouser's been employed as a gossip reporter, pushing his vile venom. We both agreed on that. And I said he (Bobby) still had been very mean, and terribly distant. He had a callous, insensitive streak that was even hateful.

Bobby said there were other things getting in our way, issues far bigger than either of us, like the South. It was exploding with anger at segregation and social injustice that had gone on far too long. The administration was trying to help right the wrongs but it was an uphill battle. Even their piece of shit VP was just playing for future votes and trying his hardest to screw things up.

Continuing south, Castro had to go. But he (Bobby) found himself riding herd over a ragtag army of incompetents, murderers and CIA beaurocrats, trying his hardest to make sure things got done. Including using Mooney Giancana, who he despised but needed 'cause the Mob wanted Castro out, too. And crazy Cubans, almost criminals, who didn't listen and refused to train. They really didn't belong within our borders, cause they were thieves and even murderers.

Let alone on risky missions where if they were caught, these mercenaries would quickly become a severe embarrassment, an undeniable problem diplomatically for the United States. Oh, by the way. I had probably been right warning him about Vietnam. Even though he had laughed at me at the time, just months ago in this very house. The Diem's were not what they appeared to be. The younger brother especially. So I replied I still admired him and that's why I was here. We had both made mistakes.

And he started to get frisky, rubbing my breasts and then my buttocks. And I said to be gentle, 'cause I was still sore. So he laughed and said, 'Oh yeah, who was I two timing him with?' So I pushed him away and told him 'this is hardly the time to demonstrate your keen sense of humor. And it was never witty to act insensitive. My reproductive system has been ravaged by a horrible operation. That YOU insisted I do. And he really didn't understand me at all, let alone women in general. I was the loyal lover and dearest friend, who never wanted to hurt him. And how I would never leave his wonderful family any more at risk than before I appeared on the scene. He was the unappreciative jackass. With emphasis on the ass.' So then he said he felt horrible. After which I said, 'good, then my words are working.'

He led me into the bedroom to 'show me something else that was working,' and we made up. Sort of. And I know Dr. Greenson is not going to be all that pleased, but what the hell. It is my life. And Bobby is clearly two people, so maybe that's why we belong together. Because as you're well aware, Red, I am two, too. Well, actually, three if you include my stage persona as Marilyn. Unfortunately, Bobby can only act mean or nice in real life.

His mood swings are even more volatile than a trained actress like myself, who can create a false world and escape into it in minutes. Quite an added benefit to be a thespian. Also helps talk you out of certain things like getting speeding tickets from motorcycle cops. Dumb.

I just reread my last statement and realize that in many ways Bobby and his older brother do too, that is, perform and then escape. They must be rehearsed actors, just on a bigger stage. And with a supporting cast of not thousands, but millions. Now that's a little scary. Especially as I continue to learn how egotistical and self-righteous both these guys can be.

Dear Red,   *April 20, 1962*

I had several very long sessions with Dr. Greenson. He has again and again cautioned me about diving right back with the General. Saying there were other men out there who were far more capable of loving, caring for and protecting me, rather than just themselves. In other words, because of where they were coming from, regarding their marital status (single) and business positions (normal) they were free to give me so much more. And I told him I was always looking, but I still cared for both brothers, rather sadly. Because they were great men, just lousy boyfriends. To which he concurred, saying he often felt they were a dangerous, white hot flame I could not resist darting around. The attraction was too great even if they could only wind up burning me in the end.

Then we got back on one of my constant themes, about men in general, and what a sorry lot they were. How my mother and her best friend Grace would just love to go out and 'have some drinks and have some fun' getting involved with various street rabble for an evening. Or at most a weekend. Not because they cared but far more likely because they didn't, neither the guys nor them. Then how shocked I was when her (Grace's) husband to be almost tore my clothes off before I escaped. And, of course, before him, with Mr. Gimmel, a guest at one of the foster homes, when he truly did molest me, when I was about nine. And how wretched I felt, especially when no one would believe me. I resent Grace, my true foster mom, for giving me up those many times, signing me into the Orphan's Home and then various foster homes.

While she was taking care of Bebe (Doc's kid) and making a stable home for her. Before she took me back, and we became a family reunited for a while.

Then, only to pass me off again, to reject me for the millionth time. The last time to Jim Dougherty when they moved East, forcing me to marry him. When in truth I wasn't her kid and I wasn't Doc's, either. And though I really liked Jim, as a friend, he was hardly someone I would choose to marry. Even if by some miracle it turned out we were a perfect match, which we weren't. Sixteen was way too young, especially for an immature girl, having just entered (and then quit) high school. I wasn't ready to wed anyone.

Frankly the only woman who was always kind and giving to me was Auntie Lower (Grace's aunt) and she died before I could ever really thank her. She gave me away at this first wedding and gave me a silver mirror and brush set as a gift and consoled me when the marriage was over. But she never knew of my eventual success even though she was the one who believed in me the most. And wasn't the victim of mental illness, like my mom, Gladys, who was and remains totally crippled in a state hospital.

I'm going over all this because, in the middle of one of these long sessions, Dr. Greenson decides it might be a good thing for me to actually speak to my mother. So I can tell her exactly how I feel about her and how much her absence has cost me. And how even now, I miss her dearly. So he dials the sanitarium and the attendants bring her to the phone. And I say, 'Mother, is that you? Its Norma Jeanne, your daughter.' And she's totally out of it, and calls me Jim, and asks me to get her out of this nuthouse 'cause they're going to kill her. So I ask her if she's ever wondered about me, and missed me.

Her response is total silence. I cry out, 'Mother!' She starts screaming 'someone's listening'. Repeats it a couple of times, each louder, then hangs up. So I'm holding the phone and I don't know whether to laugh or cry. 'Cause she's so hopeless, she's in a totally different world and doesn't even recognize me as a girl, let alone her daughter. But there she is, fearful of the phone and of people listening.

And here I am, in the very real world, and I'm in many ways the same. I'm mean I'm sure my phones are tapped and people are listening. 'Cause I still keep hearing these strange clicks, like metal on metal.

Recently, a long time friend and associate took me aside and warned me that my house was probably bugged. See, he's a major executive who is very well liked. They (the Mob) tried to get him to get me out of the house to insert these listening devices, because they knew we were friends. And this was months ago. Right before I took my first trip to Mexico, to get my new furniture, which by the way has finally arrived.

Anyhow, at that point I just threw the phone down, and got really angry at Dr. Greenson for dragging me back to this misery with my mom. Still, I guess that's his job, although I really don't see any beneficial way to work through this monster abandonment. Then Dr. Greenson says, 'But you already have. Look at all you've accomplished. You're a true star. And an effective social crusader, which is even harder to accomplish.' So I started to cry in earnest 'cause I just want my own little family on earth, who love me for me. Not because of my celebrity status. Or because I'm a woman with an occasional big mouth and balls.

Dear Red,   *April 21, 1962*

The preparation for this movie continues to fumble along, seemingly two steps back for each step forward. Still, we are at last almost ready to begin. I still have these damn headaches, with this foul smelling greenish sputum dripping into the back of my throat. Coughing spells, especially at night, almost choke me off. Shooting has now been set for April 23 but if I still feel like shit, I'm going to have to call in sick. I heard Dean has arrived from Mexico, sneezing noticeably so his condition will require further study. In my present weakened condition I must be particularly wary of anyone harboring a harmful bug, especially if this person is working close to me. Careful with everything and everybody.

I just realized I sound as fearful as J. Edgar Hoover wants me to feel. But, in truth, I think there's ample reason to feel paranoid, especially about the Director and his G men, much more so recently. See, there are these men, short hair, clean shaven, young and in suits, (my idea of what a special agent would look like if I were casting about) who have begun following me about over the last week or two; me in Mrs. Murray's Plymouth, they in this dark grey four door sedan. They usually park at the neck of the cul de sac, facing my house and wait, smoking cigarettes, drinking coffee, reading their newspapers. And when I pull out, they follow, always a few lengths behind.

But yesterday there they were when I left Dr. Greenson's office, and they just kept on my tail, even when I made two hard and unexpected right hand turns and by the time I was cutting through a parking lot, I was totally panicked.

So I drove to the local police station and stopped right at the main entrance. I just waited there for them to pass which they blessedly did. Then I waited around for another ten minutes to make absolutely sure they didn't sneak back.

When I finally did drive home, guess what? They were back at their old parking space, besides the cul de sac, smoking and reading their papers. And when I passed them to go into my driveway, they started to smile at me, and then honked twice like it was all a big joke.

Now when I described this bit of news to my good Dr. Greenson, he suggested that next time I go into the police station and make out a full report. So I asked him if he ever considered the men following me could be police, or even worse FBI? But I could tell from the way he nodded that he thought it was all a creation of my imagination.

That's why when I got home, I called my old friend and personal lawyer. Milton Rudin was one of those insiders who had tipped me off to the spying in the first place. He's defended several prominent mob figures during the course of his career. As well as celebrities with mob ties, including one rather famous or infamous crooner and actor from New Jersey with the first name of Frank. After I described what was happening to me, Milton said the agents had done the very same thing to him. A very obvious and nerve wracking tail lasted for over six months during a high profile trial. From his home to the garage and back. Milton was defending a certain union official who had been accused of embezzlement. After it was over, and his client got off, he had a little talk with one of the agents who he had gotten to know. He learned, confidentially of course, it was being done for one reason, to try to get under his skin. They did it all the time. Just a little nuisance to distract the person being tailed, so hopefully they make a few more mistakes than they normally would. Nothing personal.

Then my attorney pal asked where I was calling from. And when I said my bedroom, I could hear the sudden nervousness in Milton's voice. He said he 'wouldn't be surprised if they were listening in right now. Hoover loved to hit the phones, to hear what was being said about him. But of course with me, it could also be the crime boys cause I was like a lightning rod, attracting everyone, good and bad. Including the leaders in the present administration. The whole Kennedy family seemed to be very attracted to me physically. And if I didn't know it already, the criminal side was not especially happy with the Kennedy brothers because they felt they were being double-crossed big-time. And that's what he had tried to warn me about in the first place, when I was taking off for Mexico.' At this moment I swore to myself I would start carrying an even bigger bag of quarters and dimes around and making all my important phone calls from a public booth. Both the Mafia and the FBI could have taps on my phone lines. Gee, I wonder if they share tapes?

I'm being flip but deep down, I'm terrified. At the same time furious. I'm the one paying the taxes, probably more than all of them combined (the Kennedy's, the Mafia, and the Fed's) 'cause they have loopholes or just say screw it. And I haven't broken any laws. And here they are trampling on all my rights.

Dear Red,   *April 25, 1962*

Its morning. I just went out to call Bobby using this phone
booth at a gas station three blocks away. I wanted to warn him
not to call me at home. Or, if he did, to be extra careful not to say
anything that he might consider private. About us, or about White
House matters, because I really thought my phones weren't safe
anymore. Then I told him about the car parked down my block
and the men in the car who had chased me.

I asked him if he thought I was crazy, and he said, 'Not in
the slightest. Hoover tails and bugs everyone. That's why we, me
and him, have to be extra careful.' So I said I'm not really sure its
Hoover, because I was warned by a very good friend it could have
started with the Mafia. And he replied, 'If anything, it probably
started with your nut case ex- husband, Mr. Dimaggio. In case
I didn't know, he had maintained a constant interest in who I've
been seeing for years. Dumb Dago. And Joe, according to two
very close friends of the Kennedy's, had recently been overheard
at a very popular bar and grill. This was in New York City, talking
about both he and his brother with regards to them seeing me.
Which Bobby thought was really out of bounds, discussing he
and his brother's love life like that. Amounted to spiteful gossip
of the worst sort, clearly designed to dirty their reputations.'
And I replied, 'I agree, but what about mine? I don't want people
thinking I'm sharing my favors either.' So, he laughed and says,
'You know, that sounds kind of sexy.' Which pissed me off that he
seemed to care so little for my reputation.

Anyhow, Bobby feels I definitely shouldn't worry about the
Mafia. 'Main reason, he and his brother have the law on their
side and those dumb mob greaser's could just threaten people.' I
replied, 'The law's nice, but anyone who takes the mob lightly has
a few screws in their head.' He said I knew very little about this

topic. That it was almost funny because 'Jimmy Hoffa, who was a scruffy sewer rat, was going down in a matter of days and then all those Wiseguy goomba's would start to shit a brick. His staff at Justice was that close to getting Hoffa's indictment and Mooney Giancana was next on the hit list. Fat boy Marcello wasn't getting back in the country without a visa. And Trafficante better apply for a shitty shrimp boat license because his Tampa book making activities were just about cooked. A task force was being readied to close them all down for good. Before he (Bobby) was done, all these pieces of shit would be locked up in jail and you could throw the key away.'

When Bobby feels the slightest bit threatened he goes off on a tear, naming all his biggest enemies in a single breath. All of which I've witnessed before so by now I sort of know the rant by heart. Anyhow Hoover was an even bigger bore because with a simple type written statement from Jack, he could be retired to green pastures forever. 'With a ten dollar good-bye medal round his fat neck. And his lover's dick up his ass.' And they would promote Evans, who was already their point man, to the top spot and everyone in government would applaud them. And realize who ran things in the Capital and everywhere else too.

Then Bob says, 'Gee, I almost forgot. Would you be willing to sing Happy Birthday to the President at his party at Madison Square Garden? Because I know how very happy it would make Jack.' So I asked when was it?

And he answered 'You've got almost three weeks. Think you can learn the lines by then?'

So I told him 'not to be such a smartass, and if he knew the slightest thing about acting, he'd know it wasn't the lines but the way you delivered them. And I was doing the Kennedy brothers the favor.'

But first I had to get permission from Henry Weinstein and Peter Levathes, the new head of the studio in order to go. Because

I had already been absent from the film for over two weeks and I didn't want to mess up the production any more. And Bobby, meanwhile, should say he's sorry 'for behaving like a callous entitled prick.'

So he apologized, twice and said he was tired from directing all the undercover work on getting Castro. And they were so close to having their man in Cuba, Cubela, take the dictator out with some poisoned pellets, made by this genius chemist from the Illinois Med School. And this was really important to the nation. I replied 'a true genius did not use his wisdom in that manner. And taking a person out is not like taking dinner out.' 'Nice thought. Well, he'd see me May 15 and he could hardly wait because he loved me dearly. Also he'd waive the thousand dollar re-election contribution to the Democratic Party to attend because I was a special guest. Most important he knew his brother would be simply delighted that I chose to come and perform. It promised to be a fabulous night because so many stars were taking part.' And I told him I'd donate my time free, but his family was so rich they could give ten times the full amount and not even notice. And Bobby said if they started acting like that they wouldn't have a dime. So I replied, 'then, maybe you'd have to get a real job.' And he answered, 'sounds simply awful', and hung up.

Dear Red,   *May 10, 1962*

My good Dr. Greenson has finally abandoned me, taking
off for quieter pastures on a European vacation with his quite ill
wife. First to visit Israel and then Switzerland, where he went to
med school and still has many friends, doctors he trained with.
In truth, I fully understand and have encouraged his leaving. See,
he has postponed this trip which is a gift to Hildi for well over a
month. Mainly in an effort to see me through the early going with
the film. And its just not fair to him or his entire family to mess
them up any more.

I blame the studio and the fact a final script was never
approved. Which means constant rewrites, some partially good,
some totally bad, but all together a confusing mess. And based on
my old contract, I have no script approval. The studio has already
paid out several times what they're paying me to the seven writers.
Only problem, the script still stinks. Besides, how can they expect
me to work on a project where I'm being paid one third of what
Dean, my co-star and George Cukor are being paid? And they
both have full script approval. Tell me that's fair. Dean has leading
lady approval (like I'm chopmeat) while George has completed two
films in just this year. So he's already made major deposits and his
piggy bank is stuffed.

I don't understand how these executives can expect you to
pour your heart and guts out for them while they treat you like
complete garbage. Just 'cause it says they can based on some
ancient contract. On the opposite end of the world, Elizabeth
Taylor gets paid a cool million. Doing a ridiculous picture that's
over budget by twenty four million. Her and Burton both make
a million. So its really two million. The story has little meaning.
Definitely nothing lasting, that warrants being shown in such
grand fashion.

Cleopatra sleeps with Marc Anthony once and in return he gives her half the world. Egypt puts some black on their books. Rome doesn't miss it one bit because the Romans stole everything from all the other nations, whose only sin was they didn't have an equally huge army to defend them. Forget laws or what's right. I personally would have been more interested if they told it from the victim's side. The slaves in the boat or the one's fanning you know whose fat ass and ego.

I'm not trying to sound like an ungrateful bitch but I'm as big a studio asset as her or Burton or anyone at any studio. Surely I deserve equal pay if my films bring in the big profits. Not one of my movies has ever lost money and some have made and continue to make a small fortune. (Some in the millions each year.) And I continue to be paid less than many other stars and this has been going on for a very long time. So finally I said to myself, with the help of Dr. Greenson, until they pay me what I'm worth, I'm not going to knock myself out.

Meaning unless I feel physically perfect and my temperature is not elevated even one degree above normal, I'm off the set and back home to bed. Dr. Engelberg examined me twice during these last four days and he feels I need complete rest and sedation. Unfortunately I still have these damn infected sinuses, especially the ones around my eyes. So if they want my breathless Marilyn voice they can go to the recordings. I'll consider myself lucky if I can speak with my own damn voice. And presently it is annoyed and ready to say go shove it. 'Cause I still feel sick as a dog. And angry as a hornet.

I will only shoot one page a day, max, until I feel better. Too much work is damn draining. Pay me what's fair or you get a real pain in the ass, and believe me, I know how to be a pain right up those new executives' collective colons. New 'cause all the old ones are being retired, having bankrupted the company by spending so much. Colons 'cause that's what's attached to the assholes who picked them to take over and run things.

Thirty five million on Cleopatra, alone and its down the drain before it wraps, 'cause the film stinks. Same story, no story. No well paced plot, no heart, and an ending that doesn't come near soon enough.

So enter the bright young ones, more than anxious to start spending the house piggy banks on new stinkers. Whereas my films, even the less than great, always make a lot of money and they cost less on average than three million to make. So I may not know exactly what my value is as a girlfriend, or regular friend, but I sure as hell know my value as a movie star and comedian. For any performer, their take has to be based on the take of their films. Besides, they were supposed to give me a new contract, director and project approval, plus ten percent of the gross. Never happened.

I know I've got to start learning to trust my own judgment. Not rely on coaches, analysts, agents and lawyers who always want much more than I can give in return for their so called 'help'. And often the advice isn't the best for me but simply the best for them.

Meanwhile I have to get ready for my grand entrance as the chief heartthrob and queen of the entertainment business. Or should I say chief hard-on maker, center stage at Madison Square Garden. At Jack's mega bash Birthday Party which, incidentally is just one week away. So I'm getting rested up for that along with making sure my dress is ready. The very talented designer, Jean Louis, is creating it using absolutely sheer material. Plus a few clumps of rhinestones to cover the private areas. Hopefully just barely from afar. But when you're real close, you'll be able to see just about all of me. And that's a lot.

I'm curious to see how Jack and Bobby interact when they view my charms, face to face. Will they both want to fuck me together? I'm sure in their twisted minds, they'd really get off on a scene like that. Most especially cause they could rub against each other as they thrust into me.

Even more than doing it with a beautiful girl and film star, I'm sure they'd like to be doing it with themselves. In fact, I'm so sure, I'm taking Arthur's father, Izzy, to act as my chaperone.

Anyhow, I'm having major problems with Peter Levathes, who I really thought I'd like. He's not ready to give me his permission to take off to New York in the middle of shooting. He and our producer, Henry Weinstein, keep saying I missed eleven of fifteen days already and I can't miss another three because they're already too far behind schedule as is. But I've honestly been sick. And I can bring in two Doctor's notes for each day to prove it. I will definitely work the last three days, at least, before I take off.

Pay me more and I'll act more. Besides the publicity from something like the upcoming Garden show is going to be priceless. Even Paula says I'm right and she loves my acting work so far on this film, and doesn't want it interrupted. But she's a loyal American citizen and this is a salute to our country's leader.

I'm getting excited about my stage performance and have already started to rehearse my two stances. The second verse Danny Greenson helped me write. Well, actually he wrote it and I thanked him and plan to sing it to the President. I have already spoken to Peter Lawford and he plans to use Frankie Boy's rental helicopter to drag me away from the studio's grip. They'll pick me up on the set. Just like Jack's 007 hero, James Bond.

The chopper will come down outside the sound-stage. I'll just have to plead insanity or flu with shaking chills and fever and the studio can collect on the temporary sickness clause.

I may also tell Mr. Weinstein I have a particular heavy and painful period and run, bent over, out the side door. Before he can say no and run after me, I'll be airborne. In six hours, I should be back in my 57th street apartment, in New York, preparing and primping.

I was having some problems last week, when I started rehearsing my number in the Greenson's tub, before Joan gave me this simply charming book, The Little Engine That Could. Its about a broken down locomotive that tried and tried, finally managing to climb over the mountain. And the Little Engine keeps saying 'I think I can' as he chugs slowly upward. I will take my inspiring book, along with my beautiful dress, back to Manhattan. BUT for the next three days I have to be good on the set. I have some new dialog to learn 'cause they're still changing it. So I'd better start working on that. How can a dumbbell like me memorize so much? Because maybe I'm not a dumbbell after all.

Dear Red,   *May 18, 1962*

Well, tomorrow's the big night and I'm the last performer scheduled to go on. There's a real all-star line-up planned. Let's see, there's Jack Benny. I had a laugh riot with him a long time ago on his radio show, and he's going to play the violin and tell jokes. And Ella will be there, thank God, Ella Fitzgerald, who is the one who really taught me how to sing a very long time ago.

This is a completely true story. I know what you're thinking, Red. You mean I'm suggesting some of the other ones I put between your covers aren't. Well, yes and no. I'll often add a little, to sort of help smooth the ruff edges along. Anyhow, when I was first signed to Fox, they gave me two coaches. One for acting, that was Natasha and one for singing, and that was Freddie Karger. And while I was FALLING IN LOVE WITH BOTH of them and starting to have sex with each, Freddie gave me a record of Ella singing Gershwin.

So I went home and put it on my phonograph and just played it again and again. Truly for weeks on end, because I had fallen in love with her, also. Then, slowly it came to me, and I copied her rhythms, and the way she'd wring the heart and soul out of each line, each word.

Most of all her gentle, crystal clear phrasing. Words issued so carefully and vibrant. She's called the First Lady of Song for a reason. After I heard how much better I sounded, I called her to thank her. She was so modest and touched.

Well, about five years later I had leaped to stardom and I ran into her, live, at some children's charity event in LA. And I just couldn't let go of her hand. So I asked her how she was doing with her career?

She told me her recording career was doing fairly well as a jazz club artist. But she was finding she couldn't break into regular nightclub work, probably because she was a Negro. And having no success in recording mainstream music, either. There were simply no offers to do any albums or individual sides from any of the major companies.

I picked up the phone and called the Mogambo and spoke to the owner, who I've known for some time. I promised to come down each night while she played. And he hired her over the phone, for a two week gig. And she was sensational and two producers heard her and liked her enough to sign her for some major film work. And the press went crazy with all out accolades. And she's never had to play a small jazz club again.

So she's already called me at my apartment when she found out we were together again and we laughed like young school girls. I can't wait to see her. Maria Callas and Peggy Lee are also on the bill and they're both artistic giants. I mean absolute diva's. Peggy I've worked with several times and we get along great. And that young, extremely funny couple, Elaine May and Mike Nichols are doing one of their favorite routines. They're so brainy. I think its the one about the kids screwing in the car. RIGHT UP JACK'S ALLEY. Respect me, respect my ass.

So the full-house audience should be as ready as they'll ever be for my flag raising closing number. I'm on pins and needles but in a good way, because I'm going through final fittings.

I love having become the biggest star in all show business. I still look great, young and juicy. And I plan to show just about all of it off to the President and the entire nation. Can't wait.

Its morning of the BIG DAY. I just got a call from the stage director and he thought I was slated to go on in the dead middle of the show because I'm the highlight. So I told him I was supposed to sing last for that very same reason. He said he didn't know anything about that but he'd work around the schedule. And not to get excited. But even though he kept saying, 'calm down, Miss Monroe. He was willing to work with me', I got pretty loud 'cause I was nervous as hell.

I told him 'my dress alone would take over an hour to be sewn on me.' He asked 'what about a zipper?' I called him a dumb ass (I'm starting to sound like Bobby when he's pissed) 'cause there was no other way to fit in it. And my hair and make up, I couldn't go on until near the damn close of the show no matter when I started getting ready. Besides as far as I knew, and my agent also knew, I was scheduled to be the last act.

Perhaps he was getting confused by the fact Peter Lawford was scheduled to make some jokes during his MC'ing about me being late and perhaps he was just confused, period. But there was simply nothing I could do about my getting ready in any less time and 'to like it or lump it, my fumbling pubesant.' And the little jerk said I had cursed at him, which I hadn't and he hung up on me, the hysterical jackass. So now I'll really take my sweet time.

OK, Red, I have to get ready. See you after the party. I'm going to put you in between my mattress and bed springs 'cause I don't want to just leave you laying around. Not around here, in my apartment. And definitely not with all the strange sounds on this phone. I probably have bi-coastal wire tapping and shadowing. I'm just afraid they could break in now that they know where I'll be for the next eight hours. And steal you. Great feeling.

Dear Red,   *May 20, 1962*

It was a simply wonderful evening. Definitely worth all the hard work and preparation. Even the one week long nervous breakdown leading up to it, because I know I looked like the most beautiful woman in the world.

The dress was absolutely sensational. Jean-Louis worked 'till he was sweating. Him and his head seamstress, for over an hour and a half to get it just perfect. They started in the apartment and then did the final touches in my dressing room. Lucky for me, I was having a great hair day. And through all my emotional tumult, with the baby and Bobby, I've managed to lose over five and a half, really six pounds. I've also been working out with weights to get ready for this even dumber film. (There's a nude swimming pool scene when Ellen takes a moonlight dip to get Dean to start noticing her again.)

The fact is I'm really proud of my body and all the work I've done to look my very best from when I was a teenager up to the present. Weights and running and lots of swims. And I've never minded being naked from the time I was first coming up as a model. To be even more accurate, I simply love being naked 'cause it shows me off better than anything. In fact, I only feel truly comfortable being full out naked, even around my home or apartment. No shame. Just pride, and excitement. When I was a little girl, I always dreamed of lots of people looking at my naked body. In church, no less. And really enjoying the view. Men, and women, and it even made me less lonely. Well, last night it was in many ways like my dream. I wasn't in a pew but on stage, and the place was packed. Jack sat in the first balcony, so suave with his feet up, smoking another Castro special, I'm sure. And he kept smiling, his best smile, radiant and hungry for my charms.

His eyes feasted on my body, beautifully enhanced by that magical gown, up and down, like he wanted to be able to go in and out. I'm even proud of the subtle changes and little sags. Almost all young girls have great bodies but not that many women. And I remembered every line of the song, the first stanza I did twice. And the second to the tune, Thanks for the Memories and I brought it off perfectly. Standing room ovation, including from my Jack.

And then backstage, which was simply the best part, there was hysteria and everyone congratulating me. I greeted Izzy back stage and pulled him away from the mob and he gave me a simple red rose. It was so beautiful. So I kissed him on top of his head, his shiny egg shaped dome, and thanked him. Then I dragged him over to the President who kept looking at me like I was the girl of his dreams.

And after I introduced him as my former and favorite father in law, we all laughed. And Jack asked him if it wasn't a bit hard, being the father of a famous person. And Izzy said, 'What do you mean, Mr. President?' And Jack laughed and said, 'My Dad thinks mother Rose is the big reason for everyone's success in my family. And if it had simply been left up to him, all the offspring would have grown up to be simply monsters.' So I smiled and raised my champagne in a toast, and said, 'Your Dad is a very smart man. But none of you are near simply anything.' And we all laughed.

Adlai Stevenson, and Arthur Schlesinger, and then Bobby all came over in mass, obviously attracted to the birthday boy, or me and him, and the laughter.

Bobby almost pushed Mr. Stevenson, who is getting on in years, down onto his knees as he tried to elbow past him. And I helped catch the senior statesman.

Then I said to Bobby, 'Excuse, me, Mister Attorney General. But where did you learn your manners?' And Bobby gives me his cocky smile, and waved his lock of hair at me, and says, 'Mrs.

Smith's Finishing School for Bad Boys. Want to punish me?' And I smiled, and replied, 'Perhaps. I think you need one full month of maximum detention. With a sound spanking each evening.'

The next thing I know he's pulled me into a small cubbyhole and he's grabbing me. I mean he puts both his hands on the cheeks of my tush and squeezes, hard enough that I give a muffled scream. Then I squeal, 'What the hell do you think you're doing?' And the only thing he can say is how much he loves me. So I tell him, 'Frankly, Bobby, you had your chance to show me that two months ago.'

And he said he had to see me. I asked him if that was the case, why did he bring his wife? So did he want to meet on the stairs, alone, or back at the hotel, with her? Or we could do it, like in a couple of minutes, in one of the public toilets out front. Like animals and he'd probably like that the best. No feelings. No responsibilities. Just a straight 'fuck 'em, forget 'em.' Then I said, 'Honestly Bobby, you're short by at least a couple of inches and light by many pounds of character.' And he just kept repeating he has to see me. So I said, 'Bye. Got to go to your big brother's side.' And he said he'd call tomorrow and he loved me, and I told him 'he should move the damn phonograph needle, 'cause it seemed to be stuck on old grooves. And older lies.'

So while he sulked away to meet Ethel, I'm already halfway out the side door. I jump into the limo, which begins making a bee line to the Carlyle Hotel and one of the side tunnels that comes off a full block away from the entrance.

And I'm really sort of drunk, big time, from all the liquor they forced into me before I went out on stage, 'cause I was so nervous. But now I'm just having fun.

I wobble out the door and down into the pathway and I can almost do it blind folded. Which is a good thing, 'cause as I said, I'm pretty well intoxicated. Another good thing is that the fresh air seemed to clear my senses a bit.

By the time I made it to the Presidential Suite, the President had already removed his shirt and shoes. Better yet he was very appreciative and obviously turned on. And my man is so handsome and elegant I can't stay mad at him for more than an hour. Most of my anger was based on his brother and my nervousness about the live worldwide show, anyway. But its like I told him four months ago, 'You know I can never say no to you, you no good son of a bitch.'

So we get down to chatting. First he says, 'I heard you had taken LSD and did I have anymore 'cause he was anxious to try it?' So I shook my head and said, 'It wasn't anything great, anyway.' Then after starting on the bubbly, we quickly got back to Rose, his mother, who after Joe's stroke has taken over complete control of their family. And Jack starts complaining, saying his mom thinks the sun rises and sets on Bobby. When he is the President and the acting leader of the family. Anyhow, he thinks his brother is a truly great guy. 'And he knows Bobby really loves me and talks about me all the time. He also knows Bobby is really serious about divorcing Ethyl. And we, Bobby and me, should get married. And he'd be the best man.' So I ask him what about him? And he says sure he loves me, also, but unfortunately he is the President, and is very caught up in liberating Cuba. And Vietnam. Besides, he sure didn't want to start cutting in on his brother, not now. So I asked him if that meant he didn't want to screw me tonight?

And he drops his pants and says, 'Are you kidding? Bobby will understand. After all, its not his birthday.'

So then the man of the hour, our nation's handsome President, managed in less than thirty seconds to peel and tear apart what two skilled seamstresses took well over two hours to accomplish so beautifully. He rendered me naked, starting from the bottom to the top. And then he took me in roughly the same manner, which is one of his particular likes. What the hell? It was his special day. But then so was every day. In every month and in every year.

More than two and a half hours later, I get out of the limo returning me to my home port, barefooted and more than a little worse for wear. I greet my most loyal fan, who always waits for me, Jimmy Haspiel, at the entrance to my apartment building. And my hair, which originally looked like perfectly arranged spun gold, now appears to have gotten caught some place inside a jet engine. And my tits are almost coming out of a dress that is minus several seams which have been 'taken down' by my handsome lover. James looks me over, and gasping, says 'to be honest, Marilyn, you look like hell.' So I tell him 'I should. I've just been laid by the Fifth Marine Battalion'. So he smiles, uncertain, and says, 'well, as long as you had fun.' So I reply, 'to be perfectly frank, after awhile it got pretty repetitive' and we both laughed.

Dear Red,   *May 28, 1962*

I had a lot of fun on the set tonight. There was the big swimming pool scene I may have previously mentioned. Anyhow, there it was, Red. Time to test the waters of time. And as I'm sliding into the pool I take my skin colored suit off. And thank the Lord it was warm water.

Now I had already warned the director, so he had cleared the set for everyone but the essential crew. Then one of the first camera crew guys complained about the top strings on the suit, but he was in on what was planned, also. So I'm partially submerged, dog paddling the length of the pool. Suddenly the still photographers, I think there were three, begin whistling and snapping merrily away. Its a MSN (mess-in-neuf meaning a scene being shot without sound) so the camera men soon start in 'this is really great, Marilyn, and how about a backstroke and who was the lucky towel guy and could I do more of a breast stroke.' These clowns always think they're real comics, anyway. But I knew I was photographing well, because there were gasps coming from their vicinity, too.

So I come to the other end of the pool, and very slowly rise up and waltz into my robe. And I do a graceful turn as I teasingly tie the string around me and there's this sudden total silence. So I giggle and run back to my dressing room and they are all now applauding, everyone on the crew who is there, so I know we've made a big hit. Or as Joe would say, 'Hell, sweetheart, you knocked it out of the park.'

And by the next morning I was back, front page in every newspaper. This follows by about a week the news pictures from the Madison Square Garden party. There I also was page one, page three and back page, too. But just my front. My back on their back might make the paperboy blush.

Now all the columnists have begun making up supposed cute little quotes from me, adding to the excitement. Besides Life has already bought some of the photos and is coming out with them next week. So, suddenly I wasn't so washed up as was written about a few weeks ago. And the movie and studio has gotten a tremendous amount of free press and positive advertising. Everywhere people are writing how my figure looks better than ever, which it doesn't, but with good lighting, and the right people behind the lens, its still damn attractive.

Listen, Red, all of Hollywood is done with smoke and mirrors and airbrushes. At least I've got the raw materials to begin work with. And so much of everything is in the presentation.

Dear Red,   *May 29, 1962*

I just had the most troubling phone call from Bobby. Total change of heart. Suddenly I just want to die. He says we have to stop seeing each other, completely. 'Why??' Well, because his mother has expressed her disapproval. Rather severely, he's afraid. She's saying the family's reputation is at stake. News of us seeing each other, even being friends, would ruin any chance Teddy had of being voted in as Senator. And kill any chance he (Bobby) had to be elected to anything, but especially to follow his brother. And it wasn't fair to everyone who had worked for the Kennedy clan and their various tickets. Worst of all, his father's recovery had stalled because of this underground whispering.

I start to scream, 'Fair?! Your family knew about us for months. And what about my feelings? I mean I trusted you and all the plans we made together. You promised me you'd get divorced, you bastard. And you'd marry me. You swore on your knees.' And he says, 'Look, I'm really sorry but your friendship with Sinatra and his relationship with Giancana are powder kegs. Potentially political suicide. And my mother's insisting.'

'Really??' I yelled, 'I'm going to call dear old Rose, right now, and tell her about the abortion you made me have. Along with the fact I have absolutely nothing to do with the Mob, and its her children and her dear old husband, that model of improper behavior, who are all in bed together. In more ways than one. Screwing their whores and leading such a double life of deceit.' So he says, 'She knows already. Look, I'm sorry but in time you'll realize how wrong we were for each other. And you'll thank me.' So I yell, 'You lying bastard. I'll curse you every day of my life' Then I slammed the phone down. And I cried all night.

Dear Red,   *June 1, 1962*

Its Friday and today is my thirty sixth birthday. And I've just been handed ANOTHER EXTRA CRUEL BLOW. I tell you, Red, this is turning into my total week from Hell. See, I've just been notified by the studio that they plan to shut the film down at the end of next week. And it would be announced I had been fired. Still, I was not to take it personally because Mr. Levathes just wants to make an insurance claim. And this way the company will be able to get paid, especially if they say it was because I got sick and couldn't work and the project had been canceled because of my absence. And until they can find a suitable replacement, they will be paid up to six months. So they will continue to say this for awhile. Unfortunately.

Still, in Peter's view, I had been responsible, missing so much shooting time. George Cukor was in knots and didn't think he could continue working with me, ever. Now, they, Peter Levathes, who I was speaking to and Henry, the producer, who hid, didn't have to explain their actions. But they really had been given very little to no choice. And they had to show all the actors and actresses they were running a tight ship. And wouldn't kiss anyone's behind (these new grad school men are all so proper), no matter how important they think they were. And that includes me.

So I ask, 'what about my salary?' And Levathes replies, 'well, they didn't really know and it depended on if and when the insurance company writes out the check.' And I said, 'hold on 'cause they don't make films. We do. You fellows at the Studio and me.' Then he said, 'yes, but still, let's be realistic for a minute. Oh, they were giving me a nice birthday party on the set tonight. But they were also expecting me to fulfill my contract up through next Friday, when shooting would be officially closed down'.

So I told this disgusting Peter Meter, 'he was out of his frigging, proper for fucking, mind. And that was hardly the way the Studio I HAD GIVEN SO MUCH TO, starting when he was still playing spin the beer bottle at some dorm party, should start treating me.'

He replied, 'You've given us no choice and no hard feelings and they'd get back to me. When they were sure they knew what they wanted to do with the footage they had already shot. It was quite possible the project would be resumed at a later date. But bear in mind running a complex multilevel studio was very difficult. Somewhere, sometime it had to get down to the dollars and cents of it all, because not everything could be for art's sake alone. And there was something called tax quarters, that accountants use, and darn it, Fox would use them, too.'

So I'm off to my birthday party and then on to Dodger stadium, where I'm throwing out the first ball. Its a game in honor of the Multiple Dystrophy Fund. People who are really sick and crippled, most of them children. And I feel furious at these pompous executives and their behavior. Lousy shits. Well, I'll show them I'm not a good one to try to kick around. I still have my fans, the regular people who made me and love me and who I love in return. Its a lot more than those self-impressed big wig kids can say for themselves. Spoiled brats. And we'll see who needs who in the end. I hope they trip on their forked tongues. While Bobby falls on his slimy ass and slides straight down to Hell. They can all have a family picnic by the perpetual crackling campfire. Rose can serve the caviar.

Dear Red,   *June 4, 1962*

The Birthday Party on the set was bitter sweet. The crew
had a beautiful cake made up with me in a bikini and negligee
(opposite corners) and it read Happy Birthday (Suit). And it was
adorned with sparklers and one lone candle. So I blew out my
candle and I smiled, but I was so sad. Just chose to hide it. Because
of Bobby and what a miserable mess our whole period together
turned out to be. Not even a nice affair you can tuck away. Just
disappointments, one after another. Lies and hurt. And such anger.

Then I went to the ball park (Dodger blue) with Dean Martin's
young son, even though my heart was no longer in it. But I was
going, not just 'cause I had promised Dean and his people and his
handsome young man. But for all the children and adults in the
world who need medical care and can't afford it. I could never say
no to someone asking me to help them drum up interest to fund
research. Especially for the medical breakthroughs necessary to
free those unfortunates from their wheelchairs. Its such a special
pleasure to use my popularity for something noble and giving. Not
only does it make me feel loads better about myself. But it makes
everyone involved believe in the kindness of strangers, as Blanche
would say.

Then I went back to my home, where Danny and Joan
Greenson sat on cardboard boxes (I'm still waiting on my living
room furniture) and drank champagne and toasted me. Their gift
was this beautiful glass champagne flute with my name engraved
on it, so I'll know who I am when I'm drinking too much. And I
felt another wave of depression coming over me, mainly because I
don't think I can go back to work for the last week.

So stupid because I'm about to be fired no matter what I do,
and I don't want to ruin my negotiating power for later work. So I

called my lawyer friend and asked him to work it out for me, with those crack pots at Fox. And if George no longer wanted to work with me, there were lots of other directors who would.

Still I've started going to see Dr. Engelberg for prescriptions and have even received several injections of Nembutal.

I want to keep screaming. 'Don't take away my work, especially after I'm finally revved up to do the damn film. Let's go already because I'm ready. Learned my part and the lines and the basic story.' Well, it leaves a lot of free time for me to think about all my disappointments. I used to tell myself, hold on, Marilyn, because soon enough the General will marry you, like he said. But now I know that's a totally lost cause. There's other miscarriages (horrible word), including but not confined to the fact I'm just about to get a really bum wrap from my former studio. They're trying to blame me for all their production difficulties. And this is the one thing they may do properly. I didn't green light Cleopatra. I never even met Richard Burton.

Dear Red, June 10, 1962

Well, this has gotten rather ugly rather quickly. The newspapers are full of quotes from the Fox exec's headlined by Mr. Levathes stating 'Miss Monroe's firing was made necessary because of her willful breach of contract. It was like we've let the inmates run the asylum. Her numerous failures to report for photography has cost the Fox Studio over half a million dollars.' And that is why he plans to sue me for that same amount, and he may have to up that number if the studio finds it can not hire a satisfactory replacement for the part of Ellen.

Fortunately Dean got in the act, saying he had signed on to do this film with Marilyn Monroe and that was the only leading lady he or his production company will accept. And I love him for sticking up for me when all those sneaky pricks have rushed scripts off to Kim Novak and Shirley McLaine. Shirley, bless her beautiful soul, has already called to tell me she was going to tell those idiots it was my film and no one else could do it justice. And they were lucky to have me. And I thanked her and said, 'Actresses have a right to be treated like human beings, too. They treat us like dirt, and its wrong.' She added, 'Well, they like to get their feature artists involved in some project to start the ball rolling and then they bail at the first sign of difficulty.' And she was so kind and supportive. And Kim is tied up with another shoot and her whore-ticulture gardener.

To make it more confusing, I've been warned by one of my spies at Variety that the entire crew was now taking out a half page ad thanking me for getting them fired. Which really chills me to the bone because I've always had their best interests at heart.

I called Earl Wilson to say, 'I feel terribly sorry about the crew but it was hardly my doing. The Studio decided this. And I really enjoyed the brief time we all worked together. What more can I say? I hope we'll be back working very soon.'

Peter Levathes called and apologized for some of the quotes in the papers. I said they make me look absolutely horrible. Totally unreliable. And besides it was mostly untrue. And he agreed and said he had to say those things so the insurance company would kick in. So I told him to get the insurance company to act in their next BLOCKBUSTER. And slammed the phone down. I seem to be doing a lot of that lately.

Shit, this whole damn thing is getting more screwed by the day. And thank God, Dr. Greenson has returned to help give me some guidance. BECAUSE RIGHT NOW I'M SORT OF LIKE A BOAT WITHOUT A RUDDER.

Dear Red,   *June 11, 1962*

My Bobby nightmare keeps getting worse. I tried calling him at his work. He got furious. Saying how dare I call me on the Department of Justice switchboard, and I answered, 'but you cancelled my private office line.' And that little piece of shit, acting like I never warned him, says, 'Oh, right, sorry about that. But my electrical experts evaluated that line. Found it to be in danger of being bugged, or there may be something already present in the wiring. Seems they detected increased interference at the base line, or, in other words, from Brentwood.'

Then he replies, cold as a frozen snake, 'Its over, Marilyn. Peter told you and Pat told you and now I'm telling you, (and he starts to clear his throat, like he's trying to FINALIZE the painful hurt, the raw flash burning of being told you're not good enough) I'm not seeing you ever again.'

Then I reply, not screaming, but calm, like ice. 'Your dear mother is so concerned about hurting your career. My feelings don't matter. Your word doesn't matter. Guess what? I still have those letters you wrote me, the deeply in love ones written on official US Department of Justice stationary. I think I'll make some copies. Get them around to the various gossip column writers. They love a good scandal especially about a very high up government official and his whore. Or maybe I'll just call a press conference.'

His reply in this ultra strict tone, 'Nobody threatens me, you crazy bitch.' So then I slammed the phone down. Again.

Dear Red,   *June 18, 1962*

I'm writing in you in Dr. Greenson's private library, which
he also uses as his home office for seeing patients. Its one of
the few places I feel safe. He should come in soon. Actually I'm
early (a real rarity) because I wanted to stop before I arrived
here, and drive around in front of the police station to ditch any
'private eyes'. I gave myself half an hour, when my little avoidance
maneuver took only seven minutes. So I filled up the tank to Mrs.
Murray's Plymouth and here I am, waiting.

I want to call Bobby from my Doctor's study when my
doctor arrives so he can hear how hatefully the General talks to
me. I don't really know if he'll go along with doing this because
somehow it might confuse the issues, analytically speaking. And
there's some legal reason, too. Anyhow, my doctor just came in, so
I'll catch you up on stuff later.

Well, our session is over, two and a half blood filled hours of
misery and remorse. First issue, Bobby no longer taking any of my
calls at Justice. We discussed whether I should try calling him at
home. Dr. Greenson thought that it was the worst possible thing to
do. And I added, 'Yes, unless, of course I want to end it myself, me
in control of something.' He says, 'That's the exact point. All you
have to do is not call him and you've won. Cut him out of your life
and go on.'

'But' I break down. 'He's already done that to me. And it hurts
in my insides so much. I feel like I'm just a lousy piece of meat,
to be handed down from one brother to the other, to be used
whenever and however they desire.'

My doctor replies, 'You have to know you're better than all of
them. You can and will go on.'

So I nod. Then I stand up and go to the window. And I look out and start crying again. 'Yeah, I know I've better character. Better than that whole privileged group of phonies. In a way its really funny. I'm a Gemini. And I used to think I was crazy, because I knew I had these very different people inside me. But now, I've met these men, so powerful, who hold the future of all mankind in their hands. And I realize, they're just like me.' I stop, shaking my head.

Dr. Greenson prods, 'In what way?'

'Well, the good and the bad. The image, and the reality. They have their opposite sides and they can switch over in a blink. My problem, I got caught believing their speeches and forgot to judge their actions.'

My doctor asks me to tell him about my own people. 'Well, there's Marilyn Monroe, the sexy glamorous movie star everyone adores. She's no problem 'cause I created her. In Nana Karger's kitchen a very long time ago. With a little lisp and out of breath sound and a wiggle when she walks. She's funny and sweet and very sexy. Outgoing but without a clue. So dumb and vulnerable. Then, there's the real me, the ultra-sensitive little girl. The almost orphan who has nothing. And nobody. Who expects to be hurt because she always has been. Who is angry and suspicious and terribly insecure. Then my doctor adds, 'which makes Marilyn the patient take too many drugs, and drink too much champagne, and sleep with men who can only offer her a sliver of what she deserves.' So I break down and start crying again, because I've messed it all up. 'I believed in love and all I got were lies. So I chose to believe them.'

'My God, child.' At this point Dr. Greenson is almost pleading, 'There is the adult Marilyn, who very much believes in herself. A very hard working, bright person who forges ahead. This woman is a role model to millions, including me. You became a major success completely on your own. No one gave you one damn thing and you've already given back so much.'

I stop crying, shocked by his last statement. 'I still feel no one wants me as a wife. Which makes me think I'm such a failure.'

'Now that's truly nuts,' Dr. Greenson comes over and hugs me. 'You are one of a kind, which makes you feel lonely right now.' He pushes me slightly away so he can look at me, so caring. 'But you are a marvel who shows its as important to give as to take. With real beliefs you stand up for. My kids are crazy about you. And as for suitors, you have two or three extremely suitable men just dying to get closer.'

So I say, 'not in my present world. Well, maybe Jose, but he's a tad young. Or Joe, and I'll be the smart one. Hopefully not the bruised one. Or even Frank now that he's really acting nice to me. We both bear the disgrace of becoming Kennedy brother rejects. US Government certified persona non grata's. I know, two discards will never make four happys. But still...'

Then we both laugh 'cause it is a little over dramatic and stupid. We both go back to our respective places, he sitting at his desk, me lying on the sofa. He switches to the issue of my lack of security. My constant fears about my present safety.

I relate how I learned from both my publicist and personal attorney whose names I'd rather not mention. (Milton Rudin, my lawyer is the Doctor's brother in law. And Arthur Jacobs heads my publicity and just about everyone else's in New York And LA.) The two have between them many, many high level clients. No matter, I'm positive all my phones are being bugged right now. And I can see for myself that men are following me in cars.

On top of which, Bobby can act quite frightening when he gets angry. Several times going to the point of becoming threatening, when a month ago he was feverishly proclaiming his undying love. Now I get the opposite extreme.

Dr. Greenson asked if I would feel safer in an institution? And I replied, 'Oh, no. The thought of that dreadful Payne Whitney just sends chills down my spine.' I begged him not to send me away. 'For just awhile?' he added. 'Never' I answered.

And he said, 'Of course. He was just making suggestions. And meanwhile I could come move into his home, until I felt it was safe enough to venture out. Everything in small steps.'

I could feel my fears just vanish. This is one of the kindest thing's anyone's ever given me, the sanctity of his beloved and very normal family and their home as a refuge. So I started kissing his fingers, at the tips, and he says, 'Stop it. Are you hungry? Because we can gladly feed you.'

I laugh and we start to move into the kitchen through the dining area. And as we're walking in, I say, 'Getting old is sure scary business.' And he stops and turns to me, clearly astounded. 'Marilyn, you're only thirty-six.'

So I say, 'Well, yes, but I've already lived two lifetimes.'

'My darling child, I know you've been through a lot but didn't you ever hear that 'three times a charm?'

So I guess my doctors a gambler, too. And, hey Red, the dice are in my hands. Which means I do control the throw.

Dear Red,   *June 28, 1962*

I've just met with the studio heads, the very same men who fired me a few weeks ago. Now Peter wants to DRAW UP A TOTALLY NEW CONTRACT and make sure I'm really happy and ready to go back to work and continue on for decades. And they'll drop all their law suits and, if need be, find another director for this project. 'But number one, they want me to know they're very sorry for all their charges and threats and bad press releases. And, bottom line, they want to work with me more then ever. Mainly because everyone loves me.' In real talk, they're concerned about their bottom line, which means I'm their cash cow. And I'd better keep giving milk.

So, Red, you want to talk about a love/hate attitude, try explaining this loony group. Lucky I haven't been sitting on my ass, waiting for them to come crawling back. As a matter of fact, I've been furiously promoting myself onto every magazine cover I consider worthwhile. So to the world, and obviously my fans who have remained so faithful, I'm bigger than ever. The beautiful queen of film with a diamond tiara. I'm my own best promoter in Hollywood and the world, because I'm not bashful and I'm hardly a prude.

Over the last month I've done several photo sittings for major magazines. Big spreads. Including Bert Stern for Voque at the Bel Aire. At night, where I was naked and gorgeous. And, of course, the stills from the Something's Got to Give swimming pool series were recently printed in Life, and they were beautifully presented. Another shoot for Cosmopolitan was done just last week at Peter's house on the beach, and around the pool, with a few shots indoors near the fireplace. Positive stuff.

The Malibu beach house got me to thinking about Bobby and I started to cry. But after several minutes I went to the guest bathroom and washed my face.

And when I walked back out, I was smiling, but it was a little forced. Seems I've survived rather nicely to this point and no one sees me or my career as over. Especially not me.

Compared to Joe or Jose, Bobby wasn't all that great as a boyfriend to begin with. Too insecure and too rigid. And losing points each time we took a little roll in the hay. The General showed an increasing tendency to shoot his load before I could even get started. And foreplay got replaced with mind play, some of which I found impossible to appreciate. Let alone applaud. The killing of foreign leaders and the testing of hydrogen bombs so as to be ready to 'nuke' people in other lands is repulsive. Its morally wrong. Big power trips have never turned me on.

I have several times repeated to my therapist that 'the more I've become a sex symbol, the less enjoyment I find in sex with anyone. But least of all with Bobby. Most of the time, I wound up doing it just so he'd like me.' Seems I gave up any personal enjoyment in the mad attempt to snare my dream guy. Depressing but best accepted. Dr. Greenson says now that I've solidly elevated my stature to such heights (career wise), I should set my goals on more normal men to provide companionship and romance. Men who will love me for me, not for who I am to the world.

Why do famous people feel a constant need to cling to only other famous people? Probably because we're all so terribly insecure about our own real worth. Best way to check our celebrity status is by seeing who we're attracting and how high on the totem pole they are at that moment. How am I doing with the other A-lister's? Am I still in the Club? Why didn't what's her name talk to me?? What does it matter?

I'm jumping off that damn merry-go-round right now. I moved back to my own home four days ago because I realize I'm just as safe here. Besides, I can not just take over Dr. Greenson's place and disrupt his family's inner working's forever. It isn't fair to any of them. Obviously Danny and Joan and their mother. But even Dr. Greenson, who signed on to be my psychiatrist, but hardly to this great a degree. Four hours a day, even when you're getting paid full fee, is too much of a strain for anyone.

I'm worried I may also be messing up his practice, not allowing others to benefit from his knowledge. He feels he has fallen victim to the very treatment plan he initiated. Which is based on the belief this intensive program would best help me recover from the break down of my spirit. Well I'm better. Unfortunately the cost is proving to be severely draining on his spirit. Too much emotion. Too much wanting to help.

I simply have to start learning to depend on my self more to get by. I know I'm quite capable. Obviously. I didn't get this big by accident.

So my little house has become my refuge, MY FIRST HOME, especially now that all my furniture has finally arrived. Meanwhile, I still have several meetings at Fox, but I'm a lot less worried because Dr. Greenson has promised he'll help me negotiate with those hotsy totsy executives. So he's my psychiatrist, and agent, father, best friend, teacher, inspirational leader, everything but my husband. Unfortunately, I have to find one of those elusive guys on my own.

Dear Red,   *July 19, 1962*

Well, I've just returned home from dropping Joan off at
the Greenson house. Whew, I'm exhausted. I hosted a surprise
birthday party for my little sister and all her girlfriends from
school, in my back yard around the pool. Plus one lucky boy from
their class and brother Danny. It went really well, because she
had no idea before hand. I got my secretary May to send out the
invites. And I almost felt like a teenager, along with the rest of
them.

Someone put on a twist record from Chubby Checkers and
there was this lovely black girl who had no partner. So I jumped
right in and we danced up a storm. Lord knows I know how that
feels, to be odd girl out.

Joan got a lot of lovely presents and just seeing her happiness
was all I needed. I know the best gifts are when you give someone
something important and the person has no idea who or where
it came from. But next to that, giving someone you really care
about a true gift from the heart is wonderful. And Joan must
have thanked me ten times in her excitement over the surprise
and how well I planned it. The girls loved the food, and I got a
photographer from the studio to take head shots, just like they
were little actresses. It was a great afternoon and Joe came by to
drive some of them home. The Clipper is as popular with the girls
as the guys. Danny acted like he was the greatest thing ever. And
Joe gave him one of his signed baseballs.

On to business. I've continued to have meetings and phone
conversations with the Fox exec's and we're moving ahead with
negotiating a new contract. I'm supposed to have my salary more
than doubled, to two hundred fifty thousand, which I know is an
awful lot. That part's more than fair. Still its not the greatest movie

and I don't want to continually be caught up in doing schlock. I'm holding out for more creative control. Because I need to do more serious (let's say important) works, at least aim in that direction.

I still get my regular percent on the back end, but so far I've never seen a dime from that provision. It seems to take years and the accountants like to add in all the incidental charges, like country club and escort fees for the big wigs at Fox and who knows where else. With MARILYN MONROE PRODUCTIONS I get a substantial check each month.

I spoke to Paula who is roaming around in Europe, going to various workshops, about possibly returning. So far she's been way more of a hindrance on this project. No director is ever thrilled with her input, in any form. Most consider her a time consuming and unnecessary obstacle. And in some ways I am starting to agree. It pays to prepare.

Eli told me I was a better actress and clearly seemed to be having more fun before I ever met the Strasberg's. Maybe I should go back to my roots, find solid ground, and branch out from there. I'm pushing on, and have even managed to go out with Frank a few times, which was rather nice. And at least it keeps me in the papers, while we bicker over little things, like the booze and the pills. Old themes, old problems. But getting more controlled and less harmful. Still, without any, I just can't sleep.

Dr. Greenson has continued to be marvelous and without him, I'd be in severe trouble. I've been seeing him almost every day, along with Hymie, who prescribes my sleeping pills and occasionally gives me shots. I went to Cal-Neva once and stayed in my old suite but without either of my two boyfriends (big joke), it was depressing. Although the mountains are much cooler and we've been in a hot spell. And Frank tried his hardest to keep me amused and happy.

I've also been doing this interview with Life about fame. They assigned me one of their best young writers. Richard Meryman. So we've been going back and forth with that. Because with regards any and all questions, I need time to think about my answers. He was amazed when I asked for a list of his key queries before we even met.

But I like to prepare and don't like to be surprised in that way, mainly because I've been tricked before. And I wind up sounding stupid or self absorbed or evasive. Of course. Reporters want you to speak about you, not world conditions or politics or the economy. So I need to mull the issues over since I am going on record.

I saw a picture of Arthur in the paper with Inge. She looks big as a house, the lucky stiff. Well, he's sure not coming back. I abused him far worse than any of my other lovers, sometimes even surprising myself with my cruelty. Dr. Greenson says I have a lot of anger buried inside me and its obvious he's absolutely correct there.

I know now Arthur didn't deserve my wrath. He was right about all the pills, too, but I have tapered considerably. Actually I'm down to two reds a night which is near my all time low. So maybe I don't need electro shock, after all. I don't want my whole body straightened out. I just want to feel a little more sure of what I want and how to get there.

Dear Red,   *July 25, 1962*

Half an hour ago, Peter Levathes came to my house with a brand new studio contract in his hands, and a limp tail between his legs. He apologized profusely and blamed the pressure on Mr. Skouras stepping down, and some other major mistakes the studio had made along the way. Certainly with regards several big budget projects, plus the unexpected popularity of television, putting all the studios in deep financial trouble.

But he was offering me three hundred thousand plus my ten percent on the back end. Hal Kanter had already begun rewrites, which I could review and suggest changes. Dean was also fully on board. Most important, he, Peter, had been an idiot and coward to fire me, so he would at least be a man now and try to rehire me, himself. And he was sorry for everything. And they, everyone at the Studio, one hundred percent wanted me back and would be happy to have me consider the new agreement. And he would tell the papers he and the studio had been rash and wrong. Besides he had been misquoted badly in several of the tabloids. And we would work together on the new, more serious material I wanted to try. He would help in any way he could.

So I thanked him and took the papers and said of course I needed my attorney to go over them before I signed. Mainly because, as he surely remembered, I had been an inmate in the assylum. BUT YES, I WAS HAPPY TO RETURN TO WORK. I applauded his character, especially being able to say he had been wrong. Moving forward, I think Jean Negulso (I can't even begin to spell his name right but I loved working with him on Millionaire) would be a splendid choice to direct the film and Peter agreed and said he'd begin sounding him out. So we shook hands and hugged before he left. And I felt really wonderful, like some giant weight had just been taken off my shoulders.

Then I went into the kitchen and apologized to Mrs. Murray because she, too, had not escaped my wrath.

Then I called Paula in New York (she already traveled back home in preparation) telling her how sorry I was to have ordered her away and we were back in business. And I missed her. She's a pain in the ass but she's also a good friend. She'll be back in LA by Tuesday. So suddenly, things appear to be looking much better.

Dear Red,   *July 31, 1962*

It was simply the worst weekend I've ever experienced. A total nightmare that kept getting more and more out of control by the hour. I'm so mortified. I'm writing this down in the solace of my bedroom because I want to go over it with my doctor who I can't see until four. The curtains have been closed and the black screens have been hung over them. That way no one can possibly look in and see what I'm doing or thinking.

Not only did I totally disgrace myself but I have left myself vulnerable to blackmail of the worst sort. At the hands of the very people who are experts in this sort of manipulation. The Syndicate, the Mob, the Mafia; men who laugh at scruples and call the people that live by them saps. Horrible animals who know how to use this sort of thing to take down their enemy and keep them under their control. I was stupid enough to get in their way and fall into their trap. I'm now a mess of total confusion and anger at those who led me down this path. And feeling almost powerless by myself to stop the horrible slide that this disgusting weekend became.

I'll start at the beginning. Isn't that what Dr. Greenson always asks me to do? I was led into this degrading sex orgy by Peter and Pat Lawford, who I never thought would do anything so merciless. So spiteful. I trusted them, well, really her, the President's sister. And most assuredly I never thought she would just abandon me when I was so totally defenseless. To all those disgusting pigs who just devoured me alive, drugged out of my mind, and naked, in the bedroom, correction, on this gross round bed with an overhead mirror at Suite 52 at Cal-Neva.

The one who put everything in motion was Frank Sinatra, probably the most two faced snake who has ever lived, the little pied piper of vice. Especially when Mooney is around. Then he becomes a totally evil puppet. But I've known this for years. Its my fault, because I didn't belong there in the first place. Once it got to that point I couldn't stop any of them from using me, physically, in any manner they wished.

The attack, which came in waves, coupled with their increasing disregard for me, made the humiliation so much worse. The lousy bastards! That they acted so roughly had to have only one purpose. To leave me broken and defenseless. My insides are so raw I just want to crawl into a ball and hide. Now, this very minute, because I'm so ashamed.

It started here, in my bedroom, about two in the afternoon on Friday. Frank came bounding in with Peter in tow, both acting like I was their best friend and we were the three musketeers of cheer. And asking if I wanted to go to Cal-Neva Lodge for a weekend of fun and frolic? Now, for the last month or two, Frank has been very kind and concerned about me.

As I previously may have written, we had gone out again, dating and making love, once here and once in Frank's little palace in the hills. We had even discussed the possibility of getting married. It would be a union of the king and queen of Hollywood and most important, should drive the damn Kennedy's straight up a wall. Or in Frankie's snappy Hoboken delivery, 'We'd have our hands on a news following that would rival the Prez, himself. And that little shit, Bobby Double Dealer, would be on the receiving end of a little bad press neither he nor his big shot family could control.'

So I guess you could say we were bonding in hate and a need for revenge which is never the best reasons for anything. But what the hell, Red? We are still just regular human beings. If anything, more vulnerable, not less. Because we're used to people being nice and kissing our asses, not grinding us down, using us and then tossing the bones away.

I said I didn't want to go because I had a lot to do. Besides feeling so damn tired, maybe coming down with the flu. I was pretty much in a do nothing but lay around and feel sorry for myself mood, anyway. And I was hoping to read my new contract and the recently revised script. Call some friends like Jeanne. Take a long bath. Frank starts to talk me into it, or at least tries to, saying 'com'on, beautiful, it'll be good for you to get away from this house, but especially this bed room which is so damn depressing.' Hell, it gave him the heebie-jeebies and he was in a great mood, anywhere, any time.

Maybe I did need some sunlight and fresh air and a change of scenery. Then Frank, probably sensing my inner wavering, took it up a notch, saying, 'But most of all to show that half pint zero talent drip he wasn't going to keep upsetting you. Not one minute more. Hell, Bobby was just a two bit imitation of his big brother and Dad, anyway. He sure wasn't worth getting so worked up about.' Then Peter chimed in, adding I should go out just to show him I could enjoy myself with out him around. Take in a show, (Frank was going to sing to me), play some craps, have a nice, relaxing weekend.'

I said I definitely didn't want to go alone, that is with only the guys. Frank says, 'That's no problem. Pat and maybe one of her cousins should be joining us.' Then Peter calls his wife and says, 'Hi, Pat. Marilyn doesn't want to come with just us guys. We need you.' Then he hands the phone to me and Pat starts in. 'Please come, honey. It'll be a special favor 'cause I don't want to be the only girl and you could keep me company. And it sounds like fun. Frank has promised to fly us up to San Francisco on Sunday on our way home. There was a marvelous new spa that specialized in mud packs and naturally heated whirlpool baths and tandem pair massages. And she would love to treat me. But Frank would probably cover that too. The two girlfriends would top off the weekend being really pampered. And then Frank would fly us back.'

So I said I'll think about it and get back to her in an hour and I hung up. Then I asked Frank if he had agreed to fly us up to

Frisco and he said, sure. The place was terrific, run by a skin doc, and a health guru and some fancy diet guy and the whole shebang would be on him. Besides Mooney was coming up to the lodge. He was smart, especially on ways to fight back when you're being pushed around. He would have ideas on how to deal with the brothers.'

So I replied I could always use a good teacher, but Mr. Giancana scared the hell out of me.' Frank reacts like I've just given the finger to the Chief Angel in Heaven, and says, 'Oh, no, sugar. You got it all wrong. Mooney is an absolute prince. Wouldn't hurt a fly. Besides, he (Frank) knew he (Mooney) really liked me alot, and only wanted to do what was right by me. Making sure no one took advantage.'

Now both Frank and Peter start grabbing both my wrists and pulling me up to my feet. So I slowly walked over to the closet and began to pack an overnight bag with some slacks and a few sweaters.

Then I went to my night stand to grab a half filled bottle of reds, along with my new small inspiration book, The Little Engine That Could and threw them in, and zipped the bag.

The next thing I know I'm sitting on a plush sofa in Frank's plane, drinking champagne as we take off. The actual flight is like 34 minutes, and I take a long nap after we land. So by nighttime I'm feeling a whole lot better. Refreshed and happy to have made this decision.

I shower and brush my hair out. I do myself up real nice, and put on this simple white knit dress because it was somewhat chilly that evening, even though it was summer. We were going to all meet in about an hour but by this time I'm just famished.

I call Pat's room and she's feeling the same. So why wait? She's coming over to get me. And after borrowing a beret for her hair, and admiring the way my dress fits me, we're ready. Then we wander over to the casino, hungry, and looking for a little entertainment.

As we enter, Skinny comes running over and kisses both of us and I say we're a little hungry. Skinny says he'll get us both a cheese and shrimp platter along with a few drinks to warm us up. I ask for cold vegetables instead of the cheese, simple rabbit food. Skinny laughs and says you beautiful broads are always on a diet. Only the ones who should be, aren't. Then we start playing the slots. In about half an hour, we're ready to dine. But the two drinks they gave me went straight to my head and I'm already feeling no pain.

We wander into the restaurant area and are seated in the back, at a large round table, me and Pat, along with Frank, Peter (who is already pretty loaded), the always stylish Johnny Roselli, and Mooney Giancana, who has just flown in. The latter pair are both dressed to the nines, custom suits, silk ties, white collared shirts with stripes below. (Mooney's black, Johnny's blue).

Two young soldiers stand guard at the entrance to the annex, tough looking goombas with huge bulges at their waistline. And smaller ones under their sport jackets top pockets. Skinny D'Amato keeps coming over to make sure we have everything we need.

I had the fish, freshly caught tuna flown in from wherever, along with Dom Perignon, three bottles in our bucket.

Well, after the waiters stopped buzzing around, we were ready to talk. First we discuss my new contract and my old film and how funny Dean can be after having a few drinks. And how originally Jerry Lewis was supposed to be the funny one. And that's how they worked it when they were a team. But it turns out the really talented one was Dean 'cause he can sing, and be funny. As well as act. I explained how pleased I am to be going back to work with him. Especially since he stood up for me when the studio wanted to fire me. The same way I would forever more cover Dean's back from attack.

I've always been fiercely loyal to my friends. Especially those who have stood up for me when times got tough and I needed help. These are extremely important character issues to me.

So, a little tipsy, I chimed in 'Yeah, Dean showed me how a real man should act. Not like that scared little rat, Bobby, who turned his back on me when I needed him most. After using me like some cheap ping pong ball.'

Pat reacts like I threw a hot coal in her lap. She throws her napkin down and leans forward. 'That wasn't fair. Her brother did love me. But mother said he had to break off the romance because it was interfering with her husband's recovery. Bobby had no choice 'cause Daddy was fighting for his life. Rose and Bobby knew about loyalty. And I sure wasn't winning any points with any of the Kennedy's by speaking out, even if I felt disappointed.'

I told Pat to open her damn eyes. 'Bobby promised to marry me, again and again. And she was the one who told me how much the family LOVES me and wants him to divorce Ethel. And then I find out she was the one who introduced Jack to Judith Campbell, the twat with the turn-stile. (Frank let me in on this news a couple of weeks ago.) How could she do that to me? Or Jackie?' She said that was ridiculous and simply untrue. I was acting crazy and she was always my good friend. Besides, she would never sanction improper behavior by anyone. But especially by any of her men.

I reminded her that she'd been recruiting girls for her father for years. And I knew personally that her place on the beach often resembled a fancy cathouse. 'Because I was one of the pussies. So were you being loyal to your dear mother when you arranged dates for Daddy?'

Pat stood up and threw her napkin in my face, saying she was leaving me to my own devices and calling me 'an ungrateful, lovesick fool. I was acting like I had never heard a line from any guy. And I should never have believed him, and I was either completely naïve, or a total dunce. And I could just go to Hell.' She then ran out, leaving me with her drunk and stoned husband and the others.

Peter was by this time leaning precariously to the right, almost falling off his chair. Next step was the floor. The others, Skinny, Johnny, Sam and Frank had lit up Havana cigars and when I asked where they had gotten them, they all laughed. Johnny and Sam, almost together, replied 'Junior'. So I asked, 'which junior?'

And Johnny says, 'Santos Junior'. So I said, 'I still don't understand.'

Mooney puts his arm around me and draws me to his toned body. Puts his free index finger to my lips, then replies, 'Better keep this quiet from your boyfriends or I'm going to be pissed. But Trafficante and Castro are back in business.'

I'm shocked. Bobby's been telling me how the administration was using the Mafia to continue their assault on Castro. Santos Trafficante Jr., the big Mob boss in Florida and Cuba, had been rehired by the CIA and was their secret ace. So now it turns out he was a double spy. I shrugged and said, 'Wow. No wonder Fidel's still around. Well, it serves them right.'

Mooney made a slight grimace which made me shiver. 'Hey, with these fancy Ivy Leaquers, you got to cover your ass and then some. Sneaky bastards love the double cross. I hope you learned that much.'

I reply, 'I have no illusions. But I sure wouldn't mind getting back at them a little.' So Sam smiles and says, 'Kid, that's already in the works.'

I didn't like how that sounded, especially coming from him. And even after I prodded him several times, he never did tell me what he meant. So I got really drunk and took so many reds, I lost count (Sam calls them 'happy pills' and skinny brought a huge bottle to the table, maybe a couple of hundred.) I no longer gave a shit. I was flying.

They kept asking me about what I had to blow the whistle on either brother. I told them my best stuff were fifteen love letters from Bobby on Department of Justice stationary. Couple of shots later, I add 'I got a short tape of Jack and me in the shower.'

And, of course, my diary. But I don't want to think about that or say anything about you to them. Because if they got their hands on you, every scribble I've written in you would be broadcast around the world, proving the brothers were, at the least, immoral family men and dishonest public servants. Sure people would also say that spaced out whore got what was coming to her, fooling around with American royalty. So we'd all lose. But I already had.

Well, anyway, after I was totally polluted, I remember Frank and Johnny Roselli holding me up and leading me back to my suite. By way of the parking lot. Which I tripped over one of the curbs. I was so buzzed I thought I saw Joe up on the cliff in the distance. Then I saw the open cabin door. After laying me on that round bed, and undressing me, they both left.

Sam entered, came over and sat down, and just started rubbing my back, up high where my neck ends. And then he made love to me, I think. Followed by Johnny Roselli, him I remember 'cause he was hung, but at least he tried to be gentle.

Then Frank came in with this horrid flash camera and started taking pictures of me with Johnny and then Skinny, having sex. Then Sam brought this girl in. She was black and big, close to six feet tall, and she was naked. With pointy tits and a huge bush. She started to give me head, and I panicked 'cause it was my worst dream, to be a confirmed Lesbian, especially with that camera nearby. So I fought her off, pushing and kicking, and they were all laughing. All but Sam. He just shook his head, like he didn't want to upset me and felt bad about what had happened.

He said, 'Sorry, kid. Seeing's how Sunshine got you all riled up, we'll get her the hell out of here. And we'll let you grab some shuteye.' So they all left. And I was able to close my eyes and sleep.

But sometime during the night, first Frank and then the two goombas came in, and they all took me together, and were particularly brutal. I remember the flashes of the camera and the painful pinches in my most sensitive areas. But by then, didn't even matter.

One of them, the youngest, saw my little reader about The Little Engine on my chair. He went over and pointing at the cover, started to laugh. Said 'I was the little engine 'cause I was pulling my own train.' Then he held the book up and they all started laughing like this was the funniest joke ever.

Saturday I rested in my room, and I didn't come out all day. No one except the waiters from room service saw or talked to me. So by Sunday morning, I'm ready to leave.

Pat comes to my room. No apology, nothing. She sees how shitty I look and says, 'dear, you simply must get some rest. Why, you look dreadful. So should she cancel the plans at the spa?'

I shook my head so angrily, looking daggers. 'You bitch of a bitch. You dumped me on those pigs. Do whatever the fuck you want.' Pat started to turn back to the door. I followed her. 'I hope your drugged up husband gives you the clap. And your dear Daddy swallows his tongue and drops dead.'

Needless to say, we didn't talk on the way back to LA. Not a word. The plane touched down at Santa Monica Airport before going on to Frisco. I got out and didn't look back. Not once. I closed my teary eyes, stepped forward and prayed for a sudden ice storm.

The limo took me back to my home where I soaked in the bath for two hours and scrubbed myself with one of those stiff nylon body brushes until my skin was raw. And I threw up two times and cried for hours.

So here I am and its Monday and I've been writing for quite some time. I'm still waiting for my good Doctor to get free from his other patients so we can talk this one over. Its almost noon and Frank called to say he was sorry.

He wanted to make sure to show me the film from his camera. Prove he'd destroyed it this morning. And I told him to shove it up his ass and slammed the phone down.

Dear Red,   *August 1, 1962*

Its Wednesday afternoon and I'm once again waiting to
go over to Dr. Greenson's home office. In my safe bedroom, on
my safe bed, with the shades drawn. Writing in you, Red. So
far our sessions PO (that's post orgy) have been relatively quiet
and uneventful. I haven't described everything that went on
because I'm still extremely embarrassed. But he's got a basic idea
of what went down (me). And we continue to touch upon my
debasement.

It started Monday, in his home office. When he asked me
about my weekend, and I said 'it was bad, really ugly. They gave me
drugs and got me involved in this orgy.' And then I said nothing
for a while, just shaking my head at each little memory running
through my sub-conscious. Finally I said, 'but Mr. Giancana
thought it was a good idea, to spill the beans. And call a press
conference and tell the truth, the whole truth about Bobby and his
brother and just let the chips fall where they may.'

My Doctor cautioned me against dropping this bombshell,
saying I would be accusing the two most powerful people in the
country of severe misdeeds. Besides the fact I was a star and my
fame would greatly magnify the fallout from these charges. And it
may have a severe effect on my career, also, although we both sort
of doubted that. After all, I was clearly the victim.

We started talking about being a famous person. See, at the
same time I'm fighting for answers about how I allowed myself
to be used for so long, I've also been doing this interview with
this really nice young man, Richard. I may have mentioned him.
Anyway, its the series for Life. And the topic is Fame. We've been
discussing several things for the article. Like what I've learned
through the years about being so well known by so many people.

I finally worked it down to, 'There's a very bad side, that goes along with the admired part. You run into human nature in all its rawest forms. I wonder if its worth it, if it makes the people you care most about just treat you like dirt.' Of course I was referring to Bobby first and foremost as the dirt disher outer. And I've continued to mull over why he's become so angry with me. Probably because I will no longer do exactly what he says. He always acted like I was dumb, I mean lovable but stupid. Well, its not my fault I had such a poor education. The world took a pinup and made me the symbol of love, a goddess. So because of what I appeal to, he wanted to use me sexually. But he had to get over his Catholic guilt by saying he was in love. So he saw me as nothing but a warm receptacle. Well, I am a human being. Maybe all the Kennedy's think of women in those terms.

The word goddess is all messed up anyway because there is only one God and Moses and Jesus proved that thousands of years ago. So it is a major insult to the real BOSS. Maybe that's the reason the women who have held the title for even a short time have terrible lives or a lot of unhappiness.

Anyhow Richard wrote down all his questions about two weeks ago, and then I've met with him, this will be the third time and I speak into a mike hooked to a recorder and answer these basic queries. So another big one is what would happen if for some reason, I was no longer famous. What would I do then? After a good deal of thought, I answered, 'I'd definitely like to go back to producing films, like when I was with Milton Greene. Because I think I have a real ability to spot good scripts and I know what I like in a story.' Richard then asked, 'Well, what type of movies would you like to do?'

I answered, 'Lots of different types. Well-written comedies and inspirational stories about people fighting huge odds. Stories based on courageous women doing heroic things, and stories highlighting social injustice, making the audience want to help correct the problem.

I'd also like to try directing, probably a light short piece to begin with. I've been around sets and actors for a pretty long time by now. I definitely would know how to talk to everyone. I also know what actors and crew people need to hear to do their jobs well. Besides, as a woman, I'd sympathize with someone's problems on the set much more than the average guy would. Treat each of them like I always wanted to be treated. I had no choice but to turn to Paula. They'll be able to turn to me.

Would I feel bad about being just a regular person? I would feel bad for at most a few days. The only thing I ever wanted to be was the best actress I could. Never so well known. Certainly a better performer than I had started out. So if I was no longer famous, what the hell, at least I had it and lived it for a while. Actually, I had a very good run and what more does anyone have the right to ask for? Besides, it never warmed my bed or made me happy. Just got me a good table at some dumb restaurant.

Maybe this would be the very best thing for me. Cause I could marry an ordinary guy, who would love me for me, not because I was Marilyn Monroe. And we'd adopt some kids and grow old and fat together. I'd finally be content.

Jose Bolanos just called. He's coming into the States next weekend and I'm really excited. We had such a great time in Mexico City, and I do mean great. And on the weekend he came up for the Golden Globes, he was a perfect companion. A lot of fun to be with and just plain nice. He's such a considerate, kind man. The main reason, he doesn't care in the slightest what I do just as long as I do it with him. He grew up in a big family and would love to have his own or adopt or whatever. He tried to tag along when I went to the Mexican orphanage. When I came out, his smile lit up all day because he loves kids. He's also a terrific writer, and he's won some major prizes in Mexico. And he's so young and intent on living life.

Maybe we'd choose to live down there, away from the hoopla. He keeps telling me how much he loves me and how wonderful he thinks I am. Nice to be treated nice. I'm getting to the point where I think I'd really like that. Like it? I'd love it. I deserve to be happy and feeling loved does that to me.

Not because of my success but because I'm a good person. So Jose may just save the day. We could work together on a lot of things because he's already a skilled and sensitive director. One of the new things I do want to try is Shakespeare. Probably start with a small act on a small stage and go from there. Larry, when we were on the set of The Prince and the Showgirl thought I could do it. And if Olivier thinks I could develop into a great stage actress with hard work, then I should give it a shot.

Damn, there's the doorbell. And Mrs. Murray is out food shopping. Well, better go see who's there.

Shit. It was UPS delivery. A small package of hate. Bobby just returned the tiger I gave him. The one I christened with my own juices when we first began seeing each other. No note. Nothing. The son of a bitch. The lousy no good son of a bitch!

Dear Red,   *August 3, 1962*

Just as I was getting ready to leave for Dr. Greenson's office the phone rang. Like a crazy dream, it was Bobby. Suddenly he was very sorry and he was coming to see me this weekend. I told him he's crazier than a bedbug and I can't live with an off again, on again relationship with anyone. Let alone someone who could be so cruel and mean-spirited. He had gotten it right the first time. We should just call it quits and go our own merry way in completely opposite directions. And best of luck to him and to both of us.

Unbelievable, he starts pleading with me to give him one more chance. Almost crying as he relates how badly he feels and how we'll work something out. We simply had to. I finally had to tell him I had a medical appointment and had to go. Bye, and slammed the phone down.

Now, my doctor feels I should cut both brothers out of my life at once. The two of them have been playing a vicious tag team which makes it even more harmful to me emotionally. And I told my doctor, 'in their phony Ivy circles they're willing to pay a bundle for a kiss and a hump but five cents for your soul.' Which, of course, is exactly opposite my value scale.

I finally realize I have to go forward with what's important to me. And screw everything else. He (my Doctor) says he has never seen such a deliberate pattern of abuse, because they're both more than willing, really happy, to share me. Makes the whole thing far worse. And I agree, no if's or but's. I'm tired of being the family fuck doll.

I've also been seeing Dr. Engelberg, too much I'm afraid. He's my G.P. and over the last two weeks, he's given me several shots of Nembutal to quiet me down. Which it does but the rebound is murder.

I feel I'm being constantly spied on. Along with my phones being bugged where ever I go. I was visiting my best friend Jeannie Carmen, in her apartment house and I heard the click on her kitchen receiver. That familiar metallic click that says someone's listening in now seems to be following me around. I swear, sometimes I feel I'm coming to my wits end, its so out of control. But I have my profession and my fans and I can't disappoint them. So I think I will listen to my good Doctor's advice and cool it with both the Kennedy men. Flush is a better term.

The canceling of the General's private line and the return of my gift tiger and, worst of all, the abortion of our child, even if the doctor's report said it was a simple uterine polyp. (Lately I don't trust the doctors or their reports.) Everything says this man is not for me.

And if I can't conceive properly, so be it. I'll adopt. Hell, I don't even have to be married to do that. Although I'm thinking about Jose more and more. He's five times the lover that Bobby is. And he's in the same creative field as me but slightly different. Sure, a few times I think it all isn't worth anything. I should just put my head in the oven and turn on the gas. But almost immediately, I find myself getting really pissed off. Who the hell are they to make me feel that way? If I have to fight for my right to exist, I will fight tooth and nail. Do I want to hurt the people who have delighted in hurting me? Oh yeah. Will I?? Don't think so. That way, it will just keep on going back and forth. And its not me.

Dr. Greenson feels my best revenge would be to meet an honest normal fellow and get married and together we'd just ride slowly off into the sunset. Away from all my over privileged super rich super powerful lovers, who treat me just horribly. I need to try something different. My good Doctor feels Jose could be someone

I should continue to get interested in and he would very much like to meet him. See if my young director checks out from across the doctor's desk, from his vantage point. Which really means anyone but Bobby.

Joe called last evening and then he came over. When I gave him a quick rundown on what occurred last weekend at Cal-Neva, he became extremely upset. Said I didn't have to say any more. He knew something was up because he had talked to Jeanne Friday afternoon. By that night, he had driven up there to rescue me but the private police wouldn't let him on the property.

So it was Giuseppe up on the cliff at Cal-Neva. When I stared along the skyline as I was walking across the casino parking lot. My protector, unable to swoop down, and carry me away.

Maybe Joe could become a good husband, if he stopped being so damn possessive all the time. To which he answered, 'You do realize that's part of caring, right?' Which is true but upsetting. Because I never want to feel I'm just someone's property. Its way too suffocating.

One good thing, I feel my sinuses are beginning to clear. This is a very important thing 'cause I'm starting to feel better. Inwardly stronger and healthier. And I can now see how very much they were bothering me, continuing to shower bacteria and bad toxins into my system. I think I'll call Ralph, my masseuse, and have him come over.

My neck muscles are so tight I can't turn my head. Most of this has to be from nerves, plus exhaustion. See, I've also gotten two extremely hostile phone calls the last two nights.

From some shrill crazy woman saying, 'This is a warning, whore. Better leave Bobby alone. Or you (meaning me)'ll be sorry.' Now that I've declared myself free, even these threatening calls don't bother me much. I'm a new woman and I like the feeling. Because everyone will soon see I'm through with him. A little man with a mopsy hairdo and a crooked tongue and a split personality.

So it seems I'm ridding myself of toxins that were taking everything out of me. My sinus infection and my heartache 'caused by falling in love with the wrong man, or wrong men, from a terribly right family. Looks, charm, smarts. There was only one thing missing. That's honesty. One evades, the other lies through his eyeballs.

Dr. Greenson feels all the Kennedy men are in competition with each other, and not in a healthy sense. Jack wants to outdo his father by dating the most glamorous movie stars and beauties, thank you. And Bobby wants to outdo his brother by getting me to fall in love with him.

Which he did by constantly telling me these total make ups about marrying me and having children together. Until I finally believed him. Then he slowly pulled the rug out from under me, in a torturous campaign to break down any resistance. Clearly believing that once this was accomplished, then he could do absolutely anything he wanted with me. I'd just hang on. Like some snail with a broken shell.

You know me pretty good by now, Red. I'm a hell of a lot smarter and tougher than Bobby ever imagined.

Hardly one of the classic Kennedy women whose greatest virtue is the ability to tolerate an endless stream of abuse, while pretending to look the other way.

The male double standard of being able to do anything they want, when they want, makes us women second hand citizens and second hand people. And we will keep ourselves that way, probably forever, if we do not speak up and stand up for each other. Not just be happy its not us this time around.

Now if the brothers want to cheat and screw around, I've had as much practice as any guy. I'm better equipped and can on occasion be multi-orgasmic. I can match up and even come out on top. I just choose not to any longer. And I definitely choose not to with them. Finally, its over.

Dear Red,   *August 4, 1962*

This Saturday is becoming an all time horror show. Ten in
the morning, Peter Lawford arrives. No, he didn't wake me. Not
by a long shot. I'd already been up for hours because of a constant
nightmare, the one where I'm a little girl and I'm being chased into
a bedroom by that horrid sicko, Mr. Kimmel, the child rapist. With
his fly open and his fowl organ jutting out. And he attacks me, first
using it as a club and AFTER, my foster mother slapping me when
I try to tell her what happened.

That other horror, this one real and in the present, that angry
horrid lady who's been threatening me about Bobby called again.
But the second time was almost comical because I had already
been up for hours. So I told her, 'Look, hon, I already gave up
on that phony. See I need my men to have he-man sized pricks,
otherwise they're not fucking worth shit to me. Oh, Bobby's kids
are from eight different red neck cocks, 'cause he can't even get it
up.' So she hung up. She calls me a whore, then I'll talk like one.

Anyway, I put a call into my lawyer, dear Milton Rudin, to
see if he can somehow trace the caller, so we can make her, or
him imitating a her, stop this incessant annoyance. Then, still in
a tizzy, I made the mistake of telling Peter about her. So Peter, the
perpetual Kennedy ass kisser, starts giving me a lecture about how
Bobby's been under a very heavy strain and how I shouldn't be
putting too much pressure on him to stop anyone or anything.

Then he checks his watch and makes a call to the airport to
check on Bobby's flight in from San Francisco. Apparently Bobby
just set down or is just about to.

So he (Peter) hangs up and announces he was going to pick
Bobby up at the chopper pad at Santa Monica Airport.

He would then bring him back here. And to just relax and everything would work itself out. I tell the Rabbit his brother in law can go to hell, but not to bring him here. Because I'll call the local police. Peter informs me Bobby is the absolute Chief of all Police and can go where he feels he has to. When he feels he has to.

So here I wait. And I'm pissed that Peter on his own has dismissed Mrs. Murray for the day, once again to protect you know who. And he gave me a quarter bottle of reds before he left. He probably dropped the other three quarters in his own coat pocket. And Maf was barking up a storm when he entered, and was barking even more when he left. So intense, she was scaring me something awful. So Red, I think I'm going to put you away for a while, in the closet. Hide you away.

But I never got the chance to hide you. Half an hour later, they both arrived and Maf goes crazy. Even worse because she most likely can sense my righteous anger along with the increasing tension of all three of us, together. But this time she simply won't calm down, continuing to snap at Bobby's trousers. I had to laugh 'cause she's so little. But also so very brave. So I put her out in the yard. Peter makes some dumb ass remark about how he hoped both of us would act like adults and talk things through and come to a mutual agreement. Then he slithers out and Bobby takes over.

First off, Bobby wants to apologize for the shitty way he's treated me. Not answering my phone calls or returning my messages. But he can't get me out of my mind and he still loves me. So I ask, 'Oh, enough to marry me?'

He gives me this total bullshit statement. Probably rehearsed it for weeks, about how 'it will happen in time. I don't realize what problems the White House was facing, especially in the next few months. And I had to show a little patience and understanding. Still my absence has shown him he can't live without me. And he has to have me, now and forever. We just can't be formally betrothed.'

I erupt, saying, 'So you can come here and I can go there and you'll fuck me on the run. Not one more time in your damn lifetime! No more lies with this girl.'

He was the same old BOBBY. Only this time I hated him. And truly wanted him to leave my home this instant.

He shrugs, goes to the doorway, puts his hand on the doorknob. Then he turns back to me and says, in this really firm voice, 'Before I leave, I do need that diary.' You, Red. The record of all my thoughts and what I've been through the last couple of years. But also about my affairs of the heart, including and number one on the hit parade, him and me. Oh, and of course also his brother, the President.

So I tell him, 'A few days ago you sent me back my tiger. Now you want me to give you all my memories of us as a couple. They're mine, written by me and lived by me. You want to destroy anything that says we existed, so you can deny it ever happened?' Bobby counters, 'That's insane. Its just not safe with you. There's government secrets in there.'

I stare him in the eyes. 'Well, you'll just have to trust me to protect them. Because you're not getting my diary. Never.'

'Monroe,' Bobby begins screaming, 'I'm not leaving without it.'

He goes over to the bookcase and pulls down a few books. Starts fingering through them. Then leans over, trying to look at the rear of the shelf, like I may have hidden you behind the front row, against the wall.

I tell him, 'If you don't leave, I'll call the police.'

Bobby tosses the few books on the floor. He looks like he's ready to break a blood vessel. 'I need that excuse for a book, total pack of lies, to protect the family. I will not go without it. Its subversive, dangerous bullshit.'

Now I start screaming just as loud as him (between the two of us we must sound like old washer women), 'At least I wrote mine, myself. So its totally true to me. And as you're beginning to see, I need a few things, too. Like you in your car and my house in your rear view mirror. GET YOUR SKINNY ASS THE HELL OUT OF HERE!' And I lift up the receiver. He gets the point.

I throw him out and lock the door. I feel great. Tired, extremely upset, but also very proud of myself.

I go into the bedroom and lie down. Go back to the closet, fish you out and start to write. Well, fifteen minutes later, he (Bobby) calls back and says 'we have to talk about this further'. He wants me to come to the beach house so we can rationally discuss everything. There are neutral parties there. Come to some compromise. I tell him, 'that's the one place I'm staying far, far away from.' And I slam the receiver down.

Go back and take one of Peter's reds. Then I run back over to the phone and call my good Doctor. And beg him to please come over just as soon as he can. 'Because Bobby was back in town and he wants me to meet him on the beach. And I don't want to go. Worse, he wants to take my diary. Was tossing everything around until I threw him out.' Heck, Red, you've become part of my soul and I will defend you.

Dr. Greenson, in a very calm voice, says 'Good girl. Stay away from him. And you have an undeniable right to keep what's yours. That he respected both my decisions and thinks I've taken a major step towards getting myself well and he'll be over at four.'

Then I tried to call the White House to speak to Jack. He's in an important conference but would I care to leave a message. I ask if Kenny's there, and he's in this meeting also.

So I tell the secretary, Mrs. Lincoln, who is usually very helpful, 'Please tell the President to keep his damn brother away from me. Because he cannot hear nor does he understand the simple words NO or GO AWAY. Otherwise I might have to talk to the press about certain things no one wants to come out. Government secrets Bobby told me when we were in bed.' And she said she would tell him and she was sorry.

But then I asked her not to quote the last part. Because I couldn't hurt either of them like that, no matter how they hurt me. And she understood, and always liked me. And would do as I asked.

Then I took a bath to soak and think. With all this going on, I've come to the disturbing realization I have to give you up, Red. At least until this whole thing blows over. I'm starting to have a real fear Bobby might use some shady maneuver, trying to steal you away. Order some of his men at Justice or a group from his Project Mongoose most of them ex-Cuban ex-cons, or a few Mafia gorillas to break in and steal you. Right up their alley. Or the mob might choose to do it on their own, grab and use you as black mail.

I don't think you'd remain around very long either way. With the mob, after they're through, you'd quickly be destroyed. To the others, you're instant toast right now.

I do not want to risk that because you've become the best friend I've ever had. And I don't want anyone to just get rid of you. In proper time, probably after I'm gone, people have the right to hear my slant on things. Just as important, I feel the need to tell the people who have supported me through the years my version of this period in my life. As I saw it, through my own eyes. Because they'll want to know the truth. Someone will. So I'm writing as fast as I can, to get all the earlier events of the day in.

When my good Dr. Greenson comes, which should be in about an hour now, I'm going to make him promise he'll keep you safe and sound. Until I want you back. And he must not reveal to anyone what I have given him. For the next few years, this is just between the two of us. And, of course, you, Red. So I guess for the next couple of weeks, at least, its bye-bye.

Its just the way Bobby said 'That Diary' that has me so concerned. Knowing Bobby, I'm scared. No if's or but's. Damn, I feel horrible that I have to give you up, even if it is for a very good reason. What will I carry around? Well, I'll take notes on a pad and write them in you later. And as I scan your pages, I realize we've been through one hell of a lot together. Some major traumas, some good times. So we'll get through this one, too.

Thank God for my good Doctor, my dashing smart Romeo, who has always been there for me. Even when I asked huge and difficult things from him. He's already compromised himself so much and I have no right to ask more. But sadly, without him, I'd have nobody to help me. Not a one. And Lord knows, I do need help and protection in the worst way. Especially right now, at this important turning point in my life. Well, at least I'm no longer ashamed to ask. Especially when it regards your safety and mine. So long, Red. My beautiful, faithful friend. Hope to see you soon when everything is a whole lot calmer. And we can talk about better things.

Dr. Greenson's Final Notes

August 6, 1962

Marilyn died last night. And even though I
haven't told my family yet, we all will be going to
her funeral tomorrow, Sunday at noon. Couldn't sleep
a wink after getting back from her place at 4:45
a.m. It's now about 8 a.m. Saturday and I thought I'd
write a little in you, her diary, before I put you in
my safe in the library. I lost someone I deeply cared
for, even loved. I feel horribly guilty, compromised,
and at least partially responsible. I'm a failure as
a doctor and as a friend. What forces conspired to
end Marilyn's life? I'm not really sure. Worse, I don't
think I'll ever find out. Well, definitely not the
whole truth.

Some parts I already know because I was there.
From 10 p.m. on Friday night, after the call from
Mrs. Murray. When I first turned Marilyn onto her
back, on her bed, and breathed into her mouth, there
was something like a low sigh of air. Should I call
for an ambulance? Even though she had already been
dead at least a couple of hours. Early rigidus, low
body temperature, early livor mortis. It was hopeless
but if there was the slightest chance. Hyman, Dr.
Engelberg, arrived a few minutes later. Thought
she was obviously beyond help. Thought we could be
further implicated. Robert Kennedy, who had come
with Hyman, was violently opposed to taking her
to the hospital. I went along with their decision.
The ambulance would arrive much later, about 1
a.m. Minutes later, Marilyn's body was on the way
to the hospital, while Kennedy and I were in Peter

Lawford's car, headed in the direction of Lawford's beach house. This timing was not by accident. At the hospital, attendants took her body in through a side entrance, where she was checked by two top men, a trauma surgeon and an anesthesiologist. Both are old friends. Both said she had been dead for hours.

By the time the helicopter carrying Kennedy to the LAX airport was lifting off from the Santa Monica beach, the ambulance was returning Marilyn's body to her home. She was carefully laid on her bed, posed with her phone. By then, the massive effort to hide any evidence of Bobby Kennedy's presence in her house had almost been completed. It was a very good team assembled.

All evidence suggesting the President's involvement was also destroyed. Actually anything that belonged to Marilyn, even if it had nothing whatsoever to do with either Kennedy was thrown into bags to be carted away. I knew the material would be destroyed in a more private setting, but it would be gone and very soon. Marilyn was from that night on to be found only in her films and photographs and in the memories of those who knew her.

I know a good deal about the early part of the cover up because I sadly found myself involved. Yes, at the moment of my greatest failure, I had become a criminal conspirator, too. I was dragged into doing grossly improper and frankly illegal things. Actions that at any other time I would never have considered. I did them under the direct orders of the Attorney General. Actually I was by Kennedy's side until he took off in the helicopter. He had to make sure I didn't say anything incriminating. Only when he left was I free to grieve, not systematically go about hiding anything, including my feelings and repulsion. But I did have to return one last time to the scene of the crime, her home, to help tie all the loose threads of the alibi together.

By then, there were teams of reporters and police and neighbors on the lawn. The word had gone out to all corners of the globe. Marilyn Monroe had died, at age 36. The mentally tortured superstar was found dead in her home, most likely from an accidental overdose of sleeping pills.

So because of all these troubling pieces of information, along with the level of these distasteful shenanigans, I will attend Marilyn's autopsy, which is to be begin at 11 a.m. this morning. I need to see for myself what happened, or at least see as much as is possible. More important, I want to tell the pathologist I do not feel in any way she was suicidal, not this weekend, not this month, not for the over two years I treated her. I will not mention the soiled bed sheet, the brown liquid most likely representing feces and drugs and saline concoction. A toxic combination strongly suggesting foul play because Marilyn did not, could not administer it to herself.

Mrs. Murray washed the bedding twice, on the orders of Kennedy's team: The private investigator Otash, Lawford, Pat Newcomb, a few of Otash's henchmen. Just terrible. Marilyn's press agent, Arthur Jacobs, and Kennedy directing the destruction of all the files, papers, cards. Milton Rudin, Marilyn's attorney, making sure everything looked fairly legal. Did any of us present know who did it or how? I honestly don't believe so. But clearly there was a team who knew what they were doing and had planned the final act. They did their job quickly and quietly, and then disappeared into the night air.

Right now, I hope the coroner will listen to me about Marilyn's state of mind when I left her at before 7 p.m. last evening. After all, this is my area of expertise.

As a psychiatrist, and a full professor at the UCLA med school, I'm always asking myself one thing, "Could any patient try to harm themselves? Do they, at this moment, need medical supervision in a carefully monitored hospital?" My patient was not in any way requiring such a facility. Marilyn Monroe was fighting mad and in full control.

When I was leaving her house for the very last time, pushing through a small army of curious bystanders, some reporter shoved a microphone in my face. Asked me what I thought had caused her death. I replied with a shrug, "Possible Suicide." It wasn't, but I said it to get rid of him. Besides, I was surrounded by several of Robert Kennedy's people, and others from Fox studios. Not one of them cared about Marilyn's legacy, or the truth. Just the opposite. They wanted her to look as depressed and crazy as possible. Why else would you commit suicide? Any suggestion of criminal acts contributing to Marilyn's death would bring with it a wave of new investigations. Inquiries that would be dangerous to anyone who had been there the last day. And the President might have to resign. More than might.

4 p.m. Saturday.

I'm back from the morgue. We still don't know much. The only abnormal physical finding at the autopsy was a blue-red, engorged distal colon, over twice normal size, from the rectum up a full foot along the sigmoid colon. The doctor cut several specimens from the site. Along with taking aspirants to send to the lab. Same procedure was followed with the stomach and upper bowel. The stomach and small intestine were empty to the naked eye--no major inflammation. Externally there was noted a large hematoma, in the subcutaneous tissue. This could have been from an injection, most likely from Hymie's needle, on the top part of her right buttock, near the iliac crest.

From the autopsy and immediate microscopic studies, no capsule parts or drugs were found in her stomach. Less than trace amounts. None in her duodenum, either. So if she voluntarily ingested these drugs, swallowed them, which is the only normal way to get these pills into her system... Well, she also had to be Houdini to get rid of the remnants in the organs where they should have appeared. This is a very strong sign, a medical tilt sign, which is blinking. No oral intake, probably no suicide. So if she didn't get the drugs into her system by swallowing them, how did she get them into her system?? Some other party had to introduce them. Almost certainly from another portal. Not injection. The coroner's team very carefully checked for needle marks with magnifying glasses, top to bottom. The only other way was through the large bowel, either via a suppository or enema. We await the toxicology studies, the rectal swabs, the aspirants of colon and stomach material, the microscopic studies of the colon and stomach walls. If the lower bowel tests are positive, it's almost definitely proof of murder. The rest of the proof has been washed away in Marilyn's laundry room.

As regards to the official version, it goes something like this. Because of Marilyn's constant mental anguish, it appears she swallowed too many pills. And in her confusion, the amount ingested killed her. The diagnosis of possible suicide has been attached to her preliminary death certificate. A suicide with an excessive amount of Nembutal and chloral hydrate in her system, suggesting prolonged ingestion. If so, about thirty colleagues and I gave her the means to do it. The loaded gun was supplying scripts to Marilyn for sedatives and sleeping pills over a very long period. But Marilyn was not one to stockpile anything but her direct staff, which she faithfully kept for years, and there were few pill bottles in her present possession. This strongly suggests that there weren't that many pills around her house, definitely not enough to do this. Hymie says he gave her a script for at most fifty Seconals, and half were still in the bottle. She most likely had to have taken a good deal more. And why didn't she take them all? And where were the capsules?

Doesn't make sense in another way. When I saw her at her house between 4 and 6:30 p.m. Friday, she was relatively calm. A little drugged but I've seen her a great deal worse. Now surely she could take a great number of pills because she had steadily built up an amazing tolerance. When Hymie, Dr.Engelberg gave her 100-milligram shots of barbiturates, sometimes one in each buttock, they hardly affected her.

This is hardly a pretty tale. Besides, I am severely upset, which may taint my observations even further about what occurred during our last analytic session together.

After Marilyn called on Friday around 3:30 p.m., I hurriedly drove over to her home, wearing wrinkled slacks and a plain shirt. Marilyn greeted me wearing a white terry cloth robe. Even though she looked as if she had been crying, she also appeared level headed and almost breezy. She was excited that now she was the one who could and did reject Bobby. And saw it for the best. Saying all our talking through obviously had some effect because she finally realized how little either of the Kennedys could give her. On a permanent basis, absolutely nothing. At least the President had never promised her marriage and kids and the whole nine yards. So he was a little better or more honorable than his younger brother. However, neither one was the man she was looking for to spend her life with. They didn't want her to be anything more than a girl on the side, just to have sex with. Taking it one unbelievable step more, even if she somehow got one of them to marry her, how long could she be happy? Who wanted their life-style? The constant cheating, the politicking.

Most of her scorn was directed at Bobby, mixed with a fair dose of sorrow. Absolutely without any pity for herself. I thought her feelings were quite reasonable and totally justified. She apparently had told him off, and asked him to leave. He was concerned about only one thing. Getting her personal diary and any tapes she might have made, especially about him or the President. And when Marilyn didn't capitulate, he became this terrible, angry child.

He threatened and screamed and when that didn't work, tried searching through her things. Fortunately, she had already hidden the diary in one of her empty shoe boxes. Even better, she remained in total control of the moment. Lifted the phone and was ready to call the police if he didn't leave. So I remarked, trying to drive home the point, "He's making it very clear he's not the guy for you, don't you think?" And Marilyn sat upright and braced herself. Then a sad smile appeared. "I'd say he never was, the little shit. Well, good riddance."

The rest of this session, our last, was ordinary. Usually near the end we'd review the things she would try do once I left. This was a big part of most of our therapy. Marilyn, in her confused state, and she was normally somewhat confused, needed a list of step by step actions to do just about anything. This one was very short.

"If Bobby calls, hang up. And if he comes over, call me immediately. I'll come with help if need be," I told her. And that's the way I left it with her.

I drove to my home around 6:45 with her diary under my front seat. Transferred it to the bottom kitchen cabinet, tucked in under a few pots. And began dinner with my dear wife by around 7:15 p.m.

Around 7:25 I got a call from Marilyn. I could hardly recognize her voice. She was crying and at the same time she was shouting, really screaming at the top of her lungs. I could hear the dog barking faintly in the background. Then she said, "Doctor, Bobby's come back with Doctor Engelberg. And they're trying to inject me. Probably trying to kill me with some poison." I was aghast. I said, "Let me speak to Hymie."

She called Dr. Engelberg and he got on the phone and said, "Ralph. I have to tell you, this is one hell of a situation you got me into."

I asked, "What are you doing there?" And he responded, "I'm with the Attorney Gen…"

All of a sudden all hell seemed to break loose. In the background I heard Marilyn and someone else bitterly yelling at each other. Cursing.

Engelberg shouted, "Jesus, she threw an ash tray and it missed Bobby's head by inches. Holy Hannah! I've never seen her this agitated. She could kill someone. Ralph, I really think you need to get over here. And right now.

"Wait, Bobby just got her down. I'm going to go over there and give her a shot. Hopefully, that'll quiet her down."

And as I yelled, "Wait! Don't!" he slammed the phone down.

I sat there for five minutes, my hands shaking. I didn't know whether to call an ambulance or the police. Seven minutes later, the phone rang again. It was Engelberg.

He said, "I just gave her a shot and she seems better. We're going to let her sleep it off. I'm going back to my home, and the Attorney General is returning to Peter Lawford's house. I'm sure you have the numbers if you need us."

I asked, "May I speak to her?"

Hymie raised his voice harshly. "What are you, fucking mad? I told you she's sleeping. I need to get the hell out of here." His tone changed, lower, more pleading. "Show a little professional courtesy. Please, doctor. Especially after putting me in this stew in the first place."

I asked, "Where's Mrs. Murray?" He answered, "Not sure. Apparently, Lawford or Mr. Kennedy had her dismissed for the night. Hope I don't have to speak to you soon. But I have to tell you, Ralph, this is one hell of a referral. Can't blame me if forget to say thanks." He hung up.

I got my book and called Mrs. Murray's son. He told me she'd gone to an early movie and he didn't know what or where. I told him that when she got back, she was to immediately go to Marilyn's house to check on everything. And I would be waiting for her call.

I waited. I tried to watch television. I paced. About 9:45 p.m., Mrs. Murray called, panic in her voice. "She's dead. At least it looks that way. She's not breathing. No pulse. What do you want me to do?" I felt a bolt of burning pain deep in my gut. Can't think. Finally I said, "I'll come over."

She replied, "I'll call Dr. Engelberg. He asked to be kept informed." And before I could say, "NO! I'll call him myself," the phone is slammed down. I tried to call her back, but the line was busy. Hymie's home phone was busy, too. I ran to my car. The drive over usually takes close to ten minutes. I made it in slightly more than six. Mrs. Murray was at the front door, crying. "Where's Marilyn?" I asked. She nodded to the back hall. I ran to her bedroom. She was lying nude on her bed, on her stomach. Not breathing, blue extremities. I turned her over. Stuck my finger in her mouth. Gave her a few breaths, a few thumps on her chest. Nothing.

She was already cold. No life. I lifted her, hugged her, started to cry like I never have before. Kept saying, "I'm sorry."

I must have sat there, crying like a baby, for well over five minutes. Suddenly I heard the screech of tires out front. A minute later, Dr. Engelberg entered. Bobby Kennedy came running into the bedroom behind him. "Dammit, Doc, little late for that, isn't it?" Kennedy studied me and Murray. "I think you already lost your patient. Right?"

Then he ran into Marilyn's closet. Started pulling down her shoe boxes. She must have had over fifty, and fifteen hatboxes, piled up on the top shelf. On the floor there were more. Multiple shoe racks. And another twenty or so boxes stacked in the back corner. He started tearing them open.

I went over and asked what he was doing. "What you should have been doing since you got here." Kennedy stood up and scanned the closet. "Looking for evidence."

"Evidence of what?" I asked.

"Evidence of top secret material. Government secrets." The Attorney General's eyes darted about. "Like in that piece of shit red diary she was always writing in." His eyes focused on me. "So where do you think she kept it?"

I shook my head. He turned, ran out, and rushed to the bookshelves in the living room. Started pulling down books. He turned again to me. "Sure you don't have any idea, being her shrink, and all?"

"None," I said.

From that instant, I became part of a conspiracy to cover up or hide evidence, the same way this angry and very frightened man was ensnared. But because of his power and position in the Administration, he was brought front and center. He was quietly furious. "Any clue, Doctor?" He came forward, leaned over to face me. He was so close I could see the small beads of perspiration on his upper lip. "So Doc, you're telling me she never mentioned this book to you?"

"I knew she was keeping notes in one. " I looked him in the eye, "But as to her hiding place, I have no idea. None at all. Sorry," I lied again and will continue to lie until I'm dead. Diary, I'm keeping you safe from this terrified powerful man who wants you destroyed. That's my solemn oath. My only goal left is to keep you safe, for Marilyn's sake. Because I promised her I would.

It certainly appeared that Robert Kennedy cared about Marilyn. This didn't matter in the slightest. He was bent on destroying any connection to him, or his family, which he mentioned multiple times. The family, as if because I, too, am an American, it is my family also.

I did not want to destroy key evidence, especially pertaining to my patient, but I spent the next ten minutes with Kennedy and Hymie Engelberg, looking through boxes. Peter Lawford entered, carrying a satchel of tools. He was clearly intoxicated, weaving noticeably.

I watched them systematically break open the small lock on her file cabinet. Dr. Engelberg was against the far wall, looking down. Afraid to bear witness. The Attorney General breaking and entering, I think they call it. Tossing her papers around, tearing others, not finding anything. Definitely not the real gem, because by then it was safely tucked away in a bottom drawer in my kitchen.

To be very soon moved to a fireproof, waterproof, sixty-pound safe hidden behind the painted picture of my family in my home library and office. Where Marilyn and I spent so many hours, so much time, trying to sort things out.

I asked Dr. Engelberg what he thought we should do with her body. He shrugged.

Kennedy said, "You're not doing one damn thing until I tell you that you can. Got it?" He didn't wait for our acknowledgement. He ran into the kitchen, began making several phone calls. I heard muted words. Excited. Frightened.

He came back and said, "We have to stall until I can get the hell out of here. A private detective has been called to clean up. Otash and a few helpers. I also called Pat Newcomb for backup. A helicopter will pick me up at the beach."

He pointed to the big plastic bags brought in by Lawford. "Start cleaning up. Get all papers and pictures and throw them in the bags." So that's what we did. And Kennedy kept me by his side while we went through all her possessions, getting ready to bag them and cart them away. Then we got into Lawford's car for the ride to his beach house. Lawford at the wheel, the Attorney General and I in the rear of the closed convertible. Being stopped by a policeman because Lawford was speeding. Arriving at the house about 1:30 a.m., Lawford and Bobby talking in hushed tones on the phone in the kitchen. To Washington, probably to the President himself.

Up to the last seconds, when his chopper took off from the beach, in the back past the swimming pool, lights off, I was close to Kennedy's side. But he barely looked at me. Didn't listen to me. I was held in the same regard as Peter Lawford, who is a drunken, incompetent imbecile. Marilyn's body would be officially discovered in her bed just about the time Bobby was landing in San Francisco.

Well, Red, I'm closing you up for now. And tucking you safely away. Protected by a 10-inch, steel wall safe hidden behind a family picture. There is grief counseling to be done with my wonderful kids and wife, whom I involved far more than I should have. We all loved Marilyn as much as we love each other. We'll get through this. But first, we have a funeral to attend tomorrow afternoon to honor a one of a kind, strikingly intelligent woman, who played the dumb blonde absolutely brilliantly. And a concerned and kind human being even better.

Her death will be such a terrible loss to everyone. Those who knew her personally, and those worldwide who only knew her work. I'm sure none of us will ever be quite the same. But very few will feel as guilty as I do now.

R. Greenson, M.D.

September 4, 1963

Well, Red, It's been a sad year since they
took Marilyn from us. The final diagnosis was
"Probable Suicide." I tried to speak out against
this conclusion, urging further investigation.
No one listened or cared. There were waves of
official statements and stories, all designed to
bury any questions about cause of death forever.
All pointed to my patient's gross instability and
drug taking. The police and the coroner went along
without a whimper. Not one word was said in support
of continuing the investigation. All the lab and
pathology specimens were immediately destroyed.
So were the autopsy photos. What remained were
lab reports noting an extremely large amount of
Nembutal and chloral hydrate in her blood and liver.
It was a terrible injustice but totally expected. A
complete whitewashing of an obvious murder. I could
only speak about the case from my official position
as Marilyn's psychiatrist. Besides, what proof did I
have? Now, more than ever, I want Marilyn to have her
final word. If the real facts were known about the bed
sheets, let alone the massive cover up, I think there
would be a large outcry. Of course, until her remains
are restudied, the real truth about her death can
only be guessed at. I make my last promise, Red, with
my patient already just a memory. At some time in
some way, this diary will be released to the general
public so that it may be read and discussed. I'm sure
the legend of Marilyn will go on for many years, with
continued interest and love. Hopefully, this will
fuel interest enough to exhume the body. We owe
Marilyn at least that.

Marilyn's Attorney Reveals the Final Truth

Nov. 24, 1979

Dr. Ralph Greenson died this evening. My
brother-in-law, my best friend, died too soon. Bad
heart. He'll be deeply missed by all who knew him and
I knew him well. He and his small family were very
close. He enjoyed an extensive circle of friends,
admirers, and grateful patients. He was a very fine
doctor, a brilliant teacher and a superb human
being. After Marilyn's death, he continued his very
successful career as a psychiatrist, while becoming
a world-renowned medical author and lecturer. He
rarely talked about his most famous patient, hesitant
to open old wounds that never healed. The man had a
tremendous amount of class.

I have less. Because of my position as attorney
to various criminal elements, I knew within several
days of the tragedy how Marilyn died. She was
murdered, plain and simple. I never revealed this
knowledge directly to Ralph, as it was somewhat
in the realm of privileged communication for me. I
also saw no way this information would help him.
Could even have been dangerous if he got outraged
enough to start up a new investigation. There were
many rumors circulating through the years, but with
time, he did come to understand he was not in any way
responsible for her death. That's all he had to know,
the basic truth that pertained to him.

So what is the complete truth? Marilyn Monroe
was killed by a specially prepared enema, containing
extremely high doses of Nembutal and chloral
hydrate. This poison potion was fashioned by a

chemist, a whiz kid Ph.D. who taught biochemistry at a Chicago med school and secretly worked for the CIA. The same genius who prepared the arsenal of toxins that were designed to stop the heart of the Cuban leader, Castro, or make his beard fall out, or give him a virulent cancer.

A four-man Giancana 'hit' team pushed their way into Marilyn's home using Marilyn's friendship with Giancana's right hand man, Johnny Roselli. He got her to open the side kitchen door. They overpowered her and inserted a rectal tube attached to an enema bag, and the solution was poured into her lower colon. Thirty minutes later, they were out the door and she was no longer alive. Her death occurred around 8 p.m. in the evening.

Giancana accepted the murder contract from the CIA Director, who was trying to keep his job and prevent any potential leak from Marilyn about the Agency's working relationship with the Mafia. Especially information pertaining to political assassinations in foreign nations, including Lumumba in the Congo, Trujillo in the Dominican Republic, and multiple attempts on Castro's life in Cuba. There were rumored to be others.

One good note. Marilyn didn't suffer. She was dead within minutes of the insertion of this lethal mixture into her lower bowel. So fast was the absorption, and so deadly. The Mafia and CIA individuals who were involved in this crime had hoped to pin the murder charge on former boyfriend Bobby Kennedy, who had just returned to her side. No, it wasn't second thoughts by RFK about giving up one of the acknowledged loves of his life. The Attorney General was only trying to cover his own tracks and

obtain this potentially devastating journal so he
and his brother would not be disgraced. Draw one
more line in the sand to protect the Kennedy family's
honor. But Bobby in no way was involved in her
murder. He was the pigeon, the same as Marilyn. Not
innocent but definitely a victim.

It didn't work out the way the Mob hoped, either.
That's because the Kennedy family and their extensive
support team, including friends in the media and LA
police, went into a massive mobilization. The cover-
up campaign began immediately after her death.

This resulted in almost total destruction of all
records and pictures of Marilyn with either Jack or
Bobby, along with most of her personal papers. The
FBI destroyed all phone records from her California,
New York, and Connecticut residences before
morning. Hoover gave the order after an apparent
agreement was reached. In return for securing his
cooperation in this crime, he would be allowed to
stay on as Director past the obligatory retirement
age. Probably for a year after he stopped breathing.
No one in Hollywood was allowed to mention anything
about Marilyn's relationship with either politician.
There is an always-present threat of never again
being allowed to work, especially in this most
liberal town that prides itself on democratic values
and an absence of censorship. And it's still going on
today, and probably will never end. Big cover-ups
die slowly.

In 1975, Johnny Roselli shot Sam Giancana,
killing him instantly. This was several days before
Giancana was scheduled to testify in front of the
congressional Church Committee about his role in
the planning, execution, and cover up in the murders

of both Kennedy brothers. Roselli's sectioned body was found in an oil drum off the Florida coast several months later. I think the expression is, "What goes around, comes around."

I will give the most senior of my immediate family permission to release this book ten years after my death, or thirty years after Ralph's death, whichever is sooner, based, of course, on their discretion. I hope they will use a less involved attorney, who is more familiar with the publishing industry, and that all the involved parties will be long dead and buried. Marilyn's story needs to be told and it's too bad it has to take so long. No one realized how incredibly gifted she was until many years later, there is still only her.

Marilyn Monroe has become a true hero and a major icon, especially as a symbol of women's emancipation. Who would have thought a broken girl from a broken home, with little education and no particular training, could reach such heights on a whim and a will. First she was known for her looks, then her acting, then the men she loved, and finally by her character, flawed but marvelous. Bravo.

To me personally, it was a terrible loss. She was always a very sweet, funny, and extremely bright kid. A lovable rascal who never made an enemy. But her all-powerful lovers had many. They dug the hole and she had the dumb luck to fall in.

I still miss her. We all do.

Milton Rudin, Attorney at Law